Kensington Court
'A rattling thriller' *Daily Express*

'Kensington Court . . . will have you racing through the final pages for the brilliant, twisting climax' *Company*

Hidden Agenda
'Both a thriller – I was hooked by the very first page – and a gripping story about the power of female friendships – a winning combination!' Marika Cobbold

'A gripping and beautifully constructed story' Elizabeth Buchan

'Carol Smith has done it again, an unput-down-able thriller with a twist . . . Smith holds the reader in her grasp from start to finish, and gives us compelling psychological insights on the way' Julia Neuberger

Grandmother's Footsteps
'*Grandmother's Footsteps* . . . will keep you entertained, reading and guessing all the way to the end' *Crime Time*

Unfinished Business
'If a pacy thriller is your thing, *Unfinished Business* will suit you to perfection . . . an addictive read' *Sunday Express*

'A thriller which certainly keeps you turning those pages . . . gripping right to the end' *Daily Mail*

Family Reunion
'A gripping read' *Family Circle*

'Full of action, twists and surprises, this intricate suspense story offers a fascinating new take on the nature of family ties' *Good Housekeeping*

CAROL SMITH

Kensington Court

sphere

SPHERE

First published in Great Britain in 1996
by Little, Brown and Company
This edition published by Warner Books in 1997
Reprinted 1997 (twice), 1998, 1999
Reprinted by Time Warner Paperbacks in 2002
Reissued by Sphere in 2006
Reprinted 2006, 2007 (twice)

A CIP catalogue record for this book is
available from the British Library.

ISBN 978-0-7515-3917-2

Papers used by Sphere are natural, recyclable products made from
wood grown in sustainable forests and certified in accordance with
the rules of the Forest Stewardship Council.

Typeset in Berkeley by M Rules
Printed and bound in Great Britain by Clays Ltd, St Ives plc
Paper supplied by Hellefoss AS, Norway

Sphere
An imprint of
Little, Brown Book Group
100 Victoria Embankment
London EC4Y 0DY

An Hachette Livre UK Company

www.littlebrown.co.uk

For Sheila Lynford –
the sister I wish I'd had

Acknowledgements

My sincere thanks to Sarah Molloy, my agent; Imogen Taylor, my editor; and all the unsung heroes in the Sales, Marketing and Promotional Departments of Little, Brown/Warner, without whose valiant efforts you would not now be reading this book.

Kensington Court

Prologue

Fog shrouded the city, dense and smothering, insinuating itself into every secret place as effectively as the old pea-soupers from the days way back when coal was still freely burned. It swirled round the tops of buildings, muffling all traffic sounds and adding to the general depression which ambushes spirits on the slow, familiar creep-up to Christmas.

On one main high street, the fashionable centre of quality in the sprawling metropolis, a mammoth redbrick citadel stood impervious, spanning one whole block, preserving the privacy and protecting the lives of its occupants, barricading their privileged existence from the intrusion of strangers or prying eyes. A vast Victorian mansion block, amongst the first of its kind, erected at the turn of the century as the latest, the most avant-garde creation of a celebrated architect, still going strong after nine decades and the privations and bombardments of two world wars.

On this inhospitable night no light was showing from any window in all its five storeys. It stood as solid and unbreachable as any great monument, guardian of secrets, as old as time, seemingly deserted, as silent as the grave.

Only at one rear window, which looked out across the inner courtyard, a single lamp burned, deep within an uncurtained room. And a lone figure stood at the window, watching . . .

1

Silver dawn filtered palely through a fine autumn mist which cloaked the streets of the Royal Borough and muffled the shadowy silhouettes of a battalion of the Queen's Household Cavalry, clattering over Campden Hill on their way back home to barracks after early-morning manoeuvres in the park.

"'Watch the wall, my darling, as the Gentlemen go by,'" chanted Beatrice reflexively from somewhere deep in her dreams, then, hearing the sonorous chiming of St Mary Abbots followed, seconds later, by the more tinny echo of the Kensington Palace clock, recalled she had an early meeting with the Minister so threw back the duvet and prepared for flight. Lily, her flatmate, was already up and about, sipping jasmine tea in the kitchen as she listened to Radio 4.

'Golly,' she breathed in her soft, melodic voice, 'Guy Bartlett's dead. Killed, they say, in Cairo.'

Across the High Street, on the corner by the chemist, Rosie, the flower lady, stamped the circulation back into her feet and waved a cheery mittened hand at the austere figure of the porter going about his early-morning chore of polishing the brass on the imposing doorway of Kensington Court. It was a ritual he rarely neglected, and now he took a few steps back to admire his gleaming handiwork, then withdrew once more inside the building to warm his fingers round a mug of steaming tea. Rosie laughed as the great door closed and she watched the neighbourhood tramp shuffle from his stakeout in the doorway of the bank to perform his own peculiar ritual of shaving his face and head in the reflection from the immaculate nameplate. She knew it drove the porter wild to see his masterpiece defiled in such a way but the tramp was wilier than he was, and nimbler on his feet, so the charade continued, morning after morning.

Inside the hallway of the vast mansion block, Bonita, the cleaner, small, pert and pretty in her jeans and neat dark sweater, stood chatting by the entrance to the porter's lodge, Hoover in hand, all set to tackle the stairs. By now the building was audibly coming awake. The postman left his trolley in the hall and took the lift to the fifth floor to begin his leisurely descent on foot, delivering mail to each individual door, while a steady stream of tenants started to emerge: fathers to work, children to school, a rare enthusiastic shopper off early to the stores in an attempt to miss the crowds.

'Good God!' said Ronnie Barclay-Davenport, spreading the *Daily Telegraph* wide and spilling his coffee in astonishment. 'Says here Guy Bartlett's been killed. Out in Egypt, poor chap. Fell from a fifth floor window, which seems unlikely. Bit of monkey business going on there, I wouldn't be at all surprised. Whatever next!'

His wife, Rowena, standing at the stove behind him, thoughtfully frying bacon and eggs and not yet quite awake, shuffled across to read over his shoulder.

'Oh, the poor darling! What a dreadful catastrophe! I always told him to watch out, that it was a dangerous job. We must warn poor Gregory to take extra care. These foreign correspondents are braver than soldiers.'

'Gregory is a travel writer, dear heart. Not a lot of danger there, y'know. And come to that, I wasn't aware that Guy was exactly in the firing line. Stringer for the *Observer*. Nice work if you can get it, if you ask me.'

'Well, you never can be sure, and now you know. Rioting natives, palace revolutions, sudden bloody coups arising out of nowhere. Can't be too careful. Poor man, I always liked him a lot.'

Miles and Claudia Burdett, driving together to the office in Canary Wharf, heard the news over the car radio.

'Lord!' said Claudia, clutching her husband's arm. 'Listen to that. Can it be *our* Guy Bartlett, do you suppose? Surely not. I saw him only last week. Was chatting to him in the lift, in fact, just as normal as can be. Tuesday it was, unless I am very much mistaken.'

Miles was reflective as he manoeuvred his expensive car through the backed-up traffic on the Embankment. Curse this rush-hour scramble. No matter how early they left, they still managed to get snarled up.

'What, I wonder, will happen to his flat?' he pondered. 'I've always rather fancied that location. Top floor, glass roof in the hall, different layout to the rest of us. Might make a good investment. I'll have to investigate.'

'It's a sublet, surely?' said Claudia idly, not really listening, still shocked by the news.

'Yes,' said Miles with one of his roguish grins. 'But it's given me an idea.'

Beatrice Hunt, on her way towards Whitehall, mind now fully alert, was listening too as she sat in the rear of the car surrounded by government papers. Poor old Guy, and how jolly inconvenient. She took out her thin gold pen and scribbled herself a note. There was something here that might need investigation. Healthy, on-the-ball journalists, even ones who drank as heavily as her neighbour, did not just fall to their deaths, not without a little help. It needed looking into, and Beatrice would make sure that something was done. As soon as she'd got this dratted meeting out of the way.

The Fentons agreed that some sort of recognition was due so invited a few of the neighbours in for a quiet drink in memory of Guy. As chairman of the Tenants' Association, Digby was strongly aware of his responsibilities, and, so far as he was aware, the poor man had had no immediate relatives, or not ones he'd ever mentioned.

'He was between marriages,' said Olive. 'I rather think he had already clocked up four. Or so Gregory once told me. Not bad going for a man still in his forties.'

'It's the life that does it,' said Digby. 'I wonder if Gregory knows. I believe he's off on one of his own trips at present. Hope the poor fellow doesn't get to hear by accident. It will be a bit of a shock under any circumstances. They were always such great chums.'

The Black Widows, of course, were agog and absolutely in their element. Nothing this exciting had occurred in Kensington Court for years, and they couldn't wrap their tongues around it fast enough. They sat in a huddle in the Fentons' grand drawing room, with its panoramic view of the High Street, twittering together like predatory starlings, spilling sherry on the Persian rug in their unseemly enthusiasm. Olive, serving canapés, watched with disapproval. They were, to her mind, an evil bunch, spreading malice and doom while doing nothing for the community, this gaggle of sheltered and overprivileged old ladies. Here by grace of their dead husbands' earnings and not much else.

'I never really liked that man,' Mrs Adelaide Potter was pronouncing through pursed lips. 'Eyes too narrow, no better than he should be. Never really trusted him. Not quite a gentleman.'

'He was always very civil to me,' piped up Amelia Rowntree bravely. Though these days sagging in body, she still retained the heart of a much younger woman, and those cynical, half-closed eyes – a lot like Alec McCowen's, she'd always fancied – had made her pulses run a little faster each time she had encountered them. For the spirit of romance roamed freely within her ample chest and she still had her hopes. After all, if he'd done it four times already . . . and he'd always been so very accommodating.

Lady Wentworth was on Amelia's side. 'Definitely a gentleman,' she said with approval, pausing to hover over one of Olive's fancy pastries. 'Winchester, I believe, and Trinity. He and Gregory were two of a kind, modern-day adventurers, I suppose you might say.'

'Gregory! I wonder if he's heard!' said Netta Silcock, bright-eyed, wriggling her rump in delicious anticipation like a fat and excited spaniel, keen to be in at the kill.

'You can ask him yourself,' said Amelia in a lowered voice, and they all turned to stare at the arrival of their hero, standing outlined in the doorway, dressed as carelessly as ever, smiling his sleepy, catlike smile. She sensed a familiar slow flush rising to her cheeks: Guy might be dead but here was Gregory, dreamy and delectable as always. But the handsome Dane's eyes had already locked with Eleni's and the older woman watched, defeated, the Greek girl's sinuous advance, generous bosom undulating as she walked towards him, glossy lips invitingly apart over dazzlingly perfect teeth.

No, Gregory confided later to the Barclay-Davenports, he hadn't known a thing until this morning, when he arrived back early from a flying visit to Beirut and saw the newspapers.

'Poor old Guy,' he said bemusedly, taking a swallow of the triple Scotch Ronnie had thoughtfully handed him. 'I can't imagine what happened. He just wasn't an aggressive fellow.' He shook his head sadly and took another gulp. There was a sister somewhere, living in East Anglia. He'd be driving up there later, once he'd located her address, in order to give his condolences and do the right thing.

'Give her our best too, won't you, old boy,' said Ronnie, laying a supportive hand on Gregory's shoulder.

'Tell her we're thinking of her,' added his wife. 'You were always such good friends.'

'Yes,' said Gregory thoughtfully, staring into space. He'd tried to make light of it but it was a severe blow, nonetheless. Alone in this building, his fellow journalist was probably the person who knew him best. 'You never really know what's going to hit you – or when.'

'I wonder what will happen to his flat,' said Netta but Miles Burdett wasn't saying a word about his plans.

'Quite terrible,' repeated Ronnie Barclay-Davenport as he escorted his wife into the lift and upstairs to the fifth floor. 'Sign, I'm afraid, my dearest, of a world gone mad and growing more dangerous by the minute.'

'Quite so,' said Rowena, clutching his hand and momentarily looking her age. 'Makes you realise you never really know what's just around the corner.'

2

For as long as she could remember, Kate Ashenberry had been scared. Of spiders, of owls, of the ghost of her long-dead Uncle Ben, of going upstairs in the dark; even, for a while, of the Baby Jesus. As she grew older, these primitive terrors multiplied to include more subtle imagery: half-open doors leading into unlit interiors, old-fashioned wardrobes which might contain dead bodies, the great unfathomable mystery of death, and huge dark buildings without a light showing. Most of these fears were not at all complex and quite easily traceable – Baby Jesus to primary school, where she was first told that He was always watching her, death to the sudden and premature demise of the aforesaid Uncle Ben when Kate was still too young to understand, wardrobes to vintage Hammer horror, and looming buildings to an early childhood trip to Edinburgh, where her spine had prickled when she was confronted by the dark and somehow menacing monuments clustered too closely together in the gathering dusk of The Mount.

Virtually everything else might be put down to a thorough steeping in the savage literature of early childhood – *Struwwelpeter*, with that awful man with the scissors leaping out on the hapless thumb-sucking child, *Grimm's Fairytales*, Beatrix Potter's *Tale of Mr Tod*, the fearful flame-eyed Jabberwock whiffling through his tulgey wood, and almost anything else that her unfulfilled and slightly embittered mother, forced by circumstance to abandon a career in order to raise two children, had taken it into her head to inflict upon the younger.

Oh, and, of course, let's not forget Bruno, without doubt the older brother from hell.

Owls were obvious, and so too were frogs and spiders, especially when your childhood was terrorised by a gang of small, slightly older, bullying boys. There were cherished family photographs of the gang together, with baby Katie looking cute as pie in the wheelbarrow, their mascot but also at times their victim. But the dark, on the whole, was altogether more threatening when your home was large and old and creaking, the corridors long and the night outside frequently splintered by the skirl of seabirds or the eerie call of a mating fox. Kate could work herself into a lather of hysteria just lying there alone in her bed and imagining all kinds of unspeakable things metamorphosing through her bedroom wall – long-dead Uncle Ben; the Baby Jesus; even worse, His mother, with her vapid painted face and meekly upturned eyes. Her parents put it down to an overactive imagination, left the landing light on after dark and imposed an overall ban on anything remotely scary on film or television. What was all right for brutish boys, they figured, was not acceptable for a sensitive small girl. She would in time, they said, grow out of it, and they gave it no further thought.

The truth, however, was more banal. Bruno, always hovering at the foot of the stairs when little Katie was on her way up to lavatory or bed, poised to switch off the light halfway so that she had the split-second choice of either scampering down again or facing the last few steps in the dark she so much feared. Bruno, who regularly haunted her after lights out, draped in a sheet and making ghoulish noises, or left strange nastinesses – a dead mouse or a dog's skull – at the foot of the bed for her to find. Bruno, who once even callously traded her to a schoolfriend who pathetically admitted wanting a baby sister of his own, poor sucker.

Kate grew up with many of these fears intact, particularly a paralysing terror when confronted with a huge, dark building. She knew this fear was irrational yet never could control the residual panic, the dampening of the palms and tightening at the back of the knees when face to face with something she couldn't immediately get her mind round, something vast and immobile and showing no lights. It was really, of course, the fear of the dark all over again, for size, in itself, held no terrors.

New York, for instance, with its mind-blowing contrasts and dizzying perspectives, failed to give her any kind of claustrophobia, buffered as she was by the analgesic of new love. From the instant she stepped off the plane, in fact, she found herself bewitched by that mesmerising city with its heart-stopping skyline, its throbbing energy and perpetual buzz. She fell as deeply in love with the city as with the man and, had things worked out, would happily have stayed there for ever. For some cock-eyed reason, despite the screaming crime figures, in New York, for the first time ever, Kate felt safe.

Light, that was the key. Kate had heard many scare stories about the great power failure of the sixties and still suffered a mild frisson just thinking about it now, those blazing glass citadels rendered abruptly into looming masses of solid dark; canyons indeed, an instant throwback to her more graphic nightmares. Thus, the Time-Life building where Ramon worked was fine during office hours, a great streak of glass rocketing up from Sixth Avenue, its top floors so high they reflected the clouds. Whereas paintings of the sinking *Titanic* on its way down still brought an involuntary prickle to her spine.

Kensington Court, a vast structure which dominated the High Street, had just such an effect on Kate the first time she saw it, stepping unawares from a cab one drizzly December evening where the spire of St Mary Abbots protruded through the mist like a finger swathed in bandage, and looking upwards at the ornate façade to where, at the very top, a solitary light was showing.

She had picked up the keys that morning from the agent who, what with the pre-Christmas rush, had not had the time to come with her to inspect this sudden sublet. But it was excellent value, he assured her, owned by an elderly Kensington lady who these days lived mainly out of town.

'Needs a bit more furniture,' he had explained, 'but

otherwise it's in perfect condition and a bargain at the price. You are lucky to get it.'

Kate peered now round the vast cavernous hall, deliciously spacious with the added attraction, she now saw, of a raised glass lantern in the centre of the ceiling, one of the advantages of being at the top. It had been sealed off flush with a pane of glass but that, presumably, could be fixed. She itched to get her hands on it. A new electricity infused her battered spirits and all of a sudden she couldn't wait to take possession of this potentially marvellous place and try to restore it to some of its Victorian glory.

After the vastness of Ramon's apartment on the Upper West Side she was spoiled for space and had not expected to find it here in London, at least not at a price she could possibly afford. She had been forced into an on-the-spot decision. It had suddenly become available, something to do with the previous tenant being a foreign correspondent, just when Kate was crying out for somewhere congenial to live. This place, a mansion block, was really not her style, but anything must be better surely than the overpriced and fussily furnished bedsit she was currently occupying in Ebury Street. Right now, sanctuary mattered more to Kate than ambience. At least this colossal building was central. And safe.

For whatever Bruno had done to her throughout her childhood, he had done in spades. Just lately there was quite a lot that frightened Kate.

Seated on the Arundel train, gazing through mist at the rain-sodden Sussex landscape, Kate was numbed

by a familiar creeping misery that always set in the
nearer she drew to home. Scenes from her childhood,
far from bringing her peace, filled her with something
she had never quite been able to shrug off, something
close to dread. She glanced with apprehension round
the almost empty carriage, with its rattling windows
and worn brown upholstery. If it weren't for that one
forbidding-looking woman in the corner, immersed in
the *Telegraph* while slurping noisily on a boiled sweet,
she might almost be tempted to revert to the comforts
of childhood and suck her thumb.

These days, it seemed, she was a creature perpetually in flight and this duty visit to her nearest and
dearest was unlikely to offer much in the way of
respite. Quite truthfully, the prospect of another tense
weekend with Bruno and Lindy and their undisci-
plined brood filled her with trepidation, even though
it was eighteen months since she had last seen them
and had to put up with her brother's boorishness and
his prissy wife's unfailing disapproval. Plus, somewhere during the next two days, she would have to
put in a command appearance at the austere white
house in the shadow of the castle where her mother
had gone to ground. At times like this Kate ached for
the comforting presence of her father, but he had been
dead for years now, little more than a sepia-tinted
memory.

On the opposite seat a canvas tote bag from
Bloomingdale's bulged with cheerful packages, and
beside it sat a flame poinsettia from Marks & Spencer,
swathed in festive tissue and topped with a huge red
bow. Mother had always found poinsettias vulgar but at

this time of year there was not a lot else you could get, and since they said she was drawing more and more into herself these days, something lovely in a pot seemed the best, the only thing. Books were once the answer but now all that had gone. It was years since Grace Ashenberry had been fully of this world; at times like this Kate felt most poignantly the fact of her double bereavement and realised just how alone in the world she really was. For Bruno and Lindy, with their cold condescension and general meanness of spirit, simply didn't count.

The dowager at the other end of the carriage gave the plant an appraising sniff as she rose to alight at Angmering, and Kate, blissfully alone for the last few precious moments of the journey, took the opportunity not to suck her thumb but to indulge her craving for a rapid, illicit cigarette.

The station car park was almost empty. Though the train was more or less on time, and Bruno and Lindy had had ample notice of her visit, the circular sweep of gravel was deserted apart from a single other passenger off the London train, an elderly gent making a sudden spurt to grab the only taxi from under Kate's nose. Otherwise all was still as the gathering mist transmogrified into serious rain, and fat, disagreeable drops began to spatter all around her.

Damn them both to hell. Only her brother and his wife could induce these irrational gusts of rage in Kate, a shivering relic of childhood she had tried in vain to expunge. What was it about Bruno that had always made him hate her so much, the innocent baby sister he had once tried to smother in her cot? They hadn't got on as children but he was five years older and a boy so that she, smaller and weaker, had been helpless against his bullying and always ended up the victim. Her sole defence, her secret weapon, was the fact that she knew she was smarter, but that, at least in the family, was never commented on, perhaps not even noticed. Friends in New York had pointed out that her sole fault was the accidental one, of being born later and a girl, but for Kate that was no solace. She envied people with genuinely happy families and had longed all her life for a sister.

Her fair-minded ex-husband, Francis, though ever on the lookout for her, said it was not really Bruno's fault that he'd turned out so badly. He was a typical product of a minor public school that raised its boys as army fodder or for colonial outposts of an empire that no longer existed. Like many Englishmen of his age and class, Bruno basically feared and hated women. If he'd only had the brains, he might have followed his father into an academic career. As it was, he was now a master, disappointed and openly hating his job, at Monks, the very public school that had wrought such harm on his developing psyche. How accurate Francis turned out to have been, but then, he had always been discerning. Thinking of him now, Kate's sole regret was that she no longer had access to that candid smile and the pale, appraising eyes.

She turned up the collar of her sheepskin coat and shifted her packages back into the shelter of the station porch while she bleakly raked the familiar landscape of her childhood and waited, forlorn as an evacuee, to be claimed. Gravel swirled as the battered old station wagon swept into the station yard and there was Lindy, nodding in her chilly way, not even bothering to open the door to give her sister-in-law a proper welcome. At Christmas, too, and after all this time. When she knew full well that Kate was particularly vulnerable with another shattered relationship behind her.

'So you're here.'

Not a word of apology or even explanation for keeping her waiting so long in the cold and wet, but this was nothing new. Her brother's wife regarded Kate as an inconvenience, if not a downright nuisance. She leaned across and opened a rear door then sat in silence while Kate struggled alone with her welter of packages. And Merry Christmas to you too, she hissed to herself through gritted teeth.

'All right?'

Kate had barely closed the door and was still fumbling with her seatbelt when the car took off in another flurry of gravel and they were speeding through puddles on their way into Arundel and the rambling, down-at-heel old rectory that was Bruno's pride and joy.

'How long are you here for this time?'

Lindy was watching her in the driving mirror, her cool eyes speculative as she summed up her husband's sister.

'Just for the weekend,' said Kate apologetically.

'I meant in England.'

'Who knows? For ever. I have no real plans.'

Kate slumped back in her seat and gazed out at the sad, monochrome landscape, sneakily manipulating a cigarette from its packet and wondering if she dared light up.

'Still smoking? Surely not. Nobody does that any more, not in our circles.' Lindy worked part-time as a hospital almoner, when she could detach herself from her numerous kids. She was also a regular churchgoer and Kate found her sickeningly holier-than-thou. Well, tough shit. She lit up and took a long drag, then lay back in her seat and tried to soak up the scenery. And relax. That, after all, was supposed to be what weekends in the country were all about.

'Do you ever see Francis?' There, Lindy was at it already, talons flexed, out to draw blood.

'Nope.' Dumb question, of course she didn't.

'Funnily enough, I bumped into him last week.' Ah-ha, so this wasn't just idle chitchat.

'He was looking rather dashing, I thought.' For a man who'd been betrayed.

Kate could read her sister-in-law like a book and could always sense the lethal hidden dialogue. To Lindy, with her aspirations, cerebral power had always been a more potent turn-on than mere throbbing sexuality. Henry Kissinger would have left her pulverised and she'd always had a bit of a soft spot for Alan Bennett, despite the rumours. Odd then that she'd ended up with Bruno, poor cow.

'Smoother, better-looking somehow. Altogether more mature. And he had such a striking-looking woman with him, quite a beauty.'

Another sideswipe at Kate. Lindy didn't change. So sanctimonious on the surface but underneath a bitch to her fingertips.

'He hasn't altered a bit, though. As sweet and self-effacing as ever, and just as caring. Told me he's never forgotten my Yorkshire puddings which helped him conquer his homesickness. Silly boy, he always was a bit of a flirt. I said he should look us up some time. He's still at Jesus College, you know. I think he's become a bit of a star these days but he doesn't let it show. But that's Francis, isn't it?'

Yup, thought Kate silently, dragging on her fag. That's my boy. Always one for the line of least resistance, and even he couldn't miss this one coming from a hundred paces, even without his giglamps.

Lindy concentrated on turning off on to the bumpy, muddy track which led to her front door, then triumphantly flourished her trump.

'I didn't tell him you were back in England,' she said with satisfaction. 'Because he didn't ask.'

Bruno was already home, watching the BBC news and fretting.

'I have to be out of here by two,' he complained, then spotted his sister and gave her an abstracted nod.

Lindy bustled off into the kitchen and Kate, abandoned in the hall without so much as a by-your-leave, shrugged off her sheepskin and draped it over a chair, then crept into the untidy lounge to stash her presents. No sign here of a gift for her, but that was hardly surprising. Something hurriedly bought and carelessly wrapped would doubtless turn up on Christmas Eve, a book she'd read or a record she didn't particularly care for, with the card in her brother's writing, denoting more than anything the clear divide in Lindy's mind between his family and hers. None of that *mea casa, sua casa* nonsense in this house. Lindy made no secret of the fact that her children, her husband and her own tight family circle took precedence. Bruno's mother was an inconvenience and his wayward sister entirely beyond the pale.

Weekends at home had always been the same, Dad lingering late in his laboratory, Bruno rushing in from the pub, then out again for rugby or cricket, leaving Kate and her mother to cook, set and serve, then later to clear up. Sometimes he had a girl in tow but that made no difference. The poor popsy would not even be offered the choice between standing shivering on the sidelines, watching him play, or staying home with his womenfolk to help with the clearing up.

'I wouldn't mind so much,' Susie, his former girl-friend, had complained. 'But he will keep telling his mates how fat I'm getting. That I'll soon be playing prop for England.'

'Lunch up,' boomed Bruno now, through the door, and was already seated at the table with a beer at his side, ladling potatoes on to his plate, when Kate and a torrent of kids went to join him.

'If you want a drink you'll have to get it,' he said with his usual manners. 'Though I'd slow down if I were you or your liver will pack up.'

He smirked and wiped his nose on his table napkin. Always the charmer, was Brother Bruno. Kate never failed to marvel at how little he ever changed.

Grace Ashenberry was seated at the far end of a long, dimly lit room when Lindy dropped Kate in the porch and made a bank robber's getaway. Bruno would collect her later on his way home from the match. Kate parked her sheepskin in the hall and carried the poinsettia into her mother's presence. Grace received her kiss abstractedly, then sharply asked what had happened to tea. She looked at her daughter with accusing eyes as if groping for her name. With a sinking heart, Kate realised that it was to be one of those visits, and prepared herself for a depressing time.

In her heyday Grace Ashenberry had been something of a beauty, but now her features were gaunt and drained, and she had become a mere husk of her former self. She wore her customary faded blue, with a pale Paisley shawl around her shoulders, and her pure white hair was freshly washed and brushed back severely from her high, clever forehead, stamped with the discontent that had been there as long as Kate could remember. One positive thing about this home, they certainly took good care of her. Kate had heard too many horror stories from friends with similarly indisposed parents. It was a relief to find her own mother clean and sweet-smelling in a pretty, private room overlooking the wide, well-tended garden. Grace gazed out into the middle distance as if her mind were set on matters more deserving than the first sight of her only daughter in over eighteen months.

Kate placed the poinsettia on the table in front of her and went to the kitchen in search of a saucer.

'All right then, lovey?' asked the cheerful helper at the urn, beaming Kate the first genuine smile of this bleak day. 'Here to see your mum, are you? Ah, that's nice. Tell her tea won't be a minute. Likes her cuppa, bless her. Well, what else is there, I ask you, at that age?'

What indeed. Kate took the saucer back to the darkening room and set about unwrapping the plant and placing it to best effect on the windowsill. Soon tea, followed by Bruno, would arrive, and she could take her leave with a relatively clear conscience, though sad heart, until the next significant duty call, probably Mother's Day. It broke her heart to see her clever, élitist mother trapped like this in an institution for the elderly and deranged but, as the woman had said, what else was there for her now she no longer had a full deck? At least, thanks to Dad's foresight and prudent investing, there was money to pay for a bit of privilege for her. She wasn't living alone in squalor or, heaven forbid, forced to wander the streets. And that was about all there was to say for it.

And what about me when I get to her age? thought Kate bleakly, as she often did on occasions like this. No husband, no child and now not even Ramon. Fear gripped her chest with its familiar icy hand as she saw her present loneliness projecting on into infinity. More than anything now she longed to be able to take her mother's hand and pour all her troubles into a sympathetic ear, but those days, alas, were gone for ever. Besides, to be truthful, Grace had never been much of a one for a confidence.

'I don't want to interfere' was her maxim, whether it was Bruno's marriage or Kate's own troubled adolescence under the spotlight. No thought that these were her children who might be in need, even in pain, badly needing a mother's wise counsel. If it wasn't mentioned, it didn't exist. She'd even had that attitude to periods, so how could she be expected to cope when it came to sex?

'Merry Christmas, Mum,' whispered Kate, but she knew her mother wasn't listening.

Eventually Bruno did show up, but as usual he was in a hurry.

'Got to stop by the school,' he said as he hustled her into the car. 'The Old Boys are having a committee meeting and I said I'd drop in for a couple of jars.'

He belched. Even at this time in the afternoon, his breath smelled of beer, and she could tell he was already half-cut. It was amazing what you could get away with in these country areas, driving quite recklessly without any thought of safety. Not for the first time, Kate was glad she had never had children. Heaven forbid, they might have ended up like Bruno. Or, worse still, being taught by him.

Bruno was at his sparkling best when mingling with his fellow no-hopers. As he ushered her into the Old Boys' clubroom, with its familiar smell of stale malt and sawdust, all kinds of memories she'd rather have forgotten came struggling back from Kate's subconscious. Good God, they were all still here, pickled in brine, seated at the bar like crows on a telephone wire; smug, unambitious, going nowhere.

'Greetings!' bellowed Bruno, at his mellifluous best, passingly proud of his kid sister who hadn't yet lost her looks. 'You remember Katie? Back from the Big Apple. Still hasn't managed to catch herself a man, so maybe one of you chaps would oblige.'

Haw haw. Chuckling hugely, Bruno lurched across to the bar and bought himself a pint of ale and her a half of lager and lime. It was years since she'd encountered that poisonous concoction but he never bothered to ask, so she reverted to second-class citizen and drank it without a word. Until, as the clock neared seven, she gave him a nudge and suggested they ought to be going. Lindy was cooking dinner and had even invited some neighbours in, since Kate was there and they owed some hospitality. She'd surely be getting anxious, if not cross.

'Rubbish!' said her brother dismissively, deep in his discussion of the day's play. He belched again and knocked back his beer, then ordered himself another. It was amazing, really, how he'd managed never to grow up. In a way, she admired this relentless clinging to long-gone youth, the bonding for life with his schoolmates. Susie had left him after less than two miserable years because, in the end, she had found she couldn't even dent his hardened lack of sensitivity. He was forever on at her about her weight, her stupidity and her extravagance, not for one moment imagining that she might have feelings. Just so had he always trampled on Kate. All she could do when Susie departed was wish her well. And harden her resolution to get the hell out too, as soon as she was able.

'Don't have kids,' advised Bruno unexpectedly, on the way to the station the following day. 'Expensive, messy and far more trouble than they're worth. We must have been mad. All they do, once they reach puberty, is up and leave you. Either that or they hang around forever;

don't know which is worse. Or else they're on crack. It's a no-win situation, I can tell you.'

Bruno had always been surprisingly negative about his own brood, but he also made no secret of hating teaching. How dreary he made life seem, yet their father had always been as happy as Larry in his own eccentric way, pottering around in his laboratory, forever on the brink of some world-shattering discovery. Bruno had inherited his mother's bleak outlook. Kate at least had got the sense of humour.

'Bye,' she said as they reached the station. 'Have a great Christmas and I hope the kids like their presents.' She hadn't seen much of them this weekend. Like their father, they seemed to be perpetually out. 'Thanks too for taking care of Mum.'

'You could join us, I suppose,' said Bruno doubtfully, as if the thought had only just occurred. He stood by the car as she struggled with her luggage, paunchy and defeated in his matted sweater and muddy wellingtons. 'Only Lindy's parents will be coming, and her sister . . .'

'No thanks,' lied Kate rapidly. 'I already have arrangements.'

Anything, even four days alone in the chilly, unwelcoming mansion block, would be better than Christmas with a family who made no secret of not loving her. That, she supposed, was the purpose of these festivities; to scratch old scars and make them bleed, to strengthen yourself against more pain. You were born alone and you died alone. How true that turned out to be. The bit in between was simply to be endured. Her family couldn't give a toss what her plans might be, hadn't even asked. All they cared about was their own narrow world, and the moment she was gone, she'd be forgotten. No one had even thought to mention Ramon or ask how she was coping alone.

Which, as it turned out, was pretty bloody miserably.

3

So here she now was, three days before Christmas, fumbling in her bag for the keys while the taxi waited and the bells of St Mary Abbots rang out, heralding the festive season. There wasn't a lot for her to carry, for the flat was more or less furnished and she'd left the States with virtually nothing. Just as well, too. Not realising that the traffic in this street was one way, she had asked the driver to drop her on the corner, so now she had to schlep her bags the last few yards to the doorway of Kensington Court. By hanging two from each shoulder and one round her neck, she managed to shuffle painfully like a bag lady, then returned to collect the last two boxes.

In the dark recess of the doorway to the Arab Bank, closed for business, something stirred. At first Kate thought it was an animal invading a pile of rubbish, but when she paused to investigate, she was caught up short by a pair of penetrating dark eyes glaring back at her like glowing coals. Eyes as dark and intense as a gorilla's. Kate started and dropped one of the bags, but it was a man and not an animal, albeit a wild and dangerous-looking one, with a chiselled jaw and starkly shaven pate, wrapped in an army greatcoat and draped in old sacking.

'Clear off!' he threatened in a guttural voice as dark and gravelly as the grave, as Kate stumbled and grabbed frantically for her scattered possessions, all of a sudden gripped by a terrible fear.

'I'm sorry,' she said. 'I really didn't see you,' and fled. Oh my goodness, in a place like this too, sudden startling menace right here on her own doorstep. Accustomed as she was to walking the streets of Manhattan's Upper West Side, she had not expected to be threatened in an area as safe and conservative as this. Her heart was still banging as she unlocked the heavy front door and ladled herself and her assorted baggage thankfully into the elegant hallway.

Nothing stirred. The hall and stairwell were deserted and lit by a melancholy light as if, by swinging open that impenetrable front door, she had stepped back in time to the beginning of the century. Even the porter's lodge was in darkness, though it was barely five o'clock. The floor was thickly carpeted in a workable beige, and Kate's feet sank into its deep pile as she ferried her possessions up the short flight of steps and round the corner to the antique hydraulic lift. The wrought-iron gates were heavy but well oiled, and nothing disturbed her as she piled her bags inside, then sank on to the polished wooden bench and pressed the brass button to ascend. With a great deal of whirring and groaning, the archaic machinery ground painfully into life and slowly, slowly, like something out of a Parisian melodrama, the open cage moved upwards, giving its passenger a good view of each successive floor it passed, each as deserted as the last. What on earth sort of a place was this, and what had she let herself in for? Kensington Court, with its thick fitted carpets and solid, late-Victorian structure, was as silent and undisturbed as a museum. Or a tomb. She was glad when the lift ground slowly to a clanging halt and she found herself on the top floor, facing the door of number 25.

With hands that suddenly shook, though Kate was not entirely sure why, she put down her baggage and unlocked the door of the huge, half-empty flat waiting to suck her in or reject her. She flung her coat on to the stripped bed, found her cigarettes and settled down in the kitchen for a restorative smoke while she took a long, hard look at her new surroundings. All the rooms had fine rooftop vistas but the view from the kitchen window was particularly dramatic, framing, as it did, the floodlit spire of St Mary Abbots, fringed by the skeletal winter trees of Kensington Gardens, beyond a forest of Victorian chimneys. The building directly across the street, one storey lower than Kate's own eyrie, had pointed gingerbread windows and a steeply sloping roof, dappled with frost like a scene from a Christmas card, and a glimpse of a cosy interior through its uncurtained windows. Kate thought immediately of Hansel and Gretel, and Tom the chimney sweep in *The Water Babies*, and a familiar rush of plaintive nostalgia engulfed her. Three days from Christmas and here she was again, facing the long holiday break alone, in a city she found friendless and unwelcoming. She also thought of *A Christmas Carol*, another haunting nightmare of her earlier years, and the terrifying sound of Marley's clanking chains reverberating round just such a building. She could almost hear the scraping across the floor and her spine began to tingle at the thought of what might appear.

'This won't do,' she said briskly, stubbing out her fag. There was more than enough work to be done. She lugged her bundles into the smaller of the bedrooms and set about stashing things away in the drab, uninspiring chest and wardrobe, trying to make the place feel more her own. What furniture there was would have to do for now but it was only the bare essentials. Once she'd amassed a little money, she'd go shopping and start building herself a nest – something of her own where she could hide from the world. For this, from now on, was to be her whole existence – her workplace as well as her home. The less she saw, the better of the big tough world outside. Right now, Kate was a damaged animal who had crawled into a cave to lick her wounds and recover.

Across the cavernous hall, the main living room was huge and high-ceilinged, with two sets of sashed windows looking east towards the church. At present, it was sparsely furnished, with a couple of sagging armchairs and a lumpy sofa that had seen better days and smelled faintly of mildew, but already she could see that the room had the potential to become truly splendid. There was a wide, brick-lined fireplace with a working flue, down which an icy gale was blowing, and, on either side of the oak mantel, a couple of brass servants' bells which she thought of pressing but stopped herself just in time. Echoes of her childhood terrors came flooding back. Her parents might have vetoed the obvious scary influences of Hammer horror and *Psycho*, but they could not shield her from the more insidious frighteners like *The Turn of the Screw* or the stories of M. R. James or E. F. Benson, compulsively consumed beneath the bedclothes long after they thought she was asleep. Now, just looking at those antique bell-pushes brought to mind her favourite story, 'Oh, Whistle, and I'll Come Unto You, My Lad', and she shivered deliciously. This old building was steeped in antiquity; she hoped it didn't have a ghost and tried not to think of it, though nothing from the supernatural could possibly be worse than what she had experienced in New York.

She was standing on a kitchen chair, wrestling a dead light bulb from a rusted socket, when the doorbell rang, startling and sudden. Not the downstairs bell, heralding a caller from the street, but Kate's own front door, which was infinitely more alarming. Kate hesitated, then wiped some of the grime from her face with her sleeve and ventured into the large, bright hall to see what was going on. Beyond the frosted glass she could see a dark shape waiting. Instinctively, her heart started to pound as she checked the door chain and slid it into position before cautiously opening the door an inch.

'Good evening!'

The man who stood there, beaming broadly, wore a well-cut pinstripe suit and horn-rimmed glasses that shielded the merriest eyes Kate had seen in a long while. He was youngish, in his late thirties she would guess, with shaggy hair that would not stay in place and a wine stain on his expensive foulard tie. In one hand he carried a bottle of champagne, and he exuded the very essence of seasonal cheer. She released the chain.

'Gosh, I do hope I'm not disturbing you!' Concern clouded the boyish face as he took in her grimy appearance as well as the tension of her manner. 'I just thought I'd call and say a neighbourly hello. I'm Miles Burdett, your landlord. Number seventeen should you ever need anything.'

One manicured hand grasped Kate's firmly, and before she knew it, he was past her and inside, strolling about as if he did indeed own the place and glancing curiously at the mess. Kate was startled, and canny enough not to take him at face value. She was, after all, a dyed-in-the-wool New Yorker these days, and thoroughly streetwise. Friendly he might be, but she had learned the hard way not to judge by superficial impressions.

'I thought the landlord was a woman,' she said suspiciously. 'Mrs Benjamin or something?'

Even after an absence of several years, English charm still left her cold, one of the reasons, she was wont to say in New York, that she had never bothered to remarry. Deep down and intrinsically, Englishmen did not like women; witness the awful Bruno and his misogynist cronies. It was all to do with the way they were raised. Though this one was certainly putting on a fair enough show.

'Correct.' The smile had never left his face and he was ushering her into her own living room as casually as if it was his home not hers. 'But as of yesterday, it belongs to me. I bought her out.'

'Poor old duck,' he told Kate later, once the champagne was poured and they were slumped side by side on the sagging sofa. 'Rich as all get out, but between you and me, going a bit soft in the head. Lives in the country with an elderly retainer but owns half of Kensington, so far as I could discover. Thought I'd do her a bit of a service and unload some of her commitments. After all, in a building like this it's important to keep up standards, and we can't have one absentee landlady letting down the side.'

Despite her reservations, Kate was softening. Miles Burdett was a charmer, no mistake, but there was also something spontaneous about him that she found appealing. Instinctively, she trusted him, and for Kate that was rare. Particularly now, in the present circumstances.

'So you live here yourself. Do you own many of the flats?' He seemed young to be so affluent.

'Just three. This one, my own and number seven. Good investment, you know. These old buildings are built like fortresses and should last for ever. Compare it to Chelsea Harbour, which is jerry-built, or Lancer Square, which is already falling down, and you're laughing. And it's certainly a prime site, nothing better. You know the three most important things to look for in property?'

'Location, location and location,' chimed in Kate, joining him in his laughter.

'Correct.'

'What's she like?' asked Claudia. She had a headache and was spread out on the sofa, one hand draped dramatically to protect her eyes from the sudden light.

'Not bad. Quite nice really. Thin, tense, scared of her own shadow. Younger than us. Married but doesn't wear a ring. What else do you want to know?'

Miles disappeared into the bedroom to change out of his City suit.

'Pretty?'

'Ish. If she would only learn to relax. I wonder what's bugging her. You'd think she'd robbed a bank or something. Even had the door chain on at only five o'clock.'

'Sensible girl. You never know these days, and if she lives alone . . . Anyhow, how do you know she's married? Why would she tell you a thing like that?'

Claudia was sitting up now, fired by suspicion. Miles wandered out of the bedroom, clad in jeans and a Lacoste shirt, and went back into the kitchen.

'She didn't,' he shouted triumphantly 'I heard it from the agent, who heard it from Mrs B.'

'Why would she bother to tell you a thing like that?'

'Don't know,' said Miles, reappearing with glasses and a bottle of chilled Krug. 'Just nosy, I guess.'

'Oh Miles, don't open another one,' said Claudia wearily. 'What happened to the one you were fiddling with earlier?'

'Drank it,' said Miles as he deftly manoeuvred out the cork without spilling a drop. 'Upstairs with the popsy. She looked as though she could use a bit of lightening up.'

'You'd better introduce her to Gregory then. Or maybe you'd rather keep her for yourself.'

Claudia rose, tall and slim, smoothed down her immaculate gabardine skirt and slid her feet back into her patent pumps. Keeping an eye on Miles was a full-time occupation, but at least it had helped to chase away the headache. She glanced at her watch.

'Don't forget we have to be with the Fentons at seven,' she said, moving into the bedroom to change. 'God, how I hate this time of year. It's bad enough at the office but you'd think the neighbours could leave us alone.'

Miles snapped on the television to catch the news.

'Ingrate!' he shouted back at her. 'Be glad anyone invites you at all. Think of all the homeless and the old and unwanted.'

Think of Caroline and the girls, he might have added. Instead he engineered a diversion in his wife's neurotic train of thought.

'Gregory will sniff her out for himself, if I know my boy. Though it doesn't always pay to dirty your own nest, and Greg's not entirely the fool he sometimes seems.' Don't dip your pen in the company inkwell, was what Miles usually said, but that was sailing a bit close to the wind, especially now, when a storm was imminent. He'd broken that rule himself and been badly burned. Let it rest.

Claudia didn't bother to reply as she riffled through her orderly row of designer numbers, colour-coded and arranged according to season. At least tonight they didn't have to leave the building, which meant she could wear her new suede Charles Jourdain shoes and not take a coat. For small mercies be thankful, she thought, as she drew the shower curtain and turned on the water.

Mrs Benjamin's furniture was solid but had seen better days and did very little to enhance the homeliness of the large and basically depressing flat. Luckily Kate had savings, as well as money set aside from her last big assignment, so once this Christmas nonsense was safely out of the way, she'd start combing the local junk shops and antique markets for acceptable replacements. Things with personality, nothing too expensive. With Ramon she'd become accustomed to a certain level of South American grandeur; now all she needed was something cheap and cheerful, anything to make it feel a little like home.

First, however, there was the four-day holiday to navigate. Even though her instinct was to forget all about it and just keep working, when it actually came to the crunch Kate found it impossible to ignore the traditions she'd been brought up with and boycott Christmas altogether. She sat in the living room, with her morning coffee and the radio for company, and pencilled a list of necessities for the forlorn siege that lay ahead. From across the road, on the opposite corner, came the vigorous strains of *Silent Night*, briskly belted out on steel drums, no doubt charming for the first fourteen run-throughs but likely, she knew, ultimately to drive her crazy unless she got dressed very soon and made her escape. She flicked around the dial until she found music to suit her mood; country and western interspersed by a warm Irish accent, that was more the ticket.

Chicken bits, she wrote, then crossed out *bits*. What the hell, it was Christmas after all. The very least she could do was give herself a small culinary treat, though it would have to last for several days. And she could always turn the carcass into stock if she could be bothered. But what went with chicken?

Sausages. Slightly overcooked, with lovely crusty skins, not like the ones Lindy cooked, which were soggy in the middle.

Mushrooms, she added. Then *sherry*. No, that was stupid, since she had no one to drink it with and didn't even like the stuff. She scrubbed it out.

Wine.

Potatoes. She could have one baked instead of the wickedly fattening roast ones they traditionally had with the turkey. But no sprouts. At last she could indulge herself and miss out the overcooked mush she had hated since childhood. As an afterthought, she crossed out *potatoes* and substituted *wild rice*. Provided you could get it here, which somehow she doubted, though she'd heard Sainsbury's was always worth a visit.

God, but this was depressing. All of a sudden Kate was overwhelmed by a sharp need to be back in New York. Ramon, oh Ramon. She buried her face in the musty tapestry cushions and gave way to a moment of total despair. What in hell's name was she doing back here instead of there, where she truly belonged? Particularly now, at Christmas, the time above all when lovers should be reunited. For one giddy second she thought of phoning him, then sanity returned and she pulled herself together.

Decorations, she wrote defiantly, and *holly*. Then

dumped her empty mug into the kitchen sink and set about facing the day.

It was fairly absurd to get a tree, but the nursery was enticing so she ended up buying one anyhow. She breathed in the delicious smell of woodsmoke and frost as she walked down to the tennis courts behind Rassells in the Earls Court Road, temporarily converted into a slaughterhouse of fallen firs. She selected a humble one from the pile of four-footers, and watched while the cheerful young New Zealander knocked a block of wood on to its trunk with a couple of sturdy nails, then shoved it through the netting machine so that it emerged encased in a plastic caul to enable her to lug it home. What the hell, she bought a holly wreath too, and slung the bag over her arm while she shouldered the tree. Even Christmas alone and in flight needed some sort of a seasonal statement, particularly since her whole family had rejected her. After all, it wasn't really Christmas till you'd carried home the tree and hung up the holly.

The lift gates were just clanging shut as she manoeuvred the tree through into the hall, and by the time she had negotiated the steps the machinery was already in ponderous motion. Kate was just in time to snatch a glimpse of feet encased in sensible suede boots as the antique iron edifice disappeared upwards. Somewhere, several floors above, she heard its doors crash open. Well, at least she was not entirely alone in this mausoleum. In the two days she had been here she had seriously started to wonder. Footsteps and the sound of a key in a lock was all she heard beyond that.

Kensington Court resumed its silent slumber and Kate bore her tree aloft before remembering she had nothing to put on it.

She chanced upon the kitten later that day, as dusk was falling and she ventured to the service steps to deposit the rubbish left over from her unpacking. He was squashed amongst a row of bulging sacks and only his sharp, furtive movement made her notice him at all. In the dim light and relentless drizzle, she thought at first it was a rat, but then she saw the stricken yellow eyes peering out of pitifully plastered fur, and the small pink mouth opened in a soundless O of distress. She bent instinctively to pick him up.

He wasn't going to come without a fight and Kate found her hand dripping blood from two savage scratches, but she persevered, and he was so bedraggled that he simply couldn't put up a proper defence. Eventually she managed to trap him up against the steel door to the boiler room and wrap him, hissing and snarling, securely in her scarf to be carried upstairs for a proper examination.

'Well, you're a sorry scrap, to be sure!' she said, once he had been vigorously rubbed dry with the kitchen towel and tempted with a saucer of milk and morsels of the haddock she had bought for her supper. Though filthy and flea-ridden from living rough, he was emerging now as a handsome dark tabby with white shirtfront and paws. His eyes were emphasised by a dramatic dark mask which gave him the look of a highway robber, and she fell in love with him on the spot, despite his emphatic shrinking from her touch. He had already rewarded her Samaritan instincts with several more vicious scratches, and now he shrank into a corner under the table, his tiny mouth open in a soundless snarl. At least she now had someone to share her Christmas, even if he was a reluctant guest.

Now all she needed was the computer up and running and she might even begin to earn some money to pay for it all.

4

On Christmas morning the bells rang out loud and clear, and Kate awoke to find a small warm bundle nestled up against her feet at the bottom of the duvet.

'Well!' she said in delight, opening her eyes and cautiously wriggling up the bed to a sitting position. 'And a very merry Christmas to you! So you've decided to stay then?'

He reverted instantly from cuddly toy to wild animal, flashing off the bed like a rat out of a box to cower in the darkest corner of the bedroom, shielded behind the chest of drawers. Kate lay there drowsily, content for the while just to let him be, in no hurry to get out of bed since she had a clear day ahead of her with nothing to do but cook a modest chicken and investigate her only present. Five inches square and untidily wrapped, it was addressed in Bruno's sprawling script and had arrived, as usual, on Christmas Eve. No prizes for guessing what it might contain: a selection of arias from Gilbert and Sullivan, maybe, or Verdi's Greatest Hits, when the fact was that right at this moment, she didn't even possess a CD player. When she thought of the hours she had spent combing Bloomingdales and

F. A. O. Schwartz for just the right things for all of them . . .

Am I really that nasty a person? she pondered behind closed lids. Not to be down there toiling in the bosom of my family, helping peel spuds and scrape plates and playing mindless games with those kids? And putting up with Lindy's pious nagging, and listening one more time to Bruno's tired old jokes . . . Any guilt she might have felt dispersed when she remembered she hadn't actually been officially invited. She drowsed off, to be awoken mid-morning by tiny, cautious footsteps across the duvet. She did not move but slowly extended one hand in a gesture of friendship, and after what seemed like many minutes, the feathery tip of a small cold nose was pressed into it. The hint of a lick, even; could it be he was hungry?

'Okay,' she whispered. 'Time to shake a leg, I guess, and get us both some breakfast.'

The tree stood in isolated splendour in the hall, sparsely decorated with a single string of lights – the only box left in the shop when she'd finally got round to looking – and a few beautiful Victorian china balls she'd found in the V&A shop. She plucked a minuscule package from beneath it and tossed it to the timid kitten, who backed away, its face distorted in the silent snarl she was learning to love.

'All right. Don't open it if you don't want to,' she said, and shuffled into the kitchen to make coffee.

It was such a glorious morning, Kate decided to take a walk in the park. She had nothing much else to do apart from work, and the day stretched tediously in front of her, empty and uncharted. There was little point waiting at home for a telephone call that was unlikely to come, and in any case, this was supposed to be a new beginning, the start of a different life. Sun streamed through her windows and the bells of St Mary Abbots were once more in full peal, a joyous invocation to celebrate the Saviour's birth, as she stepped from the lift on the ground floor. For the first time since she had moved in, there was someone else waiting, a bulky woman with pale skin and silver blonde curls, parcelled up in a great plaid capelike coat with a knitted tam-o'-shanter on her head.

'Morning,' said Kate automatically, forgetting for the moment that she was not still in New York, where greeting strangers came more naturally. Then: 'Merry Christmas,' as the other woman passed her into the lift and soundlessly pressed the button to ascend.

'Oh Adelaide dear, wait till I tell you who I've seen.' Netta Silcock was so full of news she could scarcely wait to get inside her neighbour's door. Mrs Adelaide Potter took the silly woolly hat and placed it with some distaste on the hall chest.

'Come along, Netta,' she said severely. 'We've all been waiting for you.'

'The sermon went on longer than usual,' burbled Netta, sitting down heavily on the chest to unzip her fur boots. 'And then the minister had a word with each of us, such a lovely man.'

But Adelaide had already returned to the drawing room, where her other guests were waiting.

'She's here,' she announced as she poured them each

a thimbleful of sherry. 'I'll just put a light under the sprouts and then we can eat.'

Lady Wentworth sat graciously in the best armchair by the fireplace and nodded her head regally as Netta pattered into the room on her stockinged feet. There was something reminiscent of Queen Mary about the grand old woman. Even though they had lived so close for a number of years, Netta still felt quite in awe of her. Heidi Applebaum was in her usual place, at the stove, but Mrs Adelaide Potter managed to prise her away and send her scuttling in to join the other guests.

Amelia Rowntree rose awkwardly from the tapes-tried settle on which she was perched and handed around the salted nuts. Her thick tweed skirt was bagging at the seat and the powder blue twinset was a shade too tight across her heavy bust. She's putting on weight, reflected Netta Silcock with satisfaction, plonking herself down on the sofa. A brilliant shaft of sunlight hit her like a spotlight, illuminating the clear, grape-green eyes like marbles and accentuating her unnaturally pale skin. My wee lassie, the poor man's Marilyn Monroe, was what her Archie had always called her, but that, alas, was years ago; there was no one left to say it now.

'I just bumped into what must be the new tenant on the top floor,' she said. 'Small and dark, wearing a sheepskin coat.' She glanced at each of them, bright with importance. 'Going out.'

'Come along, Netta,' said Adelaide Potter bossily, ushering her into the dining room next door where a lace cloth was set for lunch for five. 'Keep that till later,

Heidi's just finished carving the duck. Pop over to the sideboard, will you, Amelia, and we'll all have a drop of wine, since it's a special occasion.'

Mrs Adelaide Potter ruled Kensington Court like a field marshal. She was one of the oldest surviving tenants, having lived there for over thirty years, the last ten as a widow, and there was little that escaped her probing and ruthlessly critical eye. It was tiresome of Netta to be one jump ahead in the matter of the new tenant. She was forced to put this snippet of information into proper perspective by ignoring it. She brought in the duck triumphantly, steaming and neatly sliced.

'Beautifully cooked, Adelaide dear,' Heidi muttered, reaching like a drowning man for the crystal goblet into which Amelia had poured her a couple of inches of golden hock.

'Not too much for me,' said Lady Wentworth. 'Not if we're going to play bridge afterwards. Now come along, Netta, and tell us about the new neighbour. A young woman, you say? On her own, then?'

The old lady didn't have a lot of time for the fussy, fat Scotswoman who didn't, she felt, fit into this building, but breeding prevented her from letting it show. What Archie Silcock had been about when he took as his second wife this Gorbals nurse, goodness only knew, though she did have the charity to admit that Netta had looked after him well, until his own premature death scarcely a year later. Ah well, these were democratic days and anyone who could afford the upkeep and service charges was, Lady Wentworth supposed, entitled to live in the building, though she could not help regretting the old days when you knew exactly who your neighbours were and, more to the point, who they were related to.

Take poor Heidi Applebaum, for instance, with her perpetual nervousness and air of constant apology. She was a funny little woman, a good soul really, if only she wouldn't fuss so much. A widow herself of some five years' standing, she treated Adelaide Potter like God and worried herself into a state if ever she thought she had done something to cause her displeasure, a not unusual state of affairs. Lady Wentworth took a discreet sip of wine and squarely faced the truth. At least they were company. At her stage in life she was lucky to have neighbours on whom she could rely. She must never, ever lose sight of that.

Kate cut down Holland Street and crossed Church Street into Kensington Gardens. A pale sun hung halfway down the sky and the air was dry and pleasantly crisp. One of those beautiful winter afternoons that took her back sharply to New York; instantly she felt a stab of pain in her gut and the old familiar sorrow welling up. She walked up past the Palace, slumbering beneath the wintry sun, and gave a fleeting thought to the lonely princess, rumoured to be spending her Christmases alone there since the failure of her own marriage. They were roughly of an age, Kate and Diana, and she wondered idly how she would be received were she to wander up to the policemen at the gate and ask if Her Royal Highness would care to come out to play. She might well get a surprise; it couldn't be much of an existence stuck inside that prison of a home, no matter how luxurious, and they could swap sob stories and cry on each other's shoulder. But she kept on walking. The way she was feeling today, she'd make lousy company for anyone, let alone a deserted princess who, like herself, had found too late that her fairy prince had feet of clay.

The best, truly magical Christmas Kate could remember was way back in her childhood when she still half-believed in Santa Claus. But the last of the traditional family ones was the year before Dad died, when her mother was still her old electrifying self, Bruno only newly with Susie and Kate just coming up to twenty-one. For once, a cold December promising early snow. Everyone, as always, converging on the house on the cliffs, with the family doubling up by choice to make room for the occasional odds and sods without whom Christmas would not have been complete. Or so Mother always said, and, make no mistake, what she said went.

The kitchen, always the focal point of the house, was its usual furnace, the old wood-burning stove belching merry sparks into the frenzied atmosphere, just like Bruno after one of his wild nights of excess, said Susie in a rare moment of wit. From the low, uneven plastered ceiling, with its genuine oak beams, hung, along with the hams, an old-fashioned airer, festooned on the night before Christmas with dripping things: dishcloths wrung out to dry after several days' hard graft; the old heirloom lace tablecloth, on an impulse rinsed out in water and sugar to be ready for tomorrow's celebration ('to look at it, my dear, anyone would believe you had finally found religion', was Dad's regular joke); plus Bruno's rugby kit, produced absent-mindedly ten minutes before the meal was due to be served, with the urgent reminder to his mother that he needed it clean for Boxing Day since they were playing seven-a-sides against the Old Merchant Taylors. That was the year, in fact, that the rot set in, when even Susie, scatty and unstructured as she was, began to recognise the truth about the brutish lout she found herself shacked up with.

'I'm sorry, Mrs A,' she had explained, helplessly waving her hands when Bruno dropped his annual offering, the contents of his reeking sports bag, on to the kitchen table amongst the bowls of peeled sprouts and closely shaved potatoes soaking in acidulated water, 'I didn't find it until the very last minute, we've both been so busy. And he really does need them for Tuesday. At Croxley Green.'

She'd shrugged her plump shoulders – what could you do? – at the assembled helpers in the kitchen, all of them women, and clearly expected some sort of applause for being such a brave little trouper. Then meekly followed him down to the pub without so much as a by-your-leave, abandoning the older ladies to cope, the aunts and the assorted hangers-on, as if it were her right as a young, arrogant and moderately nubile bimbo – yes, for Susie that was the apposite word – in thrall as she was to this insensitive, semi-literate thug. Oh Susie, as you sowed, so shall you reap. It was less than six months later that she took Kate aside on a wet Sunday walk, to talk about her sex life. Or lack of it, rather.

'It's first thing in the morning that really gets to me,' she complained. 'He farts, rolls over, scratches his belly and says, "God, I feel like a poke." He doesn't know what a turn-off I find it. Whatever am I to do?'

She turned to Kate, her boyfriend's baby sister, who gazed at her in transfixed horror and frantically racked her brains to find a way to put it tactfully without appearing either coarse or uncaring.

'If you didn't mention it the first time,' was all she could come up with, treading delicate ground – he was, after all, her closest kin – and seeking inspiration from what the agony aunts might say, 'then I'm afraid you do have a problem. Once a thing takes hold as a habit, it's hard to make him change it.'

She continued floundering till Francis, dependable as always when his mind was not on higher things, came up from behind to tweak her hair, wrap her scarf a little tighter and claim her as his own. Run like the clappers, was what she really wanted to say, but loyalty prevented it. It turned out she need not have worried. Susie clearly got the message, or reached the right conclusion all on her own. Within the year, she had left Bruno for a man nearly three times his age. Yes, really.

'Huh, it's always money that talks,' huffed Bruno. 'Mercenary little bitch, they're all exactly the same. Out for one thing and one thing only.'

But that Christmas, that earlier Christmas, when even the weather played by the rules, cynicism was the very last thing on anyone's mind. Dad came home early from the university and led the boys into the woods to fetch home a ten-foot tree, while the womenfolk, headed by Mother, swabbed the decks and made things shipshape ready for the festivities to start. There was cooking and baking and basting in droves, until the creaking old house on its precarious rooftop ledge swelled at the seams with the effluence of good living and positively sighed at being so much loved again. And the old aunts dusted and polished and complained about their rheumatism, then sat by the fire with their schooners of sherry, while the elderly widower from the corner of the common room let out one more button of his faded moleskin waistcoat and told tall tales of life in the good old days, before it all went comprehensive and sour and Thatcher's heaven failed to materialise.

It was the best of times and the worst of times – how did Dickens always get in on the act? He with his ghosts and the Spirit of Christmas Past and the blazing log fires and the fat plum puddings and the garnished turkey, enough to feed four families, and the table fireworks and walnuts and port. And then the Queen's Speech. And the men all snoozing while the aunts helped clear the dishes, and *The Wizard of Oz* and the cutting of the cake and a round of tea before it was time for proper drinks again.

And a short, sharp walk along the cliffs in a raging gale (the men again), while the aunts had a snooze and the rest of the womenfolk, those that were still active, chopped the salad and sliced the cold turkey and ham and decanted the trifle and the frozen sorbet. And set the table one more time, in the morning room for a change, and sorted the crackers and chilled the hock and opened the burgundy to allow it to breathe. Then powdered their noses and rubbed in handcream, ready to start all over again.

With sharpened pencils and clean lined pads filched from the university, ready for rhyming consequences in front of the fire while the seabirds wheeled and screeched outside and the inclement south coast weather blew itself into a storm. And tangerines were peeled and walnuts cracked, and belt buckles eased and secrets exchanged in the privacy of the upstairs bathroom or out in the stables where the billiards table was stashed.

And then, later still, when the aunts had gone to bed, the lights would be dimmed and the port and brandy brought in, and the few stalwart survivors would gather around the dying fire to tell ghost stories. And Mother, with a glint in her eye and a becoming flush to her cheek, would sing in sepulchral tones the haunting legend of 'The Mistletoe Bough', which told the true story of Lord Lovell's bride, lost during a game of Christmas hide-and-seek on her wedding night in Minster Lovell. A delicious prickle of terror would run down Kate's spine when Mother reached the final, doom-filled verse and lowered her voice dramatically to a rasping whisper:

'At length an oak chest, that had long lain hid,
Was found in the castle – they raised the lid –
And a skeleton form lay mouldering there,
In the bridal wreath of that lady fair!
Oh, sad was her fate! – in a sportive jest
She hid from her lord in the old oak chest.

It closed with a spring! – and, dreadful doom,
The bride lay clasp'd in her living tomb.'

And then she'd be too scared to go to her room alone,
so that one of the men would have to carry her, and she
would wait for Mother to come and tuck her in, and
insist on having the light on all night long, or at least
until she had fallen asleep, when Dad would come
stealthily into the room to check her covers and turn it
off.

Christmas would never be so special again, not
since, years later, Francis Pitt, the myopic boy wonder,
finally looked up from his microscope long enough to
kiss little Katie under the mistletoe, thereby sealing
her fate. And ruining Christmas for the rest of her life,
or so it seemed to Kate now, as she wandered alone
through the park.

She skirted the Round Pound, where a sprinkling of
eager children were testing their Christmas boats on its
steel-grey surface, and walked on down, past the
obelisk of the Speke Memorial, towards the Italian garden, where the fountains had been turned off. Only a
handful of walkers were out: a couple of solitary
women exercising their dogs; an old man who looked
as though he might well have been there all night; one
young couple, deeply in love, with eyes only for each
other. The familiar lump rose in Kate's throat and she
rummaged for a tissue and blew her nose hard. There
was a particularly sweet drinking fountain close to the
garden, a couple of bronze bears embracing each other.
Normally Kate would have found them cute; today

they only added to her general feeling of desolation, so she avoided Peter Pan altogether and walked instead on the other side of the Long Water towards the Serpentine.

In New York she might have crossed the park and spent a couple of cosy hours in the Metropolitan Museum before carrying the papers home for Bloody Marys by the fire with Ramon. But that idyll was over now and Ramon no longer part of her life; she dared not even think about him for fear of bringing on another attack of overwhelming grief and remorse. Diana might have her problems but at least she had those boys as consolation. Kate, childless and with two major break-ups behind her, was already on the wrong side of thirty, with nothing at all to look forward to except survival in a bleak, cold city where she no longer even had friends. That was another of Ramon's achievements. In the very short period they'd been together before he had snatched her away to New York, he'd made a point of isolating her from her existing friendships. He loved her far too much, he said, to share her with anyone else.

The sun was disappearing and the air had developed a nip. Kate wound her scarf more closely round her chin and lowered her head as she turned for home, walking close to the edge of the water and avoiding the copious droppings of the Canada geese who should, by rights, have flown south by now for the winter. Somewhere she had read that these days they were so sophisticated they migrated only as far as St James's Park, no more than a mile away, but there were certainly plenty of them still in evidence. And on

Christmas Day they were lucky to be alive. She thought of the homeless and the needy, as well as all those stuffed and garnished birds being served up in homes all over the land; there was something faintly obscene about it all. When she got home she would pour herself an outsize drink and knock together some of her favourite pasta with oil and garlic and a shaking of red pepper. The chicken could wait till tomorrow, or whenever else she could find the energy to cook it.

The tramp was still there in the doorway of the bank as she pulled off one mitten and fumbled for her keys. He had made himself a windproof nest of sacking and a mountain of stuffed carrier bags, and he sat there amongst them, draped in an army greatcoat, his coal-black eyes blazing hostilely at her like twin flame-throwers. Well, I suppose it's a life, thought Kate as she unlocked the door of the building and slid inside. At least he travels light and doesn't have to worry about tax or insurance or even finding the rent, like the rest of us suckers. And can presumably move on when he's tired of the scenery, to some other doorway with a different view. But did he have emotional worries? she wondered. Could you really turn your back on your troubles simply by opting out?

The whole interior of the building was silent. The porter's lodge was dark and the lift rested on the ground floor as if it, too, were off duty for the duration. She had seen the porter only once, fleetingly, the day she arrived, a tall, gaunt man who looked as if he might have troubles of his own, but he wasn't there now. And if there were other tenants in residence, they were certainly lying low.

There was no sign of the kitten when she unlocked the door, but he soon appeared from behind the tree, to welcome her with a cautious mew which was clearly a demand for food. Now that he had dried out, his fur had fluffed up to reveal a touch of Persian, with a tail as thick as a fox's brush. A handsome fellow indeed, with his neat white paws and dark Lone Ranger mask. His water bowl was empty and he had found and already destroyed the gift-wrapped catnip mouse. Like the tramp, this creature came from the real rough world outside and was used to surviving against the odds. Kate dropped her coat on the floor and opened him a tin of Whiskas before she even unearthed the vodka. First things first, after all, and the kitten's needs were fast becoming more urgent than her own.

The computer was neatly zipped into its carrying case, then wrapped in a blanket for protection. After she'd eaten, and listened to the Queen, Kate dragged it into the old nursery which overlooked the courtyard at the rear of the building and seemed most suitable for a study. It was a nice light room with an angled window, and caught the full afternoon sun, which would be a bonus. Also, because it faced away from the street, it was quiet and that much more conducive to work. The walls were painted a plain serviceable white, with plenty of bookshelves, and right at the end was a vast walk-in cupboard which would do for stashing files and stationery. All she now needed was a solid table, strong enough to take the computer and its printer, and she'd be back in business.

Which was not before it was due. What with her

flight from New York and the ensuing upheaval of her life, she hadn't done any real work for far too long. Now it was nagging at her mind and she could scarcely wait to get stuck in. There was nothing like throwing yourself into a job for getting over emotional upsets, that was for sure. Her father had always told her that as a child, and he had been right. Good old Dad, how wise he had been and what would she not give right now to be able to climb on his knee and share all her worries with him. But, no dice. Dad, like the rest, was gone for ever, and all she could do was try and remember his wisdom and wonder what he would advise. After all, it was entirely due to Dad that she'd ever met Francis Pitt in the first place.

She was snoozing on the sofa, with the kitten on her knee, her book open beside her on the floor, when the telephone rang. She snapped awake and sat there startled, the blood pounding in her ears, her hands shaking with an involuntary palsy. Who on earth . . .? Surely not . . . But no. Despite all her resolutions, she felt her spirits sag when she lifted the receiver and heard only her brother's voice. So what were you expecting, girl? she asked herself severely but still felt let down. The mind might know the answers but there was no controlling the heart, and at this moment, knowing it wasn't him, she missed him more than she had ever thought possible. Christmas alone without her lover.

'Oh, you're there,' said Bruno, in obvious surprise. 'We thought you were probably out gallivanting.'

'No,' said Kate, wiping one palm on her jeans and

trying to control the tremor in her voice.

'Mother's here and we are just taking her home,' he said. 'We thought you might like a word.'

In the background she could hear the babble of voices and knew they'd all be there, gathered around Granny and taking notice of her for once, on this one significant day of the year.

'Hello, Mum,' said Kate, at her brightest, as if she hadn't a care in the world. 'Had a good day, have you? Thanks for my pressie. I'll buy something nice for this lovely new flat and then you'll have to come up and see it. As soon as it's finished.'

'Hello?' said her mother, as if she hadn't the faintest idea who was speaking, then Kate heard her complaining to Bruno and he came back on the line.

'She says Happy Christmas,' he suggested optimistically, 'but she wants to go home.'

'Are you alone?' he added as an afterthought. She didn't imagine he cared, but he did sound surprised.

'Yes,' she said. No point in lying.

'Oh,' he said. Then: 'Why didn't you come here?'

'I wasn't invited.'

'Rubbish.'

'It's the truth.'

'Well, if you're going to be like that . . .'

Lindy came on the phone and, as always, chose to have the last word, slightly condescending and fairly dismissive of the two new feminist novels Kate had gone to such trouble to track down because she'd thought they'd be up her street. She was far too busy for reading these days, what with her new job and the family to take care of. And, of course, Mother.

'Guess who we'll be seeing tomorrow,' she purred. 'Here for lunchtime drinks.' She didn't wait for an answer, eager as always to twist the knife. 'Francis Pitt. He's driving over from Brighton where he's Christmasing with friends, and I'm hoping to persuade him to stay for lunch as well.'

She'd always fancied Francis, had Lindy. Kate could feel her positively preening now.

'Any message?' she asked a trifle archly, and when Kate said no, added reprovingly, 'I'm not at all surprised. The way you treated him.'

Though Kate waited all evening, Ramon never called. Not that she'd really thought he would, but the hope still refused to lie down and die. After all he'd said, all they'd meant to each other, it was hard to accept it was finally over. She wandered about the gloomy room, then leaned on the sill and gazed out over the frost-rimed Kensington rooftops as she thought back over the tempestuous rollercoaster ride her life with the wild Argentinian had been. And not all of it bad either, far from it.

Phone, please phone – you love me really. Common sense told her she'd done the right thing but still she could not suppress the treacherous litany that pounded on and on inside her head. Even though she'd barely got away with her life, and knew she must always keep on running. Luckily this phone was still listed in the name of the previous occupant and, unlike Manhattan, it might be months before the phone company got round to updating their records. Yet even that would not stop Ramon if the mood took him, and she knew she could rely on good old Bruno not to keep shtoom.

She shivered and turned away from the static wintry landscape outside, and felt something small and furry brush timidly against her ankle. In her anguish she had entirely forgotten the kitten. She scooped his tense little body up into her hands and held him close against her face, blowing softly into his fur. In a minute, she felt him relax, sad little scrap that he was, and an inner motor broke into action until he was pulsating with pleasure and gently pawing her face.

'Okay, babe?' she asked him softly, into the dim interior of the half-lit room. It was just the two of them now, against a cold and hostile world, and she felt all the better just for having him there. Outside, the landscape of roofs and chimneys was bleak and the spire of St Mary Abbots rose like a threatening finger into a leaden sky. Her troubles were by no means over but at least for the moment she was safe.

'Bed,' she said as she turned out the lights and the kitten snuggled closer and closed his eyes in trust. She checked the door chain and slid home the bolt, then carried him into the bedroom. Tomorrow they'd have a think about the future; for now, all she desperately needed was sleep.

After all, things might be worse. She could be unemployed, or HIV positive, or agoraphobic or alcoholic or humourless or covered with zits – even, heaven forbid, married to a man like Bruno.

5

On Wednesday the shops were open again and life returned to normal. Miles had an urge to go into work, so Claudia wearily agreed to tag along, even though Canary Wharf would still be virtually deserted and all she really longed to do was loll around at home and try to catch up on some of that lost sleep. But Miles was the motivator in this marriage. Besides, just lately she wasn't at all easy about letting him out of her sight.

'I'll meet you downstairs.'

She stood in front of the hall mirror and shrugged her shoulders into the soft grey wool of her Armani jacket, over a pearl silk camisole which subtly echoed the earrings which had been one of Miles's many wedding gifts. He did at least spoil her, she certainly couldn't fault him on that. She slung the Hermès satchel he had given her for Christmas over one shoulder, picked up her raincoat just in case, and double-locked the door behind her.

The lift was already occupied. The appalling Netta Silcock stood there beaming, dolled up like Bing Crosby in *White Christmas* in a pillarbox-red A-line coat and white fur hat, practically wagging her fat tail at the sight of Claudia.

'Hell*oo* there!' piped the smug little Scotswoman brightly. 'It's certainly a bonny wee day. Will you be off to the sales like me?'

Claudia gave a tight smile. The vision of the two of them breasting those hordes of rapacious post-Christmas shoppers together was more than she could stomach at this hour.

'Nothing quite so exciting, I'm afraid,' she said tartly. Not that it was any of Netta's bloody business. 'Just to the office. Some of us have jobs to go to.'

'Working again so soon?' Netta was astonished. In her eyes, the Burdetts represented money and high living. They were only halfway through the holiday break, with Hogmanay still a whole four days off. 'Why, you poor wee bairn,' she said, laying on Claudia's sleeve one pudgy white hand a-glitter with rings, each one slightly too tight. 'You ought to be home with your feet up, the way you slave so hard all year. What can he be thinking about, eh, that wicked boss of yours?' She gave a cutesy wink. 'Should I be having a word with him, maybe?'

Claudia ground her teeth. Nothing, it seemed, was ever lost on the Black Widows, that coven of ageing biddies with nothing better to do than gossip and complain. And she resented the implied criticism of her husband who, in actual fact, worked far harder than she did. What, when all was said and done, did Netta Silcock, of all people, know about honest hard toil? She, who lived the life of Riley on the ill-gotten and quite undeserved gains of a brief loveless marriage to a sad old man, was hardly in a position to comment on the lifestyle of others, especially not her social and financial superiors. The downside of living in a mansion block like this was having to put up with nosy neighbours. Left to her own devices, Claudia Burdett would pull up the drawbridge and have nothing more to do with the lot of them.

Netta's bright smile remained in place, but beneath their lustrous surface the grape-green eyes were as cold and uncompromising as pebbles. How dare this chilly young woman, with her hoity-toity airs and graces, patronise her? She who was no better than a jumped-up secretary herself, and a marriage-wrecker into the bargain, if half she'd heard was to be believed. She who had ensnared that charming man downstairs who was always so courteous, forcing him to leave his poor first wife to raise three bairns on her own. As Adelaide Potter was fond of saying, it was a disgrace what went on in offices these days and should not be tolerated. When *her* husband, Mr Potter, was still running his draper's business, he'd soon put a stop to any of *that* sort of hanky panky and quite right too.

But Archie's money was burning a hole in Netta's pocket, and the sales rails at M&S were beckoning. She'd just have a tiny look-see, in case she could spot a genuine bargain, then hop on a bus to Oxford Street to see what Selfridges had to offer. To tell the truth, these days, since she came into Archie's money, Netta considered Marks & Spencer a tad beneath her. Selfridges, which she had only discovered since her marriage, had become her new Mecca; she felt in her element there and whiled away numerous empty hours fluttering through its many departments.

The lift stopped again on the second floor and the gracious Olive Fenton stepped in, immaculate as always in mink and pearls, her hair as freshly coiffed as if the city had not been closed these past four days. She greeted both her neighbours with warmth.

'Good morning. Merry Christmas. Out and about already?'

'To the sales!' said Netta brightly and Olive caught Claudia's grimace. She smiled.

'Digby and I are driving down to Cheltenham to see the in-laws,' she confided. 'Still, it's only a twice-yearly event, so I suppose I can't complain.'

She squeezed Claudia's elbow in silent sisterhood as they all three trooped out of the lift. Claudia could seem brittle and unfriendly but Olive sensed the underlying insecurity in the younger woman and had always rather liked her. Twelve years ago she, too, had been a newcomer to this block, and there were still moments when she felt she didn't entirely fit. And Guildford to Kensington had not been that great a leap, all things considered. Despite the polished veneer, goodness knows where Claudia originated from, wearing the brand of the scarlet woman too, which the Black Widows were not of a mind to overlook. No wonder she kept so much to herself, with tongues as lethal as those in the vicinity. Olive felt only sympathy.

Miles was standing on the pavement, car keys in hand, chatting to Gregory Hansen who was lifting his suit bag and laptop from a cab.

'Well now, just look at you both!' said Gregory with real pleasure, kissing Olive and Claudia but somehow contriving to overlook Netta completely. 'What a sight for sore eyes, I must say. Can't tell you how good it feels to be home again after seven dutiful days in Toronto.'

He paid the driver and shifted his bags to the doorstep. He was wearing a camel overcoat with a red cashmere scarf thrown casually round his neck, and his blue eyes shone like chips of sapphire in the lean, tanned face. Of moderate height, with sun streaks in his thinning fair hair, Gregory Hansen was one of nature's charmers, and Netta, as she waited to cross the road, could see the effect he was having on both these married women. Silly, frivolous creatures both of them, mutton dressed up as lamb. Just wait till he catches sight of that mysterious new stranger on the fifth floor, she thought with satisfaction. Then let them see how much ice they really cut with the urbane Dane.

The computer was up and running, which was something of a relief. The idea of having to sort out this advanced technology in a city where she knew not a soul was more than Kate could have borne. She clicked on Compuserve and started to surf the Net, searching for something to catch her interest, to while away an empty hour or so before she got down to the serious business of actually doing some work. There were no messages waiting to be retrieved, which was also a relief. She had left in haste, deliberately with no forwarding address, but had a nasty feeling she might be accessible via her e-mail number. Caution prevented her from revealing her new location over the Internet, even in the vaguest of terms; you never quite knew who was out there watching. She had to tread carefully until she was confident she could not be traced.

Seeking diversion, she checked into a couple of forums but there seemed to be scarcely anyone about today. Even out there in the ether nothing appeared to be happening. She had a sudden vision of everybody in the world laid low by too much turkey and Christmas pud, sordid fights with their nearest and dearest, and being obliged to watch antique reruns of movies they didn't enjoy. At least this year she'd been spared all that. That and the washing-up.

She had dragged the sturdy pine table out of the kitchen, where it stood in the window and served no real purpose, and placed it by the nursery window, thus allowing herself an uninterrupted view across the courtyard which roughly resembled one half of a college quadrangle. Straight opposite were the mirror-image windows of the west wing of the building, while to her right was the back of the library, surmounted by the bold, gold figure of Prometheus.

It was an odd twist to be spending her days working at home on a computer when she remembered the ribbing she'd had to put up with for failing her O level maths. Dad was one of the country's leading pharmacologists, and even blundering Bruno had managed a third in biology. And as for Francis, well . . . But he, at least, had had the sensitivity not to be always on Kate's neck, making jokes at her expense. Katie excelled at all sorts of other things that were actually far more important, he said. Any jerk could add up a column of figures but where Katie scored was in her quickness of intellect and intuition. Combined with an ability to come at things sideways instead of ploughing through all the logical steps.

'She gets there faster than we do,' he would say. 'Though how she manages it, I'm not nearly bright enough to understand.'

Which was how computers worked, by short-cutting the obvious steps, and how she came to have her present job, freelancing for the newspaper she had once worked for, accessing news stories from the main-frame and then syndicating them to other papers all over the world.

Meeting Ramon Vergara on his year's secondment from *La Nacion* had radically altered Kate's life, in more ways than one. He was older, he was glamorous, with that extra edge that came from being foreign, and from the moment they first met in the newsroom of the *Observer*, he had treated her with a grave courtesy and respect for her intelligence that had, quite simply, knocked her sideways. A genuine *coup de foudre*, in fact, in all its senses. After two years in a newspaper office and four of marriage to Francis, Kate was thoroughly fed up with being treated as a bit of a joke, a cute little bundle strictly not to be taken seriously, not just by her brother and work colleagues but by her husband as well.

It was partly her size – she was just five foot two – but mainly the fault of Dad, who had refused to allow her to grow up. He had indulged her, her mother had conspired with her; the only one in the family whose behaviour didn't conform was Bruno, whose bullying had always contained an underlying streak of pure hostility.

Ramon had changed all that. She had never completely comprehended exactly what it was he saw in her, but he had seemed to single her out right from the start and focused his mesmeric charm upon her, the young, naive, childless bride just ripe for seducing. At forty-two, he was nearly old enough to be her father, as the family were quick to point out, but age appeared not to matter, at least not then. With her customary lack of thought, she had acted spontaneously on the spur of the moment and blindly followed her Pied Piper out of the fastness of her safe, dull marriage for a slice of real life three thousand miles away.

After all, her husband didn't want her; that was plain enough to see. Once the brief courtship and adjustment to marriage had been achieved – a fleeting hiccup in his busy working schedule that had to be fitted in – Francis had slipped right back into the old uncaring ways, with work coming first.

Ramon was different, exciting and passionate, and made Kate feel, for the first time in her life, like a woman and truly grown up. He marvelled at her huge lustrous eyes and the sleek blue-black bob of her glossy hair; he complimented her on her wit, her enthusiasm, her originality, the sharpness of her intuition. He made love to her at each available opportunity with his hands, his eyes, his murmured caresses, and, by seeing her as a beauty, made her beautiful. More than anything, he took notice of what she said and was not forever jibing at her ignorance, or the quaintness of her opinions. He even admired the whiteness of her thighs and never, not for one moment, ever suggested that they might be slimmer. Ramon loved her as a sensuous being but he also respected her intelligence. That was what did it. If Francis ever bothered to wonder where it had all gone wrong, it was that simple.

Francis was in the study the day Kate came home, and, flush-faced and nervous, confronted him about what really had been keeping her late in London these past few weeks. That scene would be etched into her consciousness forever, the bright concentrated light from the brass desk lamp throwing its pool of brilliance over his scattered papers while the heavy scent of honeysuckle and evening primrose wafted in through the open French windows, from a darkening garden damp with an early night dew. Francis sat eclipsed in shadow, his expression hidden by the unruly fall of hair that still gave him the air of a recalcitrant schoolboy, the lamplight glinting on his lenses. He sat quite still and silent while she spoke, so much so that for a moment she thought he wasn't listening and fully expected him to pick up his pen at any moment and get on with his work. Then, after she had stuttered to a halt, he removed the heavy hornrims and wearily massaged the bridge of his nose with thin, nervy fingers. Still without speaking.

Unable to bear the tension one more moment, Kate escaped into the twilight and sought the sanctuary of her favourite bench at the foot of the garden, close to the river. There she had sat shivering for the best part of an hour until she heard light footsteps on the grass and became aware of her husband standing nearby, clutching the lower branches of a gnarled old apple tree as he groped for adequate words. Typical, thought

Kate, of these super-erudite men. Give them a conundrum by Pythagoras and they'd have it sorted in a jiffy, but face them with one of life's ordinary little dramas and you immediately had them stumped. Pure emotion was something they simply couldn't deal with. Instead of being genital-led, like the rest of their species, eggheads tried too much to rationalise and always ended up ass-over-cranium on the floor. Well, that was no longer her problem. He'd had his chance and he'd royally blown it. She was sick and tired of feeling guilty.

'Does that mean you are leaving me?' he asked at last, in a flat, dull voice quite devoid of emotion, and when Kate nodded, too distressed to speak, let the silence hang between them as though there was nothing further to be said. Eventually he released the branch and headed back towards the house, nimbly skirting Kate's bench as if he'd already relinquished her. She sometimes wondered what might have transpired had he cared enough to try a last ditch stand; if he'd touched her, held her, even kissed her, could she have resisted him then?

'And I never even told you I love you,' were his only words as he went inside and quietly closed the doors.

Well, thought Kate now, four years on, remembering, a lot he cared. So much for Englishmen and romantic love. Within two days she was packed and ready to leave, and Francis obliged her by moving back into college and remaining there until she was safely on her plane. Since then she had had no direct word from him, just occasional verbal glimpses passed on by family and friends. There had been no talk of settlements or divorce. She had asked for nothing and, in return, received only silence. So far as she knew, he had stayed on in the house, and Lindy had confirmed he was still at Cambridge, aiming, in all probability, for the Nobel Prize.

The light was fading and Kate was just finishing her afternoon's work when she heard a clatter on the outside landing and went to investigate. Standing just out of sight beside the glass-panelled front door, she could dimly make out a lot of movement in front of the lift and the dragging sounds of heavy objects being shunted across the stone floor. On an impulse, she slid back the bolt and opened the door an inch. It sounded too bold and obvious to be burglars but even in a building this secure you could never be too careful. New York had made her super-cautious.

The opposite front door stood open and the place was ablaze with light. A tall young woman in a stylish fur coat, with a mane of luxuriant dark hair and heels so high it was a marvel she could stand at all, was struggling with the lift whilst dragging cases and roped-up boxes towards her open doorway. Inside, a much older woman, drably dressed in a brown flowered overall, her hair tied severely back in a scarf, was taking them from her, one by one, and disappearing into the flat. All the time they were laughing and conversing very fluently and very fast in some foreign language Kate guessed was Greek.

'Hi!' said the girl, when she sensed Kate's presence. 'I'm Eleni Papadopoulos, and this is Demeter.'

But the older woman had soundlessly vanished and the wide-open door was now half-closed. The dark girl laughed and shrugged.

'Always so shy. What can I do?' She straightened up and allowed Kate to take charge of the lift button, while she flicked back her hair and straightened her coat. Then she held out one diamond-studded hand as if inviting Kate to kiss it.

'So, you are our new neighbour. Welcome! We'd have been here to greet you but we're just back from Athens.'

'Hi,' said Kate awkwardly, feeling a bit of a fool for snooping. 'I was just checking everything was all right.'

Eleni flashed a radiant smile, displaying perfect teeth. 'Everything is fine, thank you, darling, and it's sweet of you to be so caring.'

She dragged out the final piece of baggage, a patent leather make-up case monogrammed in gold, and let the lift go. Then she gave Kate, in her leggings and sweatshirt, a swift appraisal and smiled again.

'I'd ask you in for a glass of ouzo,' she purred, 'but we're a little tired after all that travelling. Once we're settled and unpacked you must definitely be our guest. I love to entertain and Demeter loves to cook. A perfect partnership, don't you agree? I hope you won't find us too noisy, *cherie*.'

Kate nodded good night and thankfully closed her own door. Next to the chic and *soignée* Greek, she felt gawky and ill at ease, but she found that Continental women very often had that effect. One good thing, it was nice to know the building wasn't so empty after all, and these unexpected neighbours certainly seemed colourful and slightly larger than life. She hoped Eleni wasn't too serious about the noise.

The cat was mewing for his supper so she decided to call it a day and went back into the study to unboot the computer. Before she switched off the lights, she stood for a while at the window, slowly rotating her cramped shoulders and relishing the satisfaction of a day's hard work well done, whilst savouring the view across the courtyard. It was beginning to feel good to be here, safe at last, settled in a place of her own.

Half the windows facing her now showed signs of life. With the holiday nearing its close, other residents were clearly returning home. No longer did the building seem quite so alien. With the prickling of light across its dark façade, the feeling of eeriness was beginning to dissipate.

Right in the centre, just one floor down, a still, dark figure stood looking out. Motionless as a mime or even a waxwork, its very lack of any sort of movement caught Kate's attention and held it. What, she wondered, could the figure be watching so intently, or was it really just some inanimate object leaned carelessly against the windowsill? Or even a hat stand draped in a coat? From this distance, and in this light, it was hard to tell. Curiosity kept her there for a full ten minutes but nothing happened. Then the cat started rubbing round her ankles, demanding food, so she tore herself away and went into the kitchen to open his tin. He was right, it was definitely suppertime. She poured herself a mammoth gin and tonic – it was after all still Christmas – and put a pan of water on the stove as she felt like lentil soup.

While she waited for it to boil, she carried her drink back into the study, this time without bothering with the light. The watcher at the window was still there, but try as she might, Kate could still not discern its sex or anything about it, even if it was alive. A prickle of icy apprehension ran down her spine. Now watch it, girl, she told herself sternly, don't start getting the heeby-jeebies here, or where else are you going to run to? She closed the door firmly and returned to the kitchen, where the water was bubbling, the light bright and the radio on full blast.

6

The porter brought up some packages the next morning and made himself known to Kate.

'Septimus Woolf, Miss Ashenberry,' he said formally, solemnly offering his hand. 'Laundry's on Tuesdays and the rubbish is collected three times weekly, last thing at night. Let me know if there is ever anything you need. You can always reach me in the porter's lodge. You'll find the telephone number inside the lift.'

Tall and gaunt and probably late sixties, he made an incongruous figure in his well-pressed maroon uniform but without a cap on his distinguished shock of bushy iron-grey hair. More like a don or an actor, reflected Kate as she closed the door. What an unlikely candidate to be doing such a menial job. I bet there's a story there. Then she laughed at herself and returned to her coffee. Four years of living with a journalist had got her into bad habits and she found it hard to resist the occasional snoop into other people's lives. Strictly from a distance, of course. There was still a strong dose of caution in Kate; she hated people to get too close.

Which was why this new career was so ideal, especially in the current circumstances. As she switched on the computer she thanked her stars once more for this safe haven and the fact that she did appear, finally, to have landed on her feet. It was really just an extension of the job she had had before, updated, these days done entirely via the Internet as she accessed the mainframe of the *Observer*. Not only did she now have direct access into the lives of her immediate neighbours, but also – via the modern marvels of cyberspace – across the entire world as well.

Which reminded her. As the machine chugged into activity and grunted its way through its various self-checks, she wandered over to the window. The watcher was gone. But a filmy white curtain swept in a curve across that window, half-obscuring the interior of the room where the figure had been standing. Probably just another jaded soul, weary of the enforced ritual gaiety of the long Christmas break, thought Kate as she logged on. Bored just like me and simply killing time.

By one she was feeling peckish, so she decided to pop down to Marks & Spencer to stretch her legs and grab herself a sandwich. Her eyes were strained from so many hours spent gazing at a screen, and her shoulders were cramped. That was the down side of spending your days with a computer; headaches and the ever-present danger of repetitive-strain syndrome. It felt good to unwind, and she told herself severely that she really must sort out some sort of healthier work routine, one that would take her away from that lighted screen at least for an hour or so each day. Also, what with the tension and worry of the past few weeks, she had quite got out of the habit of eating properly. Sooner or later she needed to get organised and into the routine again of shopping in an efficient way and having meal breaks at regular hours. But with so many other adjustments to make, self-maintenance was not a particular priority. Provided the cat was catered for and she had something to nibble when hunger pains struck, Kate was content to live like a gypsy and just camp out. Until she felt more at peace with herself and ready to make plans for the future.

She was so used to the place being deserted, she was almost put out when the lift jerked to a halt at the fourth floor and a stranger got in. He was tallish and nice-looking, in cords and a fisherman's jersey, and his smile was so pleasant and his manner so relaxed, she wished for a second she had taken more trouble with her own appearance instead of merely flinging on her sheepskin over a grubby T-shirt and leggings. Better watch out, she told herself, or before she knew it she'd be turning into a slut as well as a recluse. That was how it started, the first step in the grim downwards spiral towards God knows what. Next thing she'd even be talking to herself and using the cat as an excuse. She grinned, though it really wasn't funny.

The stranger was giving her the once-over.

'Nice morning,' he offered breezily, with a barely detectable accent of some sort, soft and modulated. Automatically Kate nodded. The truth was she hadn't a clue what went on outside her windows when she was working, nor did she care. What was it about this country, anyhow, with this constant fixation on the weather? She'd only been away four years but already found herself thinking like a foreigner, harsh and intolerant maybe, but at least not banal. And from his accent – whatever it was – he wasn't even British so ought to know better. She blinked at him blearily, her eyes stinging from all that concentration on the computer screen, and wished she'd only thought to put on mascara or dark glasses. Which surprised her rather since she'd not given men a thought since her hurried departure from New York.

He was watching her steadily with alert blue eyes, and when he smiled, his tanned cheeks folded into sexy vertical creases which suddenly made him hand-some. Nice, she thought, surprising herself again, though absolutely not her type. She liked them older and more exotic; this man was too clean-cut for her taste, more the boy-next-door sort. What Bruno would probably call a regular bloke, though there was noth-ing, she supposed, intrinsically wrong with that. Provided he kept out of her way. She guessed he was a neighbour but wasn't about to ask. She had crossed the pond expressly in order to hide and lick her wounds. The last thing she needed, now or probably ever, was any sort of new involvement, however harmless.

'I guess I live directly beneath you,' said the man, almost as if he could read her mind. 'Number twenty-two. Gregory Hansen.' He held out his hand and she grasped it clumsily, feeling a bit of a fool.

'How do you know?' she asked too abruptly, and felt herself blushing. What was going on here? He was only being civil. He laughed.

'Put a tail on you, of course, what else? Now let me see, you're Kate Ashenberry, recently back from the

States, and you've just moved into Guy Bartlett's old place. Don't worry,' he added more softly, seeing with surprise her sudden rigid tension, 'we're not really that snoopy round here, at least not all of us. It's just that we're kind of a village in this building and a certain amount of gossip is bound to spread.'

His warm, sympathetic smile was beginning to get to her and she found herself smiling back. Unfair to allow two bad experiences to put her off men for life; even in this benighted country, they surely couldn't all be bastards. There were those who told her that having Bruno for a brother had been every bit as damaging as her experience with Ramon but the sensible side of her knew she must not allow herself to become hooked into a failure syndrome. Some people, like her friend Elaine in New York, had pratfall after pratfall, yet still managed to struggle to their feet again, dust themselves down and leap right back in there, back into the game. Besides, whoa – what was she thinking of? All this was was the guy downstairs asking a few friendly questions.

'I gather we're in the same line of business,' said Gregory as they stepped into the hall. Again she stiffened, which he registered with surprise. What's with this dame? she could see him thinking, and pulled herself together.

'Journalism?' he ventured. 'I am, for my sins, a stringer for the *Toronto Star*.' So that was the accent – Canadian.

'Oh, I see.' Kate wasn't about to volunteer anything but Gregory persisted. She was pretty, this strange young woman, in a slightly unusual way, but boy, was she ever tight-assed. What, he wondered, could be eating her, and why the hell take it out on him? He wasn't going to let her defensiveness get to him. Women were his relaxation. Besides, he liked a challenge.

'Miles told me you worked for a newspaper. Picked it up from your references, I gather, now that's he's acquired the lease. Well, you know how he loves to snoop . . . or perhaps you don't.'

Kate's panicked breathing visibly slowed and her pulse rate slackened. Miles Burdett, of course, she recognised the type. She must not get paranoid. She was a good three thousand miles away from danger now and this man, her neighbour, was only being civil. She was starting to feel a bit of a fool. What must he be thinking?

'All I was was a humble assistant on the the *Observer* Foreign News Service yonks ago. I don't actually write myself. Not nearly clever enough.' There she went again; she could have bitten her tongue.

They left the building together, then Gregory smiled and walked rapidly away. Cursing her own ineptness, Kate crossed at the lights and entered Marks & Spencer by way of the station arcade. She picked up a salad roll and a bottle of mineral water, then wandered the aisles of this marvellous food hall, stuffed with enough goodies to make even an anorexic drool, collecting various basic staples to keep her going for the next few days – leeks and carrots, tomatoes and olive oil, pasta and wholemeal bread. Plus a packet of grated Cheddar to sprinkle on the soup she might eventually get round to making. And, as an after-thought, a couple of litre bottles of dry French wine, to sustain her at the end of the day as well as through those odd dull moments when her fingers and eyes threatened to go on strike and she reckoned she'd earned a break. Workers in offices stopped for the occasional snifter; why shouldn't she?

Healthy eating went with regular exercise, so once she'd done her shopping, she went on walking to where she'd heard there was a good health club. In New York it was *de rigueur* to work out daily, it went with the turf. There she'd been lucky enough to live right next to the park and would jog every morning as soon as it was light, until she'd worked up a healthy sweat and could zip back home for a shower before work. Ramon used to laugh at her. In his own country he'd been a wizard on the polo field but these days he reckoned he was too old to take life quite so seriously. Besides, think of all those diesel fumes and the constant danger of being mugged. But he made no attempt to stop her; Kate was an enthusiast and that was one of the things he liked. Or so he said. Now, in hindsight, she was inclined to see it as just further dismal proof that he had never really cared for her at all.

Thoughts of Ramon always reduced Kate to gloom. As it had turned out, compared with what had happened later, a mugging would have been nothing special, par for the course. She felt the familiar danger signs, the tightening of the throat, a mistiness in the eyes, but here, right in front of her, was the doorway to the health club so she took firm hold of her fragile emotions and went boldly inside.

Only later, swimming in the pool after a satisfying

workout in the gym, did Kate finally begin to unwind and let her thoughts wander back to her dishy downstairs neighbour. She wondered idly about his private life. For someone who had forsworn men and any new romantic encounter *ever,* it was unnerving how clearly that smile and those eyes still lingered in her consciousness. Nice, well-balanced, obviously decent and clean-living; verging, if anything, on the dull side. Probably got a nice little wifey tucked away down there, possibly even a couple of bright-eyed, flaxen-haired kids.

Someone was already in the sauna, stark naked and stretched out like an odalisque on the upper shelf, where the heat was that much more intense. But she moved up obligingly when Kate came in.

'I can't get enough of it,' confessed the stranger, reaching forward to throw another scoopful of water on to the hot coals. 'Left to my own devices, I'd be here all day, in the forlorn belief that it really is doing something for my fat ass. As if!'

The accent was pure Manhattan and the laugh full and throaty. In the dim, steamy atmosphere all Kate could make out was a mass of black curls and a pair of laughing eyes with the most amazing lashes. Topping a fairly flawless figure with an impressive bosom and long, slim legs into the bargain. That was the thing about these New Yorkers, they did make a bit of a fetish about staying in shape. Aware of her own less than perfect body and heavy thighs, Kate lay down quickly, and cautiously unwrapped her towel. Here came the old inhibitions creeping back

She forced herself to concentrate on the idle chat

from the luscious beauty stretched out with such abandon on the shelf above.

'Where are you from?' she asked.

'New York. Can't you tell?'

'Sure I can. I'm fresh from there myself. How great to
find another almost compatriot!'

Connie Boyle was an actress who worked part-time in
an antiques shop in Holland Street. She had, she
explained, had an early, doomed marriage to a Brit, an
English actor whom she'd blindly followed to London
a year or so before.

'What happened?' Oh Lord, not another victim, but
she did seem to want to talk about it.

'The usual. Too high expectations, I guess; too little
dough. Not enough work for either of us, and a squat
in Brixton with a leaky roof. Nothing like a touch of
squalor for bringing you down to earth with a bang, I
can tell you. Then we realised we'd nothing whatsoever
in common and split. No big deal.'

'And since then?'

'Since then I've been on my own, more or less, and
liking it a whole lot better.'

'What keeps you here?' Kate thought wistfully of
New York, still, to her mind, despite everything, the
most exciting city in the world.

'You know something, I'm not entirely sure.' Connie
sat up and towelled her curly hair, then began to
smooth lotion all over her marvellous body in long,
sensuous sweeps.

'When I first arrived I thought I'd die of homesickness, but somehow your quaint old habits soon took a

hold on me and I found myself lingering on, even after the bastard had jumped ship.'

'What do you think of English men?' asked Kate curiously. She found herself drawn to this vivid stranger, liked her New York directness, liked everything about her, in fact.

'Zilch!' Connie pulled a face and gave her an emphatic thumbs-down. 'But you wanna know something? They're each as bad as the next one, men, so why bother? American guys are all in love with their mothers; the Brits prefer to sack down with their best friends. So where's the difference? Neither kind can make it any more, so forget it!'

Both cracked up. It was true; Kate couldn't deny it. And it made her feel a whole lot better to hear it stated so plainly by this glorious creature who must surely be able to have any man she wanted. They were about the same age, Kate estimated, and after they had dressed, they strolled back up to the High Street together.

'Oh, you probably know my employer, then,' said Connie, when she saw where Kate lived. 'Amelia Rowntree. Number sixteen. She used to run the shop with her ma but now she's on her own. I just help out occasionally between jobs. It's lovely work and helps pay the rent.'

Connie lived just round the corner, in a mews flat over a garage.

'It's tiny but convenient,' she said. 'Come up some time and share a bottle of Californian plonk. It ain't a patch on this place, of course, but then I'm just a poor actor endeavouring to make ends meet.' Again, that delicious throaty laugh. Dried off and in her jeans and sweatshirt, Connie was fairly breathtaking. She was currently doing a bit part in a soap Kate had to confess she hadn't yet seen, but was confident she'd be legging it up and down Shaftesbury Avenue again before too long.

'It's the same old story,' said Connie cheerfully. 'I'm nearly always cast as the daffy second string bimbo who gets bumped off in the first two episodes. Oh well. At least it means endless variety and I haven't yet prostituted my art through familiarity and barred myself from the Vic or Stratford. I thought about Hollywood once,' she added, just as Kate was wondering. 'But in the end, doing odd jobs here, where at least you're treated like a person if you're lucky, seemed preferable to joining the meat rack on the Coast and waiting table along with the rest of the no-hopers. And the English climate – don't you know, my dear – is so much better for the skin.'

They agreed to meet the following morning at the health club, bright and early.

'Seven's the best time,' said Connie, 'when only the serious punters are there, working out on the way to the office. There's a nice little group of us, just enough not to overcrowd the gym, but I'm sure we can move up to make room for another little 'un.'

Seven was fine with Kate. She'd always been an early riser and liked the idea of starting the day that way. Besides, the discipline would be good for her now she was working on her own. Once you began to let your standards slip, who knew where it might lead? Life needed some sort of structure; meeting Connie looked like being a brilliant start. Also, she seemed so genuine and nice; a breath of down-to-earth fresh air. First Gregory Hansen, now Connie Boyle. Things were definitely looking up.

Miles had a date downstairs with Lady Wentworth. Claudia was suspicious.

'*Now* what are you up to?' she asked him wearily, longing only to change out of her sharp little suit and collapse in front of the telly with a spritzer. 'I hope you're not trying to relieve her of some dosh. Don't forget, she's an old lady as well as a neighbour.'

Miles grinned and loosened his tie. He kissed her on the forehead, then headed towards the door, his briefcase under his arm, always an ominous sign.

'Don't worry, dear heart,' he said happily. 'As it happens, she's already a Name, passed on to her by her father years ago. All I'm doing is helping to spread her assets, make her a bit of loot, I thought, before she gets too gaga to enjoy it. Can't get much more neighbourly than that, what?'

'Get her on to your syndicate, you mean. Another poor sucker to help spread the losses and feather your own little nest?'

'What's mine is yours, my pet,' he said placidly.

True, it was her money too, but Claudia was still wary. Sharp dealing in Canary Wharf was one thing, the stuff of life to ambitious brokers like Miles, which was one reason she had always found him so sexy and his company so exhilarating. But crapping on your own doorstep was another matter entirely, and Lady Wentworth was too close to home for comfort.

Suppose something did go wrong? Miles was always telling her not to be so cautious, so *petty bourgeois*, but Claudia had learned the hard way; she didn't want to see it happen again.

'What can possibly go wrong, my duck?' Miles was fond of saying. 'If you don't take risks in life you get nowhere, and the fast track is where it's at.'

And, it had to be said, so far he seemed not to have put a foot wrong, not in all the years she had worked with him. But still. Lady Wentworth was a fine old woman, with a pedigree as long as your arm, whose family had lived in the building since the year dot. True Kensington aristocracy, the salt of the earth, and a general in the Red Cross, too, though Claudia was not at all certain what that entailed. Except that it spelled respectability and solid yeoman stock, something her own erratic upbringing had taught her to regard with a certain element of awe.

Netta Silcock, though, was something else entirely. A malicious gleam lit Claudia's eye as she opened the fridge and raked for ice. Easy come, easy go, that was what Miles always said. And if anyone was a ripe candidate for being ripped off, that awful smug Scotswoman was surely it. Or Mrs Adelaide Potter even better, with her tree-trunk legs and cowpat hats. Enough. Claudia knew herself sufficiently well to predict how this particular train of thought would develop unless she put a cork in it. She took her glass and the evening paper into the den.

She was just nicely settled when Caroline rang, hoping to speak to Miles.

'He's not here,' said Claudia, annoyed at the

intrusion, but Caroline merely asked if she'd please have him call, since there was something faintly urgent she needed to discuss. No message, no friendly greeting, but equally no antagonism; the sure way to rattle Claudia. Being Wife Number Two was not the easiest thing in the world, even if she was the winner. She was sick to the gills of the sweet, uncomplaining voice of her vanquished rival, and hated her, unreasonably, for failing to put up more of a fight. What the hell was wrong with Caroline? They'd been married ten years, after all, and shared three children; surely that must mean something? Caroline must be a wimp of the first order; just let any other woman try to come on to Miles now Claudia was holding the reins.

Amelia Rowntree arrived as Miles was gathering together his papers, looking heavy and down and sadly past her sell-by date. Which was a shame really, for he could see she had once been quite a handsome woman, if only she wouldn't favour so much brown and fawn. Her eyes brightened when she saw Miles; he was a favourite within the block. Lady Wentworth cajoled him into staying on for one more sherry. Miles enquired about the antiques trade, and Amelia shook her head dismally and slumped into an armchair like a doll with half its stuffing gone. Not good, was the answer in two words. Like nearly everything else these days, the market was at rock bottom and she had to work exorbitant hours just to cover the high running costs of her tiny shop. Her speciality was early English porcelain but now, when the tourist trade was at its lowest ebb, even that wasn't easy to shift.

'We could do with some better weather,' she said. 'what with all the big fairs coming up in June and July.' She shrugged her shoulders wearily; what could you do?

Miles studied her alertly, like a robin contemplating a worm, but could see she was being entirely upfront with him, for there was no dissembling about Amelia. Her flat suede shoes were worn and scuffed and her tweed skirt had a wavy hem. Since her mother died she had lived alone, in a small, dark two-bedroomed flat on the third floor, crammed to bursting with Victorian knick-knacks and display cases of sauceboats, cream jugs and figurines that made your eyes cross with the effort of taking them all in. The shop was much the same. If he could have done, Miles would have helped her out, but his own taste, his and Claudia's, was ultra-modern minimalist chic, all chrome and pastels and matt black leather.

Amelia's sole piece of news, apart from the dreadfulness of the weather, was that Connie, who helped her in the shop, had got to know the new tenant upstairs and reported that she seemed to be rather a good sort. Miles agreed; he had already sussed her out himself. He kept to himself the fact that he was her landlord. He didn't hold with letting the neighbours know too much about his dealings. Divide and rule, was Miles's maxim.

'But she does seemed scared of her own shadow,' he contributed. 'Almost as if she is in hiding or something.'

'Probably needs something to do with her time,' pronounced Lady Wentworth gruffly, passing the peanuts. 'If she's new to this country and lives alone, it's likely she's short of company. We can soon fix that. Find out if she plays bridge, Amelia, and we'll also rope her on to the board, if necessary. We could do with some younger blood; high time I, for one, stood down.'

Miles was thinking that she might make a nice new friend for his wife, though somehow that was unlikely. Lately Claudia had been getting altogether too clinging and suspicious, which made it hard for him to operate with his usual fluidity. He enjoyed the neighbourly attitude within this building, provided it didn't get too cloying, but missed the camaraderie of Clapham where Caroline and the girls still lived. He glanced at his watch; nearly twenty to eight.

'Better be going,' he said with a hearty smile. 'Before the old girl blows a gasket.' He nodded towards the papers he had left. 'Cast your eye over those when you have a mo and give me a buzz if there's anything you don't understand.'

He winked at Amelia as he made for the door.

'High finance,' he said, and let himself out.

What a charmer he is, to be sure, thought Amelia glumly, sinking more deeply into the overstuffed chair. In some ways he reminded her of Charles, her long-lost love, only chubbier and more schoolboyish, a little like an overgrown choirboy. What a pity he'd settled for that chilly, distant wife who seemed to find it hard to crack a smile or do so much as exchange the time of day.

Oh well, she thought resignedly, in her mother's well-worn phrase, I suppose there's no accounting for taste. In any case, what kind of foolishness was this?

He was years too young for her, even if he were available, and even at her best she'd never have been able to keep up with someone of that speed.

Besides, Amelia's heart was already taken. But that remained her secret, another story entirely.

7

On New Year's Day Kate got a chance to meet more of her new neighbours. After a miserable New Year's Eve spent alone with just the cat and a book, and a long half-hour at the window gazing out over the deserted Kensington streets while St Mary Abbots merrily pealed in another year, she called it a day and went to bed, only to be kept awake half the night by the screams and shouts of animated revellers making their way back home through the sleeping streets. Never had she felt more lonely. Earlier in the evening she had tried to phone her mother, only to be told by the brisk young woman who answered that the old lady was out. Presumably with Bruno and Lindy, since these days who else did she know?

She finally managed to sleep, and awoke to a brilliant morning and a small rough tongue working across her face, nudging her into breakfast duty. She switched on Radio 3 to bright, optimistic baroque music, swathed herself in one of Ramon's sweaters and clicked on the kettle while she fed the cat. Business as usual, she reminded herself, and at least all the sickening festivities were finally over so she could get on with her life.

She opened the door to pick up the paper and found herself face to face with her neighbour across the hall. Even in dishabille, Eleni Papadopoulos looked ravishing. She wore a pink silk negligée wrapped loosely around her luscious figure, and her glorious hair hung wild and unkempt over her shoulders as she stooped to scoop up the *Telegraph*.

'Good *morning*!' she cooed on seeing Kate, 'and a very Happy New Year to you, darling.'

For someone who had undoubtedly been revelling until the small hours, Eleni looked great: her dark brown eyes, the colour of port wine, sparkled and the wide smile was as ravishing as ever. Her feet were bare and Kate saw that her toes were as immaculately cared for as the long, extravagant fingernails.

'If you're doing nothing at noon,' said Eleni, 'pop across and raise a glass of champagne with us. We love to entertain, it is our lifeblood. Nothing formal. Just come as you are, *cherie*.'

She blew a kiss then slid sinuously back inside, leaving Kate feeling inexplicably cheered. These Greek neighbours appeared to be quite charming, and since they were going to have to rub along together, it made sense to establish amiable relations as early as possible. But not too close. And she wouldn't stay long, she promised herself. She wasn't yet in the mood for too much socialising. And work beckoned.

Eleni opened the door to her at a little after twelve, transformed from a beguiling slattern to a stylish woman of distinction, in an amber silk dress with a distinctly European cut, and a cascade of chunky gold jewellery that also bore the unmistakable stamp of authenticity. She kissed Kate warmly on both cheeks and ushered her down a long, dark corridor, sumptuously endowed with oil paintings in ornate frames and a glory of oriental rugs underfoot, into a sunny sitting room right at the end, already half full of people.

Kate wished immediately she not taken Eleni so much at her word and had made more of an effort to dress up. She really was letting her standards slip these days; instead of just jodhpurs and a cashmere sweater, she should have worn a skirt.

'Relax, darling,' whispered Eleni beside her, picking up on her anxiety. 'You look terrific. And it is only the neighbours, after all.' She handed Kate a glass of champagne and took her firmly by the elbow.

There was no one present Kate had ever seen before. Even the dowdy Demeter was tucked out of sight, doubtless slaving away in the kitchen, which seemed to be her role. Eleni propelled Kate, with a firm hand in her back, across to the window, where an elderly couple were standing, absorbed in each other's conversation. He was a handsome man in his seventies, red-faced with a receding hairline but dapper in a fancy waistcoat, with a pronounced twinkle in his eye; she a faded beauty in fine hyacinth wool, whose animated face still clearly proclaimed just what a knockout she must once have been in some earlier, more romantic era. They were as striking a couple as Fred and Ginger. Just being in their presence added a hint of glamour to the air.

'Meet your neighbours on the other side,' said Eleni,

topping up their glasses. 'Ronnie and Rowena Barclay-Davenport, absolutely my favourite people.'

Hands were shaken all round and felicitations exchanged, then the Barclay-Davenports resumed their conversation, drawing in Kate as if they had known her for years.

'We were talking about the Black Widows,' confided Rowena. 'Those dreadful old biddies always casting doom and gloom throughout the building.' Her laughter was bell-like and her husband clutched her hand in enraptured collusion, as attentive as a new bridegroom. Kate warmed to them instantly. Here was genuine compatability, fired, quite obviously, by solid lasting love. How she envied them.

'Don't you know who we're talking about?' continued Rowena in her carrying Kensington drawl, without a trace of hesitancy or reserve. 'Mrs Adelaide Potter and her cohorts – my husband calls her the Ayatollah – that poisonous old spider downstairs who tries to dominate the place. She's a positive nightmare, isn't she, Ronnie darling, and we up here have to stick together and defy her.'

'Like the Wicked Witch of the West?' put in Kate.

'Precisely.'

'Pull up the drawbridge, that sort of thing,' grunted her husband, moving aside to include in the circle a couple of new arrivals. He introduced them to Kate. 'Beatrice Hunt and Lily Li.'

'They're from the third floor but we occasionally allow them through the barricades,' added his wife with a chuckle, warmly kissing each of the new arrivals.

There was something immediately likeable about both Beatrice and Lily, though Kate found it hard to put her finger on what it was. Beatrice was the elder of the two, mid-forties probably, with a strong-boned face and slightly greying hair swathed elegantly upwards in a classic chignon. Her companion's age was harder to assess. She might have been quite considerably younger but the timeless quality of her delicate bone structure made her that much harder to date. Not that it mattered a jot. Both had an ease of manner that was immediately attractive. Within seconds Kate, the non-joiner, felt she had known them for years. Over matching jeans they were dressed contrastingly, Beatrice in a rich Amazonian wool jacket, Lily in subtly printed silk.

'Lily's a designer,' said Beatrice, noticing Kate's obvious admiration for the exquisite garment. 'Made that herself, right down to the buttonholes. Even designed the fabric too.'

'Oh, she's a clever girl all right, our Lily,' beamed Rowena, patting the Chinese woman's delicate hand. 'Be nice to her, my dear, and maybe you can persuade her to create something lovely for you.'

'I couldn't even begin to afford it,' laughed Kate. 'Right out of my league, I'm afraid.'

And then more people came into the room and one of them, Kate saw, was Gregory Hansen. She was surprisingly pleased to see him and felt a tightening in her stomach. She couldn't help glancing across at him from time to time, half hoping to catch his eye. But Eleni had both arms around his neck as if he were her personal property, and Gregory was laughing genially and patting her bottom as he greeted the other neighbours and held out his hand for a glass. They made a handsome couple, to be sure; for a fleeting second something a lot like jealousy threatened to cloud Kate's happiness, but then she saw him gently detach himself from the Greek girl's clinging arms and make his way across the room to where she stood.

'Hello there again! And happy New Year!'

Unlike many of the other guests, Gregory had clearly made no effort at all. He was wearing the same old baggy cords as before, with a sweater that was positively disgraceful, fraying at the elbows with half his shirt tail hanging out. But the charm was as mesmerising as ever. Even amongst all these well-turned-out people, to Kate he still looked pretty damn good.

'Mustn't stay too long,' he explained apologetically, as he drained his first glass and allowed Ronnie to refill it. 'I've got a deadline to meet this afternoon, and as usual, I'm way behind schedule.'

'He's very clever, aren't you, darling?' said Rowena fondly, patting his hand. 'He's our house celebrity and we're all very proud of him.'

Gregory smiled down at her, then back at Kate.

'Don't believe a word she tells you,' he said benevolently. 'She's an awful fibber, our Mrs B-D, and stirs up trouble wherever she goes.'

Rowena was delighted. 'Just like Mrs Adelaide Potter, I was saying,' she laughed. 'Now there's a dangerous woman if ever I saw one.'

Gregory grinned and nodded. 'She's not wrong,' he said. 'If there's trouble to be made, then leave it to Adelaide P. She's a miserable old boot whose sole pleasure in life comes from making things as unpleasant as possible for all around her. Believe me, I do not exaggerate.'

Everyone laughed. Kate began to relax, happy to be part of this pleasant crowd. First appearances had been deceptive; the inhabitants of this apparently inhospitable fortress were turning out to be unexpectedly nice. Normal, too. Gregory glanced at his watch and said he must dash, and Kate thought it time to make her own excuses too. It was after one; work beckoned and she had been taught never to be the last to leave. Eleni seemed disappointed, though, as she walked with them both to the door.

'Are you sure you won't stay?' she asked, with a hand on each of their shoulders. 'Demeter is making kleftades and souvlaki. Any minute now we'll be able to eat.'

Certainly, quite tantalising smells were issuing from the kitchen, but both Gregory and Kate remained resolute.

'If you're not firm, you never get away,' he explained once the door was closed. 'Talk about Greeks bearing gifts. If Eleni had her way it would be one long binge all the time and we'd all be dead from too much ouzo and general over-indulgence.'

Then he was off down the stairs on light, rapid feet, back to his own computer and his deadline, leaving Kate all alone again but strangely at peace with herself.

Down on the second floor, Lady Wentworth was also entertaining, though on a far humbler scale than that of the open-handed Greeks. Since it was New Year's

Day and she believed in doing things properly, she had invited in a few close neighbours for sherry and biscuits: the Fentons from next door and one or two others from around the building. Miles and Claudia Burdett were special favourites since she considered Miles her financial adviser, and she also included Father Salvoni who lived downstairs and was newly attached to St Mary Abbots. And, of course, Amelia, who was helping her hand things around, and Heidi and dear Adelaide. She had even, after a moment's consideration, included Netta Silcock.

Mrs Adelaide Potter arrived late and cross, Heidi Applebaum bobbing ineffectually in her wake like a tug with a tipsy skipper. Today's grievance was something to do with the porter, who wasn't on duty often enough for her liking and refused to wear his official cap. Amelia grabbed a dish of crisps and disappeared across the room to the furthest corner to talk to Miles and Claudia. Anything for a quiet life; Mrs Potter could be a right pain once she got into full throttle. Claudia looked pale and anaemic today but Miles was his customary cheery self. Once again, he cross-examined Amelia about the state of the antiques trade and showed such attentive interest that she was quite bowled over.

The bell rang again.

'Sorry we're late,' said Beatrice, and explained that they had had a prior engagement on the fifth floor.

'Those Greeks,' sniffed Adelaide Potter, and added something about foreigners and fishwives which the new arrivals chose to ignore. They sidled over to join the Burdetts and Amelia, Beatrice silently rolling her eyes as the poisonous litany continued behind her. That woman was altogether too much. One of these days someone should settle her hash, though how was not immediately obvious. Push her down the lift shaft would be Beatrice's chosen method, though even that was too mild a fate for someone with such a lethal tongue. Perhaps they should form a subcommittee of the board and pool their resources. Certainly all the neighbours were of the same mind when it came to Mrs Adelaide Potter.

Amelia stood gazing at Father Salvoni, with his dashing Florentine good looks, reflecting how distinguished he looked, far too good to remain a celibate priest. Or maybe the clergy attached to St Mary Abbots were not celibates at all. They were, after all, High Anglican not Catholic. She'd ask Lady Wentworth later; she'd be sure to know. Not that it made a lot of difference to Amelia. She picked up a plate and set off on a final fast circuit of the room.

Working the room was something most of them seemed proficient at. Miles was now deep in conversation with Digby Fenton, while Claudia, sipping plain tonic, stood in the corner with Olive, too superior, Amelia supposed, to be bothered to mix. Netta Silcock, resplendent in one of her designer sacks, this one in brilliant acid green which startlingly offset the empty translucence of her eyes, was patting her hair with a plump white hand and sucking up to Lady Wentworth like mad, while poor pathetic old Heidi Applebaum, the block doormat, was glued to the side of Mrs Adelaide Potter, attending to her every word, nodding and dutifully clucking along in sympathy with one bigoted outblast after another. How could she? Politeness was one thing, but after all she'd been through? It was amazing she could even bear to speak to the woman, let alone toady to her in such a despicable fashion. Amelia could well imagine what Mrs P. would say about Heidi the second her back was turned.

She wondered idly if the new tenant in number twenty-five might surface. She'd be interested to take a look at her. Although she realised there was probably quite a wide age difference, Amelia felt the need of a new ally in the building. Living alone could be depressing and there was practically no one of her own sort around, other than Beatrice and Lily, of course, but they both had such busy working lives and were fairly absorbed in each other.

There was Gregory, of course. Just thinking about him softened Amelia's heart and she realised he hadn't yet put in an appearance. She looked round the room. What was it with these eligible single men that made them so elusive? Her glance flicked back to find the handsome padre, but he had already left. Ah well. The story of my life, thought Amelia glumly. But she'd catch up with Gregory later; there was something quite urgent she needed to ask him.

Connie was on an exercise bike, pedalling hard, when Kate reached the gym at a little after eleven the following morning and started on her warm-up routine. Connie waved. Today she was resplendent in a Lycra outfit in icecream colours, with a matching bandeau around her forehead, holding back her curly hair. Yet again, Kate deplored her own lack of sartorial elegance, even in the gym. New York had been one thing. For jogging in Central Park the more anonymous you were, the better; besides, then she was cocooned in her solipsistic relationship with Ramon and presentation just wasn't a priority. All she had ever wanted to do was the circuit as fast as possible and get right back to the apartment and him. And even though most of the women she knew over there were forever making great dents in their Saks accounts, buying fancy clothes especially for the gym and the shore, that kind of wanton extravagance had always left Kate cold. Even though Ramon was very well heeled and she'd earned a good wage herself. Over here she'd have thought things would be more casual. But then she hadn't reckoned on running into another New Yorker quite so soon.

By the time she reached home she felt she'd done a hard day's work already, and it was still only a little past noon. She scrabbled in the fridge for a tomato to go with her Ryvita, then switched on the radio for company. She liked this new lifestyle, with its casual lack of structure. Never again did she intend to commute in the mornings if she could help it; she thought of Manhattan and that crazy stampede to and from the office each day. Enough to take years off a person's life just trying to survive, not to mention the daily threat from rapists and muggers and carbon monoxide. And it gave her premium time with her cat, who she'd decided to call Horatio. He was slithering round her ankles right now, begging a sliver of cheese, so she gave him a cuddle and a health-giving yeast tablet, then headed back to work.

She carried her coffee into the study and switched on the computer. She didn't even have to bother with what she wore most days, since she rarely went anywhere and nobody called. Sluttish it might be but it was comfortable. Her warm-up trousers and sweatshirt would do today until she decided she needed some air, when she might get round to tarting herself up a little. Or not, as the mood took her. Horatio came bleating into the room and rubbed against her ankles. She picked him up and held him, purring, against her chest.

'Bit by bit,' she told him, kissing his whiskery snout, 'we are beginning to cope. We'll show them yet.'

And then the telephone rang and she jumped as if she'd been scalded. It was Connie.

'If you're serious about buying bits and pieces for your flat,' she said, 'drop by the shop some time and meet Amelia. Strictly without strings, you understand, but why not see what we have to offer before you look elsewhere? Competitive prices and all that. After all, why keep a dog and bark yourself?'

Kate laughed. Connie was a proper little saleswoman as well as a regular tonic. She already felt they'd been friends for years.

'I've very little cash at present,' she warned. 'But I'd love to meet Amelia and I do need to stretch my legs from time to time, even after all that exercise.'

The more people she knew, she thought, the easier her seclusion would be to bear, though she had no intention of getting too close, not to anyone for the moment. An image of Gregory flashed across her mind but she wiped it. She feared he might be too much of a charmer to be safe; besides, from what she'd seen, it looked as if the exotic Eleni already had her hooks into him. Though that divine Greek lady could probably juggle more balls than one at a time. There was toughness and determination, if ever she saw it. Kate admired her feisty neighbour and wished she had some of her boldness.

She settled down to work and was quickly absorbed. Across the courtyard, motionless at a window, a figure stood watching, but this time Kate didn't see.

8

Amelia Rowntree's shop, on the corner of a pleasant, garden-laid enclave just around the corner in Holland Street, was right up Kate's alley, a treasure trove of truly wonderful things. She pushed open the door, which set a mellow, old-fashioned bell ding-donging and brought Connie hurrying out from the rear.

'Hi, hon,' she said. 'Care for a cuppa? We've got the kettle on.' Today she had changed from her flamboyant exercise kit to a more subdued, but nonetheless fetching, suede two-piece in butter yellow. She looked quite ravishing, too good to be hidden away amongst the dusty antiques of Amelia's shop. Kate said she really mustn't stop. She'd left the computer running and should get back but she'd had to pop out anyway to go to the bank.

'Then waste no more time and come right on in.'

They pushed through a bead curtain into the tiny back room where Amelia was seated, immersed in the paper, on a shabby Victorian button-back armchair with half its stuffing hanging out, shoes off, feet up comfortably on the edge of an ornate brass coal scuttle.

She beamed when she saw Kate, dusted off a hand and held it out in welcome.

'Greetings, neighbour. Good to meet you at last. Welcome to Kensington as well as to the block.'

She was square-faced and clear-skinned, with the sort of English looks Kate's mother had always put down to good breeding, with wavy brown hair, faintly greying, in a strangely old-fashioned style which might have been a perm. Her eyes were widely spaced and faintly protuberant, giving the impression that she was always slightly surprised. She was wearing a twinset which was far from clean, a saggy tweed skirt and sensible suede brogues. Kate guessed her to be in her middle to late forties but doing absolutely nothing to combat the advance of age. A British and rather admirable attitude. Amelia Rowntree was quite clearly very much her own person.

And the shop was totally marvellous. Connie took her on a rapid tour from which Kate returned with her tongue practically lolling out.

'Fantastic!' she said enthusiastically. 'I want to buy everything. Maybe I'd better just move in.'

Amelia smiled, flattered. 'You'll have to come to the fair at the Town Hall,' she said. 'The next one's in a couple of weeks and we've got a stand. I'll give you a free ticket if you're at all interested.'

Kate said she was, in theory, but had very little money to spend right now. Amelia waved that aside.

'Don't you worry. Looking costs nothing and if you see something you really want, I'm quite sure we can reach a special arrangement. In any case, furniture lasts forever. Don't forget that. Anything you do buy, provided it's good, you can chalk up to investment.'

She hefted her heavy body out of the chair, straightened her skirt and lumbered back into the main part of the shop. Kate was not exaggerating when she said she loved everything there. Amelia's taste was exquisite and the shop was crammed with eighteenth- and nineteenth-century oak and brass, all in excellent condition and gleaming with beeswax and elbow grease. If only she had the means, she would like to jettison every one of Mrs Benjamin's out-of-date monstrosities and replace them with pieces as elegant and cared-for as these. Ah well, dream on. But at least she now had space for them. It was a beginning.

They'd had the shop for ages, Amelia told her, since Mother was still alive and able to work.

'We started it when Daddy died,' she explained. 'And Ma got stifled living in the country and wanted to move back to town. It began as a hobby and just grew. Now I wouldn't be without it, though it can be a bit of a chore, even with Connie here to help out.'

'And when I win the lottery,' said Connie, bright-eyed, her eyelashes like stamens, her skin fresh and dewy and apparently devoid of make-up, 'the first thing I'm gonna do is buy myself a stake in this shop, you betta believe it.'

'Lottery?'

'The lottery.' Two pairs of eyes met Kate's ingenuous ones, thoroughly startled. 'You mean you don't know about the lottery?'

'The disease that is sweeping this country?'

'The root cause of all that is bad and degenerate? The destroyer of family life and wrecker of marriages?

The wicked right-wing pestilence? The Tory government's secret weapon?'

'I thought they were illegal here?'

Connie and Amelia looked at each other in total disbelief.

'Where have you been, lady, all these weeks?'

'You don't have a telly?'

'No.'

'Good for you!' shrieked Connie. 'Then there's hope for this benighted country yet! Mind you, you're missing nothing – except Anthea Turner, of course, and *Blind Date*. But all that's super-schlock and simply rots the mind. Truthfully, the only thing worth watching these days is *Brookside*, and *that* I could not live without. It's like a drug.'

Much laughter. Connie confessed she was working on her Scouse accent just in case the call ever came. Their cups were replenished and the conversation moved back to the much more fascinating subject of Amelia's shop, which Connie so much coveted. Kate too, now she had seen it. The stock had to be regularly replenished with trips to the street markets in the small hours, as well as out-of-town sales and house clearances. It sounded quite fascinating to Kate; she said she'd love to tag along some time. Amelia was pleased.

'Come when we go to the Cotswolds,' she said. 'We'll take a picnic and make a proper day of it. Maybe even stay overnight.'

She liked this small, dark stranger, with her bright, intelligent eyes and discerning taste. There was something about her a touch on the cautious side, as though she might be holding back in some quite integral way, but the gleam in her eye proved there was humour there too. Perhaps, when she grew to know them better, it would surface. There was too little youth these days in Kensington Court; they could do with another ally against the old biddies. In her glummer moments, Amelia saw herself developing into one of them, heaven forbid. She was lucky to have Connie to keep her on her toes. And this Kate Ashenberry seemed a more than acceptable new recruit.

'You must come down for a drink one night,' said Amelia, 'and see the stuff I've got at home.'

Kate said she'd love to, then made her excuses and hurried back.

The porter was, for once, on duty and he swiftly put aside the paper he was reading to open the lift gates for Kate.

'Good afternoon.'

His voice was mellow and his manner cultivated. Certainly not at all the type, as she'd noticed before, to be doing a job this ordinary. Again, she wondered what his secret might be. Septimus Woolf – even the name had resonance, like an actor–manager of some bygone era, or a character out of *The Barchester Chronicles*.

'Getting a little brighter.' He spoke automatically, as if his mind were on higher matters, and Kate merely smiled as she stepped into the lift. Although not particularly inquisitive by nature, she relished a good mystery and vowed to get to the bottom of this one in time. She pressed the Ascend button and the lift ground noisily into life. In a building so affluent and cared-for, it was quite a surprise that they still maintained an old relic like this, but she liked it, found it distinctive, like something out of the Science Museum, and did not begrudge the extra time it took to make its leisurely ascent. Also, because of the fancy open iron-work sides, it allowed a good glimpse of each floor as it passed. No fear of claustrophobia in this creaky contraption, you could be sure of that, though you might starve to death like a rat in a trap if ever it broke down when no one was about. Kensington Court was still stuck firmly in the nineteenth century. Anything as contemporary as a telephone or alarm bell would be an anachronism and quite unacceptable. She was getting accustomed to this dignified old building; let them leave it as it was, undisturbed by progress.

She preferred it this way.

Nice person, reflected the porter as he returned to his seat and his newspaper, but his peace was soon shattered by the strident ringing of the telephone inside the lodge. Mrs Adelaide Bloody Potter – who else? – demanding that he come upstairs immediately to collect her shopping list for the day. As though she were something a great deal fancier than the draper's widow she actually was. Really, some of these old biddies thought they were still living in Victorian times, with squads of servants at their beck and call. Septimus Woolf was heartily grateful they no longer had coal to heft. When he'd taken the job, it had not been made clear to him that shopping and doing small individual errands for the tenants were part of his statutory duties, but one or two of them were constantly on the flutter, shattering his peace and making his life hell in all kinds of insidious little ways. Small wonder their husbands had had enough and snuffed it. He popped a peppermint into his mouth, to disguise any trace of his lunchtime beer – well, you couldn't be too careful – smoothed both hands over his steel-grey hair and took the lift grudgingly to the fourth floor where the Ayatollah would be waiting.

Mrs Adelaide Potter kept her hallway dark, pervaded by the musty smell that comes with age and airlessness through never opening a window. She stood just inside the door as if unwilling to be seen, grim and unyielding in her customary dark grey and marcasite, her thin-lipped mouth drawn tight into the familiar line of disapproval. Septimus Woolf, who had known far better days than these, always had the feeling that she expected him to touch his forelock, and a vicious part of him wanted to comply, if only to shock the old harridan into the twentieth century. Except that, in all probability, she would miss entirely the intended sarcasm and merely take it as her due. The window cleaner complained that she treated him like dirt – stood by him while he wiped his boots and made him wash his hands in the scullery rather than the bathroom – while the stories that came down via Bonita, the cleaner, were almost too incredible to be believed. But they did serve to brighten his day. Nothing was quite so bad if you could laugh at it, and the howls of mirth he shared with Bonita downstairs in his lodge were sometimes enough to rouse the tenants.

Today Mrs Potter had a string of demands almost as long as his arm. She needed groceries from Safeway immediately, but also one of her blind cords was fraying and the tap in the scullery would not stop dripping and was causing a limescale mark in the basin. And she could swear she'd heard footsteps late at night on the roof. Although she did not even live on the top floor, it seemed she had hearing that touched on the supernatural and was always alerting him, at all sorts of inconvenient hours, to possible intruders she wanted him to investigate. He'd been here six years now and had learned long ago never to argue or even answer back. Mrs Adelaide Bloody Potter always knew best; he touched that invisible forelock, picked up her list and made a rapid escape.

Poor old soul, Bonita would say, lonely and left on her own by those ungrateful children. But then Bonita was a mother herself, with an incurably soft heart. The way that evil woman spoke to her, it was a wonder she had not thrown down her duster and marched out years ago, but Bonita could see the funny side of things, and besides, she needed the work. And the other tenants were nice, on the whole. It was not such a bad job all things considered, or so Bonita said. Though to Septimus Woolf, cleaning was cleaning, and any kind of servitude should these days be coped with by a machine.

Claudia was getting a headache but Miles had another meeting to get through so, with a bad grace, she called herself a company cab and went home alone. It wasn't nearly good enough. She had imagined that marriage to Miles would mean total togetherness at last, but lately she'd been seeing progressively less of him as he grew more and more bogged down in his work, leaving her to her own devices. The traffic past the Tower and along the Embankment was practically at a standstill at this hour and she wished she'd thought of taking the river taxi to Chelsea Harbour, which was faster as well as a lot more colourful. And then, to add to her general ill-humour, the sky darkened to a threatening yellow and it began to rain.

The windows inside the cab steamed up, and when she opened one for a bit of air, the rain came in so she closed it again. All she could see in the gathering dusk were the endless lights of cars travelling bumper to bumper, punctuated by the staccato flashing of their rear lights which improved neither her headache nor her mood one bit. By the time she got home it would be well after seven and she'd still have to wait for Miles before they could sit down to eat. Sometimes she hung around for him in the office, but tonight she had had enough of those echoing corridors and the bustle and whir of computers with their soulless operators intent on making money and quite oblivious to her. At times like this Claudia found herself almost regretting the early days of heartache and high drama when she'd first met Miles and her main purpose in life had been to ensnare him and take him away from his wife.

Safe she might be now, but she missed the old excitement of the chase, of those stolen kisses and dangerous secret meetings; the swift, clumsy couplings in the back of cabs or even in the office when no one much was about. In those days life had been a helter-skelter of emotion and Claudia's nerves had been constantly raw with the terror of losing him, but also the exhilaration at being the subject of so much naked animal desire. Now Miles might indulge her from time to time with a holiday abroad, a piece of priceless jewellery or a picture she wanted, but it wasn't the same. She could not help remembering that these days her possessions were his too; that the money he lavished on her since he made her his wife was not really expended, simply redeployed. She supposed that was what the institution of marriage was all about, a joining together of assets in all senses of the word. All those happy ever afters she'd read of as a child simply turned into an endless landscape of sameness; getting up in the morning to go to the office and returning home after dark, too exhausted to do more than just loll about. And lately Miles wasn't even doing it with her. Somewhere they seemed to have got out of step. A cold dart of terror shot through her but she put it down to tiredness and the onset of this damned headache.

They'd got as far as Hyde Park Corner but the traffic down Knightsbridge and into Kensington Gore was packed solid and she knew she'd do better to get out and walk, if it weren't for the rain and the fact that she was wearing her Gucci shoes. And the headache. Besides, what was there to do once she got there but lie on the sofa and watch the news and wait for her lord and master to return when the mood so took him. She thought of lovely Gregory upstairs, always so charming and alert to her needs, and, so it seemed, so entirely accessible. More than once she had toyed with the thought of starting a light flirtation with him, just to raise her flagging spirits, but Gregory was situated a little too close for comfort and things might get tricky if he were to take her too seriously and Miles were ever to find out. Though, come to think of it, even that might not be an entirely bad thing. Miles definitely needed a sharp kick in the pants at times for taking her so very much for granted these days; for just not loving her enough.

She thought bleakly of boring Caroline and those three lumpish daughters, so valiant in their determination not to be a drag on him, so positively girl-guidish in their goodness when they did get to see him, which was hardly ever. Claudia couldn't imagine how Caroline had ever been able to let Miles go, but when the gloves came off, she had simply backed off and let Claudia snatch him, with almost no resistance at all. She often wondered how they managed these days, still struggling on in that barn of a place in Clapham, with Caroline doing a little freelance editing on the side to help pay the bills. Of course, Miles still maintained them, shelling out more than he could really afford, but still. If ever she had a child, and she fervently hoped one day she would, nothing would be too good for it, no expense spared. The idea of downgrading your position to ex-wife was inconceivable to Claudia, though there was no way she could ever have allowed Caroline to win. Claudia's childhood had not been easy; it had taught her, if anything, to be a tenacious warrior. And to hang on for grim death to what she'd got.

The rain was getting heavier but they were pretty nearly there at last, honking and weaving through the solid Kensington traffic, more impenetrable than ever because of the late-night shoppers. To save the driver going all the way round the block, Claudia told him to drop her on the corner, which would mean a short walk in the rain, but would save time. She glanced into the doorway of the Arab Bank as she passed, and her gaze was caught and held by a pair of ferocious black eyes, glaring at her hungrily like a beast out of the jungle. Oh my goodness. Claudia stopped dead in her tracks in terror, almost dropping her door key, then blind panic overwhelmed her and she took to her heels and ran.

Right into the arms of Gregory Hansen, as it happened, on the point of opening the door from inside as Claudia scrabbled frenziedly with her key.

'Hold on, calm down.' He caught her in his arms and drew her safely inside, out of the rain, stroking her hair with a practised hand, pulling her head gently against his chest as if she were a terrified child. Claudia felt her heart beating like a captured bird but in a second or two the panic began to subside and she was able to breathe more normally. Besides, it felt rather good to be held like this, close against Gregory's chest, out of harm's way. A flash of distant memory claimed her for a second, of a time long ago when life was more tranquil and someone had always been there to protect her, to soothe her like this and kiss it all better. Then awareness returned and she was back to normal. Safe in Gregory's arms and liking it quite a lot. But he was not alone. From just behind him, in the well-lit lobby, Claudia became aware of another person waiting, bobbing around like a skittish mare, waiting with ill-concealed impatience to be introduced.

When he was sure she wasn't going to fall, Gregory let go of Claudia and stepped back. He was wearing his raincoat that had seen better days, with a scarf looped loosely round his neck, but the woman beside him was dolled up to the nines. Clearly going out, and on a date at that. Claudia, unused to relinquishing centre stage, felt her heart clench with jealousy.

'Are you sure you're all right?'

'Yes, yes.' She was beginning to be impatient now, annoyed that the other woman had witnessed her weakness.

'Did something happen? Is there anything we can do?'

'No, no.'

'Do you want us to come back up with you? Just in case.'

'No, don't be silly. I'm absolutely fine. I just had a bit of a fright, that's all.'

'Then let me introduce you to my old friend, Jacintha Hart, up from the country on a flying visit. Jacintha, this is Claudia Burdett.'

The other woman's hand was smooth and well-cared-for, but boneless, and the clear grey eyes held a hint of panic. She was wearing a calf-length mink coat, which Claudia considered vulgar, and her shoes and bag were genuine crocodile. She also wore gloves, dark brown suede to match the coat. To Claudia she was a creature from another planet; clearly from out of town and light years out of date. Where on earth did Gregory manage to pick them up? And why, come to think of it, would he even want to?

'You're a braver woman than I am,' murmured

Claudia coolly, indicating the coat and its endangered accessories, but her bitchy comment went way above Jacintha's head.

'Oh, I'll be all right with Gregory,' she said brightly, missing the point. 'I'm sure he'll get us a cab, won't you, darling?' And she embarrassed both of them still further by nuzzling girlishly up against his sleeve. Gregory caught Claudia's eye and gave her just the flicker of a wink. That was part of his unfailing charm: he never took sides but endeavoured somehow to remain everyone's ally.

'I'm sure in the country warmth comes before fashion,' she said silkily. 'And is politically acceptable if it's just you against the elements.'

There, she couldn't say fairer than that. Jacintha still wasn't getting it but Gregory acknowledged her remark and laughed. Claudia was past caring. As long as this woman was only passing through, she could afford to be gracious. After all, she could see him any time she cared to, for he lived in the flat directly above her. And had made no bones of how much he admired her. Of one thing Claudia had always been confident, and that was her inherent pulling power.

'Well, I must get upstairs,' she said briskly. 'Have a good evening.'

As she swept up the steps towards the lift, Jacintha Hart turned and watched her go, the epitome of metropolitan chic, cool and remote, straight out of the pages of *Vogue*.

'Pretty woman,' she tried tentatively, as Gregory opened the door and ushered her out.

'Yes,' he said, bored already.

'Married?' She knew she shouldn't but simply couldn't stop herself. It was an old habit, hard to quash. She could have bitten her lip the moment she'd spoken, but what the hell.

'Yes.'

'Oh well, that's all right then,' said Jacintha with relief, tripping along beside him, knowing full well she'd overstepped the mark but able once more to breathe. For the time being, at least.

9

Jacintha Parry first encountered Gregory Hansen back in the late seventies, aboard a TWA flight from Toronto to London, when he was a fledgling travel writer, newly assigned to the *Toronto Star*, and she a pert, perky stewardess with ambitions greater than her intelligence, ever on the lookout – as weren't they all – for rich pickings in the lusher hunting grounds of First Class. It was only later, in the cramped sleeping gallery of his rented apartment over a drugstore in Don Mills, that she learned her error – that he had simply been upgraded for that flight because of a story he was researching on airline catering – but by then it was far too late. Jacintha was hooked, as so many had been before her and since, as securely and painfully as a fully grown trout with a steel barb through its lip. Gregory was her man, and would be for the remainder of her life; the only problem was, he didn't feel a similar commitment to her.

Or, indeed, to anyone. Having discovered at the age of fifteen the precise extent of his mother's perfidy, he had swept out to earn his own living and had been alone ever since, footloose and increasingly enjoying it, so that by the time, in his early twenties, that Jacintha strayed into his net, he was already a hardened bachelor with no thoughts of ever quitting that condition. Certainly not for a fluffy-headed bimbo who got her kicks from degrading herself scrubbing his kitchen floor, taking care of his laundry and hovering attendance with a chilled martini when he came home at the end of the day. Real slippers-and-pipe stuff; enough to make any red-blooded male shy away. Because he was based in Canada and she in London, the romance had managed to survive far longer than she had any right to expect, but when she was finally grounded, ten years later, and reduced to selling tickets in the Piccadilly office, Jacintha finally stamped her tiny foot and demanded the recognition she felt she had earned.

Gregory responded by taking off to Australasia on an extended tour and failing to contact her at all for more than a year. By the time she tracked him down, resourceful in her desperation, Jacintha had learned her lesson and was a truly broken spirit. Better, she figured, to have just crumbs of him than to be banished from his life completely. In the way of women throughout the centuries, she opted for compromise, and a half-hearted one at that, and had been hanging around his life ever since, even despite her lateish marriage, at the age of thirty-seven having finally given up hope, to a much older man with a suitably cushioned bank balance.

Jacintha Parry became Mrs Clifford Hart, wife of a respected Cotswolds yeoman, and although she had failed to give him an heir, or indeed any child at all, they rubbed along companionably enough, while Jacintha now had the necessary to keep her in the style she had always dreamed of. Only with the nagging sadness of being without the love of her life. Until, five years later, promotion moved Gregory permanently to London, and Jacintha instantly resumed the chase, as breathless and hopeful as ever.

Gregory was not, at heart, unkind – merely preoccupied – and was, for sentimental reasons, reluctant to crush her more than he felt strictly necessary. Provided she kept her distance and didn't cause too many scenes, he was content to allow Jacintha a certain amount of contact on the severe understanding that she knew there was no future to this relationship, that he was, and was likely to remain, a dyed-in-the-wool bachelor who took no hostages. Secretly, he enjoyed the flattery of her adoration, as what man wouldn't? The blind devotion he seemed to inspire in a certain sort of middle-class woman helped to make up for the early betrayal by his mother, who had thrown in his face at an impressionable age the awful fact that his whole life to date had been a dreadful sham. That even the name he went by was not his own and she herself was little more than a slut.

Jacintha, grateful to be allowed any access at all, however tenuous, willingly complied but had to be content with flying visits to London whenever she could convince the unimaginative Clifford that she really was nearing the sort of emotional crisis which only an urgent shopping expedition could assuage. She would turn up on Gregory's doorstep in a flurry of perfume and carrier bags, and then proceed to drive him mad for the next few days with her fussing and cooing and the total reorganisation of his flat these visits always involved. Gregory, muttering, would retire with his laptop to the study, where Jacintha was forbidden to disturb him, on pain of permanent excommunication, until the magic hour of six, when he would emerge for the BBC news and the first martini of the evening.

She would Hoover the carpets, scrub the bathroom from top to bottom and turn his kitchen upside down, while cooking him elaborate meals, and when she left, back to the dull husband and the bland insipidness of life in the country, she always endeavoured to leave behind her some little memento of her temporary occupation; her hairspray on the bathroom shelf, an expensive silk robe on the hook on the bathroom door, a stylish umbrella leaning coquettishly and unnoticed in the corner of the hall.

Of course there were other women in his life – Gregory was a man with a healthy libido and more than his share of animal attractiveness, and also he was free. But Jacintha tried to ignore the telltale signs. Despite the occasional late-night calls, the letters in coloured envelopes, the postcards she couldn't help sneaking a peep at, she continued to fool herself that there was no real competition. Gregory's work involved a lot of travel; he was entitled to pick up a penpal or two. Only when she found the nail varnish did she finally risk losing her rag, but then the dangerous glint in his eye reminded her of the shakiness of her ground, so she suppressed her jealousy as best she could for fear of losing him altogether.

Back home in Chipping Campden she entertained her girlfriends, behind closed doors, of course, or in the sanctuary of the health club, with tales of her

London adventures that grew more lurid as the years went by, keeping from them the shameful truth, that sex with her quondam lover had flown out of the window years before, with only the occasional half-hearted grappling to keep her keen. And her secret hopes alive.

Meeting Claudia in the lobby was almost more than Jacintha could take, for here, for the first time in years, was a flesh-and-blood reminder of Gregory's life, independent of hers, and the real threat that one of these days she might just lose him altogether.

'She's very stylish,' she continued later, sitting petulantly in Wheeler's, fiddling with the clasp of the ornate bracelet her husband had bought her for an anniversary, while she debated which sole to choose.

'Who?' asked Gregory, deliberately obtuse, cursing this airhead whose presence was beginning to irritate him so much and whose company he found so irksome; determined to dump her – and finally – as soon as he could find the means.

'That neighbour of yours, the one in the hall. Claudia, was it? Married, you said. Mrs What?'

Gregory sighed. 'Mrs Burdett,' he said distinctly, as if to a child. 'Married to a devoted husband who is also one of my best friends. And they work together, too. Now make up your mind and let's order. I'm starving and I've got a deadline to meet.'

Jacintha, for once, had the sense to pipe down, so bored him instead with details of her new lounge suite and the wonderful curtains that had cost them an arm and a leg but were straight out of *Country Life* and well worth the expense. But she wouldn't forget Claudia in a hurry. Just shoved her on to the back burner of her mind, to fret about at leisure once she was home in sticksville.

'Good heavens, it's almost the fiftieth anniversary of VE Day!' said Ronnie Barclay-Davenport from deep within the pages of the *Daily Telegraph*.

'When's that, my lovely?' asked Rowena, slopping across the carpet in her flowery housecoat, a cup of coffee wobbling in one hand. It was ten o'clock on a Tuesday morning; still a trifle early, she felt, for gin.

'May the eighth, it says here,' said Ronnie. 'Just a couple of weeks away.'

'Lord, doesn't it take you back?' said his wife, her hyacinth-blue eyes alight with memory. 'And we'd been married just two years. Seems like only yesterday.'

She shuffled across to the grand piano and picked up a silver-framed photograph of a dewy-eyed young couple on the steps of the Town Hall, he in uniform, looking absurdly young, she in a tailored navy suit, with a roll-brimmed hat and a posy of carnations and stephanotis. In over fifty years she had scarcely changed at all; the eyes were as bright, the figure very nearly as slim. Only a fine tracery of lines cobwebbed across her delicate skin betrayed the fact that she was no longer in the first flush of youth. But after three children and a host of other worries that was only to be expected.

'We ought to do something to commemorate it,' she said, clapping her hands with girlish glee at the prospect of any excuse for a party. Ronnie glanced up at her and smiled. She never ceased to amaze and entertain him, this wonderful, glorious girl who had been the focus of his life for so many decades.

'Such as what, my darling?' he asked indulgently. Whatever it was, it was likely to cost, but Ronnie was long past caring. They'd got this far together and if it gave her joy . . . The children were all grown up and off their hands, with families of their own now. If she wanted a little splurge for old times' sake, then, bless her, she should have it. A chap couldn't have asked for a better wife; when he'd won her against all the odds, what a lucky cove he'd been.

'Street parties used to be the thing,' she said. 'Do you remember how we celebrated when they finally routed the Horrible Hun? It went on for days and nights on end. We were down in Rochester, weren't we – or was that when the Japs finally threw in the sponge?'

He laughed. 'We can hardly have a street party in Kensington,' he said. 'Can't you just imagine it, tables laid out along the High Street with jellies and paper hats and a band. Dancing around the lampposts with a bonfire burning an effigy of Hitler on the gallows. Do you remember?'

'Don't I just!' she said. 'And the balloons, do you remember the balloons? The first we'd seen in years. And the bananas.' She clapped her hands with joy as she squinted back over the years.

'But we could have a block party,' she added. 'That's it, my precious. Let's think about that! You, me and Eleni, and perhaps that nice dark girl in number twenty-five, she seems as if she might be fun. We could open our flats to the rest of the building and ask them all up for a glass of bubbly. What do you say?'

He rose stiffly to his feet and crossed the room to peck her on the cheek.

'Whatever you say, my love, provided it's not too tiring. Don't want to exhaust you.'

'Tosh!' said Rowena, grabbing her writing case and starting to scribble. 'Plenty of time for relaxing once we're dead. If we do this properly it might even be worth getting the old diamonds out of the bank. What a lark!'

'We're quite a little League of Nations here,' she explained later to a stunned Kate, who opened her door a little before twelve to find herself confronted by a radiant Rowena, glass in hand, keen to share her brilliant idea with her neighbour.

'There's lovely Eleni, of course, and dear Demeter, to represent the Greeks. Then Gregory downstairs is half-Danish, and Lily Li is, of course, Chinese.'

'Don't forget the Toyota salesman,' said Ronnie, coming up behind her with his whisky. 'Number eighteen,' he explained to Kate as she stood aside to allow them in. 'Company let.'

'But we don't know him, and besides, he's scarcely ever there,' said Rowena, plonking herself uninvited on to Kate's shabby sofa and clicking her fingers encouragingly to Horatio, who was eyeing her warily from behind an armchair. 'And d'you think it would be entirely appropriate in the circumstances?'

'Still, stick him on the list,' said Ronnie. 'The more the merrier, I say, and if we're going to do it properly, we really do have to include them all.'

'Even Mrs Adelaide Potter?' groaned Rowena in

mock dismay, pulling a face. Kate laughed. She already loved this woman, who was quite outrageous but clearly as nice as pie underneath.

'Everyone,' said Ronnie sternly. 'Oh, Heidi is German, and don't forget the Persians.'

Kate looked surprised. 'At numbers fourteen and fifteen,' he explained. 'A whole damn tribe of them occupying half a floor. We'll have to invite them even if they don't come. Can't afford to look racist on occasions like this.'

'And the poor dear Shah was such a pet,' sighed his wife romantically. 'And so divinely handsome in his uniform. Do you remember that time in Shiraz when we danced the night away amidst all those rose petals?'

'Yes, yes, my dear,' said Ronnie anxiously, patting her freckled hand. 'Though I'd try not to talk about it too much to them. Have to tread carefully these days, old thing. Things have changed quite a lot, y'know.'

'And, of course, there are Americans at number eight,' said Rowena, warming to it. 'Very nice people, a banker and his wife,' she explained to Kate. 'They'll join in, I'm sure of it. They love to party, those Yanks. You should have seen them in the war. They're really a lot of fun.'

She scratched a few more notes on her piece of paper and Kate, resigned, offered her a top-up to her gin and tonic.

'But you must join us, dear,' she said, clutching at Kate's wrist, and when Kate pointed out politely that it was far too early for her and she still had work to do, told her she'd have to watch it or she'd miss out on all the fun. By the time the Barclay-Davenports had departed, staggering slightly, at a little after one, the VE Day party was shaping nicely and Kate had a whole list of chores she found she'd agreed to take on, which included designing and printing out a general invitation which could then be slipped through everyone's door.

'Don't mind doing that bit myself,' said Rowena cheerfully. 'Always glad for an excuse to snoop and catch up with some of the neighbours. And since we're all conveniently under one roof, I won't even have to get out of my slippers.'

Or leave your glass behind, thought Kate. She closed her door behind them, shaking her head bemusedly at the cat, but she felt uplifted by this encounter and was grateful to be included in the core of their projected party. As if she already belonged, she thought, going back to the computer.

Eleni, too, reacted with enthusiasm. She asked if they were just going to stick to drinks or if they should also be serving plates of food.

'Just crisps and bits on sticks, don't you think?' said Rowena. 'We don't want to turn it into a soup kitchen, do we?'

Eleni promised that Demeter would make some of her Greek delicacies to hand around, saying that nothing gave the old woman more happiness than to be feeding large numbers.

'She'd have been quite at her ease with the loaves and fishes,' she said. 'She's one of those born nurturers. I have to watch my weight all the time. Now, what about people from outside?' she added. 'Are we going to include strangers or simply stick to the inhabitants of this block?'

'I thought just neighbours, don't you, darling?' said Rowena. 'Keep it family. We don't want to overdo things, do we, and there are already enough of us here to make it quite a gathering. Provided everyone comes, of course, but it is a Bank Holiday weekend.'

'Then they might be off at their other houses,' said Eleni and laughed. 'I suppose we can always fall back on rent-a-crowd if necessary. Or even include the tenants from the other end.'

'Or ask you to round up some of your many beaux,' countered the older woman with a twinkle.

Eleni's love life was a topic of much interest within the building, and the Barclay-Davenports, who lived so near, had a ringside view. They'd known the Greek girl since she first moved in, as a shy young student of seventeen, and watched the comings and goings at number twenty-four with a great deal of interest. Luckily she had Demeter to keep her on the straight and narrow. More or less.

'And when are you going to settle down and find Mr Right?' was one of Rowena's regular questions. Having married off two sons and a daughter herself, she was constantly on the lookout for another wedding to organise. Eleni laughed, and bent to kiss Rowena's faded cheek. Her dark eyes sparkled like those of an intelligent monkey and she pushed back her long, perfumed hair with one finely manicured hand.

'Not for quite a while, my darling, the way things are going,' she said. 'Men with sufficient stamina to keep up with me are not exactly thick on the ground.'

'Or rich enough?'

'That too.' She loved her elderly neighbour and was in no way offended by her constant kindly prying.

'And in any case,' she added, 'I am having far too much fun. I shan't settle until I can find someone as wonderful as Ronnie to take care of me.'

She blew Rowena a kiss, flashed her film-star smile and disappeared back inside her flat for a facepack and a lie-down before she had to get ready for the evening. Rowena, chuckling, retraced her steps to her own front door. Eleni, with her energy and exuberance, took her back to her own carefree youth, though in those days they'd really lived on the edge because of the war. There was nothing quite like a sense of imminent doom to keep one dancing with all one's senses alert. These days were tame by comparison, and, if she were honest, she often looked back with regret. But then she'd been one of the lucky ones and had come through safely with her adored Ronnie still by her side.

She rang her own doorbell to summon him to answer.

'Chin, chin,' she said, wagging her empty glass under his nose. 'Let's crack another bottle and drink to old times. You're only as young as you feel, after all!'

Mrs Adelaide Potter was disapproving when the xeroxed invitation slipped through her door, and considered herself severely slighted at not being consulted in the first place.

'It's typical of those rowdy people upstairs,' she grumbled to Heidi and Netta when they dropped by at eleven for their regular agenda of coffee and complaints. She had never approved of the Barclay-Davenports, considered them altogether too noisy and uncouth; and as for those Greeks, with their funny foreign ways, well . . . With all the foreigners who were buying into the building these days, there was no telling where it might lead and what sort of people could end up living next door. She had tried writing letters to the management and even to the council, but to no avail. Her waspish dictates regarding the control of alien invasion went unanswered, which only showed how standards dropped when you allowed just any old person to stand for election. As it was, she had those Japs next door, and a Chinese woman on the floor below. Not that Lily wasn't quiet and considerate but Adelaide Potter still didn't trust her. It wasn't natural and it wasn't right. They were quite inscrutable, these Chinks, that was a well-known fact. You never could tell what they were really thinking, particularly after Tiananmen Square. In the days when Mr Potter was still alive, he'd have had something to say, and no mistake. After all, she might have been black or anything, and then where would they all have been, unable to go out freely without risking being mugged on their own doorsteps.

'Does that mean, dear Adelaide,' asked Heidi in her usual quavering pipe, 'that you don't think we should attend this party?' She so much wanted to, but Adelaide always knew what was what. Heidi was so unsure about everything since her husband's death that she relied upon her neighbour to lead the way, especially in matters of taste and discretion like this.

'I'm certainly going,' declared Netta boldly, for once

unwilling to be overruled, particularly where a party was concerned. She had been dying to see inside some of the other flats and this looked like being her golden opportunity. And since they hadn't been asked to bring a bottle or anything, it meant free entertainment, which was even better.

Mrs Adelaide Potter's lips met in a single thin line of disapproval as she stirred her coffee and reserved her judgement. She was most displeased at being outfaced by Netta but also had a sneaking wish to be included in the party, no matter what the cost to her dignity might be. If only they had come to her first, surely only fitting after the years she had lived in the building, she could have kept things in their proper perspective by giving her approval reluctantly, after keeping them waiting for a suitable period. Things were not done correctly any more. But she'd work off her aggravation by torturing her acolytes a little and refusing to give her decision until the very last moment.

But Netta's luminous eyes were brightening and she was off on one of her chattering jags, wondering what to wear and if she would get a proper snoop at the rumoured luxury of the Papadopoulos dwelling and the Barclay-Davenport diamonds.

'Do you think she wears them often at home?' she asked. 'Or only for parties at Buckingham Palace and state occasions like that?'

'Or just to clean the grate?' supplied Mrs Potter acidly, tired already of Netta's foolish mitherings. It was one thing having her own private army, of which she was the undisputed adjutant, but class did matter, even these days, something which Netta Silcock sadly lacked. The first Mrs Silcock had been another matter entirely, though Mrs Potter conveniently forgot that Hermione Silcock had virtually snubbed her in the last few years of her life.

And now the foolish Heidi was rattling on about the party too, as if her own family hadn't been involved enough in the war, as though she thought it would be appropriate for her to attend. She was surprised they'd even invited Heidi in the circumstances; an oversight, surely, or just the ignorance of youth. She called the meeting to order by abruptly changing the subject to the laxity of the porter, and sent Heidi scuttling back to the kitchen to replenish the coffee pot. The one good thing about the German woman was that she was so biddable. Which was why Adelaide Potter allowed her to hang around.

'I don't like his manner one bit,' Mrs Potter was saying when Heidi trundled obediently back, clutching the heavy silver pot in both shaking hands.

'He hasn't the right respect about him, forgets to address me in the proper way,' she said. 'And I've had to tell him innumerable times about keeping his uniform jacket buttoned and spending too long gossiping to that cleaning woman when she ought to be Hoovering the stairs.'

'After all, it's what we all pay her for,' chimed in Netta, pale cheeks flushed with importance at the heady prospect of scolding servants. She was wearing one of her voluminous tent dresses, this one in navy patterned with fuschia that was a degree or two too hard for her pallor, and her tiny feet, beneath her puffy ankles, were crammed into Imelda Marcos shoes that were definitely a size too tight. Mrs Adelaide Potter, in clerical grey, with her tree-trunk legs respectably encased in thick grey lisle, tightened her lips still further but for once forbore to comment. Netta Silcock was vulgar, there were no two ways about it, but just for the while, at least, she suited her purposes and so she would say no more. She glanced instead at the clock on the mantelpiece as it chimed the half-hour, and, right on cue, both of her guests leapt guiltily to their feet, fearful that they had outstayed their welcome.

Heidi still lingered a few minutes longer, obedient as a trained collie, to collect the list of shopping and other errands she knew would be forthcoming.

10

A single light was burning as consciousness returned and he struggled to remember where he was and with whom. The tangled sheets that clung to his damp body were satin and the perfume in the air hung heavy and suffocatingly about him as he struggled for breath. He ran one hand cautiously over the cool undersheet but found he was alone. He sat up, slowly and with mechanical movements because of the pain in his head. The rug beneath his feet was thick and furry. Seeing in the dim light the outline of a glass on the bedside table, he grabbed for it eagerly, keen to slake this unbearable thirst, then gagged as the few remaining drops hit his abused tongue and he tasted once more the thick, cloying, sugary liquid that had been his downfall from the start. The club. That girl. As painful memory limped back, his gaze began to focus and he saw that he was in a bedroom entirely unfamiliar to him.

More light filtered in as the door opened a crack, and someone stood there, bearing a tray with glasses on it.

'Bonjour, cheri. How are you this morning? Sleep well?'

He was still wearing his watch and could just make out, in the small amount of light from the corridor, that it was 6.15. That must be a.m. Christ on a bike, what had he been doing, and where in God's name was he now? Panic struck as he groped for his Filofax, his phone, but could not locate them.

'Relax, my sweet, and drink some of this. It will make you feel better.' Slender fingers massaged his temples as she sank beside him on the bed, and a hot glass of something was pressed against his mouth. He was too weak and abandoned to resist.

He remembered the perfume which pervaded the whole room, deep and sinister and seductive. He sank back into it now as her fingers continued their exploration and all the energy he thought he'd lost began to return. *Tramp*, that was where he'd met her, but for the life of him he couldn't remember her name. Not that it really mattered. This was nice, very nice indeed . . . He'd worry about his meeting in a little while, once she'd stopped doing that to him.

It was eight when he woke again, and this time the curtains were pulled wide and sunlight battered his aching eyes. Oh God.

'Time to go, *cheri*,' said a soft voice from the door, all seductiveness fled in the brutal morning light, his clothes neatly piled on the dressing table chair, his phone and Filofax safe on top.

'Unless, of course,' with a more caressing tone this time, 'you'd care to stay for the whole day?'

The flesh was more than willing, no denying that, but some inner safety valve reminded him, even *in extremis*, of the meeting at ten that he dared not miss.

Oh no. He rolled from the bed, grabbed frantically for his pants, then tried to scrape together a semblance of dignity as he got himself ready for a speedy retreat.

'Nice place you've got here,' he offered, as he slicked back his hair with a dampened comb then tried to tie a perfect knot, even though the uncompromising light was hurting his eyes.

'Here, let me,' she said, standing too close so that he could feel the warm promise of her body through the thin silk wrapper. Her fingers moved with knowing expertise, but that he could remember from last night.

'Live here alone, do you?' He shrugged himself into his jacket, and checked his pockets for his wallet and car keys. All correct.

'More or less.' Good heavens, what was she – some sort of heiress? In the pale grey silk, with her hair all loose, she looked like a vestal virgin with her great wistful eyes. She moved towards him and he took her in his arms again, slyly checking his watch as he did so. Must get moving. Oh, but she smelled and tasted good, with none of the sourness and bitter aftertaste of a hard night on the town. His resolution wavered.

'Can I see you again?'

'Maybe.' She seemed uncertain, as if waiting for something. He racked his addled brains but could come up with nothing. It had been his shout, his car, and he'd brought her safely home. What else? Still she hesitated.

'It's not easy to maintain a place like this.' Now a sigh, deep from the heart. 'The heating no longer works and the landlord is not at all . . . sympathetic.'

She moved to the mirror and picked up a silver-backed brush to flick through her hair. As she brushed, steadily and with deep feeling, the wisp of a robe slipped gradually from one shoulder, revealing her alabaster skin and one perfectly shaped breast. Involuntarily he groaned and snatched her back into his arms, loosening first her sash and then his belt.

'No, no, I must not keep you,' she whispered with honeyed lips against his throat. 'You have that meeting, remember, the one that will transform your career? Please don't risk being late for something as unimportant as this. There will be another time for us, I promise. Provided in the meantime I can persuade the landlord to see reason.'

Then he understood her. He stepped sharply back, watching as she retied her sash and popped her breast back under the silk.

'How much?' he asked harshly, a terrible weariness of the soul beginning to overwhelm him.

For a moment she appeared not to understand, as her great dark eyes swept his face like a searchlight.

Then: 'Two fifty,' she whispered, turning back to her own reflection. 'That should fix things, for the moment at least.'

She was still brushing her hair, with languid sensuality, as he pulled out his chequebook and searched for his pen. He thought of asking if she took plastic but felt so dispirited, the joke was hardly worth it.

'Oh,' she said, before he started writing, 'and then there's the telephone bill.'

He stared.

'A contribution towards that would be nice.' She turned and flashed her radiant smile, as innocent and untouched as a bride-to-be. 'And would make me *very* grateful, darling, you can't imagine how much.'

He sighed deeply, added an extra fifty to the cheque, left it on the side table and let himself out. As he slipped off the chain and opened the heavy front door in the bright light of morning, there was movement beside him, and an elderly woman, dressed from head to foot in earthy brown, materialised silently from the room he thought was the kitchen and saw him out with a respectful nod. For a second he wondered if he should tip her too, then dismissed the notion angrily. Not quite sure what he had just experienced, the thrusting young company director ran down the stairs, too much in a hurry to wait for the lift. Guilt told him, in no uncertain terms, that he had just been royally shafted and should not even think about returning. But the flesh is weak and he knew, with a cynical shrug of acceptance, that it was well on the cards that he would.

Chuck Moran was surprised and delighted to run into his friend and neighbour, Miles Burdett, in the shower room of the Hurlingham Club.

'Good heavens,' he said, peering through the steam, 'it really is you then? What an odd coincidence.'

Miles grinned and waved acknowledgement, then returned to the conversation he was having with a couple of City brokers. At the pace Miles worked there was little time left for niceties, and he worked the Hurlingham as ruthlessly as every other arena in his life. Besides, he'd been playing this game a number of years and knew that Chuck Moran would keep. Would be easier pickings, in fact, on his own turf, at his own time. He'd already recognised the glint of interest in the banker's eye and knew the fly was successfully cast. The results remained to be seen; the rod was well and truly in his own experienced hands.

'Why don't you get to know Marilyn a bit better,' he suggested to Claudia that night at dinner. 'She seems nice enough and you must have a lot in common.' Shopping and running up exorbitant bills was what he meant, but he left it unsaid.

'No thanks,' said Claudia dismissively.

'But she must be lonely, stuck here in this town, away from Westport and the ladies who lunch. She seems fairly pally with Olive Fenton and you like her well enough.'

Claudia conceded that. Olive was someone she really respected, stylish and dignified and infinitely wise. If she became Lady Mayoress next year, which she was set to do, she would fill the job admirably and increase the Tory majority in this borough.

'So why not give it a go then? For me?' He had on his boyish, appealing look. He was up to something. He poured her more wine and gave her his special smile. She remembered how that look used to weaken her knees in the old days when they first worked together, he the City whiz kid, she his humble PA. Now she was more cautious.

'What's in it for me?' Was she reduced to this, after only six years?

'For you? For us, more like. I'm only thinking of our future together as I wear my fingers to the bone, trying to make us rich.'

Claudia sniffed. Enough of this flannel. She revolved her glass slowly, savouring its bloom, then looked her husband levelly in the eye.

'See here, Miles,' she said, 'whatever it is you're up to these days, just don't do it on your own doorstep. Understand? I've worked long and hard for what I've got now and I won't have you blowing the lot on one streak of greed. Keep your dirty dealings off this patch if you know what's good for you.'

His smile remained fixed, but behind the thick lenses, the merry blue eyes were unamused. She could be a prize bitch, his wife, when she put her mind to it, and lately she'd been showing unmistakable signs of severe insurrection. Could it be that she was beginning to take the façade of this lifestyle seriously? Did she really believe she belonged by right in a place like Kensington Court?

Smile still in place, he leaned towards her and entwined her fingers lovingly with his own.

'Do it,' he hissed abruptly, then called for the bill.

Rowena was hovering on the landing when Kate returned from the gym. They'd made it a couple of hours later this morning since Connie was doing the Bermondsey run with Amelia and had invited Kate along for the ride. Enormous fun, as it had turned out, though she'd been glad to relax in the sauna later and sweat out some of the accumulated grime. Plus the evil effects of the high cholesterol breakfast Amelia had insisted they all have afterwards, in a greasy spoon on the edge of the market.

'Tradition, my dears,' she had explained as she

treated them to double portions of cod and chips.

Even Kate had not come away empty-handed. She'd found a pretty Victorian copper kettle, only slightly dented, which she planned to polish up and hang on a hook in her kitchen, alongside the old range with its authentic green tiles.

'You've got a bargain there,' said Amelia, examining it. 'You clearly have an eye for these things. Join me in the shop any time you like. When Connie hits the big time, as we all know she is going to, and deserts us for Hollywood.'

'Careful!' said Kate. 'I might just take you up on that.'

'Only don't expect me to pay you,' warned Amelia. 'Let's not be too hasty!'

But the outing had certainly whetted Kate's appetite and she longed for the cash to be able to splurge a little more in the market and really get her flat to look as good as possible. She'd never really had a home, not one that was hers entirely, and now felt a powerful urge to build a permanent nest. This kettle marked the beginning of a new acquisitive streak. All her wedding presents had remained with Francis, of course, and when she'd walked out on Ramon she'd taken nothing with her but her clothes. Survival had been her sole motivation then, and she'd left the relationship as she'd come to it: empty-handed.

Connie and Amelia said they'd love to help, and Amelia said that if Kate spent more time in the markets, she'd soon get her eye in for the sort of thing she wanted.

'I think I'd like to stick to the period,' said Kate, 'and

try to find Victorian pieces from around the time the flat was first built.'

Amelia applauded her taste. 'One of these days I'll drive you down to Hastings,' she offered. 'I used to go there all the time for stock, since the prices are so much more reasonable. These days, since they electrified the line, the yuppies are moving out there, but it is still possible to pick up a bargain if you know what you're looking for. Particularly the sort of basic oak furniture I think you have in mind.'

'And don't forget Lots Road,' said Connie. 'One of my favourite Sunday-morning haunts.'

She told Kate about the antique warehouse and the auction rooms where you could often pick up real bargains.

'We're going to have a lot of fun,' she said. 'At least, me vicariously while you shell out the loot. If I only had the space, I'd be doing it too, like a shot.'

'So let's all pray for that summons from *Brookside*.'

'You bet!'

Rowena pounced, list in hand. Since they'd first planned the party, she seemed to have gained new energy and now the festivities were almost upon them.

'There's not a lot to do,' she explained, following Kate unbidden through her door. 'Between us, we and Eleni have plenty of glasses to cater for a whole crowd, and we thought we'd lay them out on a trestle table at the top of the stairs, just outside our front door. Ronnie's seeing to all that. One of his pals at the golf club has a table he can lend and I've dug out a suitable white cloth, part of me trousseau, don't you know, my dear.' She twinkled.

'Oh, and Amelia has uncovered a whole cache of old red, white and blue bunting,' said Kate as she switched on the kettle and ground some coffee beans. 'Left over from a scout jamboree or something. She thought we might like it to brighten the place up, give it the authentic wartime spirit.'

'Splendid,' said Rowena, ticking that off her list. 'It's just as well we're at the top or the Awful Mrs Adelaide Potter might come snooping, and goodness only knows what she'd have to say.' She laughed like a giddy young girl. 'Probably get the council on to us or something for breach of the peace.'

'Is she coming to the party?'

'Who knows. Mrs P is a law unto herself, though I doubt she could resist sticking her beak in just so she can complain.'

Heidi was coming; she'd already said so. And the Fentons, of course, who were very civic-minded. And there was no keeping Netta from anything that might involve a free drink and a snoop into other people's private places. Lock up your knicker drawer, was Rowena's advice, and had them both in stitches. Even Lady Wentworth had promised her support. She was surprisingly gracious about the event; thoroughly approved, she said, of such an important commemoration. She would probably come in her Red Cross uniform.

'Like Barbara Cartland at the Royal Wedding?' asked Kate.

'Shush, dear, you're not to mock.' But Rowena was

laughing as heartily as Kate. 'Perhaps I'll even liberate the tiara. Just to give them something else to titter at.'

'Now, what else can I do?' asked Kate once they were settled in her kitchen. 'Orders, please. I'll do whatever you like.'

'There's really nothing much,' said Rowena. 'More a question of rounding up certain things. Ronnie's ordered a couple of cases of bubbly' – they'd agreed they'd chip in equally – 'and the lovely Demeter is cooking us some delicious Greek goodies to go with the crisps and nuts. That ought to do it, don't you think? Some of the tenants won't be around and I'm not at all sure they'd all want to come, in any case. Certainly not the Japs, I would think. Or those lovely Persians who don't appear to speak a word of English.'

The plan was, Rowena told her, to lead the whole lot of them up on to the roof at eight when the Queen and Prince Philip were lighting a beacon in Hyde Park that would set off a chain of bonfires throughout the country.

'There's going to be a fireworks display after that,' she said. 'From our vantage point, up there on the roof, we should have a perfect view.'

Kate agreed. It had occurred to her that perhaps she should be patriotic and try to recapture the wartime spirit by actually venturing into the crowds in the park to savour it all first-hand. Then she'd heard on the radio that a million visitors were expected and decided to back off. She hated crowds and could think of nothing worse than the frightening claustrophobia of being trapped amongst all those people, mindlessly cheering and waving their Union Jacks, just as they had the first time around. Patriotism was all very well; on the whole, she'd prefer to view the goings-on from a distance.

It was clear that her neighbour was really in search of some gossip, but Kate resolved not to produce the gin since she still had work to do. She said she would get the bunting off Amelia and also contribute some of the snacks.

'Do we need soft drinks as well?' she asked, but Rowena thought probably not. It was really only a token get-together, after all. Those who didn't like their tipple need not stay.

'Or come at all, if they're Mrs Adelaide Potter.'

'What about Gregory?' asked Kate casually. She wasn't sure why it mattered, but it did.

'Oh, he's promised to be barman,' beamed Rowena. 'We need a man with nice strong wrists to wrestle with all those champagne corks. They do have their place, you see, my dear. We ladies are far too delicate.'

Later Kate smiled as she rinsed out the cups. Now why did she suddenly feel a whole lot better about this party?

Amelia wasn't always in the shop in the mornings so Kate telephoned her first at home. She answered on the second ring sounding, Kate thought, mildly distracted but pleased when she heard who it was.

'The bunting? Yes, I think I have it somewhere here,' she said. 'The flat's a real tip at present, since I still haven't sorted out all the stuff we got at Bermondsey.'

Kate said there was no rush and that she'd pop down

and collect it whenever it was convenient. Just then she heard Amelia's doorbell ring.

'Hang on a tick,' said Amelia, 'and I'll just see who that is.'

Kate sat idly playing on her computer, flicking over to a complex French puzzle she had recently acquired which was mind-blowing in its apparent simplicity yet almost impossible to solve. Once people simply doodled while hanging on on the phone; now advanced technology had contrived to keep them exercising their intellectual powers even at moments as trivial as this. But it was quite marvellous and totally absorbing. If she wasn't careful, she knew she could waste whole hours like this. She understood how kids got hooked.

Amelia was certainly taking her time. In the distance Kate could hear voices, then a short, sharp sound that sounded like a laugh. Or a scream. Then silence.

'Hello, hello!' she called, banging the receiver in case she'd been forgotten, but there was no response. No hurrying footsteps back to the phone, no more conversation. Just silence. And the distant click of the front door closing. What on earth was going on?

Sudden irrational panic swept over Kate and she was out of her own front door like lightning, belting down the stairs to the third floor. No time to wait for the ponderous old lift; instinct told her this might be an emergency, though she couldn't imagine what sort. The third floor was deserted and Amelia's door firmly closed. She pressed the brass bellpush and heard it ringing inside, but no one came running to let her in and no voice called out to ask her to wait. All she could hear was silence.

'Amelia!' she called frantically, pushing open the let-terbox flap and trying to see inside. 'It's me – Kate. Are you all right?'

Perhaps she had fainted, but it wasn't the sort of thing Amelia would do. Not in the middle of a phone call. Not when she had sounded so normal a moment before. Perhaps she'd suddenly gone out, but why would she do that? Not while Kate was hanging on. Even if she'd had bad news, she'd surely have had the courtesy to let Kate know what was happening. Even ask for her help.

'Amelia, Amelia.'

The door to number twelve opened cautiously and Lily Li looked out.

'Is there anything wrong?' she asked. She was wear-ing a long blue denim overall, and her hands and face were smeared with ochre paint.

'It's Amelia. I can't seem to raise her,' said Kate.

'Maybe she's popped out. I think it's about the time she goes to the shop.'

'No, you don't understand. She was there only a moment ago. I was talking to her on the phone and she just disappeared,' said Kate, seriously concerned by now. Perhaps she'd been electrocuted or something; was that possible? And what about the laugh? Or scream, the ominous voice in her head reminded her.

'Do you have the key?' There must be a perfectly rational explanation for Amelia's sudden silence, though for the life of her, at the moment Kate could not imagine what that might be.

' 'Fraid not,' said Lily. 'But there's probably one in the porter's lodge. Like me to fetch it?' She glanced down ruefully at her paint-smudged hands and laughed. Despite herself and this awful nagging worry, Kate laughed too. Lily's serenity had a calming effect; almost certainly Kate was drastically overreacting. There had to be a perfectly plausible explanation. Any minute now, Amelia would turn up and then the laugh most definitely would be on Kate.

'Don't bother. I am sorry to have disturbed you. I'm sure it's nothing really.' And she fled downstairs, trying to calm the thumping of her heart.

There was no response either to the porter's bell when Kate rang it frantically, then rattled his front door. Where was everyone this morning, and was she going out of her mind? She opened the main front door and looked up and down the street in the forlorn hope of seeing him on his way home. Where was he, in any case? He should surely be on duty at this time of day. Should she call the police, or was that too extreme? She'd no idea how to act in this sort of an emergency and her shrinking nature wished she could just go back upstairs and not be involved. If only she had not chosen that moment to phone, but that was hardly a neighbourly spirit, and how could she possibly have known?

And then the door of the sandwich bar opposite opened and there was Mr Woolf, strolling casually towards her with his newspaper under his arm and his jacket unbuttoned, no sign of a tie.

'Miss Ashenberry?' he said, instantly alerted when he saw her face. 'Is there something wrong?'

'It's Amelia,' she gabbled, grabbing at his sleeve in

her relief and pulling him into the doorway. 'One moment I was talking to her and then she went off to answer her door and now she seems to have disappeared. You've got to come, to see if she's all right.'

Probably just a meaningless scare; there was bound to be some perfectly obvious explanation and soon they'd all be laughing and Kate would feel a fool. She could see that thought reflected in the porter's patrician face as he escorted her gravely back up the steps to his lodge and made her sit quietly while he fetched the key. When he returned he was wearing his tie, and his jacket was neatly buttoned. This time they took the lift – Mr Woolf was far too stately to race up the stairs – and when they got there Lily was still hovering, joined now by a curious Iranian lady from next door, with two small, black-eyed children.

'Now let's stand back and throw a little light on things, shall we?' said Mr Woolf weightily, producing his keys and advancing on the door with a flourish. Lily, getting the message, withdrew discreetly, but the Iranian lady crowded forward, then realised from a chilly stare from Kate that this was out of place. The door was opened and the porter went inside, followed by Kate, who closed it firmly in the woman's face.

One glance showed that her alarm had not been misplaced. Amelia lay flat on her back on the floor, eyes staring wide and horribly protruding, her normally ruddy complexion apoplectic, her mouth half open to reveal her bulging tongue. Kate gasped and watched in horror as Mr Woolf stooped and felt her pulse, then straightened and pronounced her dead.

'Strangled, I'd guess,' he said, showing little emotion.

'But we'll have to get a doctor to confirm that. And the police.' And then, to Kate's astonishment, he made the sign of the cross over the body and muttered something with downcast eyes.

'What's more,' he said later, as they sat in Kate's flat, drinking hot, sweet tea while they waited for the police to arrive, 'no one came out of the building, not in the last half-hour. No one at all. I'd have seen them.'

'But you weren't even there.' Though still shaky, she was beginning to pull herself together, and her powers of reasoning were flooding back.

'Not in the hall, maybe,' he agreed, 'but I always sit in the window of Graziana's across the road, when I go over there for a coffee and a smoke. That's part of the point of spending time there, in fact, to keep an eye on the building. You get a far better view from across the road. I don't suppose you'd thought of that.'

She hadn't. And he wasn't being patronising either, just simply explaining his job.

'But who on earth would want to harm Amelia?' said Kate. 'She was such a lovely person when you got to know her. And it didn't look as if the place had been done over.'

In fact, now she thought of it, nothing had appeared to be out of the ordinary at all. Other than the grim corpse spreadeagled inside the door. Tears gathered at the back of her eyes and she realised how superficial her calmness really was. She'd come all this way to escape from violence and here it was again dogging her, worse than ever. Full realisation hadn't yet dawned; when it did, it was going to be horrendous.

Connie – they must let her know . . . but right then her doorbell rang and it was the police.

'Well, she did work in a fairly shady business,' said Mr Woolf as they trooped downstairs again.

'Antiques? What could possibly be shady about that?'

'You never know who you're tangling with when it comes to buying and selling,' he replied. 'It's all very undercover and hush-hush, like drugs. You mark my words. There's a lot we don't yet know.'

Much later, after the police and the doctor had been and gone and the remains of poor sad Amelia taken away, Kate paced her flat with a drink in her hand, waiting for Connie.

'I guess I won the lottery after all,' said a totally dazed Connie when she arrived, tears streaming down her cheeks, hardly able to grasp what had happened. Even *in extremis*, those stamen-like lashes emphasised by the raw redness surrounding her eyes, she still looked remarkably pretty.

'I'm so sorry,' said Kate softly, kissing her cheek. 'It's a rotten thing to have happened.'

Amelia's closest relative, a second cousin in Weston-super-Mare, had indicated over the phone that Connie was to continue holding the fort, at least for the time being, while they sorted out what was to become of the business. And she could move into the flat as well, he said, once the police had finished their investigations.

'Well, it does make sense,' said Kate gently, pouring her a stiff drink. 'With all those antiques and pieces of priceless porcelain down there, it needs a caretaker in residence until they can sort it out. It'll be great to have you in the building.'

She hugged her friend and they both burst into tears again.

'It seems so heartless,' said Connie later. 'When she's only just dead.'

'But I am certain it's what Amelia would want. I didn't know her long but I saw how obviously she relied upon you.'

The doctor had recommended sleeping pills and even, thoughtfully, provided a prescription, but Kate was tougher than she looked and didn't hold with rubbish like that. She knew that, like a bruise, you had to let the shock work itself out and was quite prepared for a string of sleepless nights. Better that than risking dulling her senses; she'd been down this road before and dared not lose control. In the meantime, her brain was in overdrive.

'Who on earth could possibly have wanted to harm her?' she asked. Connie simply shook her head, still dabbing ineffectually at her swollen eyes.

'More to the point, how ever did they get away? We know that Amelia let them in because I heard her doing it. But Mr Woolf says he saw no one leave the building, so where on earth did they go?'

'Up the fire escape and over the roof?'

'Perhaps. But they'd be taking a chance unless they knew the building well. It's pretty secure and the fire escape doors are supposed to be locked from the inside.'

'But only by a safety bar,' said Connie. 'Once inside, they could easily get out again and scoot across the roof to the other side and down in the other lift.'

'Provided they could get in in the first place,' Kate reminded her. 'And they could only do that with a key to the other stairwell.'

'So are you suggesting it was someone from the other half of the building?'

'Perhaps. I just don't know.'

It seemed incongruous; the situation was getting weirder by the minute, but then you didn't expect your neighbours to die quite so suddenly and in the safety of their own homes. Not, most certainly, in an area so respectable or a building as solid as this.

It was far too baffling for them to work out, particularly now, in their present shaky state, and anyhow, that was the job of the police. At midnight Connie said she felt all in, and even though Kate invited her to stay, thought she'd be better off in her own bed tonight if Kate didn't mind being on her own. Kate hugged her and told her not to worry. She was well used to terror and coping on her own. Besides, this building was supposedly as solid as a fortress and there were plenty of neighbours within easy reach – Eleni and Demeter across the hall, the Barclay-Davenports right next door, Gregory downstairs.

As she stood by the lift with Connie, she found that last thought comforting and had a sudden, overwhelming desire to run right down and see him now, for reassurance. But she stopped herself. There would be time enough in the morning to catch up with the neighbours and go through today's grisly events point by point. In just a few months, Kate realised, she had already begun to develop a sense of community living with these people. Better by far than living alone in a house, without the knowledge that other able-bodied people were so close.

She made one final round of the flat, to check that the lights were out and everything in order. Across the courtyard, in the facing wing of the building, a single light burned.

And a figure stood at the window, watching.

11

The party, of course, had to be cancelled, but by then that was quite the least of their worries. Amelia's shockingly sudden death had thrown everyone into a state of turmoil, made no better by the complete and undisguised bafflement of the police as to any kind of motivation or likely suspect.

'As far as they can make out, she had no enemies,' said Gregory, self-appointed spokesman on behalf of the tenants, who also made it his business to comfort and reassure each of the more fragile neighbours in turn. He was sitting in Kate's kitchen, joining her in an early pre-prandial Bloody Mary. Well, it was emergency conditions at present so she reckoned anything went. And besides, there was no way she would ever be able to concentrate on her work with so much going on around her.

Poor Amelia. He hadn't known her well, said Gregory, but she had always seemed so gentle and so sad.

'I think there was a broken romance somewhere way back in the past,' he explained. 'Which had stopped her getting married or making any sort of permanent attachment.'

That certainly made sense. Now she came to think of it, Kate was aware of a kind of wistfulness about the older woman. That and a touch of slovenliness to her dress, as if she had already given up.

'Poor soul. How long ago did her mother die?'

'Oh, two or three years, I would think. Nice old lady on the whole. A bit of an old termagant but the best sort of old-fashioned Brit, solid through and through, with her heart in the right place. I think Amelia missed her quite a lot, even though they were forever at each other's throats. It must be lonely when you lose the one person really close to you, particularly after a life-time together.'

Gregory fell into a reflective silence as he sipped his cocktail, and the light went out of his eyes. Kate caught a distinct whiff of melancholy about him and was surprised. In one normally so open and accessible, she sensed a vulnerability she had not previously suspected. But the moment was gone already; Gregory grinned and stretched like a cat, then glanced at his watch. Kate waved the vodka bottle in front of him and he hesitated, then accepted.

'Well, why not?' he said comfortably, allowing her to top him up. 'These are certainly unusual times. And I must say, you make the meanest Bloody I've encountered this side of the Atlantic.' Praise indeed from a North American, and a sophisticated one at that. Kate acknowledged the compliment.

'I learned from a master,' she said, a touch grimly, as she poured the clam and tomato juice over cracked ice and added lime juice, Worcester sauce and just a hint of horseradish. With a hefty slug of vodka, of course, to give it the requisite kick. Gregory leaned across and gently touched her hand.

'Some time you're going to have to tell me more,' he said. 'I sense a fellow alien despite that cultured accent. The Brits just don't seem to have the knack of making a proper cocktail. They serve them at room temperature like their beer, as if they've never even heard of ice.'

She laughed. Gregory radiated good humour again, his warm blue eyes crinkling at the corners. She thanked her stars once more for the existence of this sane, sober presence downstairs, a positive rock in this present storm of horror and uncertainty. They were disturbed by the bell; Connie come to collect her *en route* to the health club.

'What a gorgeous man!' said her friend later, as they headed down Wrights Lane. 'Where have you been hiding him, you sly puss? I thought you told me you had no one in your life?'

'No one special,' said Kate. 'In fact, no one at all. Gregory's just a neighbour. Being supportive about Amelia.'

The sparkle faded from Connie's eyes and she was once more back on the brink of tears. Kate hugged her and they covered the last few yards with their arms entwined.

'I still can't take it in,' said Connie, with a tremble in her voice. 'She was so utterly solid, so down-to-earth, and now she's gone. Just like that. Whoever would believe it?'

The second cousin, a mild-mannered country solicitor on the brink of retirement, had been as bewildered as the rest of them, totally at a loss to know what to do about Amelia's business affairs until the case was settled and the will finally executed. After a brief trip to London to talk to the police and sort things out with Connie, they had come to an understanding that things would continue as usual, with no need for any formal commitment on either side.

'That's generous,' said Kate. 'And also it makes good sense. Do nothing formal until you've all had a chance to think. And nice for you.'

'Poor man,' said Connie, with a sniff. 'It's hit him as hard as the rest of us, and I think he's relieved he doesn't have to make any sudden decisions. Which suits me down to the ground as it happens, though I feel guilty saying it in such dire circumstances.'

Kate gave her another squeeze. 'No one's going to think any the worse of you,' she said. 'Heavens, Amelia was lucky to have such a staunch, reliable pal, able to step in at a moment's notice. But can you manage? It must be a lot of work, manning that shop and presumably having to replenish the stock.'

Connie grinned weakly. 'With a little help from my friends, I guess I can,' she said. 'Luckily, fortune – as usual – is on my side. I just heard they're axing the show. Call it the luck of the Boyles. I'm getting more and more like Jonah on an off day.'

'Okay, spit it out,' she said more boisterously, once they'd worked out, had a swim and were relaxing in the sauna. 'What's with the Gregory guy – and how come he's still unattached? Or is there something nasty in his closet I'd really rather not know?'

Kate laughed. Sometimes she felt she had known Connie for ever, a much-needed tonic after the tensions and upset of the past few months. But she was not about to get into all that now. There were things, she had learned, that you did not share, not even with your closest friends.

'Not as far as I'm aware,' she said. 'He seems pretty normal to me. From all accounts he's quite a one with the ladies, though I haven't actually caught him at it yet.'

'And you're definitely not interested yourself?' Connie was teasing but there was also a note of speculation in her question that did not go unnoticed by Kate. She sat up to check the timer in the dim light; the sand had nearly run out. Almost time for a sharp, cold shower and another quick dip in the pool.

'Not in the slightest,' she said firmly, surprising herself.

'How come?'

'Believe it or not, he's just not my type.'

'You're kidding!'

'No, really.' Too mellow, too cosy. Face it, too kind. Less a potential lover, more like the boy next door. Which, in some ways, she supposed he was. That, for Kate in her present unhinged state, was far more appealing than any amount of lust. Just the thought now of Ramon, even at his most amorous, made her go quite cold inside.

Connie's humorous face appeared over the edge of the pine slats above, eyebrows raised in mock amazement, mouth hanging incredulously open.

'Says who?'

'Says me.'

'But not him?'

'No. But you know what they say, actions speak louder than words. And he hasn't made any kind of a move, so there's your answer. Not that I'd want him to,' she added hastily.

Connie lay back and laughed. 'Methinks the lady . . .' she said but there was a new note of lazy speculation in her tone that told Kate more than she knew. Well, why not, indeed? Men that special were by no means thick on the ground, and Connie was a knockout who could certainly do with a change in her luck. And fast becoming her closest friend in the world, which was odd really, considering where she hailed from. Memories of New York came rushing back and for once, Kate was just too tranquillised to resist them.

'So tell me about your husband, this Francis,' said Connie later, after Kate had coughed it all up and was still laughing and crying simultaneously after two litre bottles of best Marks & Spencer dry white French wine, lying on her floor in the cavernous living room instead of sitting, as she really should be, in front of the computer, getting on with her work.

'I really can't,' said Kate, covering her face, having had enough of everything all at once. 'Let's just say I made a mistake and leave it at that. Well, we've all done it, haven't we?' – remembering Connie's own chaotic past. 'Made fools of ourselves at an early age and lived to regret it?'

'You bet your life.'

They emptied the bottle and clinked their glasses, then saw that it was already far too late and made plans to meet in two days' time, back at the gym.

'I think I'll walk down,' said Connie, meaningfully rolling those amazing eyes and glancing theatrically towards the staircase. Kate laughed as she waved her off. Connie Boyle was quite the best news ever and Gregory Hansen would be a lucky guy if only he had the nous to grab at opportunity when it beckoned. Which, from all she had heard about him so far, was likely to be the case. So – lucky Gregory, lucky Connie. Feeling like a matchmaker, Kate closed her door with only the merest tinge of envy. Romantic though she might be at heart, she still had a very long way to go before she would be ready to risk scrambling back on to that particular merry-go-round.

Digby Fenton was thoughtful as he left the council chamber in the Town Hall and strolled the few yards back along leafy Hornton Street to his own front door. All the signs were good for the local elections next year, except for the burning issue of law and order, and this latest unfortunate happening right in his own building was not what he might have wished for at this particular moment. Apart, of course, from its publicity value; with his own personal marketing background, he would be a fool to ignore the benefits of that. Already the local paper had given it headline status – *Kensington Antiques Dealer Murdered in Luxury Block* – and judging from the regular visits from the police, it would not be long before the nationals followed suit, provided there was more to be discovered and those in the know played their cards correctly. *Mayor Elect Solves Murder Mystery* – he could see the next lot of headlines already, and it would do him no harm when it came to the vote.

He paused outside the building he knew so well, then, thoughtfully, took a walk right round it, relaxing his mind and endeavouring to see it through the eyes of an outsider. Especially a hostile one harbouring murderous thoughts for whatever reason. At first glance the place looked inviolate, solidly constructed from brick and stone at a time when quality and durability were bywords of the building trade. And this place, more than any, had been a beacon of advanced technology heralding in a new era; designed by a famous local architect in the early years of the century, with landscaped terraces, servants' accommodation in each of the purpose-built flats and, most innovative of all, even a hydraulic lift at either end of the building. Digby Fenton was proud to be part of this community, if only, by some people's reckoning, a relative late-comer. But the crucial point was that he cared. The modern villa in suburban Guildford, though luxurious and plush in the extreme, had been little more than a stepping-stone to his more serious ambitions, and now that he was here, firmly installed in classy central London, this was where he planned to remain. Provided he could be certain it was safe, for his neighbours as well as his own family.

The fire escapes, which were regularly inspected, were sturdy and could only be reached from the first-floor terrace, without any access from the street. The only way an intruder could possibly get on to them would be via the two iron gates at either end of the building which were, he was now pleased to confirm, securely padlocked. So how on earth had anyone been able to breach security in order to kill that poor sad soul at number sixteen, just one flight of stairs above his own flat? It was quite unthinkable. Particularly since Woolf, the porter, a man of integrity if slightly mysterious provenance, swore blind that he had been observing the main front door of the building at the time the murder must have taken place and that no one, neither stranger nor resident, had been in or out. Most baffling. They'd done a door-to-door search, of course, and the few neighbours at home at that time of the morning had been more than anxious to assist, even the tight-lipped Mrs Potter who had, as always, a lot to say about the sloppy management of the building. Even the police admitted themselves stumped, and the case looked like never being solved.

Which was something of a bind for Digby, the putative new mayor, and disturbing for the rest of them, in a building that had always been considered as unassailable as Fort Knox. Digby circuited the rear by way of Campden Hill Road and returned to his own front door along the bustling High Street. Olive, thank God, was a totally rational woman who had already pointed out that the building was apparently burglar-proof, but how was he ever going to explain things to that horde of under-occupied and hypercritical old ladies whose continual carping was the bane of his existence? At the thought of the forthcoming tenants' meeting, Digby shuddered. It was at times like this that he queried his sanity at having even contemplated entering public office.

He reached the main doorway at the same time as a taxi, which issued on to the pavement a slim young woman with sturdy legs and a mass of assorted baggage. As she paid the driver, Digby waited politely, key in hand. She was clearly coming this way and he felt it his duty to welcome her, in his capacity as chairman of the board. With that sort of luggage, it looked like being a long stay. He was curious to know where she was heading, since sublets were illegal without the formal consent of the board.

'Good day to you,' he said cordially, extending his hand. 'I'm Digby Fenton from number eleven. May I ask whom I have the honour of addressing?'

The woman stared back at him with a touch of belligerence, as if he had no right to address her at all, and ignored the proffered hand. Instead, she shuffled her various bits of baggage into a tidy row on the doorstep and pressed the bell.

'I'm Alice Sorensen,' she said after a pause, in a forthright voice with a distinctive Canadian twang. 'I'm Gregory Hansen's girlfriend, if you must know, and I'm here on a visit.'

'And did he know?' asked Olive, amused, as she stood at the stove putting the final touches to their supper. Her kitchen was the latest thing and as perfect as the day it was first constructed, yet somehow – miraculously it seemed – she managed to magic up these incredible meals, direct from the pages of her bible, *Woman's Journal*, even down to the garnish.

'Can't tell,' said Digby, beginning to see the funny side. 'She was still standing there when I came in.

Didn't want to intrude too much. Just to check she was really bona fide.'

'And not a burglar?'

'Well, you can't be too careful these days, and it's no use my hammering security precautions into the thick skulls of the tenants if I don't abide by them myself.'

'Quite so.'

Olive turned with a smile and gave him a crisp fried potato, as thin as her fingernail, to taste. In her freshly ironed bleached cotton apron, with its green Harrods insignia, she looked as much out of an advertisement as her kitchen. She was even wearing tights and immaculate high-heeled shoes, though they were dining alone that night.

'Ready in a moment, darling,' she said, indicating that it was time for him to wash and brush up. 'Do you think he's going to get a nasty surprise?'

'God knows,' said Digby with a grin. 'Though it's certainly high time he did, don't you think? The blighter's got away with it for far too long.'

'Jealous?'

'Absolutely not,' he said, kissing her. 'Though I would like to know where on earth he finds the energy.'

12

'It's not that I'm not thrilled to see you, sweetheart,' said Gregory weakly ten minutes later. 'It's just that it's such a surprise. Why on earth didn't you let me know you were coming? I'd have met you.'

Now that she was actually here, shoes off, settled on the sofa with a martini in her hand, Alice wasn't at all sure herself. At the time it had seemed like a brilliant idea, to surprise him, but maybe he did have a point and she was really just hoping to catch him out. She glanced round the untidy apartment, as resolutely bachelorish and uncared-for as ever, and began to feel that perhaps she'd overreacted.

'It's the end of the spring semester,' she said lamely, 'and I just got some time off from class. I thought it would be great to spend it together. It's been so long.'

'And you were right.' He pulled her to her feet and took her in his arms, as warm and arousing as he had always been. He was tugging at her T-shirt and she let him have his way, a triumphant smile softening her taut features as she felt his fingers probing deeper and the old familiar thrill beginning to rise from her groin. This was why she'd come all these miles, how it had always been with Gregory and always would be. No matter what the state of their relationship, within five minutes of their getting together he always had her in bed.

'God, I want you,' he was whispering now as he burrowed into her bosom.

'Me too,' said Alice, stroking his hair. 'I'm your woman once and for all. Always have been, always shall be. No matter what. And don't you ever forget that.'

The phone rang just then, jangling and discordant in the dimly lit room, but he took no notice and after a while it stopped. Alice tensed but Gregory just kept right on with the job in hand. That, if she were honest, was one of the things she liked best about him. He was always so relaxed and didn't allow minor aggravations to affect him. After a short pause it began to ring again.

'Shouldn't you be answering that?' asked Alice anxiously, not wanting him to stop yet strangely disturbed by the intrusion, unable any longer to concentrate.

'Uh-uh.'

'But suppose it's important? Work perhaps?' Prosaic to the last was Alice Sorensen; suburban to her blunt, unvarnished fingertips. Gregory felt his own mood of relaxed wellbeing starting to evaporate.

'Leave it,' he mumbled, his mouth fully occupied. But he knew she would not be able to. The third time the ringing started she rolled away, pulling down her T-shirt and slipping back into her briefs as if she were being spied on.

'I'm sorry,' she said nervously, sitting up and reaching automatically for her cigarettes, another thing that never failed to irritate the hell out of him. 'But I just can't do it with that thing ringing away. Who is it, anyhow?'

'How should I know?'

It rang a fourth time but he still made no move to answer it.

'Gregory?' she said, really rattled by now.

'Just leave it.'

His sunny mood was rapidly clouding; what was she doing here unannounced, getting in the way and ruining his peace? He pulled on his pants and sweater and left the room abruptly. Bloody women. Why couldn't they just leave him alone? He really couldn't be doing with this kind of hassle all the time, another of the countless reasons he'd remained a bachelor. He slammed into his study and back to his computer.

Later, puttering around in his bathroom, Alice found the nail varnish and then the shit really did hit the fan.

'I can't turn my back on you for a minute!' she screeched, aiming the bottle at the mirror but missing.

'Four months, actually,' he muttered from the other room.

'Well, you know what I mean. Who is she?'

'Oh, I don't know. Probably the char, who cares?' He'd been through all this with Jacintha already. If they didn't like it, then they shouldn't come here. They knew the ground rules but were all the same. Gregory sighed deeply and wondered if she'd notice if he escaped for an hour to the Windsor Castle, just up the hill, for a couple of fast beers and a chance to restore his sanity.

'I'm just popping out for a paper,' he said, heading

towards the door. 'Shan't be long. If you'd care to start the supper . . .'

'Women!' he exploded later to Miles, as they sat side by side in the saloon bar sharing a pint before the evening got underway. 'They're more bloody trouble than they're worth. Give them an inch and they take a mile.'

Miles grinned. 'Don't I just know it, sport,' he said sympathetically. 'At least you've never gone legal, have you? All that alimony and school fees and stuff. Put years on my age, I can tell you, and who's to say it's worth it in the long run. Keep your nose clean, that's my advice, old son, and keep on running.'

Gregory smiled. His aggravation was fast evaporating. In the main, he was an easy-going chap, and Miles Burdett was just the person to calm him. Nice bloke, Miles. Bit on the flash side for some people's taste, but definitely one of the boys.

'How's that lovely wife of yours?' It was not just a formula question; Gregory had always had a soft spot for Claudia, if only she'd loosen up a little.

'So-so.' Miles was thoughtful as he ordered another round, and his customary smile lacked some of its breezy brightness.

'You're a lucky dog, you know that, don't you? There's not much most men wouldn't do for a woman like that, I can tell you.'

'As long as she's safely married to some other poor clod, eh?'

They sat in silence for a while, thinking of Claudia, then Miles roused himself and said he would have to be on his way.

'Yes, she is pretty marvellous,' he admitted with a sigh. 'But the upkeep is expensive, I can tell you, and sometimes I'm not sure I can stand much more of the day-to-day wear and tear.'

Both laughed.

'Here, I'll do this,' said Gregory to the barman. 'And then I guess I'd better be getting back myself. Duty calls.'

Claudia was in her usual foul mood when Miles got home. The pale skin was taut across the finely defined cheekbones, and her eyes, with their mauvish shadows, were as small and mean as blackcurrants.

'You're never bloody here when I need you,' she said, hurling packets around in the kitchen as she hunted for something easy to cook. 'I wanted to go out but now it's too late. And there's nothing in worth eating.'

'Calm down,' soothed her husband wearily. 'I'll book a table at Mon Petit Plaisir and we can be there in a jiff.'

'They won't have a table, not at this short notice.'

'We'll see.'

But she wouldn't be placated. She'd changed out of her office attire and into jeans and wasn't in a mood to reverse the process.

'So come like that. You look very nice. *Très soignée, ma chère.*'

'Shut up and do something useful for a change. I'm not one of your smarmy bimbos from the office. I'm your wife and I'm tired, and sick of waiting around for you.'

She was almost in tears, he could see that. Curbing

his sharp response, he took her gently by the shoulders and steered her out of the kitchen and into the comfortable, subtly lit living room. If you wanted a quiet life, you had to keep them sweet. Miles Burdett had his black belt in manipulating the fairer sex.

'There,' he said, plonking her down on to the sofa, 'take the weight off your pins and I'll get you a glass of wine. Then I'll take care of the supper. Omelettes suit you?'

'We haven't any eggs.'

'Then it'll just have to be my old standby. *Spaghetti aio e oio* coming up. I presume we have garlic?'

In spite of herself, Claudia found the vestige of a smile breaking through. He certainly was a handful, this husband of hers, but not entirely bad. Her tension headache was hammering but the chilled glass he now set in her hand would help to make it better. Now that he was home where she could keep an eye on him.

'Not too much garlic, mind,' she warned, 'I don't want to go breathing vampire fumes all over the shareholders tomorrow morning.'

'Trust me,' said Miles from the kitchen, already chopping. 'When did I ever let you down?'

Amelia Rowntree's murder – for murder it most certainly was, even without a motive or a suspect – had certainly started a fluttering in the hen coop, and the general level of agitation rode high within Kensington Court. Little else was talked of these days; even the weather had been relegated to a very unfavoured second place.

'Just think,' wailed Heidi Applebaum worriedly, 'any

one of us might be the next to go.' Not for this had her family fled Germany. She had had the man from Banhams in to put new locks on her already overladen front door, but was still too scared to open it, even for the porter or the milkman.

'Until they catch him,' she whispered, 'we're none of us safe in our beds.' The milkman had been doing this round for years and was practically a Kensington institution, but the porter, here only six years, was still a man of mystery. What, after all, did they know of his origins or former life? She'd always had her suspicions of him. Too knowing, somehow, too well spoken.

'Pull yourself together,' snapped Adelaide Potter dismissively. 'They're a useless bunch, our board of directors, but even they must have screened him pretty thoroughly before they would give him the job.' In her head, she was already penning the poisonous note she would send to Digby Fenton. She relished moments like this; nothing gave her more pleasure than a chance to catch a neighbour off guard.

'I'll demand to see his references,' she said, hobbling to the hall mirror and fixing her cowpat hat on to her small, spiteful head with a couple of vicious-looking hatpins. 'And if they don't pass muster' – and where Adelaide Potter's impossible standards were involved, there was little chance they would – 'then I'll take the whole matter above his head, to the estate.'

Heidi looked on in awe, standing in the hallway in her wrinkled stockings and faded fluffy slippers while her neighbour briskly girded herself for fronting the outside world. The German woman greatly admired her friend, who stood no truck from the normal vicissitudes of everyday life in London but treated even the slightest encounter as a fully blown battle. Adelaide slid into her sensible black coat with its astrakhan collar, and buttoned it firmly up against the balmy spring air.

'I won't be long,' she said, reaching for her stick. 'Get the potatoes on while I'm gone and we'll have a sherry before we eat.'

She was heading for the library next door, not to choose a book but to complain about one she was reading. Heidi watched her departure, then slid the bolt and put on the door chain; better to be safe than sorry. These days, even at eleven in the morning, there was no saying what perils might be lurking outside. She glanced at the clock and wondered if Netta was going to join them today. Normally she didn't wait for an invitation but was out there hovering whenever she sensed that something might be going on, something to stick her nose into, or better still, get for free. Heidi knew such thoughts were ignoble but she couldn't help it. The matter was really not in her hands, though, so she'd just have to wait and see what happened. It was Adelaide's flat, when all was said and done, and Adelaide always called the shots. She had her own bad things to say about Netta yet also found her useful at times. And, Heidi reflected, aware of her own shaky status, these days there was safety in numbers. After what had happened to poor, dear Amelia in this very building.

Childhood had not been a happy time for Netta

McCluskie. Her father, George, was a Shetlands dentist who had migrated south to Glasgow in the thirties in order to seek a better standard of life for his wife and family. Moira, his first-born, almost as soon as she could toddle, had shown signs of having a unique musical talent which had her romantic mother making long-term plans and dreaming of Shirley Temple. Whenever there was company, Moira would be put into her prettiest party frock and brought out to entertain the guests by doing her cute little tapdance on the dining room table. She was a bonny child, with a round, guileless face and huge, heartbreaking eyes, who at three had been a runner-up in the Miss Pears competition.

Eileen McCluskie, her mother, was a simple soul who played the piano passably well and whose sole purpose in life was to take good care of her taciturn husband and this miraculous gift of a child. If the truth be told, she didn't much care for Glasgow, but George's greatly increased earnings meant they could afford a detached house with five bedrooms and an acre of garden in Helensburgh, where she spent her days cutting out paper patterns for dream outfits for her angel and fantasising about the future, which would almost certainly include Hollywood. But Eileen was not strong, and the harsh industrial winters, with their underlay of soot, quickly eroded her delicate, island-bred lungs. By their second city winter she was ailing, and by the time Moira was coming up for twelve, she was dead. The grieving George McCluskie, unable to cope alone, took, in rapid succession, a second wife – Effie – and then to the bottle, and retreated permanently into a melancholy withdrawal from which he was never to emerge. Effie stood helplessly by as both his spirits and his fortunes spiralled downhill.

Netta was the child of that second union, born when Moira was almost sixteen and already hitting the local headlines with her singing, her voice as pure and unsullied, they said, as to rival that of the recently deceased Kathleen Ferrier. Effie was a nurse, canny and practical and a total opposite to the sentimental Eileen, but even she could do little to halt the progress of her husband's chronic drinking. Within just a few years the dental practice was in ruins and the family obliged to move hurriedly on, to avoid a growing pile of debts and a few minor scandals which refused to be hushed up. The house was sold and the McCluskies moved into the city proper, to take up residence in a three-roomed flat in a squalid Gorbals back street.

That was Netta's inheritance. Where Moira had grown up with fresh air and a garden swing, riding lessons and the foundations of a solid education from the local dame school, Netta was forced to attend the local primary and run wild in the streets whence she quickly developed an accent as rough and raw as any Sauchiehall Street drunk on a Saturday night. She neither forgot nor forgave. In the cramped attic bedroom she shared with her older sister, little Netta would pore over old family albums and listen to Moira's tales of the good old days, when it seemed the sun always shone and life in the McCluskie homestead was a positive bowl of cherries.

As it happened, Netta need not have worried. Along

with her talent and sweetness of nature, Moira had also inherited her mother's bad lungs, and before she was thirty had followed her to heaven, to be quickly joined by her father, who had long ago surrendered any will to live. Like Effie, Netta took up nursing, and the two bitter women shared a drab two-roomed flat while she waited in vain for fate to come knocking. Which it did eventually, long after Netta had given up hope, in the person of Hermione Silcock, stricken suddenly with what turned out to be terminal cancer while holidaying at her weekend cottage outside Perth. Archie Silcock advertised for a round-the-clock nurse and Netta, for the first time ever, just happened to be in the right place at the right time. Hermione, who represented all that Netta both hated and lusted after, nevertheless offered her a lifeline. In her weakened state, the formidable woman, usually so astute, clung to the graceless Scottish nurse, and as soon as she was well enough to make the journey south, took her back with her to London.

So now Netta actually owned the sweetshop, but the canker of envy was not so easily assuaged.

Take Claudia Burdett, for instance; there was a snotty-nosed bitch if ever she saw one. Netta fairly seethed whenever the thought of her *soignée* downstairs neighbour so much as entered her mind. She was seething now as she stood in her own front hall, making the motions of flicking a feather duster over Hermione's precious Meissen vase and the itsy bitsy pieces of Limoges she had always been so proud of (though personally they weren't to Netta's taste at all; she preferred something altogether more flamboyant), all the time with one ear cocked for the sound of the lift heralding Adelaide Potter's return. Netta could smell the appetising aroma of Adelaide's roast pork and knew that Heidi was still in there, doubtless preparing the vegetables for lunch. She resented the fact that the German woman seemed more welcome in Adelaide's domain than she was, but that sad creature would do almost anything for a free meal. Netta sniffed. It couldn't be easy to be a widow in reduced circumstances, but if Heidi found it hard to meet the service charges, she should move. That was only fair. This was supposed to be an exclusive building and could not be expected to cater for waifs and strays. She breathed on Hermione's pair of silver pheasants and rubbed each one on her apron. That would have to do, a lick and a promise. If only she could persuade the woman who cleaned the stairs to come and do an hour or so for her, but Bonita always nodded politely and said she was too busy. Such nerve! Servants these days; who on earth did they think they were?

Claudia bugged Netta because she seemed so aloof when really she was little more than a tramp who had only snared herself a husband by sleeping with him behind his first wife's back. Everyone knew that. Netta could not bear those airs and graces which stated quite clearly that Claudia considered herself to be a cut above the rest of them. Those clothes she wore, and the understated jewellery. Considering how much money Miles was reputed to earn, it was positively laughable that his wife should always look so drab, in charcoal or navy or beige, with tiny ear studs and only a single string of pearls to break the monotony of her governess look.

Netta looked down at her own floral shirt and armful of jangling bracelets. At least she was happy to flaunt what she'd got; Archie would not have had it otherwise. He'd laughed at the way she'd spent his money, in the months before his mind began to go. She'd brought a bit of cheerfulness back into his life, and now he was gone there was nothing to stop her spending. He'd left it all to her, after all, and there were no children to worry about.

He hadn't been a bad old buffer when all was said and done, and she'd have done her duty, had it ever come to it. But the very thought of a snivelling baby made her shudder. No, as it turned out, things had worked out perfectly, and the Silcock name lived on in her, while she lived in their home and spent their cash. Which, thought Netta, remembering her deprived childhood, was no more than she deserved.

The lift gates clanged and Netta was out there in a flash, her smile as bright as her lipstick.

'Adelaide!' she purred in surprise. 'How lovely to see you. Up and about so early, too.' She glanced at her watch. 'Oh, goodness me, can that really be the time? Where does it all go, I ask you? There's me burbling on about it being so early and it's noon already and almost time for lunch.'

Mrs Adelaide Potter said nothing. Just leaned on her stick while she fumbled with her keys. Netta had her hand on her elbow, supporting her, but Heidi had also heard her coming and was unbolting the door from within.

'Why, Heidi dear,' said Netta in the same unctuous tone, taking Adelaide's bag from her and ushering her into her own flat, 'what a gorgeous smell. Would it be pork you're cooking? I was just observing to dear Adelaide here that time flashes by without your noticing it. Shall I pour us all a sherry, perhaps?'

Heidi said nothing and Adelaide observed Netta sternly as she silently withdrew the rapier pins from her hat. Heidi shuddered inwardly as she watched the workings of the implacable old woman's mind, fearful of what was to come, thankful that, for once, any abuse would not be levelled at her. Though there was just no telling with Adelaide.

Adelaide took her time. Then, her mouth reduced to an ugly slit, she nodded.

'Just an inch for each of us,' she said grudgingly, 'and I suppose you'll be wanting to stay for lunch?'

Netta fluttered and prevaricated, as if the thought had never even occurred, then deftly switched subjects to her current obsession.

'I was thinking about that Claudia Burdett.' The mean child of a mean mother, she'd learned long ago which buttons to press for the maximum success. 'Who does she think she is, with her hoity-toity airs and graces?'

'Certainly no better than she should be,' echoed Heidi on cue, anxious to please.

Mrs Adelaide Potter tasted her Bristol Cream and smacked her lips reflectively. For once her lizard-like gaze was turned inwards; she seemed oblivious to this particular conversational hare.

'Enough of her,' she said, after a while. 'Claudia

Burdett's of no importance. What we really must be putting our minds to is poor Amelia.'

They listened.

'Someone killed her, but who was it, that's the poser. And what can we do to prevent it happening again?'

13

Septimus Woolf sat in Graziana's coffee shop, jacket off, shirtsleeves rolled up, cheroot in mouth, deeply engrossed in the *Financial Times*. It was ten minutes to eleven in the morning and he was, should anyone be interested, taking an early coffee break. At his feet, in a Sainsbury's carrier bag, were the books he had just borrowed from the library, titles that might have astounded some of his employers had they the temerity, or even the interest, to investigate. Though most of them probably don't read at all, he reflected as he flashed through the market news and checked the state of the FTSE. From time to time his gaze swivelled across the narrow street to the doorway of Kensington Court. As he had explained to Digby Fenton, and again to the police in the many times he'd been interviewed since Amelia's murder, this was as good a standpoint as any for doing an efficient job, a great vantage point for generally surveying the comings and goings to and from the building he was paid to supervise.

There, for instance, went Timothy, the window cleaner, a rogue if ever he saw one but a regular on this beat. Tall and agile, with a slightly loopy smile, the young man was several sandwiches short of a picnic yet perfectly good at his job for all that. And reliable, an essential quality in a window cleaner. Septimus studied the stock-market reports and lit another thin cigar. And there, too, went that old harridan Mrs Adelaide Bloody Potter, but the less said about her, the better.

Septimus Woolf sighed to himself and prepared to return to his official post. He had had his own share of problems in his life and women ranked high on the list. Any one of the Black Widows would, to his mind, have made suitable murder fodder, but Amelia Rowntree was another case entirely, a sweet, sad lady with a depressingly lonely life. Someone who had never failed to be civil to him, with none of those airs and graces affected by others less well born. He shook his head as he sorted out his change. It just went to show you never knew what was really going on.

The old boy in the doorway to the bank was still there, guarding his territory, as Septimus strolled back across the street. Occasionally he had been tempted to stop and have a chat but the tramp had made it clear he wanted no truck with anyone, so Septimus respected his privacy and left him alone. Each was entitled to endure their own private hell in their own way. Septimus had problems enough of his own without needing to intrude where he clearly wasn't wanted. But he couldn't help admiring the dignity of the fierce old man and kept a wary eye out for him in case the law, or some other snooping do-gooder, should ever come too close.

'Morning, Septimus!'

He was aroused from his reverie by a cheery greeting

as Gregory Hansen swept out of the lift, a thin, dark-haired woman clinging to his arm. Septimus gave one of his rare smiles as he let himself into the porter's lodge. Now there was a character, Gregory Hansen, with a different woman for each day of the week. And why not indeed? On the long road through life you learned from your own mistakes, and given another chance, who knows how his own life might have altered course. As he slid back into his maroon uniform jacket in the privacy of his bedroom and flattened his springy hair with a dampened brush, Septimus reflected on the weird assortment of people he looked after in his wide-ranging duties as porter to this mansion block. They say it takes all sorts, he mused, and certainly all manner of people and relationships were grouped together here, under this one solid roof. He'd seen all kinds of happenings in the six years he'd been in residence in this job. Nothing could really surprise him any more. Not even murder. The only wonder was it didn't occur more often.

'Who's that distinguished-looking man?' asked Alice, and Gregory explained Septimus's role in their lives.

'He looks after this end of the building,' he said. 'There's another porter at the other end doing the same job.'

'Funny, he doesn't look like a servant,' she commented, and Gregory agreed. Far too aloof and intellectual for such a servile role, more like an under-cover agent or someone distinguished in hiding. Gregory had often had that thought and he sympathised. There were moments in his own life, getting more frequent by the minute, when he'd give just about anything to disappear and assume another identity. The thing about his occupation, with its constant travelling, was that he was more or less able to do just that. As a stringer on a newspaper, he answered to almost no one. As long as he filed his copy on time, they more or less left him alone, and he filled the rest of his time with freelance commissions he drummed up himself. Yes, he liked the fantasy of changing places with the porter. He'd bet there was a fascinating story there.

'The one the other end's something of an Irish drunk,' he said. 'You should meet him! As different from this one as chalk from cheese. Looks a bit like that actor from *NYPD Blue*, David Caruso. Sadly, we don't see a lot of him, which seems a shame. Only when Septimus is away, he occasionally covers for him, and he's a laugh a minute.'

Gregory was growing distinctly restive. They'd been five times to the theatre since Alice's arrival, and her constant cloying company was beginning to pall. Now she wanted to do the Tate when all he really longed for was to shut the door gently in her face and get on with his work. Women were all very well in their place, which was as far away as possible; here, on his own turf, he found them intrusive, and Alice's departure date was already overdue.

'Why don't I stick you in a cab,' he suggested, 'and see you back here for lunch?'

'Why a cab? That's ridiculous,' said Alice briskly. 'A total waste of money when I have a travel card. But won't you come to see the Turners? I suspect you don't get much culture when I'm not around.'

Gregory thought of Jacintha and all those West End musicals she so much liked; them and the Portobello Road, which she couldn't seem to leave alone. But he wasn't letting on. A martyr to his private life, was Gregory. They certainly took it out of him, these women. Small wonder he needed so much time for rest and recuperation.

'Tell you what,' he suggested as a compromise. 'Go look at your Turners and I'll meet you at Victoria Station at half past one and take you for oysters and champagne at Overton's. What say?'

Alice's taut features slackened slightly and a shine came into her black cherry eyes. She patted him lightly on the cheek and raised herself on supple toes to kiss him.

'You're really an old softie underneath it all, aren't you, hon?' she said. 'And how you like to spoil a gal. Go on then, back to your old computer, and leave me to improve my mind on my own, if you must.'

But she was grinning as she turned away, and Gregory saw, not entirely with satisfaction, that she was still as besotted as ever. Ah well. In some ways it suited him, in others it didn't. What's lost upon the roundabouts, you pulls up on the swings. Or some such damn fool thing.

He bumped into Kate Ashenberry as he let himself back into the building, but she was in a hurry to get to the bank and seemed not to want to linger. Now there was a mysterious girl, he thought as he climbed the stairs for exercise. Young, apparently vulnerable and not at all bad-looking; just the way he preferred them, in fact. But giving off no positive vibes whatsoever, almost as if his famously lethal charm were not working its magic on her at all. Maybe he was wasting his time and she'd rather be with Beatrice and Lily, but somehow he didn't think so. He'd have to find out about that some time, but there was no rush. That was the great thing about this life, he was never in much of a hurry. And when the time came and his itchy feet got the better of him, he'd just up sticks and mosey back home to Canada, where the going was always good. Or on to Australasia again, maybe, or anywhere else in the world where the fancy took him. As lifestyles went, this one was as good as it came. He smiled as he unlocked his own door and let himself into the blissful stillness of his flat.

Beatrice Hunt telephoned to invite Kate down for supper.

'We've not seen a lot of you,' she explained. 'We'd like to get to know you better.'

Kate smiled, well pleased. They were nice, those two, though she wasn't at all sure what it was about them. They gave off an aura of sanity and tranquillity which made her feel safe. She was pleased to be asked. It was lonely working on her own all day; she could do with a few more friends. She chose two bottles of the season's new Beaujolais, changed into clean jeans and a freshly ironed shirt, and went.

Lily was making green curry. The delicate aromas of lemon grass, coriander and kaffir lime leaves wafted through the flat, while Beatrice had lit joss sticks in the fireplace to add to the oriental flavour.

'Welcome!' said Beatrice, showing her into a large,

white-painted living room with bold wall coverings and Indian rugs on the polished wood floor.

'Oh, how nice!' said Kate in the doorway, genuinely impressed. One of the things she was learning about this building was the huge difference tenants could make to their own individual space. Her own flat was bright and airy because it was on the top floor and, she had only just realised, one whole storey higher than the surrounding buildings. But she hadn't even begun to create her dream yet, was still camping amongst Mrs Benjamin's musty furniture and a few spare bits and pieces from Habitat, picked up for necessity. Beatrice and Lily, on the other hand, had created a whole world of their own in a similar space, and by dint of knocking down a couple of non-essential walls, had opened up the Victorian parameters into something more like a Manhattan loft.

'The great thing about buildings of this period,' said Lily, joining them, 'is the strength of the structure.' She knocked on the wall. 'See, rock solid. If you look at some of the modern developments – Chelsea Harbour is a good example, and that place on Church Street that's already falling apart – you'll find them jerry-built and as flimsy as anything.' She ran her hand lovingly over the polished oak door. 'Look at the quality of the woodwork, too. You don't find workmanship like this just anywhere.'

'And you can't even hear the telephone from room to room,' said Beatrice, pouring Kate a glass of wine. 'Sheer bliss, I can tell you, after a hard day in the office.'

Which was Kate's cue to ask, politely, what line of business Beatrice was in, but the older woman simply dismissed it as 'just another dreary civil servant'. Kate knew not to enquire too deeply; there were people, and she well understood this, who simply didn't care to talk about their work. Well, that was just fine with Kate; the less said the better. She sank on to a low, Japanese-style couch and leaned back luxuriously against its spare back.

'Gosh, but this is comfortable!' she said, and Beatrice beamed.

'Isn't it just? We bought it from a designer friend of Lily's in Covent Garden. Deceptively simple in design but also surprisingly comfortable. Take your shoes off, if you like. We normally go barefoot at home.'

The combination of the food smells, the spacious spartan room and some soft eastern music playing from concealed speakers above the bookshelves made Kate feel luxuriously relaxed, and a wonderful drowsiness crept across her as she lay back on the couch and listened to Beatrice talk. Harmony, that was what this room had got. Lily arranged black china and minimalist stainless steel cutlery on a plain teak table in the corner. Together with the spicy jasmine of the joss sticks, the mood was one of enormous wellbeing.

'Need any help?' asked Beatrice softly, but Lily shook her head.

'One minute,' she said, noticing Kate's sleepiness, 'and we'll eat.'

The food was delicious, and Kate revived enough to clear two platefuls and still have room for the mango and star fruit salad which followed.

'Golly,' she said, when they'd finished. 'I haven't eaten that well since I left New York.'

They weren't insistent but she felt so peaceful and safe she found herself telling them a bit about life with Ramon, though she stopped short of explaining what exactly had gone wrong or the reason for her sudden, panicked flight back home across the ocean. And, bless them, they didn't ask prying questions. Just listened and prompted and took it all in, adding to Kate's feeling of extreme wellbeing and her total relief at finding herself, at last, in such a relaxing ambience, with two sympathetic new friends. She couldn't believe it when she looked at her watch and saw it was gone eleven.

'Oh my goodness,' she said, jumping up. 'My mother always told me never to outstay my welcome.'

'Which you haven't,' said Lily firmly, refilling her hand-thrown mug of jasmine tea. 'We rarely get to bed till after midnight, and it has been such a pleasure to have you and get to know you better.'

They parted ten minutes later, with hugs and promises to do it again soon, and Kate climbed the two flights of stairs to her own floor feeling calm and replete, happier than she had been in months. Bit by bit she was getting to like this building. Now she was making friends, it was even starting to feel like home.

Her own flat was in darkness, apart from the lamp in the hall, and she made her habitual round of the rooms just to check that all was in order. She stood for a while at the sitting room window, gazing out across the Kensington rooftops towards the thrusting spire of St Mary Abbots, illuminated against the night sky. The gingerbread windows directly opposite were in darkness, the occupants obviously gone to bed, but further up Hornton Street one uncurtained window was alight, a party still in progress, with sixties music booming. All life was here, reflected Kate, as she stood there in the semi-darkness, right in the centre of one of the world's historic cities but no longer feeling so alone. On an impulse she crossed into her study and looked in the opposite direction towards Campden Hill. Across the courtyard of Kensington Court a single lamp burned. And a figure stood motionless at the window, still watching.

Connie was full of exuberance; she was slowly recovering from Amelia's death and her spirits were starting to revive. She had moved into the third floor flat the week before and was already adding her own little personal touches to make it feel homey. She was also throwing all her energy into making the business work – a tribute, she said, to Amelia.

'Guess what,' she told Kate, 'I've sold that nineteenth-century French armchair, the one we had re-covered in golden leather. For the asking price, too.'

Kate was learning that the convention was never to offer the ticket price but to beat the dealer down, as in an eastern bazaar.

'To an American,' Connie continued, 'with far more money than sense. She's doing up a house in Abingdon Villas, and if I play my cards right, I guess there'll be more business from the same quarter.'

'Splendid.' Kate was delighted for her. She had hated to see Connie in less than tiptop spirits; it was good to have her sparkling again and back to her usual form.

Unlike Kate, Connie had had a chaotic childhood,

with a mother who changed partners at regular intervals, but she seemed on the whole to have survived it well. Used to a series of transitory men she knew as 'Uncle', her prime ambition from her early teens had been to settle down, get married and raise a family of her own, one on which she could lavish all the pent-up love she had been hoarding greedily in readiness for that day. Jim, the English actor she had followed to London, had seemed at first to fill all the essentials. When he defected, after only a few years, she had dusted herself down, put it down to experience, and sailed on valiantly, still in search of her one true love. She'd talked about Jim a bit to Kate, who had compared her experience with her own more dramatic one with Ramon.

'At least he didn't knock you around.'

'He hadn't the energy. Besides, I would have belted him back.'

Secretly, Connie was appalled at what Kate had let slip. She tried not to let it show, to keep up the swinging image, but no man should be allowed to get away with behaviour like that. And in every other way, Kate seemed so rational and calm.

'Why didn't you call the cops? I know I would have done.'

'Not if you valued your privacy, you wouldn't. Besides, I felt so ashamed.'

Connie understood. She hugged her friend and wiped away her tears. What fools women were, to be sure, when it came to a man. She liked to think she was as canny as the next person, yet show her a certain angle of slanted cheekbone and a pair of well-filled jeans and she was there for the taking. It was humiliating but true; all her adult life Connie Boyle had been on a quest. One of these days she was going to find her man, and when she did, she would never let him go.

'Care to come to Lots Road with me on Sunday?' asked Connie as they strolled back home. 'This same American buyer is looking for an eighteenth-century dining table and chairs and I've a hunch I may be able to find what she wants in the auction rooms.'

'Terrific,' said Kate, who, since her visit to Beatrice and Lily's beautiful flat, had had elevated dreams of what she might do to her own.

'Right, what say we leave at eleven and trawl the Fulham Road before we drop down to Lots Road,' said Connie. 'Then we can take in The Furniture Cave, too. You ain't done nothin' till you've seen that. And we'll snatch a quick lunch at Chutney Mary, if you're good. Might as well make it a fun outing.'

Connie was as good as her word. The Furniture Cave was wonderful, though the auction rooms disappointed Kate, since most of the furniture on offer that Sunday was in a poor state of repair and would need a lot of restoring, which she wasn't prepared to do.

'It's mainly for serious buyers,' explained Connie, 'buying whole job lots for the trade. Or a certain look to furnish a whole room.'

Kate only wanted the occasional piece, to fit her limited budget and make the flat feel more her own. She found a set of adorable Victorian walnut chairs with tapestry seats, each in a different pattern. There were only five, as one had disintegrated entirely, but she fell in love with them and found she could afford them, just. She checked them out excitedly and Connie agreed.

'Leave this to me,' she murmured as the dealer approached, and Kate drifted discreetly away while her friend hammered a whole two hundred pounds off the ticket price.

'See?' said Connie later, as they loaded the chairs into a taxi and squeezed in beside them. 'Everyone has a deal and no one is disappointed. You've got a bargain, she's got a sale. Nobody loses.'

'So why didn't she put the lower price on the ticket in the first place?' asked Kate.

'Tricks of the trade,' said Connie mysteriously, tapping her nose with one finger.

The chairs looked great dotted around the flat. Horatio immediately took possession of one and started sharpening his claws on the seat.

'You'll have to stop him doing that,' warned Connie.

'I try but I don't know how,' said Kate.

'In the States we de-claw them.'

'I know, but that's barbaric. And here it's illegal, too.'

'Then you'll just have to give him a regular manicure.'

'Or knit him bootees. Or paint his claws with bitter aloes.'

'What's that?'

'Something they used to put on our thumbs to stop us sucking them,' said Kate, remembering.

'What happens if you press the servants' bells?' asked Connie idly, once she had finished arranging the chairs to her own satisfaction and had switched on occasional lamps to effect the right mood. There weren't any bells in Amelia's flat; she'd had them plastered over.

'Don't know,' said Kate. 'Haven't tried.'

Connie stared at her in disbelief. Was she kidding? 'You haven't? Why on earth not?'

Kate looked at her solemnly, her straight dark hair hooding her eyes in the muted half-light.

'I'm scared of what might come,' she said ghoulishly, and the truth was, she really was. Hard to explain a childhood steeped in creepy tales, but perhaps she'd have a go when it wasn't quite so dark. And preferably when she was safely somewhere else.

Connie would only think she was totally bonkers if she ever divulged the true extent of that terror. The frisson she still experienced when she wandered into a church full of plaster saints; the prickle along her spine when anyone told her a real-life ghost story. Even, though the fear was gradually lessening, her dislike of huge dark buildings such as this.

She was to regret the levity of that conversation, which came back to haunt her later that night, when Connie had gone downstairs and Kate was alone with the cat. She stared at the brass bellpushes on the wall and they seemed to stare back at her. There was one each side of the fireplace, another in her bedroom and one in the visitors' bathroom, which still had the original brass taps and claw-footed tub. The others had been removed over the years, as the rooms were refurbished and modernised.

'Don't be silly,' she told herself firmly, her finger

hovering over one of the bells, yet still unable to make the final move.

'Now look here, Horatio,' she solemnly addressed the cat, 'we are going to stop all this fantasising and we're going to bed. But we'll leave the light on, just for a while, because there's absolutely no reason why we shouldn't.'

Or anyone to tell her to turn it off now that she was fully grown up and on her own. She avoided looking at the bellpushes as she gathered up the coffee mugs and switched off the living room lamps. And she turned on the radio while she was in the bath and listened to the Jamesons' late-night chat show to keep herself from thinking too much. Even so, it was a long time before she dropped off to sleep that night. And for once she didn't check to see if the dark watcher was still there.

14

Miles came straight to the point.

'Now look here, Lady W, I think you should sign these papers and we'll get things sorted right away.' He spread the contents of his briefcase over her leather-topped desk and unscrewed the top of his gold Mark Cross pen.

'What are they? I seem to be signing all manner of things these days.'

'Nothing to worry about, trust me. Just a spot of reinsurance to make sure you're doubly safe. What the chaps at Lloyd's call the LMX. The spiral.'

Miles flashed his appealing smile and held out the pen towards her. Lady Wentworth rose stiffly from her armchair and moved towards him, one hand on her hip where the arthritis was giving her trouble.

'Do I need my glasses?' she asked, looking round vaguely. 'And shouldn't we both sit down together and go through them properly?'

She trusted Miles, her favourite, but was still, in her eighties, a very shrewd woman. She'd had to be. Her father had died while she was still just a girl, leaving her in charge of the family finances and making her a

Lloyd's Name on her coming-of-age. And her husband, the Admiral, had possessed many virtues but had never been able to distinguish one end of a balance sheet from the other. He'd been in his grave for thirty years now, poor man, and she'd kept her own affairs in order ever since, with only a little help from the family stock-broker. But Miles Burdett had been a godsend. She smiled at him now and put one hand on his shoulder as she levered herself slowly into the upright chair at the desk.

'Ah, that's better,' she said, taking his pen. 'Now be a good chap and pour us each a sherry. The sun must be well over the yardarm by now and I think we both deserve it.'

Miles leapt to it, at the same time loosening his tie. Very nearly there and he'd have the old girl in the bag.

'No need to go through all the small print,' he said breezily. 'Terribly boring, and I think you can trust me.'

Claudia said it was immoral, but what did she know about the intricacies of high finance? She might think she was the bee's knees and the stalwart right hand on which he depended, but when it came to cutting cor-ners and the fine print of double-dealing, she was a virgin. Which was ironical really, considering the expensive lifestyle she favoured. If she'd had any real interest in the money market, the sheer visceral thrill that made her husband tick, she'd have long been aware that Mr Micawber's principles simply did not apply in the Burdett household; hadn't, in fact, since before they married.

It wasn't just having two households to support that made him gamble. It was something Miles had been born with; it was in his blood. Even at Eton he'd been famous for his backgammon school, had been threatened with expulsion on a couple of occasions when details of his winnings had reached the ears of the beak. Now he liked to think he had regularised his gambling propensity by turning it into a profession and becoming an underwriting agent for Lloyd's. Certainly it gave him complete satisfaction. The thrills of the card table and the racing track were neatly duplicated in his day-to-day life. Miles poured the sherry and carried it back to the desk.

'*Santé!*' he said, raising his glass to the old lady. And with a warm smile, full of gratitude for all the help this nice young man was constantly giving her, she reciprocated.

Eleni Papadopoulos was in the lift when he pressed the button to go up, surrounded by shopping bags and drenched in some exotic perfume.

'Miles, darling!' The radiant smile flashed on the moment she saw him and he found himself being kissed three times and clasped to her generous bosom. He liked Eleni, she was always good value, but found her a little overpowering at times. He backed away, smoothing down his hair.

'Working, darling?' She nodded at the briefcase. 'On a Saturday, too? Surely not. What a good boy you are!' And she laughed. She shuffled her glossy packages together, lining them up on the bench ready for takeoff, and glanced at her minuscule diamond-studded watch to see if it was lunchtime yet. Ten to two.

'Care for a cocktail?' she asked seductively, looking

him up and down with a glance that was full of promise. 'Or is the little woman waiting for you at home?'

Put that way it made him sound faintly ridiculous. Miles hesitated, but an idea was forming that he found hard to resist. Dangerous living, that was his middle name. He scooped up a handful of her packages, tucked his briefcase firmly under the other arm and went with her up to the fifth floor, missing the third entirely. If he played his cards carefully, Claudia need never know. He'd just say he'd been held up at the club and put up with one of her temper tantrums if need be. She was cross enough about his dabblings with Lady Wentworth; no need to let her know his plans for Eleni, which would, he knew, provoke the most colossal storm. Aged gentility was one thing. Imagine the ructions if Claudia ever found out that as of now, he also had his beady eye on the voluptuous Greek – and not just her money, either.

' 'Allo there, Demeter, I'm home,' called Eleni as she unlocked the door but there was silence. Apparently they had the flat to themselves.

'Where the hell have you been?' screeched Claudia when Miles came home at twenty past three, his tie in his pocket and his hair still damp.

'Oh, dropped in at Hurlingham for a quick game of squash. Had to wait for a court as it's Saturday.'

'So where's your kit?' she demanded suspiciously.

'In the car. Forgot to bring it up. I'll get it later.' She looked amazing when she was mad, her eyes flashing, colour in her cheeks, light years from her usual chilly self and actually quite a turn-on. Pity, but right now he simply didn't have the energy.

'Well, your *wife* just rang,' said Claudia viciously. 'You were supposed to be picking the girls up at three.'

Oh Lord. Forgot all about it. Back in the doghouse.

'Not to worry,' said Miles, more easily than he felt. 'I'll sort it out. I'll just give her a buzz.'

'She won't be there. She's had to take them to the gymkhana herself because you were too damned selfish to remember the agreement. Again.'

It was not often Claudia took Caroline's side, but she was so mad at Miles right now that practically any ally would do. Though the memory of Caroline's placid acceptance of her husband's failure to keep his word still grated. How ever did she manage to maintain that calm and still act civil? To the woman, too, who had turned her life upside down by stealing her husband and wrecking her home. Maybe there was more to Caroline than met the eye. Claudia ground her teeth in frustration and hated Caroline for managing always to make her feel bad.

Claudia's vindication to herself, if she needed one, for snatching another woman's husband had always been that her own life till then had been so shitty, she deserved fate to give her a break for a change. For the first part of her life she had been a cosseted child, raised in luxury in the country by two adoring parents, with every benefit money could buy. She had attended a private school in Sussex, learned to ride, dance, play the piano and speak perfect French, and swanned around with all the advantages life could offer until that fateful day, when she was not a lot older than Miles's youngest was now, that she returned home for half-term to find that the sky had collapsed about their ears.

She had been vaguely aware that her father was having business difficulties but knew very little about it, not even very clearly what he actually did. Something to do with money, was all she could tell her friends' parents when they asked. Something in the City, which always sounded so drab and unglamorous compared with the soldiers and judges and landowners and actors whose daughters she spent her life with. All she really knew was that there was never any difficulty about money for skiing trips abroad or holidays in France. Even visits to Covent Garden, when there was something the music teacher very much wanted them to see. If she had a privileged upbringing, Claudia was not really aware of it until – on that unforeseen black day – it was suddenly all snatched away.

Quite simply, as her tight-lipped mother tried to explain, Daddy had been having business difficulties and all of a sudden he was in court, with his name plastered all over the newspapers, as someone who had perpetrated one of the greatest financial frauds of recent times. The house was sold to cover his legal costs, Claudia never returned to the posh boarding school but was enrolled in the local secondary instead, and her mother was reduced to having to work, as a paid secretary in a boys' prep school, about the only thing she was properly trained to do. And Daddy was sent to prison for a considerable time.

Now, remembering it, Claudia covered her face in

agony as the shame came flooding back. Her friends had deserted her, her dog and her pony were sold, people had said things she'd never forget. She and her mother had moved away, to one small provincial town after another, and once the dust had settled a little, Claudia learned that her mother was divorcing him and reverting to her maiden name. The charismatic father she had always so much idolised was in future to be no part of their lives. The sentence was long since over – he had been released early for good behaviour – but he hadn't, as far as she knew, ever tried to seek them out. She had neither seen nor heard from him again, and that was especially hard to swallow for someone who had once been the apple of his eye.

Which was why Miles was so completely out of order in forgetting this regular monthly date with his own three girls. Although Claudia resented their existence and the drain it was on their own joint income, she could not escape a residual sneaking guilt at having destroyed the happiness of another family, just as circumstances had once done it to her. Her mood was quite shattered and she could no longer look forward to a leisurely afternoon lying on the sofa watching Fred Astaire and Ginger Rogers in *Swing Time*. She felt one of her dreaded migraines coming on so swallowed a handful of aspirins and took herself back to bed.

Connie and Kate were in Hastings, combing the junk shops in the Old Town and eating lovely fresh haddock and chips in a friendly little restaurant right on the promenade. They were drinking cheap red wine from a bottle with an Italian label, not what Kate would normally have chosen with fish but a must as far as Connie was concerned.

'I know it's hardly traditional,' she said. 'But somehow this particular red goes well with fish and chips. And believe me, the white here is a whole lot worse.'

She'd been coming here for years, first with her husband when they lived in nearby Rye, later on regular buying jaunts with Amelia, when they'd make it a weekend outing and load the station wagon with all kinds of furniture and things which they later sold at a profit in the shop. Kate was really enjoying herself. It was years since she last ate fish this fresh, with mushy peas and onion rings on the side, and the sharp salt air and evocative smell of nets drying in the nearby boatyard really got to her.

'You know something,' she said in surprise. 'I'm actually happy.'

It was five months since her flight from Ramon, three since she'd first met Connie, and the scars were at last beginning to fade. As they left the restaurant to resume their search the sun came out and they both rolled up their sleeves. It was a pity they'd only made it a day trip; a snooze in a deckchair on the crowded sands would be just the job to work off the effects of the wine and all that food. Not to mention an excursion along the pier. But tomorrow was Sunday, when the shops would be closed, and they still had work to do.

'Care for some candy floss?' asked Connie, but Kate declined. The way she was feeling now, she would never be hungry again.

They wound their way back into the narrow streets

of the Old Town and wandered in and out of the shops, packed with trippers and genuine collectors alike, everyone on the look-out for a bargain.

'It used to be far better pickings before they electrified the line,' said Connie. 'But you can still find bargains if you know what you're looking for. Amelia taught me a lot.'

Because they were travelling by train, there wasn't a lot they could carry, but Connie picked up some pretty Victorian floral plates and a painted firescreen she reckoned would make her a bob or two. Then they found a carved oak sideboard Kate felt she really had to have, so it became a matter of getting it delivered, which left them free to buy more things.

'It's well worth the delivery charge,' said Connie approvingly. 'Even if you add the rail fare and the lunch, things are still that much cheaper down here.'

Kate also found a black enamelled corner chair that she particularly liked, which might, the dealer said, be by William Morris. Certainly of that period; a snip at the price. She didn't really need it, what with the five Victorian chairs she'd already acquired, but it would look good in her hall against the black and white tiles, and was hard to resist. They lugged it back to the sideboard shop, to be delivered along with the rest of their booty, then slowly threaded their way back towards the station to catch the six o'clock train. The sun was still shining and it felt like summer. Kate was developing a faint tan and her skin smelled healthily of sunshine and salt.

'I've really had a wonderful day,' she said sleepily on the train. 'A bit of sea air certainly makes a change after all those hours hunched over the computer.' She drifted off to sleep and only revived when Connie prodded her awake at Charing Cross.

'Come on, sleepyhead,' said her American friend. 'I'll treat us to a taxi home.'

Connie came up for a coffee since it wasn't too late, and they were sitting in the kitchen with the cat when the telephone rang.

'Now who on earth can that be?' said Kate, noticing as she crossed the hall that her nose was really quite red. 'Probably a wrong number. Practically no one knows where I am.' Or cares.

She hoped it wasn't her family, which usually meant bad news. But there was no one there. Not a wrong number, not a bad connection. Just silence, as if someone was on the line but not speaking, followed after too long a pause by a click. She had just got back to the kitchen when it rang again. With exactly the same result.

'Someone playing silly buggers?' suggested Connie. 'Now who would that be, do you suppose?'

'Someone looking for the previous owner, perhaps. But why then wouldn't they speak?'

'Try dialling 1471,' said Connie. 'That will give you the mysterious caller's number.' But the recorded voice simply told them that the service was unavailable.

'Which means,' said Connie, 'it's probably coming from abroad.'

It rang again. This time Connie answered but still with the same result.

'I'm sure someone was listening,' she said. 'You could almost hear him breathing.'

'Thanks a bunch,' said Kate, as Connie left. 'You've

really made me feel great.' What with the servants' bells, too, and the dark thoughts they had given rise to. And that sinister, still figure perpetually at the window. All of a sudden this cosy apartment no longer felt quite so secure.

'I wouldn't worry,' said Connie cheerfully. 'Just ignore it the next time and he'll get the message and lay off.'

But he didn't. Every ten minutes or so for the next two hours the phone continued to ring but Kate refused to answer it any more. She went to bed instead, and closed the door and lay there in the dark, just listening to the distant ring and wondering.

Kate left Ramon the first time he hit her but soon went back. It was two weeks after she arrived in New York and they were both exhausted just from sorting things out. Kate was also emotionally wrung out from the trauma of leaving Francis and everything in life she cared for. It was late one Saturday afternoon and Ramon had offered to cook. It was his apartment, after all, where he'd lived alone for many years, and although Kate's basic cooking was adequate, it still left a lot to be desired, particularly with a man like Ramon, who prided himself on his gourmet tastes. Kate had been down to NYU to inquire about courses while she found herself a job, and she came back, tired and a little despondent, to find the apartment deserted, with no sign of food being prepared and virtually nothing in the icebox. Also no word from Ramon, which was unusual; no note or anything to indicate where he'd gone or when he was likely to be back.

She hung around for a while, assuming he'd popped round the corner to the deli. When he had failed to materialise by seven, she put together a basketful of washing and lugged it downstairs to the basement laundry, then came back up to wash her hair and prepare herself for a romantic evening with the man with whom she was still so much infatuated. She had her head in the basin when Ramon returned, so she wrapped a towel round her streaming hair and followed him joyfully into the living room for a hug.

'When are we eating?' was all she asked, in no way aggressively, then had been astonished when he rounded on her with a stranger's icy stare and backhanded her deliberately across the cheek. *What?* This was the man she loved, for whom she had forsaken everything – job, home, friends, family. The one, for heaven's sake, for whom she had dumped her husband. She stood there, stunned with shock and the force of the blow, waiting for his apology, for some sort of explanation; for the warmth of the lovemaking that always followed even the slightest altercation between them, but he simply turned away and switched on the CBS news. Nothing more. He acted as if it hadn't happened, but worse still, as if she were someone he scarcely knew, a mere irritation unworthy of further thought.

When it was clear there was to be no comeback, Kate had fled back into the bathroom to cry, then dried her hair, grabbed her bag and let herself out of the apartment. She despised women who put up with being abused, and was not going to stand for it herself. Saturday night on the Upper West Side is always busy, so she wandered aimlessly down to Central Park South and found herself sitting in the Oak Room of the Plaza with a brandy, shaking so hard she could barely raise the glass to her lips. Never had she been more frightened or felt more alone. In such a short space of time she had made no friends, and her only acquaintances were Ramon's. There was no one she could trust to turn to, nowhere she could go. She hadn't even any money of her own, apart from the few remaining dollars in her purse. And if she turned back now to the husband and family she had deserted, she knew what sort of reception she was likely to get. So she finished her drink, wandered on down Fifth Avenue to the Rockefeller Plaza and sat by the window in the corner of the Rainbow Room, gazing out over a darkening cityscape that had once enchanted her but had suddenly turned so sour. Eventually, as the hour grew later and she knew she had no other choice, she caught an uptown bus and went cautiously back to the apartment.

There were lights on in the living room when she silently opened the door and soft music playing.

'Katie, *chirido*, is that you?'

He sounded half-demented with anxiety as he crossed the wide hall with the speed of despair and clutched her into his arms like a drowning man.

'I've been sick with worry. I was about to call the cops.' And he sounded, too, as if he meant it.

Now came the loving she had been expecting.

'Katie, oh my Katie,' he murmured into her hair, stroking her face with an anguished hand, crushing her hard till she thought her ribs might crack. He didn't apologise – that, she was to discover, was part of the pattern – but his emotion and unspoken contrition were touching in the extreme. He made her soup – artichoke and tomato – and practically spooned her as they sat together by the fire, while he chafed her cold hands and generally warmed her up.

Then he took her to bed and made gentle love to her all night till she felt like his fairy princess once more, and the stinging of his slap, along with the faint bruising, faded along with her shock. In time she came to forgive him, a flash of temper for which she felt responsible; he did, after all, have a fiery Latin temperament. But she never, ever forgot. That was the day Kate Ashenberry discovered that even happy-ever-afters have their sell-by date; that there are certain truths you will never hear spoken, since few are brave enough to discuss them.

The day, perhaps, that she finally grew up.

15

Alice Sorensen's visit to London was not quite as
spontaneous as she would have had Gregory
believe. After fifteen years of being strung along by
him, she had very definite goals in mind and, after pro-
tracted discussions with her Toronto women's group,
was here to get him to make a commitment. Her life,
after all, was ticking away along with the biological
clock, and seeing him once – occasionally twice – a
year did not, her sisters assured her, constitute a real
relationship. Not one that counted. So she had put her
duplex on the market, intimated to the college she
taught in that she might be moving on after the end of
the summer semester, and was secretly putting out feel-
ers to London University to see if she could get some
sort of academic posting closer to Gregory.

All this reorganisation was more or less straightforward, grist to the methodical Alice's mill. Actually
broaching the delicate subject of commitment to the
man himself was another ball-game entirely. She had
been staying in his flat a full five days and still nothing
that was not strictly superficial had been raised. The
time had come to tackle him. Her return flight to
Toronto was booked for Sunday; by Friday she realised

that time was running out, that he might not, after all, give way without at least a token struggle. And in any case, there were all sorts of important issues still to be discussed.

They were sitting in the garden of the Windsor Castle, drinking ale beneath the trees and waiting for their lunch to be served, when she took a metaphorical deep breath and launched herself into the subject.

'I was thinking, hon,' she said, more cautiously than came naturally to her forthright nature, taking his hand in both of hers and stroking it gently with one finger.

Uh-oh, said a warning voice in Gregory's head, and he looked urgently towards the serving hatch at the end of the garden, desperately willing a waitress to heave into view with their order. Alice plunged ahead.

'We've known each other a long time now. Half a lifetime, you might say, if you discount the years before puberty. Some would say we're as committed as any other couple . . .'

'Alice, my dear,' said Gregory rapidly, anticipating what was coming and trying desperately to head it off, 'we have all the time in the world. That's the beautiful thing about our relationship. And you know there is no one I care more for than you.'

'Well, yes,' she said without real conviction. 'So you've always said. But neither of us is getting any younger' – she hated to admit it, but for once it couldn't be fudged – 'and I was wondering if . . . what you felt . . . well, whether you have any plans . . . Shit, what I'm really trying to say is, are you likely ever to want children?' Because, went the hidden agenda, if you do, we'd better get a move on.

There, it was out. And she felt a whole lot better for the airing of it. Gregory, temporarily at a loss for words, was saved from immediate response by the timely arrival of the food and the subsequent diversion of trying to fit two plates of hake and chips, plus all the accompanying sauces and pickles, on to the garden table which already held their beers. Plus the second round he'd had the foresight to order from the bar. But even Gregory could not prevaricate for ever. Knife and fork in hand, paper napkin on his knee, tucked into the waistband of his pants to stop it fluttering away, first mouthful of steaming fish taken and thoughtfully savoured, there was no longer any avoiding the moist, imploring, black-cherry eyes staring into his from across the table.

'Alice, ' he said again, 'my dear.'

He took a swig of beer, wondering in hell's name how he was going to get round this one, whether it would be unmanly to make the excuse of urgently needing to take a leak.

'You do know I love you. That I shall undoubtedly love you for ever.'

'*Yes*,' she said, getting desperate now. It wasn't enough.

He put down his knife and fork, pushed aside his half-eaten fish and took both of her hands formally in his. His clear blue eyes, in which for so many years she had thought the sun both rose and set, connected with her anxious, doggy ones and beamed their familiar placebo.

'What we've got, Alice,' he said in a low tone, which throbbed with real feeling as he seduced her with his eyes, 'is far better than any marriage. Think about that.'

She didn't need to. No other subject had kept her awake longer in so concentrated a way over the past fifteen years. *Thinking* was the problem. The time was long overdue for action.

'Yes, but wait a minute . . .'

He removed his hand from her tightening grip and slid it in one smooth movement under her skirt and up over her knee.

'God, but I fancy you,' he murmured, his pupils dilating with animal lust. 'Let's not bother with coffee but get back to the flat for the second course.'

He placed a pile of notes and loose change on the cheap tin ashtray which held the bill, pulled her forcibly to her feet and frogmarched her across the courtyard and out into Peel Street beyond. His hand was already under her T-shirt and tweaking her nipple brutally as she stumbled against him in her desire and felt the familiar urgent dampness invading her panties. As he marched her briskly down the hill she tried to speak, to grab at the dangling thread she had come so far to secure, but he stopped her mouth roughly with a kiss, causing a group of loitering students outside King's College to break into spontaneous applause.

'That's the stuff, old chap. Go to it!' they bellowed. And Gregory smiled laddishly and waved.

That, indeed, was the essence of Gregory Hansen, so far as the female sex was concerned, something the women's group would most certainly not be able to grasp: the sheer, brutish *maleness* of the man. Alice gave in, as she always did, as he always knew she would. And as he tumbled her on to the bed, ripping off her clothes and telling her over and over again how much he loved her, she allowed herself, yet again, to sink into compliance and believe him. She just couldn't face a major showdown right now. It was simpler than having to argue.

Gregory's Danish father was a whole generation older than his mother, but that was never an issue since he didn't stay around long enough to witness the advent of his infant son. Maudie Shaw was the only daughter of an unsophisticated, deeply religious couple in Hamilton, Ontario, who spent the summer after leaving high school waiting tables in Toronto whilst also taking acting classes and dreaming of a glitzy future in the movies. Some day soon, she fantasised, some Hollywood tycoon would just happen to be sitting at one of her tables and, with a wave of his cigar, would magic her across the continent and set her up on the Coast as the fifties' Hedy Lamarr. Alas, the dream was never to be. All Maudie found, the summer she turned eighteen, was an itinerant book salesman from Copenhagen with startlingly blue eyes and the smoothest of tongues, and the result was Gregory. Unable to support herself and a child, and still sufficiently moonstruck to believe it had been the real thing and that Sven-Erik would one day return, Maudie was forced to return ignominiously to her ageing and reproachful parents, there to raise her bastard under the guise of an infant brother. Of course the family was forced to move to another part of town to avoid the slur, and her parents were never able to forgive her for that. But they did stand by her; for that she had to be grateful, as at that period of her life they were her sole lifeline.

So Gregory grew up calling his grandparents Mom and Pop, under the impression that Maudie, who he adored, was his virtuous and God-fearing older sister. Until, on his fifteenth birthday, she deemed him finally adult enough to know the truth, and misguidedly ruined the day for him by blurting out the sordid facts of her disgrace, which was how he saw it, as well as his own besmirched origins. Gregory took it badly and found it impossible to forgive her. His inherited Nordic beauty gave him a certain aura amongst his classmates, in addition to which he was consistently a straight-A student. The cold, bare truth, delivered so unceremoniously, was almost more than he could take at that impressionable age, so that he turned and savaged the sister he had venerated and immediately blamed her for the accumulated discontents of a life spent amongst an enclosed community of much older folk, dedicated to spreading the word of the Lord. In place of the Madonna-like creature who had been his inspiration and guide, Maudie had revealed herself to be little more than a common whore.

It was the end of a lifetime's illusions, and also of Gregory's innocence. From that moment on he trusted no one, particularly not any woman, and as soon as he had finished his formal schooling, he packed his few possessions and quit his grandparents' house for ever. All he retained of his former life was his father's family name, to which he was not legally entitled, combined with a heavy dollop of the same mythical Dane's ruthless charm. One thing remained, however, in the forefront of his consciousness; his mother had never loved him, his whole secure childhood had been built on a sham. From that moment on Gregory Hansen was on his own. That was the way he intended to stay.

The phone didn't ring at all next morning, but Kate remained wary and slightly on edge. Because it was the weekend, she varied her routine and carried a pot of coffee into the sunny sitting room while she read *The Times* at leisure to a background of mellow music on Radio 3. Oddly enough, it was the ordinary little details of everyday existence that more than anything brought her a feeling of security: the aroma of brewing coffee, a bunch of fresh flowers on the table in the hall. It was, for instance, a real comfort to know that Connie was now installed in Amelia's flat just two floors down. Because of her early incarceration in academia and later flight to the States, Kate knew very few people she could really look upon as friends. Miraculously Connie had arrived to fill that gap; life was at last starting to be fun again.

Horatio sat on the windowsill behind her, grooming himself in the morning sun before sloping off for his regular morning prowl, along the ledges that skirted the top of Kensington Court. In the early days, Kate had worried about his constant popping in and out of the windows, but cats are sure-footed and there was no point trying to curb the wanderings of a spirit as free as his. She was never quite sure how far afield he actually went; she only knew he was almost always within hearing range and she had only to rattle a knife on a plate and there he would be, salivating at the prospect of another meal. He had grown fit and sturdy, with a glossy, healthy coat and a proud, bushy tail he held high like a banner. But though he had grown much more people-orientated, he remained very much a creature who walked by himself. Not unlike the porter, in fact, another being who appeared to carry a load of secrets.

Septimus Woolf was indeed an enigma. Kate couldn't make him out at all. He was calm and civil and dignified at all times, with an air of slight detachment about him as if he viewed the residents with amusement. There had to be more to him than met the eye, but no one seemed to know anything about him. Rowena confided that she'd seen him occasionally in church.

'And he's quite chummy with Father Salvoni,' she said. 'I gather they play chess together of an evening.'

Kate was glad. Loneliness was a hard enough burden to carry. It was good to know that the quiet, dignified man, who seemed so unsuited for the job, had a life of his own. One day she'd find out more if she could without snooping, though she guessed Rowena would beat her to it. Better than any grapevine was her neighbour. Far more fun, too, and livelier than a soap opera.

'I don't know how you do it,' said Kate affectionately, kissing the faded cheek when she met her in the lift.

'Easy,' said her neighbour, her eyes as bright and inquisitive as a robin's. 'When you get to my age there's not a lot else to do but snoop. And I do so enjoy it too, my dear. It's one of life's harmless little pleasures.'

Not even Rowena, however, could throw any sort of light on Amelia's murder. Time was ticking by and the police appeared to be losing interest, though some of the tenants were still quite agitated and Digby Fenton had had to call a special meeting in the Town Hall in order to calm their fears.

'Security is as good as it ever was,' he said. 'Whoever got in did so by a fluke, and we're pretty sure it won't happen again.'

The iron gates which led from the street to the first-floor terrace were firmly padlocked and the keys held by the respective porters. Each of the fire escape doors could be opened only from the inside or else unlocked from the outside by a special key. At night, along with the Town Hall and the library, the building was floodlit, and, being on a main thoroughfare, was not an obvious target for even the most foolhardy of cat burglars.

'Unless they're high on drugs,' said Ronnie Barclay-Davenport, who'd seen action in the war and was nobody's fool. 'Then there's no accounting for what they're likely to do. Young hooligans.'

'Which doesn't mean, of course,' said Digby, 'that we mustn't all be as vigilant as possible and keep our eyes skinned for our neighbours as much as ourselves.'

Another bonus, thought Kate, of living in a big communal building with a man as sound as Digby Fenton in charge.

'That's all very well,' sniffed Mrs Adelaide Potter to her cohorts, as she stumped her way slowly back from the Town Hall, key in hand to effect a speedy entry. 'But our directors are all rubbish and don't know what they're talking about.'

That was her blanket opinion on most matters.

'Quite so, Adelaide dear,' said Heidi nervously, moving her fat little legs like a corgi's in an effort to keep in step. 'What do you think should be done instead?'

'Hang them, that's the answer,' snapped the evil old woman, though whether she meant the directors or mankind in general, Kate, walking behind and eavesdropping shamelessly, couldn't quite be sure. Though with Mrs Adelaide Potter, it probably all came to much the same thing.

She was still grinning at the recollection next morning as she strolled down to call for Connie. Gregory was standing at his door, chatting to the postman.

'Morning,' he said, with his brilliant smile. 'How's tricks?'

Kate stopped to tell him about the meeting.

'I'm sorry I missed it,' said Gregory. 'But aren't we lucky to have Digby as our *führer*? What sterling work he does, to be sure. The man's a saint. He shames me with his selflessness.'

'I know. He'll make an excellent mayor.'

'You bet.'

She told him about the Black Widows and what she'd overheard, and he laughed.

'They're priceless, aren't they? It's worth putting up with their fascist views for the entertainment value.'

This morning he was wearing a teal blue sweater with a hole in the elbow, and he needed a shave. His general air of scruffiness did not, however, detract from the man's general allure. Far from it. What a love he is, thought Kate impulsively, and resisted an overwhelming urge to hug him. What was so refreshing about Gregory, she realised, was his non-Englishness. He was that rare creature, a man who truly liked women, a main ingredient of his impressive pulling power. Just then a voice, slightly querulous, sounded from somewhere within his flat, and Gregory pulled a face and retreated.

'Has he got someone living there?' Kate asked Connie as they strolled up Church Street later.

'Wouldn't know. There's been some female hanging around lately, in a dark green tracksuit and baseball cap. Looks a little like Ali McGraw with muscular thighs. Do you suppose she's connected to him? I certainly hope not.'

Connie was disappointed. Now that she had moved into the building, she was already getting faintly proprietorial towards her dishy upstairs neighbour, though she still hadn't had a real chance to get to know him.

'Maybe I'll have a house-warming,' she said, 'and ask him down for drinks. What do you think?'

'Can't do any harm,' said Kate, secretly taken aback at Connie's boldness. Not at all the way she would ever behave herself; these native New Yorkers certainly had a lot of bottle. 'Do you think it's entirely appropriate, though?' she asked, 'With Amelia so recently dead?'

Connie hadn't thought of that. 'Probably not,' she said. 'Maybe I'll just hang around and ravish him on the stairs instead.'

'That's the ticket. The subtle approach is usually best.'

Gregory had stepped out to buy an evening paper when the phone rang. Alice was packing; she took it in the bedroom.

'May I ask who's speaking?' asked Jacintha, taken aback.

'Alice Sorensen,' said Alice flatly. 'Gregory's not here.'

Jacintha was thrown into a spin. She only had a minute or two while Clifford was cleaning the mower. He'd just let slip that he'd be off playing golf at St Andrews next week, and she'd wasted no time in ringing Gregory to let him know. It had been a long, hard few weeks with the weather as bad as it was; an illicit few days in London was just what the doctor ordered. She was totally thrown off balance at the sound of this precise Canadian voice.

'When will he back?' she faltered.

'Any minute now,' said Alice. 'We're going out to dinner.'

'And you are . . .?' A cousin, maybe. Don't leap to conclusions. A colleague from the paper, passing through. The accent was certainly right.

'His girlfriend . . .' said Alice bluntly. 'Who shall I tell him called?'

'Never you mind,' said Jacintha, slamming down the receiver then bursting into noisy sobs and rushing to the bathroom for cover. This was worse than her direst expectations, final proof that her love was not entirely true to her. For a giddy few moments she thought of getting into the car and driving up to London to confront him, but what would be the use? In any case, she could hear Clifford scraping the mud off his gardening boots at the kitchen door and knew she must pull herself together fast and try to repair the damage to her make-up. She'd put it down to hay fever, that one usually worked, and then she'd think up a plan to prove to

Gregory that he didn't need anyone else in his life.

It was her own fault really, she pondered later as she prepared the beef Wellington. She'd not been sufficiently attentive to her poor boy these past few years, so of course he was losing heart and having to look for comfort elsewhere. She'd make it up to him as soon as Clifford had left for Scotland. She comforted herself, as she laid the table, by compiling a mental list of outfits to take and what she needed to buy in Cheltenham before she left. Every visit to London these days was like a mini wedding trip; no matter how many clothes she might already have, Jacintha could always light upon something new she desperately needed. Despite her anguish at the thought that Gregory might have another woman in his life just now, she remained fairly confident that she still came top of his list. It was not his fault if she had selfishly married; she would make it her prime duty to prove to him as soon as she could that her heart was still one hundred per cent his. If only they didn't live so inconveniently far apart. If only it weren't for Clifford.

As she poured the claret into a decanter and set it next to Clifford's place for him to do the honours, Jacintha thought about the small inheritance her mother had left her last year. It was sitting in the building society doing absolutely nothing except gather a little interest, and it seemed unlikely – with Clifford being as comfortably off as he was – that she would ever need to dip into it, except for purposes of purest frivolity.

'Buy yourself something special, my love.' Clifford had said that himself when he'd sorted out the estate, but there wasn't anything she had actually wanted, nothing her indulgent husband wouldn't give her himself the moment he became aware it had taken her eye.

Now Jacintha knew, as she spooned the gravy, exactly what she'd do with her mother's money. Something the old lady would have heartily approved of, had she still been here to advise. Bricks and mortar were the best investment; Clifford was always telling her that. Jacintha lifted the handsome, pastry-encased joint and carried it joyfully through into the dining room. A *pied-à-terre* in London, that was what she'd buy. Somewhere handy for shopping, in Knightsbridge or Kensington, to save the inconvenience of forever popping up and down on the train. She was absolutely certain Clifford could be talked round; it was, after all, her own money to do with as she liked. Then she could keep a closer eye on her boy and start to take care of him properly. She looked forward to that; she was pretty sure Gregory would too.

16

The idea of a mild sort of fling-ette with her neighbour, Miles, was hugely diverting to Eleni. Not just because she liked his enthusiasm, and those boyish, public-school good looks always got her going, but also since she instantly recognised a fellow rogue when she saw one. That, and the fact that his wife always cut her dead whenever they met in the lift.

'*Holy moley*,' she would say to Demeter. 'Who the bloody hell does she think she is?' And Demeter would smile gravely and wag her wise head from side to side.

'Go carefully, my child.'

Tonight he had intimated that they would meet for dinner at Quaglino's, so here she was, halfway through the afternoon, ransacking her closet for something reasonable to wear, all the time cursing quietly under her breath because her wardrobe was not in better shape and badly in need of replenishment. Demeter was off down the North End Road, buying meat and fresh vegetables at a knockdown price to keep them going for a few more days, but was bound to be back in good time to be ready with her needle and iron to pull into shape any outfit Eleni could drag together at this last-minute stage. All around her on the floor lay designer dresses discarded for one reason or another. A torn seam; sweat stains under the armpits; in one case streaks of menstrual blood on a skirt that she had not noticed last time she carelessly tossed it off. Really, Demeter was letting her standards drop. In the corner of the crowded bedroom, with its satin eiderdown and rows of fluffy stuffed toys, stood an old-fashioned coat stand with pegs from which drooped, like a row of decapitated martyrs, outfits that had done the rounds too many times and needed a good working over before they could be allowed to hit the streets again.

Thank goodness for Demeter. When she'd followed her from Athens the first time Eleni left home, Eleni had cursed her roundly for being both a spoilsport and a drag. Quickly, however, she had learned the short-sightedness of this view. Demeter had proved more than worth her weight in gold for her skill with a needle, her constant hard toil to keep them both fed and respectably clothed and her double duties as companion and lady's maid, not to mention full-time cook, which gave a front of respectability to the various homes they had shared in London before they wound up here in Kensington Court. The homespun peasant wisdom which also came with the package, Eleni usually ignored. But one thing she did know: without the cover of the older woman's dignity she would not have been able to infiltrate a building this classy.

Just lately things had not been going so well, and funds were low. She dragged out a grey silk jersey Jean Muir and held it before her in front of the glass. This was one designer you could always fall back on, but today she found the garment dreary and uninspiring. She pulled a face, then wound her heavy dark hair into a lustrous twist on top of her head and narrowed her eyes to judge the effect. Not bad. With a silver belt and strappy sandals it might just do, particularly if she borrowed Demeter's earrings that went so well with her own silver cirque.

She turned on the water in the tub and lit scented candles about the bathroom. All this for an evening with that schoolboy, Miles Burdett; really, it was laughable, what was she coming to? As she slid beneath the scented foam, Eleni closed her eyes and focused her mind on the immediate future and what she could do to buoy up the household kitty. Demeter was fine for the day-to-day slog, but the inspiration that had kept them up and running all these years was entirely Eleni's.

By five Demeter was back in the nest and stitching hard, fixing the hem. By six Eleni had done her nails and trimmed her pubic hair (she left her armpits as they were; she found most men preferred them that way) and was stretched out on the bed making phone calls while Demeter bustled in the kitchen, knocking up a delicious-smelling snack to keep up her strength until her date. Really, this woman was too much; Eleni was lucky not to put on weight, though as it was, she'd soon work off these extra calories in a few brisk rounds with Miles. Where he planned to take her after dinner, she did not know. But a man with that sort of glint in his eye clearly knew what he was about. Eleni looked forward to seeing what tonight would offer. She thought she could find it in her heart to be quite fond of Miles, particularly if she could also tap into his financial expertise and get him to work on her own fiduciary problems.

By seven-thirty, for Eleni believed in always being at least an hour late, she was sitting at her mirror, working on her face, while Demeter carefully pinned her hair into an ornate confection which she knew Miles would take delight in tearing down. Beneath the clinging silk jersey she wore nothing but a satin G-string and pale, ten-denier stockings. Tonight, she would go bra-less. Another thing she had learned about the public-school Englishman was his infantile obsession with the breast, and until she had worked her magic on him and got him under her spell, she wanted Miles to find her a cornucopia of delights. Time later to crack the whip. Eleni moued glossily at herself in the glass and carefully licked her predatory teeth.

Claudia met her in the hall at ten past eight, swathed in fur and smelling like a tart's boudoir, as she was coming wearily home from a hard day in the office, with a sore throat and the threat of another headache hovering.

'Hello, darling,' said Eleni sweetly. 'How pretty you look tonight.'

She took a step backwards and studied Miles's wife from head to toe, taking in the understated suit and sensible, low-heeled pumps. Her own delicate sandals were so high as to be a potential hazard, but a cab was waiting outside and after that the problem would belong to Miles. Eleni nodded.

'That dark grey really suits you, darling,' she said.

'Perhaps a touch of colour here and there? To lighten it up?'

Claudia smiled through tightened lips and moved past her towards the lift. How dare this foreign slut dare to question her own good taste; the way she was done up with her tits all a-jiggle and enough jewellery to grace a Pearly Queen. She'd long had her suspicions about what the Greek got up to, and now she was sure. No job, no visible means of support and that old servant woman to provide for. It didn't take a brain as good as Claudia's to add up the equation and reach a satisfactory answer. What would those disagreeable old biddies upstairs make of *that*? When they stopped sticking their noses in where they weren't wanted they'd be better occupied putting other people's houses in order.

Miles, of course, was out, but that was beginning to be nothing new. He'd muttered something about a late meeting and then vanished before she'd had a chance to pin him down, to find out exactly when he would be coming home and if it was worth waiting for him rather than having to face the traffic alone. She banged into the bedroom and threw her things disconsolately all over the tidy room. Claudia had grown up in a home where her father was absent more often than not. She was used to the mysteries of big business and a mother who tiptoed around at night in order not to disturb him, who never – in all the years of her marriage – had ever dared phone him at the office for fear of interrupting him. And then been left to pick up the pieces alone when the busies had eventually arrived and carted him off to jail.

Well, a pox on all that. Miles's business was Claudia's too, and she was damned if she'd ever find herself in a similar situation. Her mother had been altogether too meek and obliging, like so many of her generation, and look where it had landed her. Alone and ageing in a dreary seaside bungalow, still working part-time in the local hospital in order to find the funds just to survive. Occasionally Claudia felt a twinge of guilt when she thought of her mother's lifestyle compared with their own. But she and Miles were still on an upward curve; they'd take good care that her mother would be well provided for by the time she grew too old to work and wanted to put her feet up for a change.

It was already gone nine and no sign of him yet, so she'd just have to eat alone. Claudia cut herself a slice of cheese and took it, with a glass of wine, into the other room to slump in front of the television and feel thoroughly miserable and hard done by.

Upstairs Kate was also feeling glum. On nights like this, when Connie was not around, her aloneness in the world really hit her. If she'd known that Claudia was at home in a similar situation, she might have given her a call. But then, most probably, she would not. Claudia was not the friendliest of creatures and Kate had yet to get a handle on her.

'I like the way she dresses,' she had said to Connie. 'She always makes me feel such a scruff.'

'Well, with money like that, why wouldn't she? Those city bimbos really rake it in. Plus she has a husband to pick up the bills.'

'It's not fair, is it?' said Kate. 'We work just as hard as

she does, I'm sure, but I couldn't afford designer clothes. No way near.'

'Nor should you. You look perfectly great as you are – and in any case, where would you wear them?'

'Where indeed.'

As always, Connie had hit it right on the head.

'Certainly not the pub, and that's the only place I go these days. There and the pizza parlour.'

'Oh, poor love. Wait till I meet my millionaire and we'll go out on a double date.'

Connie still had hopes of Gregory, but lately he hadn't seemed to be around.

'He travels a lot,' explained Kate. 'Apart from his column for the *Toronto Star*, he's also working on a book. Guernsey, I believe, or somewhere like that.' She was a little vague when it came to Gregory. By keeping him at arm's length where her own life was concerned, she'd rather avoided asking him about his.

'Is that popsy still hanging around? The Ali McGraw lookalike?'

'Don't think so. I haven't seen her lately, but who knows? Men like Gregory always come entrammelled. They wouldn't be worth having if they didn't. It's up to you to cut a swathe through his defences, and I'd give you odds against the popsy any day.'

Connie raised one thumb in the air and gave a heavy wink.

'Atta girl!'

Connie, however, was out tonight, on a sudden stint at the Lyric in Hammersmith, who were doing a revival of *Hair* and had asked her to join the chorus.

'It won't necessarily lead to the bright lights, but they're a good company,' she explained.

'And you never know who'll be out there watching you,' said Kate encouragingly.

She loved Connie like a sister and so much wanted her to succeed. But she missed her cheery company when she was gone and was beginning to realise how much this new friendship meant to her. Not good. When she split with Ramon, Kate had privately vowed that she would always, henceforth, stand on her own two feet and never again be dependent on any other person, of either sex. She was growing used to living alone and found she rather liked it. Horatio was all the company she really needed, though it was comforting to know that she had nice neighbours should anything ever go wrong.

She sat at the computer long after her normal stopping time because she was well into her current news update and had nothing pressing to make her finish. She'd fed the cat and was simmering soup over a low gas; she could go on like this quite happily for another hour or so, while outside the summer evening faded slowly into dusk and lights came on all over the building.

From where she sat she looked straight across into the matching rooms in the opposite wing. It was slightly too far to see very clearly, but she was beginning to recognise shapes and colour schemes and felt quite cosy with these glimpses of other lives. The people dead opposite were decorating a room and had the windows open wide at all hours, with bright, unshaded lights illuminating their new pink walls. Kate longed to be able to see for herself exactly how their flat looked inside, whether it was indeed a mirror-image of her own, with the same number of rooms and so on. Because there were separate lifts and stairwells, the two sets of residents shared no common ground. Accordingly, she only ever saw them in this way, stolen glimpses of unknown interiors like Alice gazing wistfully into her looking-glass world. And somehow it accentuated her acute feeling of isolation. Those people over there had lives of their own and she could see them laughing and moving about. Could they also, she wondered, see her? A thin, dark figure hunched over a lighted box, hour after hour spent doing the same unchanging thing, like a battery hen. What a dreary life they must think she led, if they thought about her at all. And the truth was, they were probably right. Sometimes she feared that her youth was passing her by while she hid in this anonymous semi-darkness with a cat and a computer.

She yawned and stretched, then backed up the day's work and unbooted. Time to stop, even though there was not much else to do. She'd be turning into a proper computer nerd if she didn't watch out. Soon she must buy herself a television, and then she could stretch her ingenuity and become a couch potato as well. And wait till she started doing her shopping over the Internet as well. What a dismal thought; talk about virtual reality.

The sun had set over the west wing of the building and the sky was a darkening indigo blue. She rose to her feet and stretched like a cat, then strolled to the window and looked down over the court. One floor down, a single lamp was burning, and the familiar dark figure stood at the window, looking out. A jolt of shock shot right through Kate and she felt her neck beginning to tingle. There was something unearthly about the creature's very stillness, as if it were not flesh and blood at all; a tailor's dummy, maybe, or a waxwork. But when she dared to have another peek, the figure had gone.

Later, when she was putting out the rubbish, she heard voices from below, and one of them was Gregory's.

'Hi there,' she said, leaning boldly over the banister, and he turned and waved as he groped for his front door key. He was talking over the other railing to Beatrice Hunt, one floor down, also putting out her black plastic sacks, so Kate wandered down to join them. She rather liked this informal, rooming-house atmosphere; it reminded her of her flat-sharing days.

'We were just discussing house security,' said Beatrice.

'Yeah,' said Gregory. 'The main door was open when I got home, and no one was there. Woolf is off duty but someone had fixed the door open so that anyone could get in.'

'It won't do,' said Beatrice firmly. 'That's the last thing we need, even without the murder. I'll drop a fax to Digby and ask him to circularise the tenants. If we don't all pull together, what's the use?'

'Beatrice, you're a gem,' said Gregory. 'I'd volunteer for the board myself if I weren't away so much.' His laptop computer and a slim pigskin briefcase stood on the mat beside him, and he looked unusually trim in a dark grey suit with a tie.

'I've been down to Cornwall to cover the tuna war,' he said. 'For my sins. It's not all glamour, this job of mine. When my bosses in Toronto snap their fingers, I have to jump.'

He twinkled at Kate. 'There are times I really envy you. Being your own boss, calling your own tune.'

Beatrice, heading homewards, jerked her head towards the door of number eighteen, where the Toyota man was temporarily staying.

'I blame the foreigners,' she mouthed, in wicked parody of Mrs Adelaide Potter who lived next door. It was interesting how universally disliked the woman was.

'Care for a nightcap?' asked Gregory. 'I've been on the road all evening and really need to unwind.'

'Just a quick one,' said Kate, pleased, curious to see the inside of his apartment. His space was smaller than hers, with just one bedroom and a box room study. It was cheerfully spartan and smelled slightly of socks and sour milk; rather like her own flat, she thought, when she'd first taken possession.

He led her into the untidy living room, awash with old newspapers and unopened junk mail. It was pleasantly cosy, a real bachelor pad, with a comfortable sagging sofa and a threadbare carpet, though through the open door she could see that the kitchen was immaculate.

'Goodness,' said Kate. 'You've certainly got a lot of books.'

They were piled everywhere, all over the desk and the dining table, even in great stacks on the floor. He grinned.

'One of my little weaknesses, I'm afraid. Can't stop buying them, it's a kind of sickness. I keep meaning to do something about more shelves but somehow there's never time. And I'm not much cop with a screwdriver, I'm afraid. Never was much of a hand about the house.' She could see that.

'You don't need to go to all that trouble,' said Kate practically, remembering an old trick. 'Just planks on bricks works perfectly well, and actually looks quite nice. At least it would get them from under your feet.'

'And would mean I could occasionally find one when I needed it,' he agreed, fetching glasses and a jug of water from the kitchen to go with the Scotch on the mantelpiece. 'It's a good idea. One of these days I'll maybe mosey along to that timberyard in Church Street and see if they can fix me up.'

He waved Kate into an armchair, then stretched out comfortably on the sofa.

'That's better,' he said contentedly, cradling his glass on his chest. 'So tell me all about yourself, Kate Ashenberry. What is it that makes you tick?'

Kate hesitated. It was not her habit to talk about herself, something instilled in her from childhood, and even with Connie she felt uncomfortable when it came to discussing private matters like emotions. But something about this man put her at her ease and made her feel inexplicably safe. Unlike the other men who had been prominent in her life, there was nothing remotely macho or aggressive about Gregory; he had a feline softness that was almost asexual and made her feel she could trust him. She sipped her whisky and slowly relaxed and felt her tension beginning to drain away.

She looks like a scared little rabbit, thought Gregory; he mustn't rush her or do anything to alarm her. Listening was the thing he was best at, the real secret behind his success with women.

'Man trouble?' he asked at last.

Kate nodded. She felt embarrassed and was still at a loss for words.

'That's why you're here? In London, I mean?'

Again, she nodded. 'Of course, why else? Isn't it always the case?'

'*Cherchez l'homme*,' said Gregory comfortably, leaning across to top up her glass. 'Transatlantic romance? Those things rarely work out.' And I should know.

She smiled in relief; he understood. 'It wasn't so much long-distance,' she said. 'In fact, we were scarcely apart from the moment we met.' Now she felt the threat of familiar tears and was worried she would cry. Gregory thought about proffering a handkerchief but didn't. Don't break the spell, let her get on with it. There was so much obvious need there, bursting to come out.

'It's just that he was foreign, Argentinian, and I suppose I didn't know him as well as I thought.' She dragged a crumpled tissue from her sleeve and dabbed at the corners of her eyes.

'Was he violent?' asked Gregory softly. Kate was appalled. Was it that obvious?

'Don't worry,' said Gregory, observing her panic. 'I really don't mean to pry but sometimes it helps to talk. To someone not involved, I mean, and I promise it will go no further.'

Kate thought of all the absentee men in her life: her

father, always working; Bruno, who never listened; Francis, constantly preoccupied; even Ramon who towards the end had always shouted her down. Gregory was still lying there motionless, eyelids heavy, totally at ease. Outside, beyond the half-open window, a rare nightingale was beginning to sing. The air was balmy, the night was still. At this height, even over the busy High Street, the noise of traffic could scarcely be heard. It was a moment of pure tranquillity. Her limbs felt heavy and she wanted never to move again.

'It was usually my fault,' she admitted, after a while.

'Of course,' said Gregory, with the slightest of smiles. 'It nearly always is.'

What? Then she looked up and saw his expression. He was laughing at her, but only gently, and she saw from his eyes that he really understood. And just the telling was making her feel loads better. It was a long time since she'd properly got it off her chest.

'Of the lot of them, I suppose Francis was the most reasonable,' she continued ruminatively. 'Dad was wonderful, of course, but never, ever there. But even though he was just as preoccupied with his work, somehow Francis always found the time to listen. I miss that.'

Gregory's eyes opened wider. Had he missed something?

'Francis?' he enquired.

'Francis Pitt, my husband,' explained Kate. Hadn't she mentioned him before? Probably not.

Gregory sat up straighter, suddenly alert.

'You were married to Francis Pitt? The Cambridge don?'

'Yes, do you know him?'

'Well, no, not exactly. But I've heard of his work, of course. A very brainy sort of guy, from all accounts.'

Kate smiled shyly and looked at her hands. No doubt Gregory was as startled as the rest to discover she'd managed to marry a man of that calibre. Well, he needn't be too impressed, as it turned out. She hadn't succeeded in hanging on to him.

'I ought to go.'

'Please stay a little longer. I want to know much more but I meant what I said; it'll go no further, I promise. I may be a journalist by trade but I'm not Rowena.'

'Or Netta Silcock,' said Kate, beginning to smile.

'Or the Ayatollah. Precisely. Though there's always Father Salvoni you could talk to – or even the porter, at a pinch.'

'Why do you say that?' asked Kate, startled.

'I'm not really sure. It's my business to observe people, and there's something about him I can't quite put my finger on. Something that doesn't fit, as if he's wearing borrowed clothes. You mark my words.'

'I always think he looks like a don. Or an actor, perhaps.'

'Indeed. I rest my case.'

Now, at last, he had her laughing, and a healthy glow was returning to her cheeks. If he weren't so bushed, he'd feel like pouncing, but it wasn't the moment, and she'd keep.

'So tell me more.'

And she did, sketchily outlining her days at the *Observer* leading to the fateful first meeting with

Ramon, followed by the heady time in Manhattan where she'd thought she'd remain for the rest of her life. She still missed it dreadfully, she said, though London was an easier city.

'But duller.'

'Well, yes. But at least here you can walk the streets in safety and don't have to be quite so manic about locking up.'

'Even if neighbours get butchered in their own homes by a character who must have been the Scarlet Pimpernel, at the very least, for all the traces he left behind.'

Oh Lord, he was right. Kate's smile vanished again and he watched as she clenched her fists on her knees.

'Who do you think did it?' she whispered. This man seemed so wise, so reassuring. If anyone had the answers, it would be him.

'No idea,' he said. 'And neither, by the way, do the police. I've spent quite a lot of time with them, you know, assisting with enquiries, helping them sift through the evidence. I'm sorry to tell you they're as stumped as the rest of us.'

He looked exhausted; it was time to go. She rose and slowly stretched, then walked to the window and looked out. His living room was, she saw, directly below her study, with the identical view across the courtyard. But now there was no sign of the watcher; the blinds were drawn, the room in darkness.

'What are you looking at?' Gregory came silently to stand behind her, hands on her shoulders, leaning gently against her in the most natural way in the world.

'Nothing really. Just the place across the courtyard.

There's often someone standing there. No sign of them tonight.'

Gregory wasn't really listening. He was wondering whether to kiss her.

'Those flats are rentals and half are unoccupied. Not like us, where we're mainly owner-occupiers.'

Kate could feel his breath warm on her cheek and was very much aware of his physical presence, standing so close. Her heart beat wildly and she hoped she wasn't blushing. If she didn't go soon, she was scared of what might happen. And she wasn't ready, not quite yet. Though the thought was not unappealing.

'We'll do it again very soon,' said Gregory. 'When I'm less tired.'

And the kiss he gave her was more than just a neighbour's friendly peck, long and lingering, filled with promise.

17

Envy and greed were Netta Silcock's driving forces. She couldn't bear to think she might be missing out on anything someone else had. The merest hint of laughter in the corridor and she was out there snooping, hoping to get in on the act. And the pungent cooking smells from a neighbour's kitchen were sufficient to have her ringing the doorbell on almost any paltry excuse, in the hope she might be invited in to join them. Netta wasn't much cop at cooking but she did like to eat. Living one floor down from the Greeks was enough to keep her salivary glands working overtime, while the nectar that wafted upwards from the Iranians was sometimes almost more than she could bear. In a frenzy of thwarted greed, she could often be found hovering somewhere in the middle, which was how she came to observe so closely the various movements of her nearest neighbours.

The day she happened into the lift and caught Eleni Papadopoulos with Miles Burdett had her hopping up and down like a mad thing and wanting to broadcast it to the building at large. Miles, watching her shrewdly, anticipated her interest and decided to kill all rumours stone dead on the spot.

'Well, thanks a lot,' he said cheerily to Eleni, as he got out on the third floor. 'I'll get the papers drawn up and then you must come down and sign them. Claudia's been nagging me for ages that it's long overdue we had you in for a drink.'

He nodded benevolently, with far more gravitas than he felt, and Eleni, instantly catching on, just laughed.

'He's quite a star, isn't he?' she said dewily to Netta as she pressed the button to descend. 'So clever with money, such an asset as a neighbour. I mean, what do we poor women know about the finer complications of high finance?'

She spread her hands eloquently and put on her little-girl-lost look that never failed to have an effect. Netta listened alertly. If anything mattered more to her than food or scandal it was money. What did this sluttish Greek girl know that might be of use to her? If there was anything going free in the building, then Netta Silcock meant to have some. She got out on the second floor for coffee with Lady Wentworth, and no sooner was she inside the flat than she started to spill the beans.

'Oh yes,' said her gracious hostess calmly. 'Eleni's right, dear Miles is such an asset. He's quite a financial wizard and so very generous with his time. I really don't know what I'd have done without his help these past few years, not since all this awful Lloyd's business started.'

Breeding forbade her to discuss such matters but Netta was not to be so easily diverted. Terrier-like she clung to the subject.

'What exactly is it he does for you?' she asked baldly,

ignoring the older woman's slight frown and the pursing of the lips that should have warned her she was overstepping the mark.

Lady Wentworth took her time answering, fussing with the sugar tongs and straightening the dainty lace traycloth until it was mathematically aligned. Netta coughed to regain her attention.

'What was that, my dear? Oh yes, Miles. He's such a clever investor – part of one of the smarter syndicates, you know – and has sweetly offered to oversee my portfolio and try to improve my investments. Quite out of the goodness of his heart, you understand. Such a dear boy. Just when I was wondering what on earth I was going to do.'

Her hand shook slightly as she handed Netta a delicate Crown Derby cup and saucer. She wasn't going to say any more, for Netta represented trade and was slightly vulgar, but the truth was that Miles Burdett had virtually saved her life. Just as Lloyd's were beginning to press their claims and things were getting financially quite ugly, along he had come with his cheery smile and valiantly offered to sort it all out for her. Nice boy. And all from the goodness of his heart. It was only a pity he hadn't married a more suitable girl. Claudia Burdett was full of nonsense, with her airs and graces. She might fool some but you couldn't pull the wool over eyes as sharp as this old lady's, who had in her youth been lady-in-waiting to Princess Alice of Athlone.

Netta was thoughtful as she took a taxi to Selfridges and ordered the driver to drop her at the main door.

Her eye had been caught in the latest catalogue by an opulent burgundy velour leisure suit with appliquéd gold braiding on the shoulders; just the thing, she thought, for coffee with the neighbours or even one of Olive Fenton's At Homes, should she ever manage to wangle an invitation. The Fentons were people she watched very closely; they had such style. Olive always contrived to look so *soignée*, though secretly Netta found her choice of colours dull. The burgundy suit would look well with her gold calf slippers. She jangled her many bracelets in anticipation and brusquely ordered the driver to extinguish his cigarette.

So Lady Wentworth was into some money-making venture, and it looked as though the Greek girl was in on it too. Netta's shallow grape-green eyes grew speculative. Archie had left his money well invested but she sometimes wished she could have a flutter and make it grow. It was, after all, hers now. Both Archie and Hermione were safely in their graves, so what was to stop her indulging a fantasy while she had the chance? On an impulse, she bought the leisure suit in aquamarine too and rode home in triumph feeling like her idol, the Queen Mother. All she had to do now was get to know Miles better. And the way to a man's pocket, so she had learned, was very often through his wife.

Kate sat with Grace in the garden, under the shade of a vast cedar tree. It was far too long since she had last made this journey but these days her mother lived such an internal life that she seemed scarcely aware of the passing of time. Kate looked into the faded old eyes and wondered just how much of the real world she was still able to comprehend. A constantly recurring memory that came back to haunt her when she was having a guilt attack was of a conversation she had once had with Grace, years ago, when she still had all her faculties. Out walking along the cliffs one afternoon, Kate had asked her mother to tell her the single most terrifying nightmare she could think of, and without hesitation, Grace had replied:

'To be buried alive.'

'Really? Why that?'

'Don't know, but it's something that has obsessed me since childhood. I can't seem to get it out of my head.'

On that light-hearted afternoon, Kate had flippantly promised to see that it never happened.

'The moment you begin to lose your marbles, Ma,' she had said, 'I promise I'll push you downstairs.' Yet here she now was, trapped for the rest of her life in a mind that no longer functioned properly, unable to articulate what she was really feeling, cut off forever from normal everyday intercourse.

Oh, sad was her fate! – in a sportive jest
She hid from her lord in the old oak chest.
It closed with a spring! – and, dreadful doom,
The bride lay clasp'd in her living tomb.

Maybe that was why Grace had so much liked to sing that sepulchral song. Kate could only hope that such morbid fancies had faded from her mother's consciousness along with rational thought.

'Come on,' she said briskly, jumping up. 'Let's take a

little walk around the garden and see what flowers we can find.'

She held out both hands to help her mother rise, and Grace took them trustingly and staggered to her feet. Slowly, with Kate walking backwards and continuing to hold both hands, they circled the beautiful garden, stopping every few yards to look, admire and smell, or sometimes simply for Grace to catch her breath. It was an oddly moving ritual, this walk, which never failed to touch Kate profoundly, the absolute trust the mother put in her daughter's supporting hands; a direct reversal of the learning process when Kate was toddling her own first tentative steps.

On the train back to London, Kate thought about the profundity of life, which somehow brought her back to Gregory's kiss. Something significant had happened between them that night. It was early days yet and she was in no hurry, but feeling was beginning to filter back into her heart. After all these months stifled by the thicket, the sleeping princess was slowly beginning to revive.

Claudia was astonished when she opened the door that night and found Netta standing there, clad in some maroon monstrosity that made her look like Mrs Michelin Man. With nasty gold braiding squiggling over the shoulders as if, with her bulk, she needed to accentuate her width.

'I've brought you your newspaper, dear,' said Netta, smiling hopefully and making no move to go. Under her arm was a clutch of copies of the local free sheet, snatched from the hall in a moment of inspiration, the perfect passport, surely, for gaining admittance to her neighbours' flats. Claudia, who never read it, nonetheless took one weakly, ignoring the other woman's obvious desire to be asked in. Netta, still smiling broadly, was bobbing and ducking, trying to get a good look past her into Claudia's domain. Just as the door was beginning to close – no nicety of manners where Claudia was concerned – Netta's eye fell on a watercolour almost out of sight on the hall wall.

'Oh, what a lovely painting!' she piped, grasping at straws. 'Mind if I pop in a moment, dear? I'm not a great one for art myself but I certainly know what I like.'

Claudia ground her teeth as the great red blob bounced nimbly past her and into the coveted sanctuary of the flat. Once inside, it was clear she had no intention of budging, so Claudia, defeated, gave in with a poor grace and reluctantly offered her a drink. What did it matter, anyway, since Miles was not yet home and showed no sign of imminent arrival. The meal was spoiling, she needed a pick-me-up. Might just as well grit her teeth and get it over with, then, with luck, they wouldn't have to do it again for a while.

The Burdetts' minimalist tastes did not at all appeal to Netta, but she bounded from room to room in her ridiculous gold slippers, exclaiming at everything she came upon until Claudia wanted to shriek.

'You'll have to come upstairs to my place, dear,' said Netta coyly. 'Far more cluttered than yours, I'm afraid, but I've got some good pieces you might like to see.' For the first time ever she was glad of Hermione and those wretched pieces of Meissen porcelain. Her own taste ran to mail-order commemorative plates, but they mingled nicely and she wouldn't expect this cold-eyed young woman to know the difference. Who was she, anyway, but a trumped-up trollop no better than she should be?

'I'm afraid my husband's not home,' said Claudia after a while, glancing at her watch. 'And it very much looks as if he's not coming.'

'Oh dear.' Netta was quite transparent. 'I was rather hoping to catch him for a consultation.'

Claudia stared.

'My investments, you know,' said Netta, lowering her voice. 'I hear from Lady Wentworth that he's an expert on capital growth.' She smiled ingratiatingly and assumed her Marilyn Monroe wide-eyed gaze which cut no ice with her hostess. She looks like Henry the Eighth, thought Claudia savagely. In his best mock-Tudor polyester lounging pyjamas.

'I'll tell him,' she said gravely, rising to her feet to indicate that the audience was over. 'Maybe he'll give you a call. I can't promise, mind, since Miles's business affairs are nothing at all to do with me.'

Too late she realised that Netta would know she was lying, but what the hell. She showed her unwanted guest to the door, then indulged in a secret smirk as soon as she was safely alone. Greed and envy, two of the cardinal sins. Claudia was almost light-hearted as she mashed the potatoes and prepared to eat, knowing full well what Netta was in for. And jolly well serve her right.

If Kate had a problem with her growing feelings for

Gregory, it was Connie, quite overlooked until this moment, as they sat together in Kensington Place, where she was treating them both to a slap-up lunch to celebrate a major sale.

'Not only the table and eight dining chairs,' she exulted, 'but an eighteenth-century walnut tallboy, too, and a carved mahogany sofa. Can you believe it? All I need now is a couple more buyers like her and I'm set for life.'

'What happened to stardom?' asked Kate, amused. 'And the call from *Brookside*?'

'Oh, that old thing. Guess I can fit them both in, should it ever come to it. But being a dealer beats hanging around in draughty rehearsal halls, I can tell you. And it's also more lucrative.'

Today Connie was radiant with happiness, her skin as clear and translucent as porcelain, her eyes as blue-black as Victoria plums, setting off the healthy, milky whites. Kate envied Connie her complexion as well as her figure, displayed to perfection in a lime green body cinched by a scarlet elastic belt. Their starters arrived – grilled goat's cheese salad and celeriac vichyssoise – together with a nice chilled bottle of the house Chardonnay.

'Here's to us, darlin'!' said Connie exuberantly, raising her glass to the restaurant in general. 'Now all we need is a couple of fellas and we're set to conquer the world!'

Oh Lord, here we go. Any minute now and she'd be back to the subject of Gregory, and just at this moment Kate couldn't quite face it. She felt so guilty yet nothing had really happened. Just a simple kiss between good neighbours and what was so spectacular about that? Yet she still couldn't bring herself to mention it.

'Thanks but no thanks,' was all she could mutter, wishing she sounded sincere.

'Not yet, maybe,' said Connie happily, digging in. 'But any minute now, who knows? You can't mourn for ever, it just ain't healthy. I still have great hopes for you, my friend.'

Kate smiled with genuine affection. No one was dearer to her than this funny, zany American, and she'd do anything she could to keep it that way. Friendship, she had learned the hard way, was far more valuable than unreliable love. Treacherous, lying men were thick on the ground; give her the true friendship of a loyal girlfriend any day.

'Say,' said Connie, popping a piece of grilled bruschetta into Kate's mouth, 'what's with the divine Gregory these days? I haven't heard a peep from him in ages.'

Jacintha Hart was with Gregory, that was what, arrived unheralded and all aglow with the thrilling news of her marvellous new plan. She plonked her overnight case in the hall and followed him, chattering, into the kitchen, where he was ineffectually attempting to make Welsh rarebit.

'Wow!' she said, looking around at the mess. 'What on earth have you been doing in here?' Practically every single implement he possessed was piled on the draining board, drying, while the bits and pieces and makings of his lunch were scattered all over the work-top.

'Here, let me,' she said, reaching for the pan, risking her expensive couture silk. 'Better still, why don't I treat us both to a restaurant?'

She was radiant with excitement; seeing her beloved Gregory was always cause for celebration, and Jacintha was up on one of her buying jags, her chequebook red hot in her handbag. But she planned to tread carefully; she needed to wheedle him into the right mood before she sprang her surprise. Clifford didn't even know about it yet; she had thought she'd start by talking to the man in her life who really counted. Right now, however, was hardly the time to do it.

'Sorry,' he said, snatching back the pan with ill-concealed bad grace. 'I'm in the middle of building bookshelves. If only I'd known you were coming.'

I'd have run a mile, was the hidden text, but Jacintha was too smitten to recognise the truth. Even Gregory, normally so placid and accepting, was beginning to have had enough, and felt one of his extended foreign trips coming on. The book on Guernsey was progressing slowly and he could usually find stories to cover in parts of the world that were more far-flung. Just looking at Jacintha now, in her tastefully accessorised little two-piece, with foolish Doris Day stars in her eyes, was enough to make him slip into those vagabond shoes and vamoose. Right now, however, there wasn't a lot he could do but grin and bear it. Fifteen years was a long time, after all, and he wasn't entirely a monster.

'Want to see what I'm doing?' He took her by the hand and led her into the bedroom.

'Wow!' said Jacintha. 'I see what you mean!' The

room was in total chaos, the books all stacked at one end, while the bed had been dragged away from the wall where Gregory was in the process of doing his construction work. Not a particularly professional job, she could see, but certainly serviceable. The whole wall was almost covered with planks of pine balanced on new red bricks.

'Want me to help you?' She loved being useful, particularly around this flat.

Gregory looked doubtfully at her little silk number and shook his head. 'Not dressed like that, but thanks for the offer. I think you'd do better to cut along to Harvey Nicks, and with luck, by the time you return I'll have everything shipshape again.'

He glanced meaningfully at the littered bed and she got the message. If her luck was in and she was a very good girl, who knows . . .

'See you later, sweetie,' she said, blowing him a kiss. She'd buy him something nice in Knightsbridge, spoil him a little. Once her latest little plan came into operation, she could finally see her dreams coming true. ·

'Guess I'll give him a ring,' said Connie, thoughtfully spooning her *crème brûlée*. 'What do you think?'

'Why not?' said Kate uncomfortably, still feeling guilty. He wasn't her property and Connie had equal claims, even if he had kissed her that night and sent her hormones into overdrive. And anyhow, what could she do? If there was more to tell, she'd confide in her friend, but she was horribly scared of looking a fool. It could simply be the product of her imagination. Gregory was a decent sort of guy who'd seen she was upset. Very likely all he was doing was trying to comfort her; she must hang on to that thought and not get carried away. She escaped to the loo and ran cold water over her wrists. The last thing she needed right now was any kind of new emotional trouble, but try telling that to your neglected nether regions. Besides, Connie was so much more glamorous, there really wasn't a contest. She pasted a cheery grin on to her flushed face and went back to the table.

'By the way,' she said casually, as Connie settled the bill, 'do you have Annie Russell's number? I reckon it's time I got a new haircut and smartened up my act.'

Miles laughed when Claudia passed on Netta's message.

'Does she, indeed?' he said speculatively, as Claudia served him burnt stew with a helping of turgid mashed potatoes. His excuse tonight, sincere for once, was Caroline and the roofing problem. He'd found himself detained in Clapham longer than he'd intended. He was dreadfully sorry but he'd forgotten the time and the traffic had been bad. The truth was, Caroline's cooking had always been far superior to Claudia's, and he really hadn't wanted to leave. That, and the welcome sight of her dear face, uncomplicated and undemanding above her faded old cotton skirt and T-shirt, asking nothing more of him than the answers to a few straightforward domestic problems, and perhaps a bit of company for a while.

Claudia, for once, seemed uncaring, eyes bright with malice at the prospect of getting back at the vulgar Scotswoman who these days was her principal bugbear.

She sat across from him, elbows on the table, and listened attentively as he outlined his plan.

'It depends a lot on how much she's willing to part with. Don't want to alarm her, these *nouveau riche* widows are all much the same. Not used to handling money, scared of doing anything very dramatic. Best to tread carefully – softly softly catchee monkey, that sort of thing.'

He'd have to be a little cautious because of her propinquity, but he agreed with Claudia, the prospect was delicious. Snatching sweets from children. And it really couldn't happen to a more deserving person.

'Tell her I'll call on her but it's doubtful there's anything much I can do. Too much work already, not worth my time unless it's a considerable investment.' That always got them; he could just imagine the avaricious gleam in the wee biddy's eye. Combined, of course, with the snobbery angle; sheer bloody basic psychology. If she already knew Lady Wentworth was involved, she'd be led by the nose as meekly as a lamb.

'Probably not rich enough for Lloyd's, but you never know. And these days, for God's sake, who are we to be choosers?'

Hard to tell how much that sort of man might have left; he'd need to look him up in the records. But there weren't any direct heirs, that much he did know, so with luck this old trout would prove fair game. Miles smiled fondly at Claudia and stroked her cheek. If she'd any idea just how close he was to being deeply and totally in the shit, she would not be gazing at him so fondly right now. But luckily he still had his secrets, even from this trusting little wifey.

He stretched and yawned and rose from the table.

'Think I'll hit the sack,' he said. 'It's been a hard day. And you can join me if you play your cards right.' Less exciting than Eleni she might be, but far more dependable. And despite his other extracurricular activities, he did still love her. In his fashion.

18

Ronnie was getting seriously twitchety. It was the opening day of Royal Ascot, and any minute now the car would be here, but Rowena was apparently still nowhere near ready. Which, after all these years of living with her, should no longer come as a surprise.

'Don't fret, darling,' she said as she drifted about the flat in her sweet pea silk wrapper, checking that the guestrooms were suitably tidy, with clean sheets (even if a little crumpled; Mrs Bates's eyesight was not what it had been), empty hangers, towels, bottles of Malvern water, Agatha Christie paperbacks, the lot; and that the spare bathrooms were equipped with soap and sufficient loo paper for the annual invasion of the Barclay-Davenports in force, at least the racing faction. Family they might be but Rowena believed in putting on as good a show as possible, provided it didn't take up too much energy or time.

'Do shake a leg, old dear.' Ronnie was as nervy and on edge as the White Rabbit, his starched collar giving him the customary hell, already uncomfortably hot in his mandatory black wool morning coat and dove grey waistcoat. By some strange quirk of providence, and regardless of any weather patterns that might have held throughout the first six months of the year, Ascot Day usually contrived to fall on the hottest, and therefore least comfortable, day of the sporting calendar even though within the same few days the course very often ended up waterlogged.

'I shan't be a jiff, my darling,' called Rowena from the bedroom, where she was putting on her hat. 'Get the lift, why don't you, and I'll be right there.'

Ronnie stood on the landing, shooting stick propped against his leg, picnic hamper at his feet, together with a case of the best champagne – the Barclay-Davenports' contribution to the day's events. Every year for as long as he could remember they had done Ascot on all four days, joining up with the same gang of perennial returners and between them managing to sink enough bubbly to float the proverbial battleship. Last season, on one day alone, he had totted up the empties, which came to more than fifty in one afternoon; disgraceful really, but what was the point of the thing at all if you weren't going to enjoy it to the full? At least these days he didn't have to do all the driving. Rupert and Dolly were doing the honours today and would be parked outside, blocking the traffic and infuriating the wardens, if Rowena didn't hurry up and get her skates on.

Now she was here, gorgeous in sugar pink with a hat with an eyeveil that was all made up of little white dots, but just as he was holding the lift gate for her the door of number twenty-four burst open and out stepped Eleni, looking like a heavenly slattern in her nightdress, to pick up the papers. Then, of course, it was all kissy-kissy and darling this and darling that and Ronnie was obliged to let the lift go in order not to antagonise any of the downstairs neighbours. Rowena had the knack of turning the slightest encounter into an hour-long marathon; even though she saw the Greek girl almost every day of her life, there still seemed to be an enormous amount of vital information they needed to exchange without delay. Only by re-calling the lift and ostentatiously humping into it the hamper and the shooting stick and the champagne did he eventually manage to snatch her attention and carry her bodily away. Women. Infuriating creatures, bless their hearts, but whatever would we do without 'em?

As the Barclay-Davenports, with a great deal of squawking and guffawing and a flurry of binoculars, folding chairs and other vital props, fluttered through the entrance hall and into the waiting Rolls, Claudia and Miles Burdett followed in their wake, also in their fancy best and, as it happened, headed for the same destination. Claudia looked icily beautiful in a narrow cream Bruce Oldfield outfit, suitably short-skirted, and an understated Italian straw hat, which made Rowena, by contrast, resemble a bridal bouquet.

'I bet they're in the Royal Enclosure,' she hissed as they watched the Rolls glide smoothly away. A basic bitterness in Claudia's character prevented her from ever quite achieving her heart's desire. How ever high she was to fly – socially, professionally, financially – it never seemed to be quite high enough. Claudia Burdett was a discontented woman hiding behind a façade of hauteur. Like a child prematurely deprived of its toys, she wanted too much too soon and was bound, there-fore, never to achieve full satisfaction. She had snatched another woman's husband but today even he was not coming up to scratch. Miles in his morning suit lacked the inborn elegance of a Ronnie Barclay-Davenport and was cheerfully bursting out all over and looking positively Bunterish.

'Look at your hair,' she snapped as they stood on the pavement. 'Where's your comb?'

Miles smiled easily and dragged his fingers ineffectually through his sandy mop.

'Not on me. A gentleman never carries one, don't you know?'

He wandered off to fetch the car, leaving his wife fuming on the step. Somehow, apparently without even trying, Miles often contrived to put her down and, even if he was unaware of it, Claudia was liable to seethe for hours after. She walked slowly along the street towards the corner, clutching her neat little Hermès bag that went so exactly with the Ferragamo pumps, devoutly wishing she had been born with class instead of just marrying it. She had forgotten entirely the menacing tramp who dwelt so permanently in the doorway to the bank and so was rudely startled by a low-pitched wolf whistle right behind her.

Claudia turned and glared but encountered only those impenetrable black eyes as inscrutable as a gorilla's. His head was shaven to a shiny poll and even on this scorching June morning he was huddled into an outsized army greatcoat, buttoned to the neck. Claudia threw him a glance of disdain and was severely shaken when he held her gaze and stared right back. For a second she was unable to avert her eyes, mesmerised and held fast by the man's much stronger will, but then Miles pipped the Porsche's horn beside her and effectively broke the spell. He stepped out of the driving seat and came round to open her door and just as Claudia had folded herself neatly inside, as gracefully, she liked to think, as the Princess of Wales, the tramp leaned forward from where he was squatting and spat viciously in his direction. A great gob of mucus landed accurately on the shiny toe of Miles's shoe, and when he looked up in appalled disgust, he found that those frightening eyes were mocking him, something close to a smile on the twisted, inhuman features.

'Come on, let's get out of here,' muttered Miles hurriedly, as he skipped round the car and back inside. 'Doesn't do to tangle with these fellows. They let them wander and say they're quite harmless, but then some poor blighter goes and gets knifed to death on an underground station. Just for minding his own business, too. Blame it on the jokers in this government. Far too lax with the social services, if you ask me.'

Claudia said nothing, simply handed Miles a tissue with which to wipe his shoe. Something about that man's sheer intensity had frightened her deeply; it would be a long time before she got those penetrating eyes out of her memory.

Netta Silcock would have liked an invitation to Ascot too, but no one ever asked her. It really riled her, since she knew that Archie had once been quite a regular racegoer and even the saintly Hermione had been known, in her time, to like the occasional flutter. Or so they told her. She'd have gone there alone, she had the money, but she didn't know how to arrange it, or even if it was quite the done thing. She thought of asking a friend to accompany her and she'd hire a car and do it in style, but the sad truth was she had no friends, and even her neighbours were inclined to treat her with caution. So instead she turned her abstinence into a virtue as she listened to the ringing laughter from the Barclay-Davenports as they departed.

'Vulgar couple,' she remarked to Heidi. 'Noisy and ill-bred. My poor Archie would have taken me there like a shot, only I've never cared for conspicuous consumption.'

She cast her eyes, the colour of envy, down in mock humility, then narrowed them in malice at the thought of yet another social scene from which she was excluded. She took it out on poor old Heidi instead.

'Your problem,' she said, in her most demure mock-Morningside accent, 'is that you're built like a hamster, all body and no legs. My fashion consultant tells me to make the most of what I've got – great legs and a wonderful white skin, just like Marilyn Monroe, he says.'

She raised her lily-white arms to demonstrate her point, sending her bracelets jangling down to her elbows, as the yellow and orange paisley-patterned silk rippled back to reveal rather more than she intended of her flabby upper arms. But the squat little German woman eyed her with no malice. Crushed by Netta's cruel and pointless attack, she inwardly collapsed, as she did so easily, and worried instead about her own physical shortcomings. Thank heavens, she was thinking despondently, for true friends like Netta who can always be depended on for the truth. Then looked around for a stone under which to hide.

Claudia was standing discontentedly near the grand-stand, bored already with the racing and wishing she could escape from this unruly and overexuberant crowd, when Miles returned, beaming, from placing a bet and told her he had wangled them an invitation into a private box.

'You don't mean it!'

'It's a bloke from Gooda Walker. He owes me a favour or two,' said Miles nonchalantly, but secretly hugely pleased. 'Come along quickly before the next race gets started.'

He congratulated himself on another deft piece of gamesmanship. In one stroke, not only was he able to wipe that disconsolate scowl from his wife's face but also, very likely, be in a position to do a little light can-vassing for business amongst an altogether better-heeled crowd. A networker by nature, Miles did not believe in wasting any time at all. His idea of pure pleasure was an occasion like this where Claudia could trot out her glad rags and be seen while he was sliding his business card into some of the most prestigious pockets on the social scene.

Nice one, Miles. First Lady Wentworth in the bag, then the delectable Eleni toppling on the brink, while today who knew what else might happen. Whistling with sheer satisfaction, he made brief introductions, parked Claudia with his friends in their box, where at least she'd be in her element, and swaggered off to place five hundred each way on the Queen's horse,

Phantom Gold. There were days he felt he couldn't put a foot wrong. This was definitely one of them.

Claudia, tired already of the banal chitchat of her host's wife and her friends, wandered off into the paddock, where she spotted the Barclay-Davenports several yards away and thought about going to join them. At least they looked as though they were having a great deal more fun than she was so far, and judging from the noise they were making in the middle of their jolly throng of friends, the champagne they were drinking so freely was not the first bottle they had quaffed today. She glanced several times across at them, hoping they might see her there and rescue her, but both seemed entirely engrossed in the racing and the ambience, and Claudia was just too buttoned up to make the first move to greet them. Though she knew from years of warm hospitality that she would have been royally and extravagantly welcomed. Where the Barclay-Davenports were concerned, everyone in the world was an instant friend. There were times when Claudia envied them their easy open-handedness and wished she could be more like them.

Eleni Papadopoulos was beginning to weigh more heavily on Miles's conscience than he cared to admit, even to himself. What had started off as a bit of a light-hearted romp, some rumpy-pumpy on the side entirely between the two of them and hurting no one, with perhaps a modest financial gain for Miles somewhere in the future, for the lady maintained an extravagant lifestyle and was clearly loaded, was beginning to occupy a disproportionate amount of his thoughts.

While he worked the turf of Royal Ascot, her image was ever in front of him as he pushed his way between the bevies of chic, long-legged beauties in their designer outfits and extravagant hats, and compared each one unfavourably with her. Quite right, too. Miles was yet to see one penny of her reputed wealth, yet he prided himself on being a fine judge of a thoroughbred woman, and Eleni was about as good as they came. He had a horrible fear he might actually be beginning to fall in love with her, and that was something he certainly wished to avoid. At this particular point in his life, Miles was in sufficient trouble without incurring another involvement of that kind.

Miles's financial dealings were, to say the least, erratic. To put it at its crudest, he was currently alarmingly overextended, and there were commitments and half-promises he had made that not even Claudia – not just his wife but also his PA – knew anything whatsoever about. And that was how he intended things to remain. He was entirely confident it would all come good in the long run. Sailing close to the wind was second nature to Miles; in fact, he had practically invented it, for life without a gamble would be very tame meat indeed. But right now he was in serious danger of biting off slightly more than he could chew. All this dreary business with Lloyd's was dragging on interminably, and even though he had been sure he would soon be out of the wood, right now he found himself blindly and alarmingly wandering round in circles, still stuck firmly in the thicket.

Lady Wentworth and her cautious investments had proved a bit of a lifesaver, as it happened. She still professed herself profoundly grateful for all Miles was doing; the truth was, without her funds at his disposal just when he needed them most, he would have found himself in a bit of a jam. Claudia had no idea, of course. She'd murder him if she ever got even one whiff of it. But with her unfortunate background, that attitude was only to be expected. Her old man had faced ruin and disgrace in quite a major way but he had been a fool and allowed himself to be taken. That, when it came down to it, was where the essence of it lay. Miles, with his Eton and Balliol background, was a great deal more fly than any self-made parvenu. Guts were what was required in this game; guts and stamina combined with nerves of steel. Miles came from a long line of gamblers; dirty dealing was in his blood, though in his circles they preferred to call it market speculation.

Which didn't in the least help his current dilemma over the delectable lovely presently dominating his nocturnal fantasies. There was something about Eleni he couldn't quite fathom; maybe it was simply that she was foreign. On the few occasions he had been inside her flat – entirely above board since they were supposed to be discussing her financial affairs – he had been disconcerted by the number of times the telephone rang and the constant dialogue she had with that old crone in the kitchen, Demeter. Who appeared to have more say in Eleni's affairs than seemed quite proper for a family retainer. All most odd. But sooner or later he'd get to the bottom of it. Miles prided himself on his acuteness and also his way with women. It was really just that this time around, he was skating on ice that was scarcely there at all. If Claudia, heaven forbid, were ever to suss this out, she really would have his guts for garters. And his balls moreover, what was left of them, as earstuds. If there was one thing he knew, it was his missus.

Rather to his surprise, Claudia was in a benevolent mood when Miles completed his second circuit of the enclosure and sheepishly homed to her side. She was engrossed. Nearby, Joan Collins was holding court, wearing a neat little something almost identical to Claudia's though with a big, flowery number on her head that gave Claudia (at least in her own perception) the edge. She was slightly flushed and almost beaming. Rumour was that the Princess of Wales was here, though she hadn't actually seen her yet, and the champagne was finally filtering through to the places that mattered. Miles smiled and patted her on the bum. With the right amount of bubbly inside her, provided it was vintage, Claudia could mellow into something resembling human. Which was probably why he'd married her in the first place, though these days he couldn't honestly remember.

'Isn't that that slightly chilly neighbour of yours, Mater?' Ivo Barclay-Davenport was saying right then, his eyesight slightly blurred after a gruelling five hours in the Ascot sun.

'Probably, darling,' said his mother without turning. 'But if it is, do me a favour and don't breathe a word.'

It was one of those rare moments when Rowena was off duty. The warmest, kindest, most agreeable person in the world, there were occasions like this, really enjoying herself and surrounded by her absolutely favourite people, when she relished a bit of privacy and mentally kicked off her social shoes and just had a good time. She had spotted Claudia hours ago but was ashamed to admit that she had managed to turn a blind eye. Claudia was all very well, poor darling, with that reprobate husband with the saucy eyes, but she was far too uptight and a tad pretentious to be sucked into an intimate group like this, people Rowena truly valued; the sacred inner circle who had been behind her through thick and thin. Including that rogue, her son, and his impossibly pretty new wife, Veronica. Rowena waved her glass at them then waited tipsily for Ronnie to replenish it. Some time in the future, she reminded herself, she'd take a closer look at poor little Claudia Burdett, for something was obviously not quite tickety-boo and normally Rowena had a heart to encompass all the world. But not today. Nor indeed this week. For this was Royal Ascot and Rowena, for once, was inclined to be selfish.

All the way home in the car that afternoon Claudia smiled and hummed softly along with the Eurythmics tape she so much loved. Her hat was thrown on to the rear seat, allowing her hair to blow free, and she'd long ago kicked off the tight and slightly conservative shoes she'd bought mainly for their status value. Miles kept quiet, though he loved to see her in this mellow mood. All in all, it had been a good day. The Queen's horse had romped home at twenty to one; his Gooda Walker colleague had taken him aside to make encouraging sounds; and furthermore, he'd picked up at least a couple of likely contacts in his trek around the enclosure. A day well spent, with, from the look of her, promise of a night to remember to follow. Now all he needed to do was sort out the elusive Greek.

The Rolls was there before them as they swung into Campden Hill Road and tried to make a right into Hornton Street. But the road was blocked. A couple of squad cars were parked at right angles on the corner outside the library, and blue and white police tape effectively sealed off the whole of the front of their block. What on earth . . .? Miles wound down his window but Ronnie Barclay-Davenport was already outside, deep in conversation with a hovering policewoman, coming over now to talk to Miles.

'What's going on?'

'Sorry, old chap, but there seems to be a bit of bother.' Seeing Claudia half asleep, in happy repose in the passenger seat, Ronnie cocked an eyebrow and silently invited Miles to step outside. Which he did. Now that he was free of the confinement of the Porsche, he saw the ambulance pulled up discreetly right in front of the entrance to Kensington Court. And the stretcher-bearers in the process of leaving, their burden covered with a blanket.

Indescribable dread clutched at Miles's heart. Nothing he had anticipated could be remotely as bad as this. Today had been a sunshine day, when everything turned out right. Ronnie saw his ashen pallor and put a comforting hand on his shoulder. These youngsters were all very well with their dash and panache, but insubstantial with it, he'd long been aware of it. Look at

Ivo, look at his other son, Max. Splendid fellows in their way but without the grit of his own generation. After all, they'd missed out on a war. It had to make a difference.

'It's like this, old chap.' He lowered his voice out of deference to Claudia and led Miles several paces away. 'It seems there's been another murder. In Kensington Court this afternoon. While we were all enjoying ourselves at the races.'

Instinctively, Miles shot a look at the doorway of the Arab Bank, now empty.

'Where's the tramp?'

'In custody. Along with the porter. This time, I'm glad to say, the police are taking it seriously.'

19

Poor Heidi Applebaum had been slaughtered in her bed some time that afternoon, as she took her customary nap after lunch. They'd only found her when she'd failed to turn up for supper with her next-door neighbour, and Mrs Adelaide Potter, for once entirely accurate in her suspicions, had summoned the police and insisted they should break in. She lay on her quilted bedspread, poor soul, face down in only her slip and pull-on stockings, and her head had been so badly stoved in that bits of her scalp and brain were spattered like stippling all over her blush-pink walls. There appeared to be no motive. Nothing had been stolen or even disarranged. Whoever had been the perpetrator had acted swiftly and with precision. The silver-tipped swordstick, one of her late husband's few artistic extravagances, that had been taken from the wall in the hall and used as the weapon, still lay on the floor beside the bed. Ingrained with blood and brain tissue, of course, but entirely devoid of fingerprints. She hadn't even had time to grab for the telephone, still securely there on the bedside table, under its crocheted lady. There were no signs at all of a struggle.

The door to her flat had been so heavily barricaded the police were obliged to break it down. There were three Banham locks in a row, all locked, with a sliding brass bolt and a door chain, both still in place.

'Whatever was she so scared of?' asked the patrolman as he took notes. 'At that time of the afternoon in a building this secure?'

'Whatever it was, she was right.' His female colleague was more practical, tight-lipped with horror at what lay before them but unwilling that he should see. In her book emotion spelled weakness and in the force it didn't do to let it show. Not in front of another rookie who might not be trusted to keep his mouth shut.

In the flat next door sat Mrs Adelaide Potter, for once disconcerted and numb with shock, nursing a restorative glass of port. Netta Silcock sat beside her and so did Lady Wentworth, drawing on her reserves of strength after a lifetime's affiliation to the doughty Red Cross.

'I can't believe it's happened,' Netta was repeating, over and over again. 'Right under our noses, mind, with us not hearing a thing.'

Secretly the whole event had given her a kind of vicarious thrill. Excitement had brought a rare flush to her pallid cheeks and the translucent green eyes were bright with a kind of eager horror. Whatever next? Why, only a few hours before the murder she'd been chatting to Heidi just as normal as could be. It only went to show that you never knew what was lurking round the corner.

They'd already been over it endless times, first with

the police and later amongst themselves. Even though both Netta and Adelaide had been home at that time, not a sound had permeated the rock solid Victorian walls, and without Mrs Potter's formidable insistence, poor Heidi would in all likelihood still be lying there in a pool of her own blood. It didn't bear thinking about. Netta gave a theatrical shrug and gathered her cardigan more tightly about her shoulders.

'And her just between us, Adelaide,' she whispered. 'Who's to say it won't be us next?'

The police, though less emotional, were having similar thoughts. After hours of scouring the building for evidence and cross-examining those tenants on the premises at the time, they had drawn a total blank and arrested the porter. Well, taken him into custody to 'help with their inquiries', which to Mrs Potter's mind was the next best thing.

'I never did trust that man,' she said now, darkly, sipping her port and doomfully shaking her head. 'Surly fellow with a great deal too much lip about him. I can't imagine what those dozy directors thought they were about when they hired him. I could have told them all along it would only end in tears.'

And the tramp? Mainly because he had been abusive when the squad cars arrived, the police had scooped him up too for good measure and carted him off to the station, swearing and cursing, together with the sorry cache of stained plastic bags and bits of old sacking that seemed to comprise his worldly goods.

'Quite right, too,' said Mrs Potter, continuing to shake her head and sink her chin grimly into her neck.

'Vermin like that has no place in a respectable street. He ought to be put down like a rabid dog.'

'Was she, er, interfered with?'

'Miles!' shrieked Claudia in disgust. 'Not here. Not in front of our neighbours, please.'

'Well?' It was a perfectly reasonable question, he thought, though frankly who would go to all that trouble just to see to a faded old trout like that, he really didn't know. Still, there was no accounting for taste, and they did say the tramp had been arrested, the one who had spat so disgustingly on his shoe.

'Actually, no,' said Ronnie Barclay-Davenport, who knew the answer. 'And neither, indeed, was poor Amelia, who they now think must have been done in by the same intruder.'

Rowena shuddered. 'Quite dreadful, isn't it?' she said. 'That poor old darling who wouldn't hurt a fly. And after all she'd already been through, too.' Both Burdetts looked at her in surprise. 'Escaping from the Nazis only to end up bludgeoned to death in Kensington.'

This was news to them. Heidi had been so self-effacing they'd scarcely so much as given her a thought. The thing about death was it brought out all these interesting subtexts in people's lives. Claudia, who secretly had foreign blood too, though certainly she would never let on, felt unexpected sympathy for the murdered woman. All these years they had nodded to each other in the lift, yet the only impression Claudia had formed of the little, stoop-shouldered elderly woman was her terrible dress sense and the way she was always dancing attendance on the grim and horrible Mrs Adelaide Potter.

'What about Mrs Potter?' she asked now. 'Why haven't they arrested her?'

Rowena brightened considerably.

'What a spiffing idea, darling. You are clever!' she said in delight. 'Perhaps they'll drag her away and put her in a dungeon, never to darken our doorsteps again. What do you think, should we tip off the police?'

'You could drop them an anonymous note,' said Ronnie, opening more champagne now that the gloom was beginning to dispel. 'Come along, everyone, drink up. We can at least raise a glass to the poor old duck.'

And to Phantom Gold, thought Miles silently, patting his pocket.

'And be glad we're all still here safe and well,' added Rowena.

News of the murder spread like wildfire through the building and also the rest of Kensington, where the local paper had it on the front page in hours. *Phantom Killer Strikes Again*, was the not terribly original headline, and some of the tenants found themselves accosted in the street by a grubby young man in a T-shirt, with a shorthand notebook and bitten fingernails, hopefully seeking out further titbits to add to the editorial he was writing. Amelia's death had been a tragedy, of course, but lack of evidence had helped make it fade more quickly than it should. Nothing had ever been established to form a link with any possible suspect. Somehow the neighbours, and probably also the police, had begun to assume it was just one of those random killings, done by someone with no connection to the victim and therefore impossible to trace.

But this time round things looked a lot more deadly. Not only was the murder itself considerably more gruesome and apparently planned, but once again the police could find no trace of forced entry – or any entry at all, since all the door locks were firmly in place and there was no sign whatever of a struggle. And how had the intruder left without being seen? The first time round had been puzzling enough, but at least there had been the chance he had left via the fire escape and over the roof. This time all the windows were securely locked too. Unless she'd done it herself, which was impossible, the killer really did appear to have vanished into thin air.

'If she'd burned to death it could have been spontaneous combustion,' said Connie helpfully, sitting with Kate in the kitchen as they bolstered themselves with copious glasses of wine.

Both of them were shattered, especially Kate, who'd flown all these miles in order to escape from violence. The great thing about this building, she'd always thought, was its solid walls and total inviolability. Even so, she'd painstakingly each night remembered to lock the mortice lock, slide the bolt and slip the door chain into place, only to find that someone was able apparently to walk through walls. She started to doubt her wisdom, now, in having taken on this expensive sublease.

Connie gave her a hug. She had gleaned enough about Kate's history to deduce what she was thinking. Over the months they'd been friends, bits of her awful past had come seeping out, and Connie was quick to recognise naked fear when she saw it.

'Come on, sugar, chin up. It's not going to happen to either of us, so quit worrying.'

'How can you be so sure? Would you have pinpointed either Heidi or Amelia as victims?'

'Well, not of the physical kind. No, I see what you mean. But there has to be a solution and the police are bound to crack it this time, with so much more evidence to go on. We've all got window locks and enough hardware on the doors to provide ammo for another war. Unless this murderer really can walk through walls, there has to be an obvious solution, and they're bound to find it soon.'

Though she was not convinced, no way. Her hand shook a little as she topped up both their glasses, then followed Kate through the hall and into her spacious living room.

'Maybe he came down the chimney,' said Kate, kneeling on the hearth and trying to squint into the murky darkness above.

'Not in Heidi's flat, he didn't,' said Connie. 'Her fireplaces are all blocked up.'

They drank in silence, gloomily brooding.

'Where's Gregory?' asked Connie suddenly. 'He usually has a theory and the police seem to trust him.'

A dose of that luscious dish from downstairs was just what the doctor ordered. She was preening in front of the mirror when Kate dashed her hopes.

'Not here, I'm afraid. I rather think he must be off on one of his trips. I certainly haven't laid eyes on him for days, not that that means anything very much.'

She hadn't heard him coming or going but that didn't necessarily mean he wasn't there. She was just disappointed he hadn't been in touch. After that magical moment together in his living room, the lingering imprint of his lips on hers, she'd been waiting on tenterhooks for him to follow it up. But there was no way she was going to tell Connie that, at least not yet. Men had let Kate down all her life: Dad by dying too young; Bruno by just being himself; Francis by not loving her enough; Ramon perhaps by loving her too much. She had tried so hard to resist the charms of Gregory but now had to admit she had failed. She longed so much for his warmth and sympathy and hoped upon hope he was not going to reveal himself as just another common or garden rat.

'I wonder why he chose Heidi?' Connie was musing.

'He who?'

Connie stared at her. 'The murderer, clot,' she said. 'Who did you think? What is it we've been talking about all afternoon? Please pay attention.'

Kate laughed. 'I haven't a clue. Amelia either. I'd say because of her china collection, only nothing appears to have been taken.'

'And there's better stuff in the shop, which would also be easier to enter. Maybe he's just working through the building, knocking them off at random.'

'Connie!' Kate was genuinely shocked.

'Well, we have to face up to it, whatever sort of kook is doing it must have some kind of a game plan if this is the way he gets his jollies. With luck, it'll be the Ayatollah next. How's about leaving him a note to point him in the right direction?'

She caught Kate glancing at the clock and took the hint.

'Okay, okay. Just let me knock this back and I'm away. And don't worry, darlin', it ain't going to happen to you. Me neither, I can tell you. I'm far too foxy a lady for that!'

In the end, as usual, it was Digby Fenton who came up trumps, after five gruelling hours at Earls Court police station standing surety for Septimus Woolf. In the early hours of the morning, having sifted what meagre evidence there was over and over again, they grudgingly allowed the porter to go, on Digby's firm assurance that he would not leave town without first informing the police.

'Poor man,' said Olive, serving tea and scrambled eggs at some ungodly hour, 'why on earth would they pick on him? To my mind he's the most responsible and law-abiding person in this building. I don't know what we'd do without him and, if necessary, I'd stand up in a court of law and say that. Yes, I would,' she continued, pulling her hand away when Digby attempted to pat it. 'And please don't patronise me. I know what I know about people and they don't come much better than good old Septimus.'

She glared at her husband from across the kitchen table and sobered his mirth with a glance.

'I know,' he said, aware of how late it was getting. 'Why do you think I've been down there half the night? They were only doing their job. He's the one person with keys to all the flats, and he's only been in the job a relatively short time. Also, there are suspicious blanks in his CV which, even when threatened with possible disgrace, he refused to fill. At least in my hearing.' He passed one hand wearily over his eyes. 'Give me a break, sweetheart. It's at moments like this that I really regret getting involved in running the tenants' association in the first place.'

'Not really?' She allowed him to take her hand and hold on to it. The harsh strip lighting she found so serviceable when cooking was shining on his hair and revealing how grey it was getting. Time was passing; they were no longer young. What was happening in this building was too horrible to contemplate, but at least they still had each other and were safe.

'Come on, darling,' she said, extinguishing the lights and leading the way. 'We'll talk all about it in the morning.'

But as she slid out of her housecoat and finally between the scented sheets, she couldn't help asking: 'Tell me the truth. Who do *you* think did it? You must have some sort of theory.'

This was the man she'd married at twenty, the tycoon, the manager of people, the man of principle; with luck, the Royal Borough's next mayor.

'I haven't the faintest idea,' said Digby frankly. 'That's what really scares me.'

Through lack of evidence, they let the tramp go too, after a couple of nights in the cells and a thorough wash and brush-up. Although Digby had secretly hoped that this salutary lesson might do the trick and persuade him to move on, he noticed that by Monday morning the vagrant had returned to his pitch, plastic bags and bits of sacking and all. In an odd way, Digby found that faintly reassuring. There were, after all, traditions to be observed, and the tramp was turning out to be one of them. It was a bit like the ravens at the Tower of London or the monkeys on Gibraltar. Just as long as they stuck around, things couldn't be as bad as all that.

Naturally, Mrs Adelaide Potter and her cohort – for they were, as Rowena naughtily observed, diminishing by the minute – had a deal to say about the scandalous nature of things when the police could let two potential murderers loose in the community, as bold as you please, without first coming up with any convincing alternative suspect. But on the whole, the residents of Kensington Court had faith in the system and were relieved to have their porter back, if not the tramp. Still, the mystery remained, more enigmatic than ever now that the obvious solution, that of the porter's keys, had been eliminated.

'I don't know,' said Miles the next day. 'If it wasn't the porter – and I'm glad it wasn't – then what precisely do we have to go on? What's the point of all this security if someone can get in as easily as that and murder defenceless old ladies in their beds, right under our noses? I mean, what on earth is this country coming to?'

Claudia, severely frightened, was still brooding on the tramp.

'I can't believe they'd let him go, just like that,' she said. She couldn't get those eyes out of her mind, the way they'd bored into her, the inner knowledge. The way he'd looked at her as if she were naked, the sheer presumption of it all.

'Of course it was him,' she snapped, one hand already on her forehead in anticipation of the headache. 'It has to have been. They should lock him up and throw away the key. So that the rest of us can lie easy in our beds.'

'But he's innocent,' said her husband, mildly surprised at his wife's unaccustomed vehemence, particularly in a matter that did not directly concern her.

'What makes you so sure?'

'Simple. If he weren't he wouldn't still be here. There are plenty of other doorsteps in London he could choose, with better views and better pickings. So what's so special about ours? No, the johnny we're looking for, mark my words, is far more devious than that. I hate to say it but I have a nasty instinct that this is only the beginning.'

She ran to him and he took her in his arms.

'There, there,' he murmured, kissing her hair as he felt her trembling. 'Chin up and let's see you smile. Nothing's going to happen to you. You've got me to protect you, remember?'

20

It was Saturday morning. Kate had just gone wild in the antiques arcade in Church Street and carried home a glorious Lalique glass bowl, palely opalescent and ornamented with blue lovebirds, that she simply could not live another moment without. It was far more expensive than she could possibly afford but love is love and that was that. Since hanging around with Connie she'd developed quite an eye for old glass and Lalique had been one of her impossible favourites from way back, something to yearn after and save for and which, with luck, should prove to be a lifetime's investment, all the while appreciating in value.

'I'll take it back any time you care to bring it in,' said the man in the shop as he wrapped it carefully, and you couldn't say much fairer than that. Provided that rampaging cat with his great swishy tail kept clear of it, it was both a work of art and a nest egg for the future. She carried it home as delicately as a baby and arranged it with care on the Hastings sideboard where the light from the window shot darts of amber and aquamarine right through it.

The phone rang. Kate answered. There was no one

there. It rang again, twenty minutes later. Again, no
one. She cursed and went back to what she was doing.
It rang again five minutes later, and again in another
five. Then on and off, twenty-seven times in all, during
the next hour. She tried dialling 1471 to see if she
could check the caller's number, but whoever it was
was smarter than that. The calls were coming from a
public phone box; that was all she could deduce. She
tried leaving the receiver off but then all she got was
that irritating operator's voice asking her to please
replace her handset. By twelve she was sick of it – it
reminded her too much of the old days and brought
back too many bad memories – so called it a morning
and went round the corner to the Elephant and Castle,
where she found Gregory sitting outside having a beer.
With Connie.

'Hi!' they chorused, as if they were the most established duo in the world, and Connie obligingly moved
along the bench to make room for her beside them.
Kate accepted Gregory's offer of a drink, and when he'd
gone to the bar briefly outlined her reason for flight.
Connie gave her an all-enveloping hug and planted a
kiss on her cheekbone.

'Poor sweetie. I thought you were looking a tad
drawn,' she said, sparkling with obvious happiness,
the unmistakable light of near conquest in her eye.
Kate tried not to notice; it wasn't her business, anyhow.
That intrusive phone had shredded her nerves to the
point where she felt like screaming. Who on earth
could it possibly be? Not *him* again, she hoped. She
rubbed her eyes and massaged her temples ferociously.
Gregory reappeared with her drink and gave her

shoulder a light squeeze as he slid back into his seat the other side of Connie.

Connie told him about the calls, but Kate wasn't keen to dwell upon it. It made her sound incredibly wet, and talking about it only added to her feeling of unease.

'It's really not important,' she said. 'These things happen. Almost certainly just some nutter who has picked on my number at random.'

On this bright, warm morning Connie was wearing white calypso pants with a truncated T-shirt that flaunted her flat, tanned midriff. Lucky girl. Her ankles, in their brief thonged sandals, were equally tanned, and her toenails painted a bold, immaculate scarlet. One of the things Kate envied most about Connie was her ability to put herself together to the very best advantage. Her cheeks were glowing with a tan that could only be fake, and her lustrous black curls showed all the signs of having been recently and expertly raked through to give that entirely natural look. Annie Russell, Kate would bet. The famous, ultra-chic hairdresser's tiny salon was just across the road, tucked down the alley which led to the church. Part of this small, exclusive village Kate was only just beginning to know. Gregory was in his customary workpants and crumpled denim shirt. And he hadn't shaved, which might, or might not, be indicative of something.

'Can't stop long,' said Connie excessively brightly, glancing at her tiny watch almost surreptitiously. 'Gotta get back to the shop. All of a sudden, with the tourists in town, there's an upsurge of business.'

'Good for you.' Out here in the sun, with the beer

and the scent from the window boxes and the comforting hum of conversation from the handful of
lunchtime drinkers, Kate felt a whole lot safer, and also
rather silly. It was absurd to look for menace in every
single occurrence. Since she'd put down her roots in
the heart of upmarket Kensington, she'd probably
never been safer in her life. She smiled at her companions, noticing that Connie's hand lay suspiciously close
to Gregory's. Well, good luck to them. It was none of
her business.

Gregory, however, was looking straight at Kate with
his sleepy, comforting eyes, and she felt a surge of affection for him for being such a reliable pal.

'All right?' he said softly, and she nodded.

'Right,' said Connie positively, banging down her
empty glass with conviction on the table. 'Time to
make a move. Much though I hate to leave you guys, I
gotta shop to run and a living to make. Pop by on the
way back,' she said to Kate, 'and I'll give you a coffee.
And as for you,' nudging Gregory's foot with one gilded
toe, 'I guess I'll see ya around!'

She leapt to her feet, stretched theatrically to give
the world the full benefit of her amazing torso, with its
fine full breasts and tiny waist, then blew them each a
kiss and was off.

'She's marvellous, isn't she?' said Gregory relaxedly,
finishing his beer and reaching for Kate's glass. 'All that
energy and pizzazz. I just don't know where she gets it.'
But the look he directed at Kate was for her alone;
searching and intense, full of understanding and
understatement.

By the time they'd had the second round and a ham

sandwich, and Gregory had gently stroked Kate's arm and lulled her back into feeling secure again, there really wasn't time for coffee with Connie. Kate banged on the shop window and gesticulated, pointed to her watch and mouthed, 'Later,' then hotfooted it back to the flat with renewed enthusiasm to plunge herself into her work. The phone rang. Kate answered it with a snarl. It was Bruno.

'Ho,' he said heavily, at his most pompous. 'What sort of a welcome do you call that?'

Kate was nonplussed. It was six months since she'd heard her brother's voice, and now he was calling out of the blue. And expecting a civil reception? He told her it was the Lord's test match next week and he'd be coming up for the duration.

'I suppose it's all right if I stay with you?' he said, and Kate was lost for any sort of words, let alone an excuse.

'Why not?' was all she could come up with, as she groped in her mind for where he was going to sleep. Oh well. She'd been meaning to get a divan for the dining room so that it could double as a guest room. Now, she supposed, was as good a time as any, though why she was making such a concession for a brother who never reciprocated, she really couldn't say. She put it down to basic cowardice combined with unresolved guilt; an anxious need to prove to herself that she was more family-spirited than her brother. Which was maybe the truth; she really didn't know. All she did know was that Bruno, who had always dominated her, had obviously not lost the habit.

*

Connie, always glad of an excuse to go shopping, joined her on a trip to Peter Jones.

'All this for a brother you can't stand?' she said. 'Sounds pretty suspect to me.'

'It's the truth, though not just for him.' Kate wasn't keen to go into too much detail but she missed a family home and wanted this flat to be more than just a temporary refuge. Somehow, with each new thing she bought, she felt she was building a nest. But a nest, this time, with solid brace-and-belt-built walls, designed to last forever. Never again was the big bad wolf going to get a chance to come huffing and puffing around her establishment; that was for sure.

She bought a serviceable convertible bed that folded easily back into a handsome sofa during the day, in bright cerulean blue that would look wonderful against her coral walls and would also pick up the lovebirds in the Lalique bowl. Connie was impressed.

'You know, hon,' she said in admiration, 'you certainly do have an eye.'

'Well, I'm getting there,' said Kate modestly, more delighted than she cared to admit. All she needed now were matching blue candy-striped sheets and duvet and the room would be complete, as a guest room if not as a dining room. Not just for Bruno, but for anyone else who cared to come to stay. As her fear level diminished, so did her hospitality plans grow. Although she'd been out of touch for a while, there were several good friends in New York City she'd be proud to have as guests any time. Not to mention the new friends she was making, should they ever, for any reason, be in need of a bed.

Over pasta and a glass of wine in the garden of La Familia, at the far end of the King's Road, Connie talked of Gregory, and Kate got the impression she was probing. She stalled. In any other circumstances, Connie would be the one person she confided in, but on this occasion caution made her hesitate. What it boiled down to was quite straightforward: Connie was a darling, so why risk spoiling her happiness by letting on she had any sort of feelings for him herself? Nothing very grown up had passed between them – just a kiss. Not of any significance at all, certainly not to him. In the six months they'd been neighbours, Kate was aware how popular Gregory was. She hadn't seen all of the visiting popsies but there was enough gossip around the building for her to know about them. Still, as her mother might have said, there was probably safety in numbers.

'I'd go for it,' she said to Connie brightly, squeezing her hand.

'I intend to,' said Connie. 'He's far too much my kind of guy to let him get away. I mean to mount a big offensive. Do you think he'll turn tail and run, or what?'

'There's one sure way to find out.'

He'd certainly done it countless times, if all she'd heard from Rowena and Eleni were true, but that was not to say that Connie couldn't win. Not if she set her mind to it, and this was one feisty lady. Kate swallowed a minor twinge of regret and joined enthusiastically in her friend's plans for conquest. By the time they'd paid the bill and left, Kate was halfway to feeling sorry for Gregory.

*

Bruno, having said he'd be arriving too late to eat, turned up at eight expecting a meal. Kate, who had just rinsed off her solitary salad plate and was trying to fit in a few hours' extra work, was hard put to find anything suitable in her fridge. She poured him an interim gin and tonic while she foraged, and Bruno strode importantly back and forth across her kitchen, telling her all about school.

'Will bacon and eggs do?' she asked at last. Bruno grunted. Something more substantial was what he had had in mind; trips to the big city to him represented a bit of a binge. Still, bacon and eggs it would have to be if that was all there was on offer. Pretty poor show, though. He hadn't thought to bring a bottle, or anything at all, so once he'd finished the gin he opened a bottle of Kate's Chianti and went on drinking. She asked him careful questions about the children as she cooked but he wasn't really interested, and settled down instead to read her paper.

'Too bad you haven't got a television,' he grumbled. 'I wanted to watch the late-night replays.'

He was up and off early the next morning in order to get to Lord's in good time for the start of play. The match was going brilliantly well; it looked like being a walkover victory for England, for a change.

'Will you be back for a meal?' Kate found herself asking, but Bruno didn't know. 'Only it would be more convenient if I knew now whether to expect you.'

'Why?' he asked, surprised. 'You're not doing anything else, are you?' Kate could not believe he treated Lindy this casually, but undoubtedly he did. She hated herself for it but found herself trekking off to Safeway the moment he'd gone, just like a regular little *haus-frau*, to replenish her fridge in readiness for a siege. She bought steak, potatoes, whisky and cans of beer; all the things she didn't much care for and rarely stocked. Even though the chances were he'd not come home and the food would be wasted. People like Bruno didn't realise that Kate lived quite a different life. And, fur-thermore, lacked the income to sustain these unbudgeted splurges. He might complain about his schoolmaster's salary; what he didn't realise was that she had no regular income at all. Simply a retainer from the paper, plus commission on any syndication sales she succeeded in making.

When she went into his room to straighten up, she found he hadn't bothered to make the bed and had left yesterday's underpants scrunched up in the middle of the Lalique bowl. So much for that, she thought, leav-ing them where they were. Away went any residual guilt about not seeing more of her brother. Bruno was a boorish pig, plain and simple, who over the years hadn't improved one jot; so-called maturity had merely exacerbated his faults.

Septimus Woolf was sitting in his lodge, tie off, jacket undone, sharing a couple of snifters with Rhodri O'Connor, his opposite number from the other end of the block. Behind them, a fitting counterpart to their conversation, Wimbledon was droning on in muted tones on the black and white portable, contributed as a gesture of magnanimity by the tenants.

'Miserable old sods,' Rhodri had pronounced, as he produced his half of Johnny Walker from a discreet brown bag. 'Ye'd think they'd a coughed up something a little smarter, considering the hours you work, old fella.'

Septimus smiled but made no comment. Television played so small a part in his life that the seven-inch screen was more than sufficient for his needs. And who needed colour for tennis, anyhow?

'Is there any news of the murders?' asked the Irishman, loosening his belt and settling down for a good old-fashioned chinwag. Life had been a great deal chirpier for him since the building had hit the head-lines and the hacks had come crowding round, some of them prepared to give quite substantial back-handers for a tasty bit of gossip.

'Not that I'm aware of,' said Septimus, underplaying his own small involvement in the drama. 'The police are continuing with their inquiries. That's all I can tell you.'

'Sure, and it's a damned strange thing that someone can kill two pairsons, bless their souls, and then walk free without a trace of anything.' Rhodri took a deep swig from the bottle, then wiped the top and handed it to Septimus. Grimacing slightly, Septimus fetched him-self a cup and poured an inch of the liquor which he then topped up with water.

'Indeed,' he said. 'But that's how it is. Though I have my own theories, I don't mind telling you.' He tapped the side of his nose but refused to be drawn.

They were interrupted by stealthy movement in the hall.

'Hang on a moment.' Struggling into his jacket and putting aside his cup, Septimus emerged from the lodge in time to prevent the stranger from entering the lift.

'Good evening, sir,' he said, at his most respectful. 'Can I help you?'

'Oh,' said the stranger casually, from his prosperous air and trace of accent clearly a foreigner. 'I was just on my way up.'

He wore an expensive raincoat, odd at this time of year, and his eyes were shadowed by inscrutable dark glasses which entirely eclipsed his expression. Septimus knew for certain he'd never seen him before, and instinct told him not to trust him. Besides, it was his job to challenge all comers.

'To which flat, if you don't mind my asking, sir?' he said, stepping adroitly in front of the lift to prevent the stranger's entry. 'We are very strictly security-conscious here and I am afraid I will have to announce you.'

The man looked fleetingly annoyed, then thought for a second and turned in his tracks.

'Don't worry,' he said as he walked briskly away. 'It's not important. I'll be back in a while, when I'm certain there's someone home.'

'May I leave them a message? Who shall I say it was that called?'

'No message,' said the stranger, without a backward glance.

'You see,' said Septimus, resuming his seat inside. 'It's just that easy. If I hadn't been here, with my eye on the door, he'd have been straight on past us and up in the lift. Doing who knows what and getting away with it too.'

'So how did he get through the outside door? Without a key or anyone to let him in?'

'You know as well as I do, old son. Rang a couple of bells at random, claiming to have forgotten his key or some such claptrap, and – bingo – they fall for it every time. The same old biddies who make my life hell, yours as well I shouldn't be at all surprised, reading the riot act if I'm ever late with the papers or slow at picking up the rubbish of an evening.'

'Sure, but it's quite criminal,' agreed the Irishman, taking another deep swig. 'I don't know what the world is coming to, indeed I don't, there's so much petty crime around these days. And these benighted old besoms, well.' He paused for effect then spat for emphasis into a convenient pot plant. 'All I can tell you, my good fellow, is that they deserve every single damn thing that's coming to them. And isn't that a fact?'

Amen to that, thought Septimus with amusement, then surprised himself by feeling guilty.

The match, to Bruno's huge enjoyment, had ended with a resounding triumph for the English team. Despite Lara's brilliant batting, the West Indies had ended up being roundly trounced, and Bruno seemed to take it as a personal success. He strutted around the flat, radiating cheerfulness, drinking copious gin and tonics and regaling Kate with stories of old classmates she hadn't heard of in aeons, not since she was a teenager, in fact, but who were obviously as relevant as yesterday's news in her brother's static life.

What had happened to Bruno? she wondered, as she

cooked him the meal he had ordered. He lived in a timewarp from which he had never emerged, an ageing Peter Pan probably afraid to grow up. Painstakingly she baked frozen chips to go with the prime steak he'd requested, with grilled tomatoes and mushrooms on the side and a fresh salad she'd felt she must include, even though she knew he was unlikely to eat it. Vegetables had never been Bruno's thing. It was an old childhood fad, dating from God knows when, which she was fascinated to observe several of his children had also assumed. It was odd what heredity could do. She herself, as a child, had been declared a fussy eater. Now she knew – and her mother, before she lost her marbles, was nice enough to agree – that all it had ever really been was a natural aversion to meat. Kate, by inclination, was a vegetarian, yet here was Bruno gorging the steak down half-cooked and pushing aside the green stuff, just as she'd known he would, as if it were something obscene. Fascinating.

Now what was he on about? Another of those tedious team-mates she had no longer any recollection of having ever known.

'There was a chap there in the Members' Enclosure,' he went on, 'who I could swear I'd met before. Odd sort of cove. Joined our group for a couple of drinks and hovered around the edge of the circle as if he wanted to speak but didn't. Wandered off just as I was going to go up and quiz him. Reckon I know who he was, y'know. One of that bunch of Argies who played against us at Sunningdale, just before the outbreak of the Falklands War.'

While Bruno pondered, mentally Kate yawned.

She'd switched off proper listening long before. This was the Bruno Ashenberry she'd known all these years and heartily abhorred. Third-rate, droning, self-obsessed. Did it never occur to him to think even fleetingly about other people? She toyed with her salad as she dismally watched him demolish the meat, while the talk just went on, and on . . .

'Look,' she said suddenly, rising from her seat and beginning to gather up the plates. 'All right with you if I grab an early night? There's plenty more to eat and drink, just help yourself from the fridge. And I'm sorry I don't have telly yet but there's a perfectly good radio in the other room. And a bath too, if you want one. Will you be staying another night? Only tomorrow I won't be here since I've got to go out at the crack of dawn . . . for a meeting.'

Actually she was doing Bermondsey again with Connie, but who was he to know the difference? She only knew she couldn't bear to spend a single moment more in his company, that was the effect he had on her. Bruno, in full spate, chewed furiously, with bursting veins, to finish his mouthful and speak. At least he had that many manners, though these days nothing would surprise her.

'Can't, unfortunately,' he said, with no irony at all. 'Got to get back to school tomorrow to supervise nets practice in the afternoon. Okay if I leave the keys with the porter chappie? So that I can pick up my stuff at lunchtime?'

'No problem,' said Kate solemnly as she swept the dishes into the kitchen with a lightened heart. He was leaving, he was leaving – that, at the moment, was all that mattered. Provided she stayed away until he was well and truly gone, she felt she could consider this visit a cautious success. They hadn't had words or any major falling-outs. No insults flying, no childish feuds renewed. They had stepped around each other, tippy-toed with a caution not natural to either one of them, but the end result was that they had survived. For which she was sincerely grateful. True, he hadn't asked questions or shown any interest or complimented her on anything. But equally he hadn't been too rude, had liked her cat, had finished his food, and her gin into the bargain. He had stayed two nights, a compliment in itself, and had only told her once that she was putting on weight. As competitions went, it was a bit of a knockout. She could even almost forgive him the incident of the Lalique bowl.

'Sleep well,' she said, with a degree of real affection, as she slipped into her bedroom and closed the door for the night. Poor Lindy, she thought as she nodded off to sleep. But Lindy, when all was said and done, had actually chosen him.

The day had been great, the market successful, and she'd stayed out a whole lot longer than she'd intended. Driving with Connie in the bright, light glory of dawn through deserted streets towards the East End of London, when only the lorries and neurotically early commuters were around, had filled Kate with a soaring of spirit she had not experienced for more years than she cared to count. Being alive was what counted, young and free and unencumbered; travelling through a city she loved with probably her best friend in the world.

'Happy?' asked Connie, perceptive as ever.

'You bet.'

Getting away from Bruno was one thing; being out and about and on the road quite something else. Connie had a long list of things she wanted to hunt for. All Kate cared about was the essence of it all and the chance she might stumble upon some extra gem for her rapidly improving nest.

'Wheee!' she cried exultantly as she watched the dawn light strike bronze flashes off the river.

'You know something?' said Connie fondly, manoeuvring around a juggernaut too big and ponderous for its own good. 'You're an idiot. And, what's more, I love you for it.'

Yes, well. Here she was at a shaming ten minutes to six, sailing back into Kensington Court, clutching to her bosom the five Victorian plates she had salvaged, plus the copper lamps in a plastic bag and the wonderful brass Dutch coffee pot clearly dated 1765, which needed only a bit of sustained polishing to restore it to its former glory. And, oh yes, some time a nifty piece of antique oak on which to display it. They'd seen an eighteenth-century lowboy that would have been just the job, but, alas, Kate's purse could not extend to it.

'Which is probably just as well,' said Connie, ever the sage. 'Else how would you ever justify coming out on the rampage with me again?'

The rest of the day had not been idle, far from it. Kate had helped Connie load the mountain of wonderful bits and pieces of oak furniture they had found in a cache in a street just off the market, and drive slowly back to the shop in Holland Street to unload.

And carry it carefully, piece by piece, into the rear of the premises, where they'd then gone mad, after Connie had parked the van, with vinegar and lemon juice and loads of beeswax and elbow grease, slowly restoring each piece to its original splendour, ready to grace the showroom of Connie's exclusive establishment. A day well spent; Amelia would have approved, and both of them knew it.

Glancing finally at the clock, Kate experienced a chill of conscience.

'Oh Lord,' she said. 'Can it be that late? I really ought to be off; things still to do in the office, you know.' At least Bruno would have been and gone.

'I know,' said Connie, hugging her. 'And you've been such a pal. Far more than the call of duty and all that stuff. Whatever would I have done without you? Go now and we'll meet in the morning. And be sure to soak in a long, leisurely bath. You must have hefted enough today to have sunk two brickies.'

Almost too tired to walk home, yet floating on a cloud of contentment, Kate bowled down Hornton Street, thinking only of that bath and a drink. There was nothing like physical effort to put an edge on an appetite, and she hadn't felt this content in years, certainly since her arrival back in London. She remembered the early days with Francis, moving into the first small flat they'd shared, painting and papering and gathering together furniture, setting up an independent home, away from the creaking old house on the cliffs. Those were happy, carefree days; a mist of regret threatened her eyes and her mood, and she brushed away the memory before it could take a hold. She'd been happy then, happy and uncomplicated, with a golden future stretching ahead with nothing in the world to ruffle it. Francis, the only man she'd truly loved. Why, then, had it all gone so unexpectedly wrong?

'Oh, Miss Ashenberry, one moment.' Septimus Woolf stepped out of his lodge as Kate, aching but cheerful, walked through the hall on her way to that promised wallow. In his hand he held a small white card; she glanced at it as she stepped into the lift and pressed the button for the fifth floor.

What she saw made her eyes start out of her head and her blood run cold. Three thousand miles she had flown, just to be safe from this menace, but all her efforts had been in vain. Ramon Vergara was here, in London, and furthermore he knew where she was living.

21

Miles Burdett could sniff out a potential victim at fifty yards, and now he was on the look-out for another. He'd had his hopes of Amelia, if the truth be told, but had been deprived of his prey by her untimely death. Now things were getting slightly hairy; he hadn't a lot more time to waste. Kate Ashenberry had looked like perfect victim material – soft voice, nervous disposition, a tendency to shyness combined with a total unawareness of her own rare attractiveness. Best of all, she was apparently all alone in the world, with no one older or wiser to advise her. On closer investigation, however, he had decided she didn't really have what it took. Her flat was only rented – from him – and whatever work she did appeared to be freelance. Certainly no heiress here, and Miles was looking for larger game. He was rather afraid it would have to be Netta Silcock after all.

'Well, don't, whatever you do, go inviting her down here,' warned Claudia. She disapproved entirely of her husband's methods but was resigned to letting him play his little games. To a point. The thought of that smug little Scotswoman setting foot in their home ever again set her teeth on edge.

For this visit Miles dressed down; cavalry twill pants, tweed jacket with elbow patches, jaunty yellow cravat and floppy Hugh Grant hairstyle. Just the job, he reckoned, admiring himself in the glass. Trumped-up *nouveaux* like that, who didn't know their arse from their elbow, expected men of substance to dress like country landowners. As a final touch, he folded the *Financial Times* under his arm and went off whistling. Even Claudia was amused. He could be such a clown, her husband, but on the whole an effective one. Provided he retained a little caution and didn't go overstepping the mark. For too many years Claudia had lived the life of a rootless cuckoo; she wasn't having him risk her home now that she finally had one of her own.

Netta was thrilled and flattered when she opened the door. She was wearing wide patio pants that, if she did but know it, served only to accentuate her girth, under one of her floppy, multicoloured shirts. The flat was in apple-pie order, for it had just had a thorough going-over, and there was little Netta ever did to muss it up. Life without Archie was really rather dull. She'd never been able to master the rules of bridge and was tired of watching endless Australian soaps and soaking herself in *Hello!* and *Homes & Gardens*. She needed a bit of something new in her life; and here, miraculously, right on her doorstep it was.

'Come in, come in!' she fussed, with her most ingratiating smile, surreptitiously licking her teeth in case there was lipstick on them. 'Oh, but it's been another bonny wee day. Come in and sit down and let me fetch you something to drink.'

The living room was small and overcrowded, with plump, self-important brocaded chairs and a plethora of small, spindly tables that Miles felt in danger of knocking over. It was rather like a slalom course; he wove his way amongst them carefully to plonk himself on the velvet-covered sofa his hostess was indicating.

'Now what will you be drinking? Campari? Dubonnet? Gin and French? Just say the word and I'm sure I have it,' said Netta magnanimously.

Miles inwardly cringed; it was only half past five and the thought was fairly nauseous, but what the hell. In for a penny and all that, and if he wanted this particular killing, he had to be prepared to make small sacrifices. He asked for a small martini, then realised too late that it almost certainly would not be dry. Ah well. He supposed he'd drunk worse in his student days and survived. Netta disappeared for a full five minutes, then returned smiling coyly with a brass tray bearing her Dubonnet and his disgusting concoction, together with nuts and crisps and bits of things on sticks, enough for a feast. She perched precariously on the arm of a chair, knees crossed provocatively, one high-heeled fluffy mule dangling, and gave him her most seductive of smiles. He was years her junior but people told her she was well preserved. And from what she was beginning to know about Miles, it seemed he was none too particular where he hung his hat.

'I'm sorry it's taken so long,' he started, 'but my wife tells me you might be interested in a little investment. Would that be correct?'

As he talked he was rapidly casing the room and took in with approval the Meissen pieces, together with a whole showcase of Chelsea porcelain, chosen with discrimination and probably worth a small fortune. In the forefront of the room, on the spindly tables, were a couple of cutesy Hummel children and some Copenhagen figurines, on which he was not so keen. But still worth a bob or two if you found the right buyer. Old Archie Silcock had had his own aluminium works oop north and must have been worth a pretty penny by the time he died. Provided this silly bitch hadn't squandered it all. There was a collection of disgustingly kitsch ornamental plates clustered together in the corner of one wall, but Miles averted his eyes from these.

Netta simpered and put on her reading glasses to look more important as she leafed through the box file containing her broker's letters.

'May I?' Miles leaned forward politely and firmly relieved her of the lot. Now that he clearly had her trust, the rest should be pretty much plain sailing.

'You know what?' he said, as he flicked through the file. 'I'd love another of those dynamite martinis.'

What he'd really far rather be doing right now, instead of exchanging sugary platitudes with this insufferable woman with her twee turn of phrase, was seeking out Eleni and giving her the rogering of her life. But she hadn't seemed to be home for days and that weird old woman never answered the phone. Miles was feeling anxious. He hoped the magic wasn't wearing thin. Eleni was an expensive hobby, one he could ill afford, especially now, but it was too late for being sensible and backtracking; he was hooked.

*

With Netta's cheque securely in his pocket, Miles thought he'd pop upstairs and pay a visit to the Barclay-Davenports, just in case. From the life they lived, there must be oodles of loot up there, and at least he knew he would get a decent drink. And there was nothing like striking while the iron was still hot.

'No use approaching us I'm afraid, old chap,' said Ronnie with a laugh. 'We've hardly got two ha'pennies to rub together these days, and what with death duties and inheritance tax, our children look like ending up paupers themselves.'

'Luckily we'll have Max and Ivo to look after us in our dotage,' said Rowena cheerfully. 'Though we don't want to be a burden on them, poor souls. They've got quite enough to worry about as it is, the way they're beginning to breed. Lucy too, now that she's finally settled. It's high time you started a family of your own, my dear, and found out for yourself what it's all about.'

Too late she remembered Caroline and the children. She clapped a hand theatrically over her mouth and rolled those magnificent eyes in mock distress.

'Oh, my dear, what a truly awful thing to say! Me and my big mouth! Do please forgive me and let me freshen your glass. How are the girls these days, anyway? It's a long time since you brought them to see us. They must be quite grown up by now.'

Too right. Two uncomfortable Sunday lunches *en famille* had been more than enough for Claudia. These days the girls were banned from the flat and Miles had to use all his ingenuity thinking up outside treats for them, for the alternate weekends he was allowed to see them. It was a pity, really, for he could not imagine

more loving role models for his children than the warm
and energetic Barclay-Davenports, grandparents incar-
nate. Their hearts were so big and their hospitality so
generous, they had more than enough love to lavish on
all the children in the world, not just their own. Ah
well.

'I must be going,' said Miles. Claudia would be waiting and there was still the chance he'd encounter Eleni,
who must, surely, come home sooner or later, if only to
change her clothes.

'Take care,' said Rowena, accompanying him to the
lift. 'And give that lovely wife of yours my love.' She
still felt slightly guilty about having ignored Claudia at
Ascot.

Jacintha, feeling jubilant, was on her way to London to
share her triumphant news with the blessed Gregory.
Clifford, handled with a subtlety born of many years of
skilful marriage, had raised no objections to her plan
for investing some of her mother's capital in a London
pied à terre, provided she was careful where she looked
and aimed at an area unlikely to depreciate, preferably
in a purpose-built building with effective security.

'No point lumbering yourself with a potential white
elephant,' he said, quite reasonably. 'And if it's to be
unoccupied most of the time, you want to avoid
attracting vandals.'

Yes, yes, she was aware of all that but was smart
enough to know when not to argue. Chelsea or even
Kensington seemed most suitable, and even Clifford
agreed that a mansion block would make the best
sense. A lot of the modern monstrosities they were

sticking up these days were little more than jerry-built rubbish; best to stay with the tried and true, solid, reliable Victorian bricks and mortar. He cautiously offered his assistance and was relieved when she told him firmly she could manage. She, who was always popping up to shop, knew far better than he did her priority areas, within handy reach of Harrods and her Sloane Street hairdresser and, of course, as close as possible to Kensington High Street and Gregory. She was going to enjoy searching; in fact, could hardly wait to get on the scent.

Gregory, only recently disencumbered of his Alice problem, was none too pleased to receive Jacintha's breathy call but crumpled, as he nearly always did, in the face of her determination and agreed she might stay a few days while she made an initial recce of possible purchases. Provided she kept away from his particular patch, he reckoned, this latest harebrained scheme might even end up to his advantage. It would certainly knock dead any future excuses for moving in on him and might prove a suitably engrossing hobby to take up some of the space in her empty head that was usually reserved for him. Or so he hoped. Hampstead might be the best place to start, he pondered; or Islington, which was up and coming, especially so with the recent emergence of the Blairs. Alternatively, Barnes or Putney, with the riverside frontage, might do the job, or even, come to that, Greenwich. As a man of the world and a travel writer to boot, he reckoned it shouldn't be too difficult to edge her in the right direction, as far from comfortable Kensington as he could manage.

He mentioned Jacintha's plan to Miles that night in

the Windsor Castle and a light flashed on in the broker's head, though he was careful to conceal it. He went right home and suggested to Claudia that it was high time they did some entertaining, since they owed the neighbours so much hospitality. She pulled a face. She loathed cooking and was really not at all a social animal, certainly as far as her fellow residents went. But Miles was persuasive and she had to concede he had a point. They did receive a lot of invitations, largely through Miles's indefatigable networking, and sooner or later she supposed they'd have to reciprocate. At least if they made it drinks at six she could settle old debts in one deft throw and then go safely back into seclusion for a while.

So they fixed on a Friday and drew up a list. Definitely the Fentons, Claudia's absolute front-runners, and also the Barclay-Davenports because of their connections. Likewise Lady Wentworth, but emphatically not her cohorts, the nightmarish Mrs Potter with her lethal tongue and the smugly smiling Netta Silcock.

'Yes, I know you've got her in your pocket,' said Claudia, anticipating his resistance, 'which is all the more reason not to see her socially. Business and pleasure really don't mix, you know. You've been telling me that for years. And that dreadful woman is just too pushy for words.' Common was what she really meant but Claudia believed that even the use of the word might tar her with a similar brush. Even with Miles she felt the need to be on her mettle; he had a cruel tongue and could be merciless in his mockery if the mood should ever take him.

Gregory, of course, was a must, and also the hand-some Father Salvoni, always so agreeable and silkily polite.

'If he drinks, that is,' she said as she added the priest's name, but Miles was positive that he probably did.

'What else has life to offer him, poor bastard?' he chuckled. 'It's bad enough that he has to do without the floosies.'

Then there was Lily, and Beatrice of whom Claudia was quite in awe, and that gutsy American actress who was holding the fort for poor dead Amelia. And a cou-ple of other Americans, the Morans, whom Miles knew from Hurlingham and was currently courting. She'd be tempted to ask the porter too, if only he weren't staff.

'I suppose you'll want your girlfriend from the top floor,' said Claudia tartly, giving Miles a momentary start of panic. Claudia was slowly growing curious about Kate and inclined to get to know her better. Though she drew the line at those Greeks which was, Miles thought, probably just as well in the circum-stances. He'd not seen a lot of Eleni recently but this, most definitely, was not the occasion to try to strengthen that relationship.

'I guess that's enough,' said Claudia thoughtfully. 'Champagne and kir, I think, since the weather's so warm, and I'll get the canapés catered.'

'A baker's dozen,' said Miles, totting up. He'd have liked to include the Iranians from next door but one, but knew it was no use mentioning it to Claudia. Besides, their country's customs might well prevent them from being where alcohol was likely to be served. You couldn't be too careful these days.

'I'll get Sylvie to knock out some invitations first thing tomorrow,' said Claudia grandly, and promptly started worrying about what she was going to wear. Not that there was likely to be much competition in this building.

Damn, thought Gregory when he opened the invitation. Just the week Jacintha would be here; he supposed he'd have to let her tag along. Though he really hated the idea of her getting too cosy with any of his neighbours, particularly Connie, who he was just beginning to explore. Still, Gregory had been juggling dates almost as long as he could remember and was now something of a past master at it. To be honest, it was the essence of his *modus vivendi*. Without the extra zest of life on the edge, he sometimes thought he had it in him to become a very dull dog indeed.

Jacintha, needless to say, was ecstatic when she heard the news. She'd not brought anything up from the country, not in any of all those bags, remotely suitable for hobnobbing with Gregory's neighbours, so she postponed her first viewing appointment and rushed instead to Harvey Nichols to see what she could find in the summer sales. And why not, indeed? It was all part of the same overall game plan, getting to know Gregory's nearest and dearest with the long-term purpose of generally infiltrating his life. Gregory gritted his teeth as he sat hunched over his laptop. Letting Jacintha loose in Kensington Court was a little like allowing a cheetah to frolic amongst sheep, but what the hell. If things grew too hot, which they usually did in the end, he could always disappear.

'Who's that rather pretty woman over there,' asked Connie.

'The one with the eyelashes, disguised as a butterfly?'

'The same.'

'Don't know. Someone from Gregory's lurid past, I'd imagine. She certainly looks as though she's about to devour him whole.'

'You don't think it's someone of Claudia's, then? A sister, maybe, or a bosom friend?'

'Not a chance.' Kate didn't want to be unkind but there was nothing whatsoever to link the slender naiad with the silvery laugh to her sallow-skinned hostess, watching her now from across the room with wintry disapproval.

'I think I'll mosey over and take a closer look.' Connie, with her provocative cropped top and smooth brown midriff, was being deliberately casual but she didn't fool Kate. Not for one second.

'Why not?' she said with a grin. 'Go to it! At least you'll be doing a service for Mrs Danvers. That basilisk stare would put Medea to shame!'

Claudia, who hated any sort of competition, was not a happy hostess this particular evening. There were several handsome women gathered together in one small space, and even though it was she who had issued the invitations, there were at least two too many for comfort. If, however, she'd known the true thrust of her husband's devious game plan, she'd have been considerably less sanguine.

'Gregory mentioned you might be in the market for some real estate,' Miles was saying cautiously to Jacintha, once he'd succeeded in detaching her from Gregory. He was showing her the dining room, since she'd been so flatteringly enthusiastic about their minimalist style. 'Only I might be in a position to put something your way. Provided you keep it to yourself for the time being.'

Number seven Kensington Court had been sublet for a couple of years to three noisy nurses from the Cromwell Hospital whose partying and erratic hours were causing quite a ripple amongst the hen coop of the lower floors. Now that he had the leasehold firmly in his possession, Miles was working on getting them evicted. Regular rent had been a useful source of capital in his more affluent days; right now a hefty injection of cash could be just what the doctor ordered. He studied Jacintha with a connoisseur's eye. Expensive clobber, if a little on the fancy side, and jewellery that had cost more than it looked. The haircut, shoes and handbag might make Claudia sneer but what more could you expect from someone who lived in the sticks? But Gregory had mentioned a loaded husband, complaisant in the extreme, who rarely came into town, and from the way she was gobbling Gregory up with her eyes, too close would not be close enough. Besides, Miles was desperate. So far Lady Wentworth's patrician good manners had prevented her asking too many uncomfortable questions, but Netta Silcock possessed no such forbearance; it could now only be a matter of time.

Miles and Jacintha found they understood each

other, and within a matter of minutes the deal was done.

'Mum's the word,' he said with a wink, as they wandered back to join the rest of the guests, and he knew from the excited flicker in her eyes that his secret would be safe with her. What Gregory would say when eventually he found out was another story entirely. But just for now Miles had more pressing worries.

Kate strolled home alone the following night, across the park from an exhibition of avant-garde art at the Serpentine Gallery. It was still quite light and throngs of people paraded along the Broad Walk, having to stay nimble on their feet and keep their wits about them to avoid the hordes of fancy-footing rollerbladers. The sky was streaked with lavender and pink and the surface of the Round Pond was so incredibly still and mirrorlike she paused for a while at the edge of the water to gawp and marvel at the evocative scene.

Her mind was still reeling at the shock of Ramon's card. How on earth had he tracked her down, and where was he now? She was almost too scared to return home in case she found him there, waiting for her. There was a sweet official notice on the railings, asking people to respect the privacy of the family of cygnets, newly hatched, whose father liked to parade them each day across the grass to the safety of the pond, and Kate laughed to herself and reflected that you'd never see a notice like that in New York, no way. Or, come to that, anywhere else in the world. Which meant there was still quite a lot to say for this stuffy old country, despite the hoots and jeers in the popular press about the current state of the economy and the government. Law and order were still effective and people were basically decent; there had to be ways to stop a lunatic like Ramon molesting her. If necessary, she would go to the police.

Lupins and red hot pokers grew informally in the private gardens of Kensington Palace, and on the serenity of the lawn, only feet away from the public concourse, a family of rabbits was boldly grazing, oblivious to the gaze of onlookers. It was evenings like this that restored in Kate a sense of wellbeing and cautious joyfulness; at being at home and once more her own person, in the heart of one of the world's great capitals where she was rapidly beginning to sink new roots. It felt good. She thought once more of that lonely princess, locked in her cage of misplaced destiny, and reflected how far their paths had separated since her first walk through this same piece of ground, alone and despairing at Christmas. Well, Diana might have her bodyguards and policemen but Kate still had her freedom. And now she also had neighbours who really cared about her – Connie, and the wonderful Barclay-Davenports; Eleni and Demeter; Beatrice, Lily, the Fentons and the rest. And Gregory.

The sky was finally fading into a clear, true Prussian blue, and a bright half-moon hung boldly over the Barkers building, now the home of the *Daily Mail*, with its fine glass art deco turrets dominating the High Street in a blaze of amber light. Almost home. Kate dug in her pocket for her keys as she turned the corner by the Town Hall and gazed up affectionately at her own bedroom window, where a lazy cat would be waiting for his supper. In just six months this place had really worked its spell on her and the roots she had already put down were deeper than she realised. Kensington Court, to Kate, spelled harmony, a haven of peace and tranquillity. And safety.

'Are you crazy?' Claudia was screaming at that precise moment. 'You have to be out of your cottonpickin' mind!'

She hurled their pasta plates into the dishwasher and slammed it shut with enough force to break it. Miles turned from rinsing glasses to observe her with mild consternation.

What, dear? said his expression. What wickedly depraved sin have I committed now?

'You can't allow that woman into this block.' Oh, that. He might have known. 'To begin with, what do you suppose Gregory's going to say?'

Aha, the old familiar green-eyed beastie. Miles's bespectacled face broke into a benevolent smile as understanding dawned, and he caught her by the shoulders from behind and nuzzled her neck. Claudia shook him away with irritation.

'In any case, why do you do these things without first discussing them with me? We're supposed to be a partnership.'

'I didn't see any harm in it. Thought she'd be a nice new neighbour for you to shop and lunch with.'

Claudia scowled and swept a cloth across the melamine tabletop as if she were wiping the smirk off his face. She didn't live that sort of life and well he knew it. She *hated* her husband when he was in this mood; playful, almost mocking in that supercilious upper-class way that really got to her. Of which Miles was aware. Having grown up an only child, with a father whose first language was not English, teasing was something she had never got used to, even from her husband in the privacy of her own kitchen.

'Well, it's done now so put it out of your head,' he said with a hint of ice in his voice. 'She wanted it, I needed the dosh; it's done. I can't see what it's got to do with you. Or Gregory either, come to that.' And he picked up the evening paper and left the room, master in his own home.

Beneath the veneer of easy urbanity, however, Miles was a little tense. Gregory *would* mind, of that he had no doubt, and would curse him for a thoughtless, interfering numbskull. And he'd be right. It was just that Jacintha's pansy eyes and open chequebook had got him in his most vulnerable spot, and before he'd had time to think properly, or sober up, the transaction had taken place, with assurances on both sides that all would remain confidential until the vendor was ready to spill the beans. Worse still, even the handsome lump sum now residing, temporarily, in one of Miles's accounts would make hardly a dent in the gigantic overdrafts he had accumulated over the past few years in several City banks. The only mildly good thing was that Claudia, so far, had not the faintest suspicion of just how dire the situation really was. When that happened, well . . . Miles couldn't even begin to imagine such a catastrophe.

What he needed now was a bit of R & R, and he needed it fast.

'Just going out for a while to stretch my legs,' he shouted, then beat it to the corner to call Eleni from a payphone.

He was in luck. This time the sultry Greek voice did answer, and after a pause, she agreed to meet him at the Connaught for a late supper. The fact that he'd already eaten didn't in the slightest bother Miles. Always a trencherman, he was adept at this kind of deception; besides, he had learned the hard way that you didn't pull birds of Eleni's calibre with just a few jars at the local pub. But keeping up this pace of living was not easy and did nothing to assuage the growing strain on his wallet. He eyed Eleni's racehorse legs as she stalked through the bar towards him, followed by every other eye in the room, female as well as male. This was one classy filly; he could only hope her reputed fortune was in equally good nick.

Her mission accomplished with the minimum of effort, there was nothing really to detain Jacintha, so she prepared to go home. She had been suitably vague when Gregory asked questions, so that, with an immense leap of relief, he received the impression that she was cooling on the plan; that her dream of spending more time in London was just another of those ephemeral feminine fantasies. If so, he reckoned he'd got off lightly. He treated her with special care her last couple of nights, inadvertently raising her expectations to a frenzy of desire. Just wait till she told him – but a promise was a promise and the surprise would be that much more magical when all the details were sewn up.

Before she left, she gave the flat a thorough going-over. She cleaned the kitchen from top to bottom and polished the old brass fitments till they shone. She scrubbed the bathroom and replaced the towels with prettier ones, she sorted through the cabinet and finally disposed of the nail varnish and a suspicious-looking bottle of herbal shampoo she hadn't seen before. She took a duster to his brand-new wall of books. She stripped his bed and lugged everything to the launderette; once she was installed in her own place two floors down, there'd be no stopping her. She'd see to his laundry as a matter of course, along with her own, and she'd also replace those curtains and the tatty old bedspread while she was at it. Jacintha, at last, was right in her element. For fifteen years, since that first fateful meeting, she'd dreamed of becoming Gregory's wife. This was nearly the next best thing, and who knew where it might lead?

Finally, when he popped out to file a story, she opened the bedroom closet to sort through his clothes. And that was when she discovered Gregory's little secret.

22

The dark woman seemed to be following her; at least that was how it appeared to Kate. She'd started encountering her on the High Street, on her way to the post office at the end of the afternoon. Always in exactly the same spot, by the Children's Book Centre just before she reached the Earls Court Road, and always walking purposefully, rapidly in the opposite direction. Slim and dark and striking, with overly stylish clothes and neatly bobbed hair, not a lot unlike Kate's own. But taller, more dramatic somehow, not entirely of this time.

'Perhaps she's a ghost,' suggested Connie, who had yet to see her, picking up on Kate's train of thought.

'Perhaps. She certainly looks . . . unusual. With an overstated chic that's no longer fashionable.' That was the best she could do. But it made her uncomfortable. Particularly as something about the woman was distantly familiar.

'How do you mean, *following* you, if she's coming from the opposite direction?'

Kate couldn't really answer that. She just knew the woman was always there, regular as clockwork, and it didn't feel quite right. Connie laughed.

'Honestly, hon, are you sure you're not hallucinating? Too much Internet for too long spells? Too much solitude? Too much gin?'

'No, really.'

'Then lead me to her and I'll unmask her. Connie's here, have no fear!'

'Okay. If you're prepared to do the last-minute five o'clock dash.' Kate usually had mail to send; ten past five was her zero hour if she wanted to be sure of catching the last post. But she knew if Connie came with her that the woman would somehow not be there. She wasn't going barmy; she'd noticed her for weeks now and her routine rarely wavered.

Connie laughed. It sounded suspiciously as though her little friend had a screw working loose.

'You probably need a holiday,' she said kindly, which was almost certainly true. 'Come on, let's go to the gym.'

The woman was tall and very striking, with dramatic make-up and elaborate couture clothes. She always wore high heels and sometimes gloves, and she favoured navy or black for her smart, impeccably cut dresses and suits. They never made direct eye contact but Kate was transfixed by her. Wherever she was headed, striding along so purposefully at precisely fourteen minutes past five, she certainly had a definite destination in mind.

'Maybe she's a female impersonator.' Believe it or not, Kate had already thought of that. It was something to do with the woman's exaggerated femininity; career women today were inclined not to look quite so polished. Her fingernails, when her hands weren't covered, always matched her lipstick exactly, and her shoes matched her bag. Kate was turning into quite an expert.

'Well, next time turn round and try following *her*,' said Connie helpfully. 'Two can play at that game, you know. There has to be some sort of explanation. Probably just some bored Kensington housewife heading towards Barkers for a little light shopping.'

'At that time in the evening?' Besides, she definitely wasn't the Barkers type. Nor was she one of the journalists in and out of Northcliffe House. You could tell that, just looking at her. Kate continued to be intrigued.

Gregory, meanwhile, had given them all the slip again, which to Kate, at least, was something of a relief. He'd left without another word, off on one of his foreign junkets said Septimus Woolf, who made it his business to track the various residents even if he kept the information to himself. Woman trouble, mark my words. For a man who had sworn himself to misogyny, the porter was a surprising expert on the subject.

'It's a lot easier when you don't have to give it a thought,' said Father Salvoni as he moved his rook to block his opponent's queen.

'But can you put it behind you, just like that?' asked Septimus warily, studying the board to see if he could be trapped.

'I did,' said the sloe-eyed Italian quite simply. 'It may be taxing on the spirit to begin with, but with regular prayer, you usually get there in the end. God is merciful.'

'I don't think I have sufficient courage,' said

Septimus sadly, making his decision and leaping in for the kill. 'Check!'

'God will provide,' said the priest as he zapped the porter's king. 'He always does in the end. If you have faith.'

This time she was dressed from head to foot in black, with cherry red fingernails and matching lips. Her tights were pale, glossy ten denier and her sleek hair was freshly set as she bounced along at a rapid pace with all the confidence of a model on the catwalk. Kate, in her usual frantic dash, was as scruffy and dishevelled as ever, but she slowed in her tracks when she saw her and made a rapid decision. Connie was right. Now was the time for action, or else she'd never get to the bottom of this particular mystery and would simply keep on bombarding Connie with wilder and wilder speculations. The mail would keep. There was nothing in there that a day would affect; the time had come for a bit of serious sleuthing.

She spun round, trying not to look too conspicuous, but the woman was already yards ahead of her, arms swinging, pace unaltered, pausing now to cross the road opposite Jaeger. Hoping to look as if she'd forgotten something vital, Kate fell into step behind her, excited now that the chase was on; not expecting any particular revelations but determined to see the game to its conclusion. It might be a sad reflection on the fun factor in her life these days but at least it should be good for an anecdote. Often as good a reason as any.

Past the Chinese emporium she went, past the boarded up C&A. Past Safeway without a second glance then smartly across Campden Hill Road to the corner of Kate's building. For a second she slowed her pace and Kate thought she was heading for the bank, but no, she was fumbling in her chic little bag for keys and – lo and behold – was unlocking a door and disappearing inside. Into Kensington Court itself. At the other end.

It wasn't exactly news but she passed it on to Connie nevertheless. For what it was worth.

'Well, well, well,' said Connie with amusement. 'So she's a neighbour, after all. It's probably she who watches you. Had you thought of that?'

Kate had. That was what it was about the woman that had been bugging her all these weeks, something about her stance. She walked to the window and looked down but the blind was firmly drawn, with no lights showing; it looked as if there was no one home but if so, where had she gone? Kate felt an icy frisson run lightly down her spine.

Horatio hadn't been home for a while; Kate was growing concerned. A wild, free spirit with a life of his own, he was nevertheless inclined to stay fairly close to base, certainly usually within calling distance. But today suppertime came and went – he was always fed on the stroke of six – and there was still no sign of him. Kate paced the flat, calling his name, opening cupboards in case he were trapped inside one. In the end she rang Eleni's bell and caught her, fresh from the bath, preparing for a date.

'Have you seen my cat?' asked Kate, feeling a bit of a fool, the stay-at-home slattern confronting the fairy princess.

'No, darling, but please do come in,' said Eleni, dragging her through the door.

' 'Allo, there!' she called. 'We have visitors, Demeter!' And almost immediately the older woman appeared from the kitchen with a shy smile and placed a plate of Greek savouries in front of Kate.

'What does this cat look like?' asked Eleni, as if the roof of Kensington Court were teeming with wildlife, rubbing her dripping hair with a towel as she walked barefoot around the room. Kate described Horatio and Eleni solemnly translated for the sake of Demeter, who appeared to understand no English. The old woman's wrinkled face expanded in a wide smile as she gabbled away in Greek.

'Ah,' said Eleni, face lightening up, 'she says she sees this pussycat very often.' Demeter was gesturing and nodding her head. 'He comes many times along the ledge and looks in the window.'

They debated a little further, then Demeter shook her head and spread her hands expressively.

'But not tonight. I'm sorry.' Eleni looked genuinely concerned and implored Kate to stay and have a drink with them.

'But you're going out.'

'Ah, pouf,' said Eleni dismissively. No one of any importance, and he would keep for a while.

'Please,' she said, 'sit.' Then hurried from the room to fetch a corkscrew and a bottle of wine.

After half an hour or so of chat, and several glasses of the mellow, fruity wine, Kate managed to break away and urged her generous hostess to get on with her dressing and please not delay her date any further.

Eleni laughed. Her attitude to life and men was obviously considerably more relaxed than Kate's. She worked on the principle that there was always another taxi; if Miles had gone by the time she showed up, no big deal; there'd be someone else to take his place and buy her a drink into the bargain.

When Kate got back to her own flat, slightly tipsy, Horatio was sitting in the middle of the kitchen, giving himself a thorough wash.

'Where did you come from, you bad boy?' scolded Kate, picking him up and noticing as she hugged him that his coat smelled slightly of dust and dankness. But he seemed quite unperturbed, just hungry. She fed him, then went back into the office to do a little after-hours tidying. The door to the big wall cupboard stood ajar; Kate was positive that was not the way she had left it. Her old childhood spook of half-open doors would have prevented that; a cupboard was much like a wardrobe after all. There was no telling what nastiness might be lurking in its depths, waiting to jump out at her. She went to shut it, then saw that a pile of cardboard boxes at the back had toppled over, revealing a small door in the outer wall less than three feet high, which she had never noticed before. That door, too, was slightly ajar.

Intrigued, Kate dropped to her knees and found herself gazing into impenetrable darkness. The door appeared to lead into some sort of tunnel, off to the right, just inside the outer wall of the building, roughly the same height as the door. She found a torch, relic of a previous tenant, and shone it along the tunnel, revealing nothing but dust and rough brickwork with a tangle of ancient copper pipes and cables running along it. Where on earth did it lead? she wondered. All around the building by the look of things, but she wasn't about to crawl along it just to satisfy her curiosity.

Mr Woolf was fascinated by Kate's find. She led him through into the office, where the doors to the cupboard and its small inner sanctum both stood open, and the porter bent his tall, spare frame to peer into the darkness beyond.

'Ah yes,' he said. 'That's the original tunnel that runs right round each floor, carrying the water pipes and electric cables. Someone slim enough,' he glanced thoughtfully at Kate, 'could slide along it and work themselves right round the perimeter of the building. At least, in theory.'

Just thinking about it appalled Kate; solid darkness and all that dust . . . not to mention the spiders. Supposing you got stuck in the wall? Or the next door along, wherever it was situated, turned out to be blocked up? Just thinking about it made her feel quite faint with claustrophobia.

'Does that mean all the flats have similar entry points?' she asked.

He nodded. 'Presumably. Unless they have been blocked up, which seems unlikely, in view of the fact that things occasionally do go wrong and pipes and cables, particularly old one, need repairs.'

'Then the building is not as solidly secure as I thought.'

He laughed.

'Secure enough. How many cat burglars that skinny do you know? And they would have to gain access from the outside first, which is simply not possible. No, don't worry, my dear.' Don't worry your pretty little head. 'You are perfectly safe in Kensington Court. It was built to last and last it has. For almost a century, and still going strong.'

'So what about poor Heidi?' Murdered in her bed by someone who had used neither the windows nor the door. And Amelia? Whose assailant, by the porter's own admittance, had not been spotted leaving the building. 'Do the police know? Has anyone bothered to draw their attention to these tunnels?'

Her tone was sharper than she intended, but Mr Woolf appeared unfazed.

'Good point, Miss Ashenberry,' he said, with his customary grave courtesy. 'I shall not hesitate to make sure they do.'

Beatrice was knackered and wanted only to get home and run herself a long, tepid bath with a whisky on the side. It had been a week of meetings and committees with a delegation of Eurocrats, and now that the weather, belatedly, was finally getting a grip on itself and beginning to shape up for Wimbledon, the streets of central London, The Mall and Birdcage Walk in particular, thronged with tourists so that the homegoing traffic was virtually at a standstill. Beatrice cursed. She rarely took her car to the office but had needed it today for an afternoon meeting south of the river, so now found herself stuck in a stream of scarcely moving motorists in a car that would have been uncomfortably hot were it not for the air conditioning. One perk of her senior-ranking grade maybe; she would far rather have had more flexible hours or fewer papers to lug home at night so that she could revert to the carefree habits of youth and simply hop on the tube at Westminster and be home in twenty minutes. Not that she was old now, mind; barely in her prime, as Lily was forever reminding her, though there were times lately, like today, that she certainly didn't feel it.

There was a sudden spurt in the traffic and she was cheerfully passing the Palace and heading up Birdcage Walk before she remembered that Lily was at a party tonight at the Roof Gardens and she'd said she'd join her. Now she really did curse. The last thing in the world she felt like doing was mingling with a bunch of Lily's arty friends, but she'd given her word. And at least the venue was, for once, acceptable and, best of all, nearby. This balmy summer's evening was the perfect setting for that glorious private garden, built in the thirties on the roof of what used to be Derry and Toms and now privately owned but still leased out for functions like tonight's. Something to do with the Designers' Federation, of which Lily was a founder member. Beatrice would have liked to pop home first and shed the trappings of her formal, governmental weekday persona, but there wasn't time. As it was, once she'd got there and found a place to park, the party would be nearing its end, and she hated to disappoint Lily.

In the lift she tidied her hair and tried hard to psych herself into a party mood, but her heart sank when the doors opened at the top and she found herself facing the sort of mindlessly frothy throng she most of all detested, the design world at its loudest and most pretentious, clustered together in one cavernous art deco room to the ear-blasting sounds of Cotton Club jazz issuing from the rostrum at one end. Oh dear, another night of noise, mayhem and too much to drink. Beatrice steeled herself, lifted a glass of disgusting-looking pink champagne from a passing tray and strode forth in search of Lily.

She eventually ran her to ground, not in the crowded interior with its mindlessly braying hordes, but, as she might have expected, out in the fading sunshine, at the far end of the spacious Spanish garden, seated on a white wrought-iron chair serenely in conversation with one other woman.

'Hi.' Lily raised one slim hand in greeting as Beatrice strode towards her across the grass, and the other woman glanced at her watch, commented on the time and cheerfully relinquished her chair.

'Whoo,' said Beatrice, lolling back, glad to be off her feet and away from that noxious crowd, 'now this really is something like it!'

Lily smiled. 'Isn't it great? At one time I used to be up here all the time, whenever we had a spell of good weather and before the restaurant closed at lunchtime. Did you walk round the other side and see the flamingos? They seem to have been here always, but surely they can't live that long, can they?'

'Don't know,' said Beatrice with her eyes shut, her face tilted back to catch the remainder of the sun. 'Parrots do, so I don't see why not.'

'I'll look it up in my bird book,' said Lily thought-fully. Unlike many people, for whom the intention was sufficient, she always followed through and got things done. Which was partly the secret, Beatrice knew, of her unostentatious but remarkably steady success. Continuing the avian imagery, the Chinese woman was a rare bird of paradise amongst this flock of indiscriminate gabbling geese. Or so Beatrice had always thought, though usually she kept it to herself.

'Come on,' she said, draining her glass, 'let's go. Lovely it may be but I'd sooner be in my own home with my shoes off, enjoying a proper drink with some Mozart on the stereo.'

Lily looked at her with her gentle smile and put a restraining hand on her knee.

'Not so fast,' she said. 'All that will still be there when we get back. How many nights like this do we get in London, and when else are we likely to be here, to enjoy this lovely garden?'

She was right, of course. Beatrice left her chair, but instead of forcing her way back through the thinning crowd within, contented herself with a leisurely stroll around the garden which they still had virtually to themselves. Across the road the spire of St Mary Abbots gleamed golden in the setting sun, and right on cue, the bells began to peal forth their insistent carillon. Beatrice glanced at her watch.

'Thursday,' she said, for that was the night they practised. Someone, a keen amateur bell-ringer, had told her that this was one of the last of the great peals, and it never failed to give her pleasure just hearing the bells ring out, even though it was more years than she cared to remember since she'd last set foot on hallowed ground for other than purely aesthetic reasons. Once, on a flying business trip to Strasbourg, she had heard the bells of the cathedral and recognised immediately that they were computerised, which had impressed her colleagues from the Ministry no end. The benefit, though she hadn't confessed it, of living for so long in the shadow of a great church. It was amazing what trivia a person could pick up in the course of everyday life.

She linked her arm loosely through Lily's and they leaned companionably against the wall, looking out over the High Street towards their own building.

'I hadn't realised,' said Lily, 'that the Gardens were quite so close. Catty-cornered to Kensington Court; all we need is a willow-pattern bridge and we could be home.'

'Now whose flat is that on the corner, the one we are looking right into?' pondered Beatrice.

'Eleni's,' said Lily. 'See, there's her circular window at the end, with the lovely alabaster lamp just inside. And next to her, to the right, is where Kate Ashenberry lives. Look, there's that darling cat of hers out for his evening stroll.'

They laughed as they watched a nonchalant Horatio glide with sinuous tread past Eleni's open windows and round the corner towards the front of the building with its dramatic main pediment.

'I wonder how far afield he actually goes,' said Beatrice, fascinated. 'He was born wild, so theoretically there's nothing to stop him just going on and on. And it's all his territory, since there aren't any other cats in the building. None, at least, with access to the roof.'

But something, some subtle noise undetectable to their human ears above the hum of evening traffic, halted him in his tracks. He stood, one foot still raised, ears cocked like a lemur, then retraced his steps at a more determined pace to disappear out of sight through Kate's living room window.

'Home for supper like a good chap,' said Lily, laughing.

'Come along, blossom,' said Beatrice, tugging gently at her arm. 'That's precisely what we should be doing too, before they chuck us out.'

23

The woman fingering the ornate carving on the oak chest was unusually well turned-out for the average Saturday-morning browser. Connie put aside the gilt gesso brackets she was delicately restoring and pushed through the bead curtain into the shop.

'Sixteen ten,' she said, wiping her fingers on her overall. 'Pretty impressive, huh?' In the months since she'd been working here she had gained considerable knowledge of the antique furniture trade. This particularly splendid piece she had snapped up at a house clearance outside Bath; she had been amazed when she had it dated to find out quite how valuable it was. She drew the woman's attention to the fine detail on the arcaded front and the lozenges at the sides.

'You won't find carving like that outside of a museum. Just imagine, nearly forty years before the birth of Grinling Gibbons. Pretty spectacular, eh?' She was really getting the hang of the sales pitch, too, and found her stage experience a definite asset. 'And pretty indestructible, too. Probably used for storing linen or even something more valuable. It would be a pretty hardy moth or mouse that found its way into a sarcophagus like that. Just try lifting the lid. Impressive, huh?'

The woman ran an immaculate, silk-wrapped fingernail delicately along the carving, then turned with a smile and confessed that she was really only looking. Her voice had an attractive mellifluous lilt; east coast Canadian, reckoned Connie, most probably Montreal or Toronto. She wore beige wool trousers with a narrow Gucci belt and a fine silk shirt under her well-cut blazer. Her hair, which was dark and sleek and enfolded her face like the petals of a poppy, was really brilliantly cut. All right for some, thought Connie. I suppose if you've got it you might just as well flaunt it.

'Actually,' said the woman, 'I'm afraid I'm rather here on false pretences. I was looking for Amelia Rowntree. Is she about?'

Connie paused for a while, gripped by a sudden dread, then held aside the bead curtain and invited the woman to enter.

'Better come inside,' she said. The next part of the dialogue looked like being truly painful but she guessed it had been bound to happen some time. As it turned out, however, the woman had never actually met Amelia. Was out to meet her as a fellow collector.

'I heard about her shop from a friend back home,' she explained, 'and thought I'd look her up while I was passing through.'

The card she fished from her elegant bag just said *Madeleine Kingston*, with an address in Quebec, and she was interested in early English porcelain, in which she'd heard Amelia was something of an expert.

'What a dreadful thing! How exactly did she die?'

she asked with real concern, and Connie, sensing genuine sympathy, put the kettle on and settled down for a bit of a gossip. She missed Amelia exceedingly; it was good, after all this time, to get a chance to talk about her.

'You mean they've never picked up a lead of any sort?' The alert eyes narrowed with interest, and to Connie's surprise, the woman snapped open her bag, took out a slim leatherbound notebook and scrawled something inside. Then she smiled.

'Forgive me,' she said, tucking it away. 'I have such a butterfly brain I have to write things down as they occur. I've just been looking at some Staffordshire dogs round the corner and wanted to record the price while it was still in my mind. Please go on. Did she have no family or anyone to put pressure on the police to sort things out?'

Connie told her all she knew. The closest relative was the second cousin in Weston-super-Mare who would sort out the details of Amelia's estate once the will had passed probate. In the meantime, she was acting as caretaker, both to the shop and also the flat. She sensed a certain heightening of interest in her visitor.

'You have access to the flat?' she said alertly.

'I am living there. Why? Is there a problem?'

Madeleine recrossed her elegant legs and relaxed a little.

'No, no. Please forgive me for what must appear my unseemly curiosity. It was just that my friend back home told me she thought Amelia had a private collection that she rather wanted me to see. Chelsea figures? Does that ring any sort of a bell with you?'

Connie's mind flashed to the glass-fronted cabinet in the sitting room filled with little bits and pieces she'd never particularly liked. Chelsea, that was it. She remembered clearly Amelia's dissertation and had meant some day to take the time to study porcelain properly. The beautiful oak furniture and brass accoutrements that made up most of the shop's main stock filled her with such admiration that she'd really not had time to involve herself in Amelia's other interests. Madeleine was watching her intently, on the brink of saying something but obviously not quite sure. Connie smiled and offered her more tea. Madeleine shook her head.

'*The Girl-in-a-Swing*. Does that ring a bell with you? And is it possible she's got one, perhaps tucked away at home?'

Connie thought fast. The so-called Chelsea toys, she could remember the exact conversation.

'Yes,' she said excitedly, 'I rather think she does.' Then, finding Madeleine's eyes fixed pointedly on her, added: 'Why not come round some time and see them if, you're interested?'

'Do you normally go letting total strangers into your home?' asked Gregory with amusement. Connie was busy dusting and tidying in readiness for Madeleine's visit. She laughed.

'No, of course not, but she's perfectly safe,' she said. 'Just a keen amateur collector, as far as I can make out, and from the way she dresses, probably loaded. There's surely no harm in showing her Amelia's things. Sooner or later old Doodah of Weston-super-Mare is going to have to make some decisions, and it might well be he'll be glad to unload himself of the porcelain collection.' And me from the flat, she couldn't help reflecting, but that was a bridge she had yet to cross. 'Stick around if you don't believe me, and judge for yourself.'

Gregory laughed. He was on his way to the library with an armful of books and had just stopped in to see what Connie was doing later.

'Nothing much, once the collector has been,' said Connie. And agreed to meet him at eight in Arcadia, an atmospheric restaurant just off the High Street beyond Barkers.

Connie was pleased with the way things were developing with Gregory. For a while she had thought him quite unassailable, but lately there had been a definite warming in his manner towards her, and now that the pansy-eyed bimbo appeared to have vamoosed, he seemed to have quite a lot of time on his hands. Long might it last. Apart from a few unsatisfactory one-night stands, Connie's love life had been a veritable desert these last few years, and sometimes she had fears she was never going to fall in love again. Or even in lust. Now she seemed to have hit the jackpot with a vengeance; Gregory Hansen was quite the dishiest man she'd met in a long while, white, Anglo-Saxon, single and straight. And, most extraordinary of all, he lived just upstairs. Which went to show what could happen eventually if only you kept the faith.

'Thanks, Amelia,' she mouthed once he'd gone. She had a warm feeling that the dead woman was really looking out for her. 'I'll not let you down, I promise.'

But the first thing she meant to do was to clear all

those other women out of Gregory Hansen's life. Connie Boyle was not by any means the most exacting of souls, but infidelity was the one thing she would no longer tolerate. She'd been through all kinds of shit in the past with her husband and subsequent males. Life was just too short for messing around, and she still had sufficient pride not to be willing to share.

Back home in Chipping Campden, Jacintha was cooking a special candlelit dinner and dancing a positive jig of delight as she thought about Gregory and their future together. At last, at last; it had even been worth all the waiting. Gregory, she now realised, had always been a bit of a free spirit and had needed the advance into early middle age to sow his wild oats and think about settling down. She thought back to the many times he had hurt her, but in her current mellow mood felt only forgiveness for him. He'd been young, he'd been impetuous, but also impossibly clever. And so good-looking. The first time she'd met him, with his silvery-blond hair and clear, Nordic, ice-blue eyes, she'd thought him the handsomest man she'd ever seen but she realised now that, in a subtle way, he was even better now he had aged a little. Less dramatic, maybe, but definitely more mature, the hair dulled slightly from its original blaze, the eyes as vivid as ever but warmer and far kinder.

She didn't know a lot about his background except that at an early age he'd been hurt in some deep and integral way by his mother, in all probability the main reason he was so reluctant to put down roots and settle down. There'd been a lot he needed to get out of his system, the travelling and all those oats to sow, but lately she'd begun to feel he'd become considerably calmer. People matured at different rates and girls were always that much more precocious than boys. It had been worth hanging on; she saw that now. As an unloved child, he'd also had to learn how to show affection, but now he seemed to be finally getting there, in time to share the best years of his life with her.

The shock of finding all those clothes in his closet had set her back quite a bit, she didn't mind admitting. Just as she had fixed up to move into his building, too. Her first reaction had been hysteria and a strong desire to open the windows and fling the whole lot out. Then common sense had taken over and she'd gone for a long, hot bath instead, with a couple of tranquillisers and a shot of brandy, while she thought about what to do. Fortunately, Gregory had been out of the way or there was no telling how it might all have ended. But she'd calmed herself and finished her tidying, and by the time he'd finally got home, it was to a perfect flat, supper on the table and Jacintha all perfumed and prettied up and completely back to normal.

They had dined in style and drunk quite a lot, then taken an early night together because she was leaving next day. And, after several hours of passionate love-making, when he'd convinced her over and over again that he really did love her, she'd mentioned the clothes, and of course there'd been an explanation. Which only went to show you shouldn't jump to conclusions without first hearing all the details.

'What a silly bunny you are, to be sure,' he said tenderly, as she nestled in his arms. 'Don't you trust me at all? Even after all these years?' And he smoothed her hair and kissed her nose and made love to her all over again.

No, he told her later over a late-night cigarette, there was absolutely no mystery at all. If only she'd thought to ask he'd have explained immediately instead of letting her fret like this. Just a few old things belonging to the boring Alice, the school teacher from Toronto who was forever plaguing him, dumped here last time she was passing through because she had bought a load of new textbooks and didn't want to pay excess baggage. As simple as that.

'She uses me as a sort of depository,' he said with a grin. 'Too bloody mean to leave them in store.' He ran a practised hand over Jacintha's generous breasts and felt her nipples harden with the return of her desire.

'Everything okay now?' he asked a long time later, and was relieved when she simply nodded and curled up to sleep.

Which just went to show how misunderstandings could arise if a couple were apart too often and for too long. It wasn't Gregory's fault if other women ran after him, she saw that now; just one of the crosses he had to bear, as he liked to put it. Besides, as he'd often enough pointed out, he didn't own London and couldn't stop them coming. At that point she'd almost broken her promise to Miles but had stopped herself just in time. Her word was her bond and Miles had things to sort out before they could formally exchange contracts. And, in a way, it simply added to the pleasurable suspense. She had waited long enough; another few weeks could do no harm.

Jacintha sprinkled fresh rosemary over the rack of lamb and gave it a final basting. Tonight, as a celebration, she was wearing black lace, with her strawberry-blonde hair swirled high on top. Clifford didn't know what all the fuss was about but he did approve of the flat acquisition and agreed it sounded a pretty good bargain. For him, that was sufficient. He had no spirit of adventure whatsoever and was grateful to be left in peace to live his life as he liked it. She slipped into the lounge, where he was sitting quietly with his good friends Brian and Sheila, Len and Yvonne, listening to his beloved Mantovani and boring them rigid with his stamp collection. Bless his heart. He was a good man, Clifford, who had always seen her right, and she'd never stop being grateful for that. She didn't want to hurt him, had no intention of doing so, but she had a life to lead too and if she didn't start now, her time would be all used up. Besides, when love beckoned . . .

It was getting dark and the breeze through the open French doors was developing quite a nip.

'All right?'

She switched on a few side lamps and pulled the doors closed to cut out the draught. Sheila, in her serviceable beige, made signs of coming to help her in the kitchen but Jacintha signalled her to stay put. She was almost ready. She lit the taper candles on the dining room table, then carried in the new potatoes and fresh, minted peas. A lovely late summer supper with the people she was closest to. She'd miss it, this peaceful, rural life, if she ever had to give it up completely, but just for now that was not the option. Goodness, she'd not even broken the news to Gregory. She could hardly wait to see his face when she did.

Perhaps a simple gathering like this, with some of his nearest neighbours, would be the way. Lovely Miles Burdett, to whom she owed it all, though she was less sure of his chilly wife, with those coldly accusing eyes. But the rest of the neighbours seemed really friendly and terribly fond of Gregory. She'd think it out over the next few weeks and perhaps make a bit of a splash when the flat was finally ready. There was so much to plan and look forward to, she hardly knew where to start. Luckily Clifford had his stamps and his golf and would scarcely miss her for the periods she was gone. Jacintha surveyed the perfect table and clapped her hands silently in delight. It had been a long, terrible wait all these years, but at last she felt she was really getting there. She slipped out the Mantovani tape and replaced it with Rita Coolidge. That was more like it.

'Come along, everyone,' she cried gaily through the sliding doors. 'Dinner is served. Come and get it!'

Madeleine gave a cursory glance at the Chelsea collection but stopped Connie getting it out, piece by piece, for her to inspect.

'It's far too precious,' she said hastily, 'and might get chipped. We don't want to risk that.'

She seemed more interested in the flat itself and wandered the main room thoughtfully, studying Amelia's pictures and effects, even tapping the plaster in places and rolling back the rug to look at the floorboards. Connie watched her with surprise; what on earth did she think she was up to?

'I'm sorry,' said Madeleine, catching her eye and realising that her behaviour was a little untoward. 'You really must excuse me, but real estate is what I'm in professionally, and I can't seem to lose the habit of prying!' She laughed and gestured towards the bedroom. 'Would you mind awfully if I had a little snoop in there? Talk about a busman's holiday but these wonderful buildings are something else, aren't they just? Did you ever see anything like this back home in the States?'

Only the Dakota. Connie followed her as she cased the joint, enjoying her visitor's enthusiasm, not even minding the invasion of her privacy. Amelia certainly did have some lovely things, scattered around amongst the junk, and in any case, Connie was all too aware she was only there on sufferance herself.

'What about the neighbours?' asked Madeleine thoughtfully, as if she were thinking of making an offer. 'Nice, are they? Do you know them well?'

'Quite well.'

She supplied a quick verbal sketch of the ones on this floor – the upwardly mobile Burdetts, the amiable gay couple at number twelve, the horde of Iranians she hardly knew whose cooking smells permeated the whole building when they were feasting.

'It's a mixed bag,' she said with a smile, 'but a nice one. Friends on every floor, a good community spirit. You feel you'd be amongst kindred spirits if ever there was trouble.'

Which, of course, there had been; in abundance. She told Madeleine about Heidi's murder, which had momentarily slipped her mind. It sounded absurd and heartless but it was true. Connie had barely known the fussy little German woman and was still absorbed in the aftermath of Amelia's death. But thinking of Heidi gave her another idea.

'I tell you what,' she said with sudden inspiration. 'There's a woman upstairs with one or two quite good Meissen pieces, if you're interested.' She'd already been cornered by Netta more than once, keen for any professional tips on the provenance and value of Hermione's legacy. It was not impossible she'd be willing to sell, especially if Madeleine could fork out good money. And, thought Connie, with a flash of cold commercialism, there could also be a nice little commission in it for her. Well, why not? She was a professional dealer now.

Madeleine looked thoughtful and said she'd certainly think about it. 'Netta Silcock, number twenty-one, you said?' and wrote it in her notebook. But yes, she agreed, Connie should make the introduction should it become necessary. It was really only a question of whether she had the time. She asked a few more questions then checked her watch and said she had to go.

'You've been really helpful, thank you so much,' she said. 'I'll take a note of your number, if I may, and maybe call round again for a further chat? In case I decide to follow up on the porcelain,' she added quickly, though Connie had a shrewd suspicion she wasn't nearly as interested as she pretended to be. At least, not in that.

She was tidying up and clearing away the tea things

when her doorbell rang, in three short, sharp bursts, and someone rattled the letterbox urgently. It was Kate.

'You'll never guess who I've just seen,' she said, bursting in. Connie laughed; she loved her friend's impetuosity, she always took life so seriously.

'Who?'

'The phantom follower, the mysterious stranger. In Hornton Street, just leaving this building.'

Connie paused.

'Tall and chic with a haircut to die for?'

Kate nodded. 'The same.'

'And pale beige pants and an Italian shirt? With a purse that must have cost an arm and a leg?'

Again the nod.

Connie paused for effect, then laughed out loud.

'Sorry,' she said, 'there must be some mistake. That was a Canadian porcelain enthusiast, just passing through. I met her in the shop this lunchtime and invited her to pop round later to view Amelia's private collection.'

But Kate wasn't convinced. She shook her head vehemently and stood her ground.

'I'd know her anywhere, that walk, that stance. Those timeless clothes, that glossy patina. The way she has of holding her head.' She was getting quite agitated.

'Calm down,' said Connie, inviting her to sit. 'That was a bona fide transient collector, I promise you. Look, she even gave me her card.' She dug into the pocket of her jeans and flourished it triumphantly. 'She's from Quebec and that's where she's headed back. You've simply mistaken her for someone else.'

Kate shook her head again.

'I don't care what you say,' she said. 'Bona fide collector or not, that woman is the one who has been following me. For weeks, even months. And,' she added, crossing swiftly to the window, 'watching me from the other end of the building.'

Later that evening, Bruno called. He had nothing really to say, no word of thanks for her hospitality, the meals she had provided, even an appreciation of her new apartment. All he wanted to know about was the cat. Horatio had worked his usual magic and Bruno, always an animal lover, had obviously joined the club.

'By the way,' he said, as he was ringing off, 'you remember that Argentinian johnny, the one I saw at Lord's and couldn't quite place? Well, I've just remembered who he was. Found you, did he? I gather from old Plunkett he was asking for your address. Odd he didn't come and talk to me himself, but then I never did much care for the fellow. Slimy sort of beggar; I'd watch out if I were you.'

24

'Damn,' said Madeleine crossly to her colleague. 'I think I may have inadvertently blown our cover.' She patrolled the length of the stark, sparsely furnished room, running nervous fingers through her glossy hair, cursing herself for such deplorable lack of professionalism. And after so many months, so much meticulous research; he watched her passively from his seat in the shadows but offered no comment.

'There's certainly a great deal to see there,' she continued. 'And I may well need the excuse to go back in. Provided my story holds up. *Damn.*'

She cast her mind back briefly to the exuberant American who had fleetingly made her so welcome, with her poise, her enthusiasm, her all-round professionalism. Connie Boyle was a joy to do business with, a far cry from some of the people Madeleine had been forced to tangle with in her brief sojourn in this town. But Connie wasn't the problem.

'I really need to get into that flat upstairs. Via, it would, it seem, a woman with a Meissen collection.' She laughed. Who ever would have believed it, back there at base, after so many years of top-grade tuition and training? There was just no telling where a person was likely to fetch up in this job; at least she couldn't complain that her life lacked variety. But it was the other one who was the problem, the small, dark, suspicious one. Kate.

'I know she saw me. I don't know if she recognised me. And even if she did, does it matter?' That was the crucial question.

She made a few more turns of the room, tugging at her hair. Finally he spoke from his remoteness.

'But did you do it? What you set out to do?'

'Oh yeah. No problems there. Now, theoretically, all we need do is sit back and see what we can pick up.'

If only it were that easy. She wasn't at all sure. And the waiting was beginning to make her feel positively ill.

The tramp was back in his makeshift camp, Mrs Adelaide Potter saw with disapproval as she passed the bank on her way to the chiropodist. It really was disgraceful, the way these things went on in this supposedly respectable part of the so-called Royal Borough. She was heartily sick of lodging complaints, with the landlords, the council, or anyone else who would listen, and getting no return – and furthermore, no thanks – for all the trouble she took as a private citizen on behalf of the community. That Digby Fenton, with the wife with the airs and graces, was no better than he should be. *Councillor* Fenton as he liked to style himself these days, as if he cared a jot about anything more than self-promotion and running for mayor so that he could get his picture in the papers dressed up in all that flummery, with a fancy chauffeured car to drive around in when he should be stopping at home and attending to more important matters on his own doorstep. Like ridding the streets of this filth. She cast a look at the tramp fit to kill but, for once, received in return no more than a benevolent stare. Which for some odd reason made her even crosser; even on a good day, there was just no pleasing Mrs Adelaide Potter.

Two hours later, when she came limping back, he was still there, sunk into his greatcoat and army blanket as secure as a papoose, rolling himself a cigarette between gnarled, nicotine-stained fingers. Mrs Adelaide Potter sniffed loudly as she passed; it was an outrage that scum like that should find the wherewithal to buy tobacco. The porter was standing in the hall, gossiping with the cleaner. Mrs Potter drew to a halt before both of them, giving them a look to set them on their way.

'Have you finished the stairs, Bonita?' she barked, just as if this were a private mansion and she its chatelaine. Then, to the porter: 'If you've nothing better to do with your time, you can fetch me a loaf from Safeway. Plain, white sliced. Marks and Spencers is too expensive.' No offer of payment upfront, he noticed. She always seemed to assume he had money in his pocket, ready to satisfy these sudden whims of hers.

Septimus leaped ahead of her to open the lift gates, and he and Bonita stood in respectful silence, watching her shuffle her way inside like a very much older woman. Then they both broke into wide, silent grins and Bonita stuck her thumbs in her ears and cheerfully waggled her fingers. Mrs Adelaide Bloody Potter kept them both mindlessly entertained for hours, if she did but know it.

'Sour old cow,' remarked Septimus, buttoning his jacket.

'I'm sorry for her,' said the gentle Bonita. 'She's all alone for most of the day, with no one but us to talk to.'

'I'm not surprised.' He was off out of the main front door, glad of an excuse to stretch his legs. Mrs Potter was the absolute bloody limit but inwardly he agreed. Bonita did have a point. He knew too much about solitude himself; it was no fun to be so alone in the world, even if it was your own pure nastiness that had driven people away.

On the fourth floor Mrs Potter encountered Netta, lurking close to the lift, as usual watching the comings and goings of her neighbours. For once the grim old woman was glad to see her obsequious neighbour, and, muttering, permitted her to follow her into the dark, airless flat.

'Disgraceful,' she pronounced as she unpinned her hat. And went off into one of her tirades about the insolence of servants these days and the laxness of the police and social services. Netta, with her eye firmly fixed on the sherry bottle, for once held her tongue and waited to be invited to sit. Archie Silcock in his heyday had far outranked Potter, the dead draper, Netta knew that. But today greed took priority over precedence; besides, she was still a little in awe of her formidable neighbour.

'We have to do something about security in this building,' pronounced Adelaide grimly, once the sherry was poured. 'No one but me seems in the least bit concerned, but if we just do nothing, we may all end up murdered in our beds. It's all very well for those namby-pamby directors to sit back complacently and tell us not to worry, but someone has to take responsibility, otherwise who knows where it all may end.'

It was true. It was hard to conceive of anyone much more harmless than timid little Heidi Applebaum, but look what had happened to her. And poor Amelia also. Quiet, respectable *gentle*women, that was the word. Not like that Greek strumpet upstairs, or the brassy American on the second floor. Or those noisy nurses who kept such irregular hours and had no respect for the privacy of others. Since the board of directors appeared to be so lacking in gumption, Mrs Potter would have to take matters into her own hands. As usual. She gave a weary sigh and allowed Netta to refill her glass. Soon, if Netta were lucky, the old woman would start to feel peckish, and then perhaps she might even be allowed to stay for lunch. Standing in for Heidi wasn't exactly her idea of fun but it did occasionally have its up side.

Digby Fenton had been going to do it in any case, though of course there was no convincing Mrs Potter of that. He called another emergency meeting in the Town Hall to address the tenants one more time on the subject of security. Which, he said, was clearly now of even more vital importance. And this time he had a crime prevention officer from Earls Court police station at his side to emphasise his point.

Olive, seated loyally at the far end of the long table,

silently observed her neighbours and privately assessed each one. Not all of them were there, of course, but as many as possible had been persuaded to turn up, or else had sent a note of apology. They were a mixed bag who never failed to give her secret pleasure, with their attitudes, their bugbears and their funny little mannerisms. Talk about a village under one roof; all kinds were grouped here today, exuding emotions which ranged from anxiety and bewilderment to plain, simple boredom.

Gregory Hansen, for instance, was doodling on his lined pad, occasionally moving his protecting arm to allow a squint to Connie Boyle, sitting so cosily beside him. From time to time she would give a muffled snort and then Digby would focus her with a penetrating gaze and pause for absolute silence before he made his next point. Olive was interested to observe that new connection; from what she could see it was pretty obvious that something was going on between the handsome couple. And why not, indeed? Even she, happily married as she was, got a buzz just talking to Gregory. He was one of the nicest, most sympathetic men she had ever known, and it was long overdue that he found the right girl and thought about settling down. And, by anyone's standards, Connie Boyle was a knock-out. In the years she had known him, Olive had watched a stream of foolish hopefuls sucked like lemmings into Gregory's dynamic slipstream only to be politely but firmly parachuted out on the other side. Women could be very silly, she reflected, especially these days when everyone banged on about equality. What, she pondered, had resulted from the valiant efforts of our grandmothers? There were times when it seemed that their struggling and privations might have been in vain.

On the other side of Connie sat little Kate Ashenberry, dark and intense and taking it all so seriously, ignoring totally the muffled hoots of merriment emanating from that corner of the table. Olive was a little intrigued by Kate, who she still needed to know a lot better. Something was troubling her, it was clear from the solemn eyes, probably something more than just the recent horrors in this building. Her eye travelled on. Ronnie and Rowena Barclay-Davenport, divine pair, were sitting together like the Duke and Duchess of Plaza-Toro, nodding and smiling and tossing words of encouragement to all around them. What absolute pets they were, to be sure. Olive smiled and returned Rowena's wave. Solid gold through and through, both of them; authentic old Kensington to their fingertips and proud of it.

Lady Wentworth came shuffling in late, more arthritic by the day yet still full of dignity and regal bearing. She inclined her head graciously to the assembled company, then sat down next to Olive.

'Quite a turn-out,' she said approvingly. It took a subject as emotive as this to bring the Kensington Court tenants out in quite such force. The old lady's eyes brightened as Miles came hurrying in, his tie all askew, followed by Claudia with scarcely a smile or acknowledgement for anyone. Now what *was* chewing at her? wondered Olive. She still had a soft spot for Miles's wife but there were times when it wasn't easy to remember why. She had so much going for her, after all: beauty, brains, youth and an attractive, attentive husband. Yet her manner could be so offhand at times that Olive had the urge to slap her. One of these days she'd have to get Claudia on her own and try in a gentle way to probe her. If something was making her that unhappy, there had to be a cause. Listen to me, thought Olive with a smile. Trying to be den mother to all and sundry. I must be getting old.

Beatrice had meetings and couldn't make it but Lily came as her stand-in, as still and serene as the flower whose name she bore, and every bit as exquisite. And next to her sat the benevolent Father Salvoni, dark-skinned and rather exotic in his soutane. How utterly charming they looked together, as they smiled and chatted. And how contrary of nature to play such pernicious gender games.

The other seats were occupied by the stately and dignified paterfamilias of the Iranian family, who listened courteously and intently to all that was said but proffered no comment; the polite Japanese Toyota executive, who nodded and smiled at every point that was made; and, seated fiercely in the furthest corner, gnarled hands clasped belligerently about her stick, the overbearing Mrs Adelaide Potter at her darkest and grimmest, wearing one of those hats, and surrounded by empty chairs on the one side and Netta Silcock on the other.

Having sketched the basic reasons for this second meeting and outlined the areas of concern in order of importance, Digby ceded the floor to the crime prevention officer. Diligence at all times was the watchword, they were told. There were certain precautionary steps that should be taken – burglar locks on windows, additional mortice locks on all front doors. Alarm systems in certain cases, though these were less vital in a building like this, provided all outer windows and doors were secured. Gregory raised his hand to tell them that he already had an effective internal system, with hot spots that would detect any unusual movement within his flat, and time switches on his lights for when he was off on one of his trips.

'I travel so much,' he explained, 'I find it wise not to advertise the fact too much.'

Above all, there must be concerted vigilance about who was let into the building.

'Never, at any time,' said Digby, resuming the chair, 'should any of us admit anyone who buzzes over the intercom unless they are known to us and have a definite appointment.'

Someone raised a hand to suggest they install a closed circuit television system, and Digby was able to confirm that this was already under consideration.

'Can we not create a form of Neighbourhood Watch?' suggested Gregory. There were murmurs of assent all round. 'If we all agreed to look out for one another, but in a structured, formalised way, might that not work? Nothing too organised, just an agreement amongst friends.' He glanced round the table, his blue eyes keen, soft fair hair flopping forward like a schoolboy's.

'Absolutely, old boy, I'm with you there,' said Ronnie. 'Like the fire watchers in the war.'

'Oh, what fun!' breathed Rowena in delight, ever on

the alert for an excuse to party. 'And we girls can sit home and cut sandwiches and make tea. Though gin would be more patriotic, don't you think?'

Digby, with a patient sigh, called the meeting to order. He was an exemplary chairman who had held the position for years and justly deserved his probable elevation to the office of Mayor of Kensington and Chelsea; a cinch, thought his long-suffering wife, after keeping this lot in line for so long. What it boiled down to, he wound up, was additional security in the form of locks and alarms, plus a heightened awareness of the possible perils outside. Look out for your neighbour, should be the watchword; he declared the meeting closed.

As they walked back from the Town Hall, Gregory came up between Kate and Connie and linked arms with both of them.

'Chin up, girlies,' he said cheerfully, aware of Kate's preoccupied quietness. 'All very hairy, I know, but if we join forces I'm confident we'll repel all intruders. And provided we have the Ayatollah running scared, we must be doing something right.'

Kate smiled. It was hard to stay too serious in Gregory's company. She glanced at Connie and intercepted the look of pure love she shot him. So that was how it was, already. Well, good for them, and they should pursue their happiness while they could. They were, after all, her two best friends, currently the people she was closest to in the world. Her new family. Any feeling she might have for Gregory herself, she was willing to suppress. It was Connie's turn for a bit of happiness and, in any case, Kate was feeling far too rattled just now to have room in her thoughts for anything else. Survival was her priority; all the black memories had come rushing back and she wasn't at all sure what she was going to do.

'Come on up to my place, guys,' she said spontaneously. 'That is, if you've nothing more important on the agenda. And I'll knock up some spaghetti or something else easy.' She could use a bit of company, and as long as they were there, it would prevent her brooding.

'And we'll all get pie-eyed together,' added Gregory comfortably. 'Sounds pretty good to me. How about you, doll?'

Connie smiled and snuggled against his shoulder. 'Just what I need right now, I'm starving. How about we drop off at my place and pick up a coupla bottles of vino? I've also got some wonderful runny brie that needs eating fast before it melts completely.'

'Five minutes, then. I'll start the water boiling.'

But she guessed from the way they were looking at each other that it might be considerably longer than that. Oh well. They were young, they were happy, they were generous with their affections. And, goodness knows, she had plenty else to occupy her thoughts this night. Kate poured herself a glass of wine and set about organising a meal.

The doors to St Mary Abbots were standing wide open to let in the fine sunny weather when Septimus Woolf, in shirtsleeves and uniform trousers, slipped into a rear pew and bent his head in silent prayer. Father Salvoni was not in evidence this afternoon, for which he was much relieved. He'd bent his friend's ear so often in recent months that he did not want to abuse their closeness by taking too much advantage of the priest's calling. Problems were meant to be sorted out in solitude; it was the Lord's way of stiffening your spine. Life for Septimus in the last six years had been a wasteland of loss and exile with which he was only now beginning to come to terms. Taking this menial job had been a step towards saving his sanity; it was also a supremely effective way of disappearing completely from his former life.

And in some ways he quite enjoyed his new subservient role, amanuensis to a bunch of clucking women, with its attendant benefits of a small, cosy flat and sufficient aggravation to keep his mind moderately occupied during the day and away from the grief and confusion gnawing at him from within. It was only at night, when he sat alone in his lodge with his books and a bottle of whisky, or at moments like this, in congress with his Maker, that he allowed his mind to dwell on the past and all he had thrown away in that one rash, unpremeditated act.

He raised his head from his clasped hands and gazed upwards at the stained-glass window above the altar. With the full glory of the afternoon sunlight blazing through it, it seemed that his Lord was not just listening but pretty nearly visible, and he quaked as he felt Him looking right into his tarnished soul. For several years, after he had fallen, he had abandoned his faith and kept his bitterness out of the house of God. But a lifetime's calling and deep commitment cannot be so easily relinquished. This new refuge, in the shadow of so glorious a church, had proved in the end too much of a draw. Now he was once more a regular worshipper and his heart was that much lighter to know he had at least made peace with his Lord.

But the agony in his soul had not diminished, far from it, and he sensed he was still being tested, driven to the edge as a further tax on his endurance. He had made his penance, surely he had by now, but the pain had not lessened, it still hurt just as much. The church was empty on this slumbering afternoon so that only the tombs and Victorian memorials and perhaps the eye of God watched Septimus sink his head on to his arms and sob.

Anna, oh Anna. Why have you forsaken me?

25

They'd found the Barings trader, Leeson, and now he was in a Frankfurt jail awaiting extradition to either London or Singapore. It was all over the newspapers, with pictures of his loyal wife pleading on his behalf, the innocent pawn crushed by a pitiless system. Miles shuddered slightly and rapidly turned the page. There but for . . . He glanced instinctively at his own loyal wife but she, as usual, was paying no attention, sunk in her habitual early-morning gloom. It would not do. He'd been living too close to the edge for far too long; any minute now, unless he had a stroke of the most colossal luck, his own time might come and it would be Claudia's mugshot out there, plastered all over the tabloids, while he would be the one in the arrow-covered suit, languishing in some prison cell. She'd always lusted after fame and recognition but that, he had a shrewd suspicion, would be going a tad far even for Claudia. So the only alternative was to do something fast; the question was what.

As if on cue, Claudia raised her lovely, disgruntled head and said: 'Oh, I forgot to tell you, Lady Wentworth was up here last night, asking for you.'

In the lift on his way to the office Miles was further

discomfited by a face-to-face confrontation with the dreaded Netta Silcock, off on one of her early-morning pillage sessions, dolled up to the nines in something garish and unsuitable (he tried not to look) and giving him a knowing nod and semi-lascivious wink, just as if they were bosom buddies instead of victim and predator.

'Will I be hearing from you soon, Miles?' she asked coquettishly, almost as if their association were amorous rather than starkly financial, and Miles was forced to smile and prevaricate and let her continue to believe, for as long as he was able, that her money really was safe with him and that any minute now she'd be reaping the benefits of her shrewd investment. Things were hotting up, there was no escaping it, and the latest news from Lloyd's was bleak in the extreme. Drastic action was called for, PDQ, and since he'd already milked his neighbours for about as much as he was likely to get, there was only one avenue left to him.

He called her from the office, remembering this time to wait till after noon, which was when she started taking calls.

'Hello, there – Eleni?'

'Miles, *cheri.*' She sounded deliciously languid and rumpled from sleep, and he could just imagine her lying there, in her pewter satin slip of a nightdress or, better still, nothing at all, her hair a glorious, perfumed tangle on the pillows. What he wouldn't give to be there with her right now . . . but sex for once was not uppermost in his mind; he had matters far more momentous to sort out. He plunged straight in. Could she meet him that night for a spot of late supper, and if so, where would she like to go? Her wish, as always, was his command. A light sweat broke out on his brow as he heard her pondering; this chick had the most expensive tastes he had yet encountered and to give her free choice was courting potential bankruptcy. But needs must when the stakes were as high as this; situations this dicey demanded similarly drastic solutions. And he comforted himself by remembering that it was all good, solid investment.

Eleni was feeling in a holiday mood. The weather was hot and unusually muggy, and something a little on the nautical side had the most appeal. So The Canteen in Chelsea Harbour it was, and Miles was able to breathe more freely and be thankful that she hadn't had her mind set on Cap Ferrat or Monte Carlo. With Eleni you just never knew. But tonight's little piece of financial dallying was crucial; he'd have taken her on a trip down the Amazon if he'd figured that was the only way to crack her.

Claudia was not pleased when he popped his head round her door and let her know, casually, that he wouldn't be dining at home tonight. Something had come up – and here he tipped his head towards the boardroom and gave her an extravagant wink, then withdrew quickly before her secretary left the room and she was able to give him the full third degree. Miles breathed more easily as he slipped away. Just lately the ice he was skating on had become so thin, he might have given Torvill and Dean a tip or two.

Back in Kensington Court, Eleni replaced the receiver, stretched luxuriously and gave her throaty laugh.

'Aha!' she said. 'The sucker is finally on the run.' She told Demeter to run her a bath then made another couple of leisurely calls before she rolled off the bed. Her dalliance with Miles was beginning to bore her; tonight the tedious fool was in for a larger surprise than he'd bargained for.

Downstairs, Connie was preparing for work, reluctantly. It was almost lunchtime and the shop remained closed; poor Amelia would be turning in her grave at such slackness, particularly now, when the market was so torpid.

'Don't go,' said Gregory, still in his bathrobe. The night had been a long, glorious romp; they'd finally made it into the sack and it had certainly been well worth the wait. Connie was padding around with her hair still wet, draped only in a bath towel. She was more in love than she could ever remember being, and still could not believe her luck in having at last snared this heavenly man. And this time it really was for keeps; she felt it in her bones. Just wait till she could get to a telephone and spill the beans to Kate. One of the more delicious aspects of newly fledged love was the sharing, and Kate was such a darling, Connie knew she'd exult in the fact that her friend's luck had finally changed.

'What are you going to do today?' she asked Gregory fondly, as she perched on the edge of his writing table and watched him sort through the mail. Her skin was peachy from the recent massive injection of testosterone and her eyes shone like a child's on a visit to Disneyland. Gregory, slicing open envelopes, witnessed her look of blind adoration and inwardly quailed.

'Nothing much of any interest, I'm afraid. Just an article to finish on last week's trip to Andalusia, then I suppose I really should be doing something about the book.' He reached out a hand and idly stroked her flank, which Connie took as a signal to drop her towel and start all over again. They rolled in ecstatic abandon across the threadbare rug and wound up under the table, rocking it so violently that they risked serious damage to Gregory's precious computer.

'Enough already!' he said eventually, dragging himself reluctantly from between her athletic thighs. 'Unhand me, woman, if you please. I really do have to get back to work.'

'Me too.'

But she continued to lie there provocatively on the rug, limbs splayed, showing him everything she'd got. This time, however, he really was in earnest and she saw from his sudden detachment that his mood had already swung. Connie took the hint. She scrambled to her feet, dropped a kiss on the nape of his neck and went in search of her clothes. He was right really, she supposed; they had all the time in the world and nothing at all to hurry for. Delicious.

'How about tonight, hon?' she asked when she walked back into the room fully dressed, her damp curls beginning to dry beguilingly in frondlike tendrils around her face. Gregory glanced at her abstractedly. The last thing he needed right now was another amorous entanglement, but Connie Boyle was certainly spectacular, in more ways than one. And his for the picking; wait till he told Miles.

'Don't know yet, love,' he said vaguely as he faced his computer. 'Let's see how I get along with this. Call you later. Okay?'

Step by step, that was the way to do it. Nice and easy and don't allow it to get too heavy this time. Though he rather feared he was already too late; he had glimpsed the familiar too avid gleam in her beautiful eyes that inevitably spelled disaster. Why did women always do that? Ruin things before they'd even begun?

Of course she was late, but he was used to that. In a way it was a relief, since it gave him time to think. He sat looking out over the sluggish Thames, sipping his perfect martini and watching the coal barges chugging by and the skittish movements of the early-evening sailors. What a life indeed, if only you had the money. He'd always rather fancied Chelsea Harbour, even though he'd watched it being built and knew his money was far better invested in the solid structure of Kensington Court, which even an earthquake was unlikely to budge. If only he dared to continue living there and hadn't put quite so many dubious eggs in one basket. This place was far more his style, if he were honest. It was Claudia, with her cloudy origins and her inbuilt snobbery, who had directed him to Kensington in the first place, to live in a state of permanent siege amongst people with breeding and inherited wealth who probably looked down their noses at the likes of him. No matter what his schooling might be, or his family's recent pedigree.

Chelsea Harbour was far more his speed, with the same allure that had attracted him to Sydney. If he had to get out in a hurry, which seemed likely, that was where he'd head, with whatever he could salvage, for a brand-new start in a newish country, far enough away for him to be able to relax. No miserable sojourns for Miles Burdett in a dreary foreign slammer, that was for sure. But he was ahead of himself. The game was not yet up, provided he kept his head, and who knew what tonight might bring? His little Greek friend was a lovely lady and, like all her compatriots, clearly loaded. No wonder she'd chosen this faintly nautical setting for tonight's little rendezvous; shipping was in her blood. He respected her for that.

By the time she did arrive, even later than usual, Miles was faintly in his cups, and Eleni was not alone.

'Hi there, sweetie,' she cried with her fruity mellifluence from the doorway, then strode across the crowded restaurant, nodding and fluttering fingers to left and right, followed by a vapour trail of at least three dazzling acolytes, as gorgeous and expensively attired as she was. Miles hadn't known her nearly long enough to realise that Eleni Papadopoulos preferred to hunt in a pack.

'Miles darling,' she said when she finally reached him, wrapping sinuous arms about his unresisting neck. 'Here are Monique and Haldora and Marie-Christine come with me tonight to cheer you up.' She nibbled his ear and ruffled his hair. 'We thought we'd go on later somewhere to dance. I have told them how generous you are.'

Miles glanced in panic at the gathering crowd around him, and four pairs of predatory eyes returned his gaze.

'But first, *mon cher*, we are feeling a tiny bit peckish. What a great place to have a snack, don't you think, *mes amies*?' And she grabbed the menu and began ordering almost too fast for the dazzled waiter.

Jacintha, at least, was not about to renege on Miles. That was one consolation to keep him going at this most difficult of times, though he did still feel a trifle guilty at keeping his secret from Gregory. The nurses had been effectively dispatched, and the flat given a thorough going-over by a benevolent local painter and decorator. The cheque had been presented and banked, though not in an existing account where it would have been instantly swallowed into the maw of the vast and reckless overdrafts Miles had now incurred.

Once the immediate need for secrecy was dispensed with – Miles had acted swiftly before they'd had recourse to a rent tribunal – Jacintha had decided she rather liked the idea of putting one over on her long-time inamorata. She wanted to make things as perfect as possible, to put the final touches to the fantasy love nest before she spilled the beans and let Gregory into her wonderful surprise. It wasn't easy to achieve but Jacintha managed. By keeping a close check on his professional movements, she knew when the coast was likely to be clear, and would scurry up to town for a few days' fast activity while he was safely out of the way. Occasionally she would bump into another resident, but either they'd never seen her before or they simply failed to connect. Or they just weren't interested, which was mainly the case. The only person, other than Miles, who really sussed out the score was the porter, but he certainly wasn't saying anything. Not his business what the residents got up to; furthermore, more than his job was worth.

Jacintha wrought a total transformation on the formerly cramped and badly decorated flat. By the time her practised hand had had its way, number seven was fast becoming a worthy candidate for a magazine spread. She thought of contacting one of the glossies or even the ubiquitous *Hello!* but decided against it because of the luck factor. And in any case, she was wary of raising her husband's suspicions. As long as he believed it to be nothing more than a convenient overnight stopping-off place for Jacintha when she wanted to shop, he was not likely to come and stick his nose in. Clifford was very much a countryman, whose dislike of the big city increased as he got older.

What enormous fun it was. Jacintha shopped to her heart's content and, as her masterpiece neared completion, happily envisaged the culmination of fifteen years of hopeless dreaming. Olive Fenton knew the score, of course, since Digby was chairman of the board of directors, but nothing would have induced her to share this knowledge with Gregory or, indeed, anybody else. Digby found the situation amusing but that was men for you. Olive was far shrewder and anticipated trouble. What right had this foolish, featherbrained woman to meddle in Gregory's affairs or invade his territory in quite so intrusive a manner? All that could possibly come of it was tears; Olive fervently hoped she wouldn't be in the line of fire when the shit did eventually hit the fan.

*

These days Connie was positively lyrical in her new-found love. Kate could not have been happier for her, yet feared she might be moving too fast and hoping for more than Gregory was yet prepared to offer. Her own experience of impetuous romance had ended bitterly; she would do anything within her power to protect her friend from a similar disaster. Yet really there was no comparison between the two cases. Ramon and Gregory could not be further apart in temperament while Connie was certainly a lot more streetwise than Kate had ever been, especially at twenty-five. The wild Argentinian had been moody and unpredictable, with a firecracker Latin temper and the shortest possible fuse, while Gregory was far more even-keeled, calm and well balanced, infinitely wise and dear. An observer, a philosopher; the best possible of friends. Her heart swelled with love for both of them.

'What will happen when Amelia's estate is settled?' she asked cautiously, not wishing to throw any kind of a dampener on Connie's bubbling happiness. But there was no chance of that.

'I guess I'll move in with Greg,' she said confidently. 'There's plenty of room once we've done a little re-arranging.'

These days she was constantly on the move, up and down the stairs between the two flats.

'It's a pity the flat isn't actually mine,' she said. 'Or we could knock a hole in the ceiling and convert it to a duplex.'

'A spiral staircase, that's what you need.'

Perhaps when things were finally settled, Connie would get a chance to purchase Amelia's lease. Though how she'd afford it was another matter entirely. She didn't have that sort of money and could see no prospect of ever being able to raise it. Being an actress wasn't sufficiently secure, and her stint in the shop was also only temporary.

'Greg'll know what to do,' she said comfortably, making Kate's flesh prickle with apprehension. 'I guess he's pretty well heeled. I know the paper pays him well.'

Bold words indeed so early in the relationship, but it wasn't for Kate to comment. She was far too nice even to speculate why Gregory had eluded marriage so long. Or to ask impertinent questions on the subject of commitment. He was away just now, on a flying visit to Goa, but Connie seemed to have his life well in hand, taking care of his day-to-day shopping and doing his laundry along with her own.

'I must get him to give me a set of keys,' she said. 'Then I can really give it a going-over when he's safely out of the way.'

Oh dear. There was something about Connie's unthinking confidence that made Kate uneasy, yet it wasn't her business to interfere. Despite Connie's extra maturity, this bright-eyed, rapturous, giddy-headed creature reminded her ominously of herself four years ago. Ramon had made his cataclysmic entry into her life, and after that nothing had ever been the same. And just four years later, blind infatuation had spiralled downwards into blinding terror.

By three a.m. Miles had had enough but the girls were still going strong. More's the pity, he thought ruefully.

Not one of the four showed any sign of flagging, while the pressure on his wallet grew heavier by the minute. There was nothing remotely emancipated about this lot; those silly vanity bags carried little more than a comb and lipstick, together maybe with an extra little something to account for the renewed vitality and shine in their eyes each time they returned from a visit to the powder room. From The Canteen they'd progressed to Les Ambassadeurs and then, by unanimous vote, to Madame Jo Jo's. The music was too loud to talk over with any comfort, and they were all such seasoned clubbers that three of them were usually away from the table at a time.

Miles was feeling positively middle-aged. It was time, he felt, to call it a night, though he shrank from the prospect of having to ferry the entire crew home. He was getting nowhere with Eleni tonight, that was for sure, and would have to start negotiations all over again when he'd shaken off the acolytes. And when his head was a little clearer. Besides, it would not be appropriate to arrive back at Kensington Court together. Eleni was in the Ladies when he slipped away, having paid the bill and left a couple of extra twenties to cover the tip. She'd be all right, he was confident of that. This babe was used to playing the town and she'd got the bimbos for company. The important thing was, he'd given her a good night out, which must surely count for something when it came to settling his account.

For Miles was reaching the end of the road, and without the Greek girl's rumoured fortune was in deep trouble. He'd been in similar scrapes before and always won through, but this time things were that much more complex and his energy was starting to flag. The heat was still as thick and clinging as a blanket as he stepped out into Brewer Street and hailed a cab. What was badly needed was a short, sharp thunderstorm to clear the air, but that was the least of his concerns when he reached his own door and saw that the lights were still on.

'Where in hell's name have you been till now?' screeched Claudia, her face a mask of fury. She stood in the hall in her satin robe, her eyes dark pools of rage above her fishwife's snarl. Miles stood there wearily, for once at a loss for words, finding himself far drunker than he had realised. This was all he needed right now after such a frustrating evening. The little woman going for the jugular when all he really wanted to do was weep.

'Your banker friend's been on the phone, four times in all this evening. And Lady Wentworth still awaits your call. What have you been up to, you stupid fool? If you've been messing with the neighbours you've only yourself to blame and I want no part in it.'

She slammed the bedroom door in his face and left him alone to sweat.

26

Chuck Moran was on the doorstep first thing next morning, arousing Miles from a troubled sleep. There was no sound from Claudia. When he glanced at the spare room clock he saw that it was already after eight. She must have gone to work, the bitch, and left him to oversleep.

'Sorry to disturb you, old man,' said Chuck, looking distinctly hot and bothered. 'But we really do have to talk about my investments and I couldn't seem to rouse you at all last night.' In his stiffly starched shirt and pinstriped suit, he looked the epitome of the successful banker, in sharp contrast to crumpled Miles in his paisley pyjamas and slipperless feet. Miles felt terrible. His head was pounding like a steam-hammer and the inside of his mouth was quite obscene. He gestured for his neighbour to come inside and made a vague attempt to offer him coffee.

'Not now,' said Chuck, abrasively. 'I have to be in Curzon Street by nine.'

For once, his affable American charm was absent and the round red face, with its bulldog jowls, was set in an expression of grim determination. His watch chain strained across his ample waistcoat and he seemed on the point of bursting his collar stud. Chuck Moran was clearly not a happy man.

'Look here, old boy,' he continued. 'This simply won't do. Got to give some sort of accounting to my colleagues and you've been giving me the slip for weeks. What gives? It's not that I don't trust you . . .' His voice trailed off and at last he looked acutely embarrassed. What he really wanted to do was punch Miles in the mouth but the pathetic slimeball looked like nothing on earth this morning, not even worth so much expended energy. Through his hangover and the fog of depression that was rapidly beginning to engulf him, Miles gave him the usual muttered platitudes and packed him off with a definite promise to be in the Chase Manhattan offices at three sharp to give a full account of his negotiations.

After the banker had left, Miles leaned against the closed front door, eyes shut against the morning light, wondering what in hell's name he was going to do. No point in phoning Eleni at this hour; if she were home at all, she'd be sleeping it off and all he'd get, if anything, would be that batty old Greek woman not understanding a word he said. There was always Netta Silcock, of course, but she had lately been showing decided signs of discontent and he wasn't at all sure that he could push her any further. Not just now, until she had realised a few of the promised dividends. Lady Wentworth was out of the question and that, more or less, wound it up in this building. He glanced at his watch. Unless, unless . . . He had a shrewd idea that today Jacintha was moving in. With a little luck, he might catch up with her before he had to go to Canary Wharf and face much bigger trouble, his wife.

Kate was ironing and listening to 'Midweek' when Horatio appeared at the window, growling fiercely and carrying a brown paper bag.

'What on earth have you got now, you silly animal?' she said, as he carried it triumphantly through the scullery window and into the kitchen to lay at her feet. He was really so endearing, this rooftop scavenger, and brought her all kind of treasures in place of the mice and birds he should be hunting. A potato, a tiny ornament, once one of her earrings; anything he could easily carry that happened to take his fancy. She was always careful to pet and praise him, though she sometimes worried about what might be coming next.

Today it was a bag of fresh tomatoes, snatched presumably through an open window. Though what it was about them that had caught his fancy was not easy to fathom. He stood there expectantly, tail held high like a banner, so she picked him up and gave him a cuddle, then filled his breakfast bowl with food.

'Good boy.'

As soon as his back was turned, she would sling them in the rubbish. They looked okay but you never quite knew. One of these days he would get himself in trouble, but it was a cute habit and was doing no harm. Just his way of earning his keep; how could she scold him?

'You're the dearest puddytat in the world,' said Kate, 'and I love you lots.'

*

It was Miles's further misfortune to run into Netta in the lift, and he saw from the gleam in her chilly green eyes that his assessment had been accurate and his troubles were only just starting.

'Ah, Miles,' she said, dispensing, for once, with the sugary greeting, 'I need a wee word with you. I'm thinking of taking a cruise to South Africa and need to have exact details of where I stand financially.'

It was twenty to eleven and about as hot as Hades. His mouth felt scoured and that much less disgusting, but the headache hadn't even begun to budge. Netta wore one of her floating shrouds and a daft little straw hat on her platinum curls, presumably in tribute to Mrs Adelaide Potter. With white gloves too. Her greedy, glossy mouth and those little piggy eyes filled him with a rage so acute he felt he wanted to strangle her. Instead, he got out on the second floor.

'I'll telephone you later,' he said smoothly, and pressed the Down button to dispatch her on her way, though sawing through the main cable might have made better sense, the way he was feeling.

To his overwhelming relief, his hunch had been well founded and Jacintha was in the process of moving in. She came to the door with a brilliant smile, in an overall and big rubber gloves.

'Miles!' she said. 'My hero!' making him feel better in an instant. She gave him a big sloppy kiss then stood aside to let him view the property, and out of tact and natural good manners, he allowed her to take him on the full circuit while he edged towards the subject of the day.

'Very nice indeed,' he said approvingly. 'You've certainly got a gift for it.'

Claudia would hate the way she'd done it up, all chintz and fancy drapes and tastefully framed hunting prints, but it certainly was effective, a far cry indeed from the squalor in which the nurses had once wallowed. An army of muscular young removal men was trekking steadily through the flat but Jacintha was fully at ease, in her element in this domestic setting, more content than she'd been in years. She offered him coffee but he said he hadn't time. She saw from his expression, though, that all was not well with him and listened to his pitch with a flatteringly grave courtesy. When he'd finished she fished out her chequebook and wrote the figures firmly in her round, unsophisticated schoolgirl script.

'There,' she said decisively, blowing on the ink. 'You've been good to me, Miles, so the least I can do is reciprocate in kind.' Clifford normally took care of her finances, but spending Mother's money had given her an unexpected adrenalin surge. It made her feel fully grown up for the first time in her life and beat buying frocks and cushions, that was for sure.

'Is this enough as an initial down-payment?' she asked anxiously and Miles's headache shifted a fraction as he said it was and pocketed it speedily. Not enough to keep him out of prison maybe, but a tidy little increment nonetheless, to help him stay afloat till he could get to the bigger money.

'Thanks, Jacintha, you're a pal,' he said. 'And you're making the right decision, I assure you.' Words, words. It was all so easy provided you kept your head.

'Now don't forget,' she said gaily as she saw him out. 'Dinner here on Thursday at eight with Claudia and

Gregory. And meanwhile, mum's the word!'

She blew him a kiss as she closed the door, and Miles ran down the final two flights with a renewed lightness in his tread. If he could only survive the next few days, then he might just possibly make it. Provided he kept his cool and his wife didn't slaughter him when he finally had to confront her in the office.

Netta was in Barkers, guzzling Black Forest gâteau while she waited for them to reburnish her curls. Time these days lay heavily on her hands; Marks & Spencer had little new to offer – it was that period of the year – and there was nothing on at the Odeon she remotely wanted to see. She sighed with discontent as she swallowed the last luscious mouthful. That child at the sweetshop window she had known so long was finding it increasingly hard to satisfy her longings. She flicked through the upstairs departments before entering the beauty salon, thought about a plush pink jewel box which played 'Lara's Theme' when you lifted the lid, turned up her nose at some marked down Edinburgh crystal and managed to resist a terracotta pig which grew parsley out of its back once you'd planted the seeds. Goodness, what was happening to her? A terrible malaise had taken over Netta's spirit and she badly needed some sort of atonement. Though for what, even she was not quite clear.

The truth was, she wanted a new husband, though where she would ever find another sucker like Archie, she really couldn't imagine. She had enjoyed playing the married lady, and resented her reduced status, after such a short time, to merely widow. No one in the building took her sufficiently seriously; a new husband would fix all that. She allowed the girl to massage her scalp and even apply a little conditioner, though privately Netta thought these extras a terrible waste of money. She sat there scowling at herself in the mirror and thought about the bad things she would like to do to some of her neighbours; to the overbearing Adelaide, the supercilious Claudia, to Connie Boyle who always seemed so pleased with herself, even this day to Miles, up till now her blue-eyed boy.

Miles was not playing quite straight with her, she felt it in her water. This whole Lloyd's business was, she suspected, the most gigantic scam, but she'd hurried into it with barely a second thought because she knew Lady Wentworth was involved, and later, also, the hugely reliable Chuck Moran, who was, after all, a banker by profession. And a Wall Street one at that. No, what she felt cheated by, the more she brooded on it, was her lack of involvement in what was going on at the nub, her non-inclusion in Miles's inner circle. Unlike Lady W and the Fentons, who seemed to be forever hobnobbing with him and his stuck-up wife. It was grossly unfair. She was sure if she were younger and prettier, it would be another story entirely. Or if she had a husband to settle their hash.

Connie was just going into Gregory's flat, her arms full of freshly laundered sheets and towels, when Netta got out of the lift, her platinum curls recoiffed. She scowled in response to Connie's ebullient greeting as she fiddled with her own door key. Brazen hussy, with her painted toenails and cut-off shorts. Flaunting this new liaison for all to see. Just wait till Mrs Potter got wind of it; they'd not hear the end of it. Netta made a mental note to be sure to drop an appropriate word as soon as possible. She'd light the blue touch paper and just stand back, a surefire recipe for mayhem where Adelaide was concerned.

'What's eating that sad old sausage, I wonder,' said Connie gaily as she swanned into Gregory's bedroom and started briskly reorganising his drawers. Gregory sat at his desk, tapping away at his keyboard, and barely raised his head at her entry, not even when she dropped a kiss on his head as she passed. She was loving every minute of this cosy new arrangement, discovering dimensions of domesticity in herself she'd never suspected were there at all. Now that she'd done the sheets and towels, she'd tackle the bedroom curtains, which looked as if they'd been there since the year dot, so grimy and faded you could no longer distinguish a pattern. But she'd better wait till he was out of the way before she started. He'd only think she was fussing; she'd prefer to make it a surprise.

'What shall we do for supper tonight, hon?' she called, as she sorted through his laundry bag to see what still needed doing. Five shirts and seven pairs of pants, all of them frayed and fairly disreputable, some quite holey and threadbare. First thing tomorrow, before she even went to the shop, she'd pop across to M&S and buy him a whole new set. Colour co-ordinated, with socks and ties to match, to keep him going until their relationship was a little more official. Men! Connie smiled fondly to herself as she bustled into his kitchen to see if she could scrape together the makings of a meal. Otherwise, it would have to be a pizza *again*, which was wreaking havoc with her waistline.

God, thought Gregory wearily, why can't she just lay off? He was batty about Connie, of course he was, if only she'd stick to the ground rules. The very last thing he needed right now was another interfering woman underfoot, fussing through his things and sticking in her nose where it was not wanted. What was it that happened to the whole damn lot of them the moment you took them to bed? They instantly transformed from free-wheeling individuals to clones of the same anxious mother hen, clucking around his bachelor pad, attempting to turn it into a nest. What had attracted him to Connie in the first place was her great sense of humour and feisty independence. Here was a woman, he'd spotted immediately, with whom to have a few good laughs and some raunchy, uncomplicated sex with no strings attached. But look at her now. They'd scarcely been at it for more than a week and already she was out there in his kitchen, changing the shelf paper and tidying the knife drawer. Alice had been bad enough, not to mention Jacintha. All Gregory really wanted was to be left alone.

Fat chance of that.

'Sweetie,' called Connie from the kitchen, 'how do you feel about mushroom risotto? If I pop downstairs I've got some arborio rice and dried *funghi*. And I can knock up a salad from the dribs and drabs you have in your fridge.'

She doted on this man, could eat him alive. The best thing that had ever happened to her, and when she was least expecting it too. Next time he popped across to Toronto she'd tag along with him, no sweat. Give her a chance to meet his folks and then they could drop down to Brooklyn together so that he could get to know her mother. And throw a few dinners in the parental home for Paige and Phyllis and the rest of the gang. They'd all been so thrilled for her, she could hardly wait to show him off.

Gregory gritted his teeth, pretending he couldn't hear. He hated her affectations when it came to food and cooking. Next she'd be growing basil on his windowsill and getting friends to bring back first pressing olive oil from private vineyards in Tuscany. And balsamic vinegar. And making him lay down wine; there was no end to it once they got started. He'd been that route before, so many times. Which was why he continued to travel the world and live the life of a nomad.

'You work so hard, my darling.' Her voice was close to his ear now, as she nuzzled his neck and peered over his shoulder at the game of Solitaire on his screen. 'Naughty baby, caught you! If that's all you're doing, you've time to take a breather.'

And before he could speak she'd got hold of both his hands and was hauling him to his feet, back to the bedroom for an energetic work-out.

Two floors down, Jacintha was also having the time of her life. The removers had finished their job and left, the unpacking was more or less done. The brand-new kitchen equipment was up and operational; there was champagne in the icebox and caviar in the fridge. A roast was quietly cooking in the oven, the vegetables had been cleaned and scraped. And hanging on the freshly painted cupboard door in the bedroom was an understated little nothing in crisp summer cotton that had set her back a whole four hundred pounds. It was twenty past six. Time, once she'd had a facepack and a half-hour nap, to start putting her plan into action, as soon as she'd checked that her other guests were there and still co-operative.

Claudia was not amused when she picked up the phone. She and Miles were still barely speaking so naturally he hadn't told her of Jacintha's invitation; even if he had remembered it, which he hadn't. She was rude to the point of extinction.

'I'm afraid my husband's not home,' she said. 'And I'm certain we have no plans for going out tonight.'

Jacintha Hart, she pondered once she had hung up. Now who's she when she's at home? The name did ring a faint bell; the bimbo, the butterfly, the one with the hots for Gregory and a convenient elderly husband stuck at home in the country somewhere. Despite herself, Claudia began to smile. How divine. The woman in mink, the innocent from the boondocks. The cloying fool who thought she stood a chance with him, who had seemingly blown her cover now by buying a lease in this building. Now how on earth had she managed that? To Claudia's certain knowledge, there was nothing at all available at present. She'd have to ask Miles, if he ever did come home. In the meantime, to satisfy a sadistic streak in herself, she dialled the number Jacintha had left and told her, a great deal more civilly, that she'd just remembered, it had quite slipped her mind, and they would indeed both be there that night. Depending on Miles and what time he got home.

Connie had her clothes on again and was back to fussing about the evening meal. Gregory was past caring; it was almost eight and he was feeling distinctly peckish. If only she'd cease her blather for a minute and put some meat and potatoes on the table.

'I'll just pop downstairs,' she told him again, 'and see what I can throw together.'

If she moved quite quickly she could get across to M&S and he'd never even suspect it. A ready-made salad would be nice to go with the risotto, and some grapes and nectarines, maybe, plus a fresh baguette for the cheese. Decisions, decisions; she'd forgotten how complicated love could make everything seem. And a couple of bottles of really good wine. She tripped down the stairs on fairy feet, too impatient to wait for the lift.

It seemed only minutes before she was back again, ringing the doorbell and dragging Gregory once more from his desk. Oh my Lord. He'd give her a key, only he knew how often she'd use it. Women, they were far more trouble than they were worth. He flung open the door with a show of bad grace . . . to come face to face with Jacintha, dressed like a milkmaid and holding forth a silly little china teacup, an expression of leering triumph on her face.

'Hi,' she said, posing prettily. 'I'm your new downstairs neighbour, sir. Could you let me have a cup of sugar maybe? And what are your dinner plans for tonight?'

27

The second time Ramon hit her had been even less expected. Friends of his from Buenos Aires had been visiting, and the two of them had taken them out on a tour of the Manhattan highspots, then prepared together a feast of such sumptuous proportions, even they had been impressed.

So maybe she did show off just a bit that night, talk too much, be a little heavy-handed with the wine, but that was because she was enjoying herself and the visitors were enjoying it too. She bonded with Alicia, the best friend's glamorous wife, and soon plans were being made for them to do it all again, very soon, only next time in Buenos Aires. Which was when it first penetrated Kate's awareness that Ramon was no longer part of the conversation; was sitting detached at the far end of the room, smoking a cigar and looking a touch menacing. And all for no reason she could possibly deduce, not after she had tried so hard and managed so well.

His mood was getting to the guests too, so soon they were saying they were tired and must be getting back; that the day had been a riot and they'd meet again as soon as could be arranged. And everyone was shaking hands and kissing all round, particularly Kate. And she stood in the doorway in a frenzy of ecstasy, waving as they climbed into their cab on Central Park West, blowing kisses to her new-found friends, about as happy as a person could be.

Until she closed the door and went laughing back into the room and he hit her. Just like that. Bloodying her nose and rocking her front teeth in their sockets so that they'd been loose ever since. And all for what reason? That she'd put herself out to be welcoming to his friends? That she'd spent a week preparing for the meal and had acquitted herself as a chef most admirably? That she'd loved him enough to make this evening special?

'You're drunk!' he snarled, hitting her again. 'You behaved like a whore in front of my oldest friends.' Then he'd torn at her clothes like a thing demented, thrown her to the rug and raped her savagely, all the while thumping her with skilful fists, like a trained thug in a police cell, knowing where to hit to hurt the most yet show the least damage.

She should have left him then, when he'd finally had enough and swept off to bed, locking the door so she'd had to sleep on the couch. If she'd only had the courage to grab her passport and the ruins of her pride and beat a swift retreat that night he might well have been history by now. Instead she'd hung on, guilty and contrite, for a further two and a half years. Until he'd behaved so badly that even she could no longer turn a blind eye, and she'd done it and put an ocean between them, planning never, ever to see him again.

The room was stifling in this hot weather, and Madeleine was beginning to fret.

'Take your jacket off,' he said. 'Make yourself comfortable. No point in torturing yourself for the sake of fashion when no one's going to see you.'

'Other than you.'

He smiled. He didn't count, and well she knew it. He was there to do a job, that was all. Once the mission was accomplished, he'd be straight off, back to his real work, with no further thought of her. As it was, he was getting impatient. They'd been here too long with no tangible results.

'The trouble with this goddam country is the lack of air conditioning.' Madeleine was in the habit of overdressing. It was an ingrained habit, born from her early days under cover, which had now become part of her identity. She liked to look good, made something of a cult of it. Appreciated approving glances, enjoyed giving out false signals. But this boffin, this *Englishman*, just about took the biscuit. It surely wouldn't hurt him to tell her occasionally how nice she looked but somehow she knew the thought would never even enter his head. He simply wouldn't notice.

She poured them each a glass of mineral water and touched up her make-up in her pocket mirror. Today she was wearing svelte dark blue, a three-quarter jacket and the shortest of skirts. With four-inch heels and sheer satin tights; all wasted on him, of course. She sometimes wondered if he had a real life at all, was anything more than a highly developed brain. But his smile was nice, she'd grant him that, and there were times she suspected he had a sense of humour.

Across the courtyard there was sudden movement

and then it was all stations go. He disappeared behind his equipment and she resumed her post. At the window.

And now it looked as if Ramon was back in London. The thought was almost too terrifying for Kate to bear, and she paced the flat when she should have been filing stories, chewing her nails and waiting for the second shoe to drop, almost too scared to do anything. Yet what, if she were rational, could he possibly do to her now? If he'd followed her all this way, which seemed unlikely, it could hardly be in order to do her an injury. For why should he bother? If he despised her as much as his behaviour would have her believe, then getting her out of his life could only have come as a relief to him. She wished she could believe her own common sense, but each time the telephone or the door bell rang, she started with terror. If he had bothered to come to the block and leave his card with the porter, then he wanted either to see her or scare her; she wasn't quite sure which alternative was worse.

And if he simply wanted to put things right between them, how come he had not been in direct touch by now? She was certain now that those silent calls must have been Ramon. If he hadn't made himself known by now, then she could only put the more sinister interpretation on his actions. He was silently stalking her but for what reason? Goodness knows, she had enough to scare her as it was, without the wraith of Ramon breathing down her neck. She longed to talk to Connie and Gregory but hesitated to bother them, particularly now, when she knew they had more important matters on their minds.

'God, it's noon already,' said Connie, prancing naked from the shower and leaping on him from behind as he stood at his desk. She pressed her naked, still damp breasts against his narrow back and cupped both his buttocks in her prehensile hands. Gregory laughed and turned to face her, pinning those hands in his own where they could do no harm. This woman was insatiable; was there nothing he could do to calm her down? Once, as a younger man, she'd have been his ideal wet dream. Now, a little older and wiser, he liked to have time to savour his pleasures. And there were other things he had to do.

'It's almost lunchtime and I need a drink,' he said. 'Then I've got work to do, an article to finish and some urgent calls I really have to make.' Jacintha, he had to reach Jacintha. What she had done was quite inexcusable but the look on her face when she'd caught him with Connie was anguished beyond imagining. And no matter what her shortcomings, faithful Jacintha did not deserve that. Not after fifteen years' hard service. He was not that much of a monster.

'It's that woman,' said Connie, immediately catching on. 'You're not going to grovel to her after what she did?' Lord, she'd thought they were beyond all that. She was a married woman, after all, and surely not of any importance. Not a threat to herself and Gregory. Not now, when they'd reached this marvellous understanding.

'Get dressed,' he said, slapping her bare backside,

'and I'll take you round the corner for some fast nosh.'

It hadn't been fun, the showdown with Jacintha, even if she had had it coming and had done the unforgivable by poking herself in where she definitely was not wanted. Remember the ground rules, he'd told her more than once. Keep off my patch and you get to hang around. Or words to that effect. But did she listen? Did she heck. They were all the same, these women; tarred with the same brush and quite incorrigible.

And here came Connie, dressed at last, twining her arms around his neck and smothering his face with kisses.

'Come on, let's go.' While she was still on her feet and not pushing him back towards the sack.

Miles was in the hallway, chatting to the porter, paying an unaccustomed flying visit to his flat in the middle of the day. Gregory invited him to join them for a noggin but he said he hadn't got time. He'd come home to pick up some papers, he explained, but in reality he was still hoping for a word with Eleni.

'All right for some,' he joked, seeing them together. 'Most of us poor blighters have work to do at this time of day.'

'I believe Miss Papadopoulos has just gone out,' said Septimus discreetly once they'd gone, enjoying himself enormously. He'd seen her swanning by just ten minutes earlier, dressed to kill, which was unusual for her at this time of day, obviously off on something more than just a shopping spree.

Damn, thought Miles. What a wasted journey. All

the way from Docklands, too, in this blasted heat. He should have phoned first but he hadn't wanted to alert her. And it was quite unheard of for her to be out and about at this hour. He'd look in on Jacintha then, just to see how the land lay. But when he rang her bell there was no one home.

'Why Miles,' said an unwelcome voice from the flat next door, 'my husband was keen to speak with you. Have you a moment now?'

'Sorry,' shouted Miles from the stairs, in rapid retreat. 'Got to get back to the office for an urgent meeting. Tell him I'll catch him tonight if I'm not too late.'

The sight of Connie, so obviously at home in Gregory's flat, had been almost too much for Jacintha. To have waited so long for the fulfilment of her dream, to have got so far, only to be thwarted at the ultimate moment by this gorgeous, exotic American woman in revealing T-shirt and the skimpiest of shorts, had brought her close to cracking point. Had she had a weapon handy, she'd certainly have used it, though which of the two of them she would have destroyed was a moot question.

The wheeze of using the teacup as an excuse for ringing his bell had seemed so cute at the time, so appropriate, that she'd giggled to herself all the way up in the lift, dying to see his face when he opened the door. Instead all she'd got was undisguised dismay, followed, almost instantly, by the clang of the lift-gates behind her and a throaty voice saying cheerily:

'Wait till you see what I've got us for supper. Lobster do you, hon?'

'Jacintha!' said Gregory in weary surprise. 'What on earth brings *you* here?' And then he had shattered her illusions entirely by introducing her to Connie as 'an old friend up from the country' and almost forgetting to invite her in. Inside, the true situation could not be disguised. The kitchen was upside down with activity, the bed unmade and Connie's sandals halfway across the floor where she'd kicked them off as she strode through the door. This woman was very much in occupation and making no bones about letting her know it.

'I'm sorry,' she said to Jacintha, with wide, guileless eyes. 'I only got two lobsters. If I'd known you were coming . . .'

'Don't worry,' said Gregory rapidly. 'Jacintha's not stopping. How about a glass of something before you go? And you still haven't answered my question.'

Feeling suddenly quite faint with despair, Jacintha sank on to an armchair in her Little Miss Muffet designer sundress, and clapped her hand theatrically across her eyes. Words for once evaded her. All she felt was sick to her stomach as well as the most colossal fool. Then she remembered the sneering Claudia and her reckless invitation to dinner. It was five to eight; they'd be there any minute.

'Sorry,' she said, biting back her tears. 'I really have to be going. I've things to do downstairs.'

In the event, the evening went better than she'd envisaged, and even Claudia turned out to be quite nice. It was clear when they arrived, on time for once, that something drastic had happened to Jacintha and that she was in quite a degree of distress. Neither knew her well enough to ask direct questions but Miles took

over the pouring of drinks and after only a few minutes' careful shuffling around the subject, managed to
extract the whole dire story in a gush of despair and a
torrent of tears.

'I really thought he loved me,' she wailed, not
entirely truthfully, and Miles leaned across and patted
her hand while Claudia managed to keep her face passive though secretly jubilating inside. So the country
bumpkin was not as much in charge as she had
thought; Claudia could afford for once to relax and be
charitable.

The meal was very good indeed, at least Jacintha
had got that right, and once she'd stopped snivelling
and calmed down, it began to be clear what Gregory
had seen in her. Jacintha was by no means sophisticated but she was still a passably attractive woman,
even in her early forties, with a certain guileless softness about her that Claudia knew men liked. She was
also a superlative hostess, and pretty soon the three of
them were relaxing and chatting away like old friends.
A supreme relief for Miles, who'd had one of those
days, and for Claudia, who couldn't quite decide
whether or not she was speaking to him.

They sat in the pretty, chintzy parlour and talked
about Gregory instead. Jacintha carried in a tray of coffee and Miles did the honours with the liqueurs.

'I suppose it was love at first sight,' she said simply
as she poured, remembering that first meeting on the
plane and the way his easy-going manner and the
bright blue eyes had caught her fancy right from the
start. She did not tell them she'd been a stewardess,
or that the fact he was travelling in first class had

heightened her interest. Only the barest details in fact; just that they'd been an item by the time they'd disembarked. She sighed as she looked back.

'He was so attractive in those days,' she said. 'Still is, I suppose.'

Claudia thought so but wasn't about to say. She begged a rare cigarette from her husband, leaned back in her comfortable chair and realised with some surprise that she was actually enjoying herself. They should do this sort of thing more often, informal dinners with casual friends; no sweat, no underlying business agenda, not even very far to go home. Jacintha, she discovered, was the sort of woman she actually rather liked. Unsophisticated, yes, but also stylish, socially aware, with even a sense of humour when she relaxed enough to let it show. Well heeled, too. The snobby side of Claudia could not find a lot to fault. Most important, she realised now that Jacintha was no threat.

'So tell us more about Gregory,' she urged. 'Why do you suppose he has never married?'

Jacintha sat back and pondered. 'I don't really know,' she said. 'He gets on with women amazingly well and, unusually, actually likes them.' She paused a moment and groped for her hanky; the tears were still pretty close to the surface. She would not forgive in a hurry this latest treachery, nor the humiliation that accompanied it. 'In fact, I guess that's the problem. He likes them rather too much . . . and they like him.'

Claudia threw Miles a venomous glance through a thin exhalation of smoke. He needn't think he was off the hook; there was unfinished business still to be settled. But she was finding this whole exchange fairly engrossing. The dashing Dane had always fascinated her, though why, she was not quite sure.

'So you think it's a matter of not being able to make up his mind?'

Jacintha considered it, then slowly nodded. 'I guess so. He needs to be everything to all people.' It didn't make him necessarily bad, but there it was. If she'd only been more forceful when their affair was first at its height, who knows how things might have turned out. *Cosmopolitan* was forever running articles about catching your man, but where Gregory was concerned, even after all these years, she found herself still putty in his hands. At the moment she felt like murdering him, but she knew that feeling would pass.

'Actually,' she said quite simply, looking to Claudia for support, 'he should have married me. I'd have kept him out of trouble.'

And Claudia, despite her cynicism, thought she was probably right.

'Let's do lunch,' she said with a sudden brilliant smile, astonishing Miles. 'Some Saturday, perhaps, if you're ever up here at weekends. With maybe a little shopping thrown in.'

Connie, upstairs, was giving Gregory a bit of a going-over. Well, she wouldn't have been quite normal if she had not. She didn't sling the lobsters, they were far too good to waste, but while she was making the mayonnaise and tearing up leaves for the salad, she let him know in no small way exactly what she thought about men who two-timed.

'I was only gone a couple of minutes,' she scolded. 'You must have known she was coming. Why else would she be in this building, if not to see you?'

A good point and one he found hard to answer. Just wait till he got hold of Miles and found out the truth about this secret property deal. Treachery amongst the troops just wasn't on; if you couldn't trust a drinking crony, then who else was there? He spread his hands with his customary vagueness, then held out his arms and implored her for a hug.

'Don't be cross with me,' he said, like a schoolboy caught out in a bit of a jape. 'I don't own London, and who am I to stop her coming? She's her own person, for goodness' sake, with a husband in the country to pick up all her bills. Is it my fault that she finds me irresistible?'

He pulled such a face and looked so mock-woeful that Connie forgave him everything on the spot and dragged him off to the bedroom for a quick aperitif.

'But don't let me catch you doing it again,' she told him much later. 'You've got me now to keep you in line.' And she meant it; boy, did she mean it.

28

Netta came in that afternoon, hot and weary from a hard day's shopping, to find no one around and the porter off duty. She pulled open the creaking lift gates and piled her purchases on to the wooden seat, then pressed the button to ascend and slumped thankfully down beside them. Gosh, but it was hot; London wasn't used to this sort of weather. The reports were saying it was breaking all records, not just for August but for the century. Her silk dress was clinging uncomfortably to her thighs, and her fat little ankles were overflowing the too-tight shoes. What she longed for more than anything was a nice cup of tea; what she'd do once she got through the door was first have a wee then put on the kettle. The lift seemed to be moving more slowly than ever; the aged machinery wheezed and groaned as it toiled its painful way to the fourth floor. From the glass roof in the dome the sun beat down relentlessly, turning the stairwell into a funnel of heat and the openwork lift into a furnace. She'd have to have a word with Digby Fenton and get him to organise blinds or something. This heat was positively disgraceful; the tenants of a building of this calibre should not be expected to suffer in this way.

The lift began to judder as it passed the third floor, then halfway between the third and the fourth it stopped. Abruptly, just like that. Netta could hear the anguished metalwork groaning and contracting, rather as if it had given up trying and was closing itself down for the night.

'Hello,' she called, peering up at her floor. It had halted exactly halfway so that she was suspended in space, unable to open the gates.

'Hello,' she called again, unable to believe her bad luck. She'd heard many scare stories about people getting stuck but this was the first time it had happened to her. There was no alarm bell, no telephone; no way of attracting attention other than by calling. Her bladder was beginning to give her urgent signals and she couldn't hear a single sound throughout the building. She remembered, with sinking spirits, the firmly closed door of the porter's lodge as she'd passed. For all she knew, he'd be off duty till the morning, but somehow she had to escape before then.

Luckily, because of the lift's open ironwork sides, there was no particular feeling of claustrophobia. She could just sit quietly here on the hard wooden seat and wait patiently for someone to find her. Or else scream her head off to bring them all running, which was far more her style and which she'd rather do,

'Hell-*oo*-oo there!' yodelled Netta, in sudden desperation, rattling the gates with two fat hands and praying for some response.

She'd been there an unbelievable half-hour by the time she heard the footsteps, and by then she was weeping with fear and annoyance and was limp with perspiration, stuck like a rat in a trap and frightened half to death. She peered upwards at the floor above and saw two reassuring legs standing right by the lift gates, quietly waiting and listening.

'Why, you're in a pretty pickle, aren't you?' said a voice she knew well and trusted. 'I suppose you want me to get you out.' Yes, oh yes, what on earth was the delay?

'Quickly, quickly,' she said in agitation. 'I really can't bear to stay in here one more minute.' Her feet in their tight shoes were killing her, and she dared not think of the state of her underwear.

'Don't panic,' said the voice, and the footsteps strolled away. Strolled, not hurried; she was very much aware of that.

'Help me, help me!' screamed Netta in despair, losing control entirely and beating her fists against her iron cage. She heard a door closing then opening again, and the feet came strolling back, in no hurry at all, and something was rattled against the top half of the lift. A long wooden pole with an S-shaped iron piece at the end, used for opening and shutting the old Victorian sash windows, was pushed through the latticework and into Netta's grasping fingers. But what on earth was she supposed to do with it? Batter her way out?

'Greedy, greedy,' said the same soft voice, filled with amusement now. The pole was pulled free, then poked her savagely in the chest, so that she lost her balance and fell heavily back on to the wooden seat. 'You're like a bird in a cage, aren't you, Netta,' said the voice. 'So let's hear you sing.'

This time the pole swung round in an arc and caught her sharply round the ear, bruising her cheek-bone and bringing tears of pain to her eyes. This wasn't a joke; what on earth was going on? The pole caught her again before she'd regained her breath, this time round the other side, tearing the earring from her ear-lobe and knocking her to the floor.

'Not so much a bird in a cage,' said her tormentor. 'More like a shark, and a dangerous one at that. Or else a fat little piggy going wee-wee-wee all the way home. Isn't that right, Netta?'

She opened her mouth to scream this time, but the metal hook at the end of the pole caught her full in the mouth, silencing her effectively and shattering one of her expensive crowns. Then it beat her twice on the head for good measure and came back, as fast as light-ning, to catch her in the chest again, this time with full force.

'Did you enjoy Punch and Judy shows when you were a child?' asked the voice, conversationally. 'Or weren't you ever a child?' And two strong hands drove the pole back into her chest.

'Aaargh,' said Netta dully, as she slid to the floor, her glass-green eyes rolling back into her head, blood trickling from her battered mouth. The hook had gone in four inches and the pole was sticking out of her chest like a picador's lance. Just at that moment there was a grinding of machinery from way down in the basement and the lift began slowly to move again, descending at snail's pace to the second floor, the pole going boing, boing, boing against the metalwork all the while, as it worked its way still further into Netta's unresisting flab. And all she'd have been able to hear, had she still use of her faculties, would have been foot-steps walking softly away and the sound of a distant door closing.

'What the heck?'

It was like one of those ghastly recurring night-mares, something he'd hoped never to experience again. Septimus Woolf had just returned from church and was unlocking the door of the porter's lodge when he heard an agonised cry from somewhere above, the sound of a person profoundly in pain. He pressed the lift button but nothing happened, so he abandoned his dignity and raced up the stairs. There, on the second floor, was a horrifying sight – Chuck Moran standing transfixed in the open gates of the lift, clutching in one hand a bloodstained pole with which he appeared to have just stabbed Netta Silcock. The cry was Chuck's, for she was too far gone.

'What's going on?'

'Jesus, man, I just called the lift and there she was.' The banker's normally ruddy complexion was ashen; he swayed slightly on his feet as if about to faint. Netta lay sprawled like a huge broken doll, half on the bench, half off, blood pumping steadily from the deep wound in her chest and soaking the flimsy silk of her summer sack, her alabaster skin an ugly mishmash of bright red weals and darkening bruises.

'I thought I heard someone calling but there was no one there. Jesus.' He mopped his face with his hand-kerchief and leaned heavily against the wall to steady himself.

'Dead,' pronounced Septimus, though he hardly needed to check.

'Honey? Is there anything the matter?' called the banker's wife, opening her door when she heard the commotion, then screaming full blast when she caught sight of Netta. 'My God! What's happened?' she asked, then screamed again, bringing the rest of the tenants tumbling out on to their landings.

Digby Fenton took command and ushered the Morans back into their own flat.

'Better have a brandy, old man,' he said in quiet, measured tones. 'And give one to the little woman, too. We'll call you when the police arrive, don't worry. But the fewer of us out there now, the better, and you look as though you could use a bit of a sit-down.'

'Everything all right down there?' called Ronnie Barclay-Davenport from the stairs, in slippers and braces with a glass of Scotch in one hand. 'Only we thought we heard someone calling and Rowena sent me down to investigate. Lift doesn't seem to be working. Oh, good heavens!'

And soon there they all were, massed together on the second floor: Digby and Ronnie (Olive was tending to the Morans); Miles Burdett strolling down from above with, for some reason, Eleni Papadopoulos; Lady Wentworth, standing in her open doorway and holding her side; a small crowd of silent Iranians; Beatrice, looking very grave indeed, with Lily; Mrs Adelaide Potter, somehow shrunken and suddenly looking tremendously frail. And Kate. Then suddenly Gregory, thank the Lord for that, bursting down the stairs from his fourth-floor flat, in shabby denims and bare feet, taking in the scene with one fast glance, full of contrition and wise counsel; ready if needed to take over and do the necessary.

'Bless him,' said Rowena, who'd also trickled down, with tears in her eyes. 'Always here when we need him. Ready to cope.'

The police had been called, and while they waited for their arrival, Gregory conferred with Digby and the porter, then took control.

'Look here, chaps,' he said apologetically, opening his hands in a gesture of total helplessness, 'there's not a lot any of us can do just now to help this horrible situation except stay out of it.' He glanced compassionately at the body of Netta, still lying there in the open doorway of the lift. 'Poor lady,' he said in a much lower voice. 'I think she deserves a little respect, don't you?'

And, having intimated that all would be made clear at a suitable future time, he did the impossible and persuaded them to leave.

'She was coming to me for supper,' said Mrs Adelaide Potter in a broken voice, and Kate took her by the elbow and gently led her away.

'Well,' said Connie, who'd missed it all by inches. 'Tell me every detail and don't miss out a thing.'

It was quite like old times. They were sitting in Kate's kitchen, sharing a bottle of Marks & Spencer French wine, and Connie was avid for every bloodthirsty detail she'd missed. Gregory was still downstairs, conferring with the police. There wasn't really a lot to tell. Kate herself had only chanced upon it because she usually

went to the post office at that time and had run down
the stairs when the lift failed to appear.

'Don't laugh,' she warned, lighting a cigarette, 'but it
was a bit of a riot, I have to confess, what with the
blood and the shouting and all. And that awful
American woman having the screaming heeby-jeebies
all over the place. And her old man looking as if he
were about to have a coronary. And Digby being grave
and noble and terribly mayoral, as if he thought the
reporters might show up any minute. And Septimus
playing to the hilt the Porter-with-a-Secret. And Miles
sashaying in, right in the middle, with Eleni on his
arm. So to speak.'

'What!' cried Connie, leaping to attention. 'There's a
turn-up for the books! Tell me more.'

'That's all I know,' confessed Kate. 'They arrived
together when things were at their hottest and I somehow got the feeling they hadn't just met on the stairs.'

'Or in the elevator,' she added after a pause, and
although it was in the worst possible taste, they both
exploded with nervous laughter and had another
drink.

Gregory hadn't a lot more to offer when he finally
got away from the police and sought them out.

'All I know,' he said, taking Connie in his arms and
placing a consolatory hand on Kate's knee, 'is that
something nasty happened to Netta some time this
afternoon when nobody appears to have been about.
She met her Maker in the lift, so to speak, and that,
until the autopsy, is all that anyone can say.'

'Did nobody hear her?' asked Connie. 'Surely she
must have screamed or something?'

'Some of the residents claim to have heard something, hence the crowd on the stairs, but remember how thick these Victorian walls are. You could get away with damn near anything in a building this solid.'

'Poor Netta. I never much cared for her, but she didn't deserve this. What a truly terrible way to die, poked to death in a cage, unable to defend herself. Horrible.' Kate was immeasurably moved at the thought; tears came into her eyes.

'Who've they arrested this time?' asked Connie, but Gregory shook his head.

'No one,' he said. 'At least, not yet. The tramp, for once, is right in the clear, and the porter wasn't even on the premises. With witnesses this time to prove it. Unbelievably, he was at church.'

'What about Mrs Adelaide Bloody Potter?'

'Don't know. She lives right next door but claims she heard nothing. The police have taken a statement from her but until they have some evidence, their guess is as good as ours. Besides, she may be many things but can you really see her doing something like that, spearing her one remaining friend with a ruddy great window pole? With those pathetic arthritic old hands, she can barely lift her own teapot.'

Connie hugged him tighter and kissed him full on the lips.

'Sweetie, don't worry, just joking,' she said. 'But someone must have done it. And this time the possibilities must be far fewer.'

'I don't know,' said Kate thoughtfully, lighting another fag. 'She wasn't much liked, not by anyone in this building. Always pushing in where she really wasn't wanted. I've heard them talk about her often enough. In their eyes she was still an outsider.'

'But that's no reason to kill her.'

'I know. I'm simply telling you what I've heard.'

They sat in silence, the three of them, drinking their wine, thinking dark thoughts. Eventually Gregory looked at his watch and suggested they really must go.

'Will you be all right?' asked Connie, with a sharp eye on Kate. 'Why not come downstairs and join us for some supper?'

'Can't,' said Kate, 'but thanks a lot.' She'd got work to do, urgent stories to syndicate. Too many interruptions of this kind could play havoc with her schedules.

'Well, call us if you change your mind,' said Connie.

Kate saw them to the door and held her friend in a long, tense hug. Terrifying times, but somehow they had got to learn to cope.

'Brace yourself,' Madeleine was saying nearby. 'You're not going to believe what has just occurred, and right under our noses, too . . . This isn't funny, what's happening here. We ought to be able to stop it, with what we know already.'

'But we can't,' he said passively. 'Not till we have enough evidence. I know it's a hard one but it's why we're here. Watch and wait, that's really all we can do until we get the official okay from upstairs. Meanwhile we just have to trust our friend, the reliable London bobby.'

'PC Plod,' said Madeleine sneeringly. 'Well, I just hope you're right and we haven't left things too late.'

He didn't bother to answer that, but she saw from his eyes what he was thinking.

'I never did get to see that Meissen collection,' she lamented later. 'If only I'd been quicker off the mark, but who was to say she'd be the next one?'

It wasn't an easy assignment, but then she'd never thought it would be. She'd been over here for most of a year, stuck in this flat with only a taciturn backroom boy for company, and at times like this she began to lose hope and think despairingly of jacking it all in. Why couldn't the Metropolitan Police just crash in now and make an arrest? Before any more catastrophes occurred; more innocent blood was spilled. She had to keep reminding herself that this was a delicate mission; that she'd been specifically selected because of her training and experience in the field. Where undercover work like this was concerned, caution was the byword. Just one false move could blow the whole operation, waste years of detailed work and planning; worst of all, allow their prey to go free.

'Why not take yourself off for a walk,' he said tactfully, observing her torment. 'Following the established pattern, nothing's likely to happen for a while now. You might just as well get some fresh air.' And calm down.

Right across the courtyard, Beatrice Hunt was experiencing similar anguish, monitored by the equable Lily, whose Zen-like stillness helped to both calm and defuse her.

'Heads will roll, they're bound to,' Beatrice was saying, as she patrolled the polished floors of their tranquil apartment, an oasis of sanity amid the surrounding horrors. She pulled a couple of efficient pins from her Grade Five hairdo and allowed it to cascade around her shoulders, instantly enhancing and softening her appearance at the same time as she kicked off her shoes.

'Much better,' said Lily approvingly, placing a mug of jasmine tea in her hand. 'Come sit and tell me more about it. You're surely not saying they'll blame this one on you? How come it's always your fault?'

Beatrice smiled, and the taut lines in her face softened. 'Because the buck has to stop somewhere,' she said. 'That's what the Civil Service is all about.'

Mrs Adelaide Potter was positively out of her mind with terror; this creeping horror, whatever it was, seemed to be mowing down all her friends one by one, and who knows, she could well be the next. Olive Fenton took to dropping in but to little avail. All the old lady could mutter, over and over, was that it must be stopped, but how – and what? If Olive had the answer, she'd certainly give it, but she and Digby were as perplexed as the rest. The murders seemed to happen without rhyme or reason, and if there was a pattern, it was so subtle it had managed to elude them all. That was the most worrying part of all. They were no closer to any sort of a solution.

'The police still don't have a clue,' said Digby, after one of his sessions down at the station. 'No fingerprints, no motivation, no apparent access to the building. Even no obvious contact between the three unlucky victims, apart from the fact of being neighbours and friends.'

'Poor old Adelaide P is positively spare with worry. Say what you like, but I can't help sympathising. Can't sleep at nights, she tells me, for fear of being next on the hit list.'

'As well she might indeed. There's a lot of folks in this building who would shed few tears if anything happened to the Ayatollah – grim, maybe, but true. She's made a career out of being unpleasant. The world might think it high time she got some sort of come-uppance.'

'But who do you think it can be?'

'Search me. Short of arresting everyone in Kensington Court and sectioning them until the murderer's caught, I can't really see what more the police can do. Until he makes a mistake, which they nearly always do in the end.' But he still wasn't entirely convinced and had thought about taking Olive away for an extended holiday. Until he remembered his civic duty and dropped the idea. It would certainly not look good if the Mayor Elect were to abandon his post when the going got sticky. He knew Olive would understand if he ever got round to telling her. In the meantime, all they could do was be extra-specially careful.

Jacintha was in a quandary. She'd not had her show-down with Gregory because Connie simply wouldn't allow it, but she had spoken to him on the telephone, several times, so he now knew the details of her secret purchase and how she'd been able to facilitate it.

'I wanted it to be a surprise,' she wailed, 'for you as much as for me. But all I seem to have achieved is to drive you away still further.'

Gregory, calm as ever, was conciliatory. 'Nonsense, my love,' he said placatingly. 'Nothing has changed between us at all. You're still my best girl, though no need to let Connie know that. And what has Clifford to say about all this?'

Jacintha brightened a little. After all those years of living off crumbs, she could not abandon her great passion now, not when she had got so far as acquiring keys to Gregory's actual building. And Connie Boyle was so new on the scene, chances were she would not last long. She returned to Chipping Campden battered in spirit but with a renewed spark of hope in her heart. Clifford need never know of her bitter disappointment. She still had the *pied-à-terre* in a highly desirable area of London; Mother's money had been well invested and that was all that need ever concern him.

'You know something,' said Beatrice thoughtfully. 'There's a lot more going on in this building than meets the eye.'

Lily, engrossed at her drawing board, said nothing but she was listening. Beatrice methodically watered the plants, paying particular attention to the basil on the windowsill, then wiped the spout of the little brass can and replaced it tidily on the kitchen shelf. She walked barefoot back into the main room and removed a few dead leaves.

'On the surface it seems quite bland and ordinary, like a pack of old-fashioned Happy Families cards. But don't be fooled; there is darkness underneath.' She opened the sandalwood box on the coffee table and lit a gold-filtered Russian cigarette. Then she sank gracefully into the lotus position on the floor and lapsed into a thoughtful silence. This was the best part of the day, the golden hour between seven and eight when the sky was mid-blue and streaked with pale crimson, and distant voices from the street below reminded them it was summer and central, a pulse point of one of the greatest cities of the world. On the tape deck a wailing saxophone was playing, something melancholic and surreal that set your teeth just slightly on edge, like the hint of lemon in a glass of pure, sparkling water.

'And?' said Lily after a while, still drawing, arousing Beatrice from her reverie.

'And,' repeated Beatrice slowly, 'I think it's all going to work out in the end. Painful though the process may turn out to be.' She gazed reflectively at her dear, dear friend, etched now in pure golden light by the setting sun.

'If I didn't, my dear, I'll tell you quite frankly. I'd quit this lousy job right now and be heartily glad to see the back of it.'

'Look!' said Lily suddenly, glancing up. 'There's that cat from upstairs, Horatio, just walking by as bold as brass!'

Beatrice laughed and sprang lightly to her feet. 'How on earth does he find his way down here? Two floors. And whatever has he got in his mouth?'

She stuck her head out of the open window and watched Horatio carefully manoeuvring something large and unwieldy along the ledge. 'Looks like somebody's supper,' she said. 'I hope you didn't leave the kitchen window open.'

'Did you hear about the pigeon he killed? Kate told me she had feathers all over the flat.'

Actually, it was a rock cake. At the sound of Beatrice's voice he dropped it and stood protectively over it, holding it down possessively with one paw.

'Ha,' said Beatrice, in pure delight. 'Some poor soul around the building is doing a little baking, blissfully unaware that there's a cat burglar at large.'

'Why would he take a cake?' said Lily.

'These feral cats will snatch anything they can find, it's in their nature. Even though he is well looked after, he'll never lose his thieving ways.'

She retreated from the window and they both watched the jaunty swish of the retreating tail as Horatio took his booty home in triumph to present to his doting owner.

'I sure hope she appreciates it,' said Beatrice. 'Now, how about stopping that and pouring us both a drink?'

29

It was August, hot and humid, and the British people were beginning to flag, unused to the unaccustomed fine weather. Grace was out in the garden when she got there, a little after twelve. The sun was bright but in the shade of the trees it was really quite pleasant and Kate was glad to sit down and kick off her shoes. Grace sat in an upright chair, an ancient volume of Dryden on her lap, unopened.

'Happy birthday, Mother,' said Kate brightly, kissing the pallid cheek, but Grace made no response, simply flinched slightly and pulled away. She was neatly dressed in pale grey and white, with a cardigan round her shoulders, and her thin hands, despite the temperature, were as cold and clammy as always. Kate wondered if her mother recognised her today. The tattered memory came and went and some days she was more lucid than others. It was hard to tell. Kate had brought her a hydrangea in a pot and displayed it proudly on the lawn. Grace was not interested.

'I'll put it in your room, out of the sun,' said Kate, 'and then I'll bring us a gin and tonic. I'm sure you'd like that.'

Her heart was heavy as she carried the plant back into the house and along the shaded corridor to the room at the end which was her mother's. She hated these visits, put them off for as long as possible. She knew she was wrong, that she neglected her mother, but the confrontation was always so painful and dredged up childhood memories she'd far rather keep buried. No matter how hard she tried, it seemed to Kate she could never succeed in attracting her mother's interest or approval. Even now, as a brain-damaged old lady, her residual bitterness was still close to the surface; the long-dead dreams of a discontented woman forced to put aside a career in favour of marriage and children.

The room was airy and pleasant, fine lawn curtains fluttering in the breeze. On the table by the bed lay Gogol's *Dead Souls*, face down, and when Kate checked she saw that her mother had reached page 113. So she did still read, encouraging to know, even if these days she rarely communicated. On the centre of the round table by the window, where Kate had planned to display her own floral tribute, was a vase of bluebells, Grace's favourite flower, filling the room with their pungent, distinctive scent. Lindy and Bruno? She rather doubted it. They usually brought chocolates, because they were easier, and it was highly unlikely that Bruno would know his mother's taste in anything.

She poured two tumblers of gin and tonic and carried them out to the shade of the trees.

'The bluebells are lovely,' she said. 'Who brought them? On your birthday too, so appropriate.'

Grace accepted her drink with scant enthusiasm, then sat and gazed into space without comment. It wasn't clear if she'd even heard her. Kate knew there was little point in repeating the question.

'Your husband,' Grace said suddenly, as clearly as anything, as she took a sip. 'He always remembers that they're my favourites.' For a second the austere face softened and almost a smile caressed the bloodless lips. Kate was startled. Her mother must be confused.

'I have no husband, Mother,' she said. 'Remember, we split four years ago?'

Maybe she did mean Bruno after all. Perhaps she was confusing Kate with Lindy. With Mother these days there was really no telling; it was tragic to watch so fine a brain wither and die like an untended garden.

'Your husband,' Grace repeated stubbornly. 'He always remembers.'

'Francis, you mean?' She was startled.

This time Grace nodded, emphatic. 'Francis Pitt,' she said quite clearly. 'Never forgets my birthday, never has.'

'Can it be true?' Kate asked the matron later, when she popped in to say hello and to check up on her mother's general health.

'Oh yes,' said the woman, beaming. 'Dr Pitt comes to see her several times a year and always brings her bluebells, when they're in season. Such a nice man.' She nodded approvingly. 'Quite the gentleman, if you know what I mean.'

Kate knew. Compared with Bruno even a chimpanzee would pass muster, but Matron was clearly impressed. Well, fancy that. Kate felt a sudden, unexpected glow in the pit of her stomach, the ember of something that had once consumed her. So Francis still visited; no one had told her. Now why would he do that? Out of deference to Dad, of course, it must be. Her father had been a major influence on Francis Pitt's life. It was warming to know that he remained so loyal when he'd every reason to have defected completely. She helped her mother back to her room and arranged her in the chair by the window, along with her books and her memories.

'I'll come again soon,' she promised as she kissed the withered cheek, but she knew already it would be longer than it should be. She found this extended mourning just too painful. Even though her neglect made her as guilty as hell.

On the train going home, she thought about Francis, about the shy gawky boy he'd been when they first met him, stooping slightly because of his great height, a curtain of thick fair hair eclipsing his eyes, but a razor repartee once he conquered his awkwardness. Francis Pitt, the scholarship boy; Dad's proudest contribution to the world of science to which he had devoted his life. She smiled despite herself. What summers they'd been, when they were growing up, eternal sunshine (or so it seemed), picnics on the beach, blackberrying in the woods, rambling with Dad over the downs, and the conversation, the endless exchange of ideas, accompanied as they sometimes were by some of Dad's colleagues from the university. A golden childhood by anyone's standards, with impromptu cricket on the village green, hide and seek in the outhouses of the nearby farm, and the lengthening shadows on the fading grass as they turned at last for home, tired and thirsty, sunburned and replete, back to the creaking old house on the cliffs and the makeshift tea in the low-beamed kitchen, with Mother presiding, book as always in hand.

Why he'd chosen her, she'd never quite been sure, but he was the one who had captured her heart right from the first time she saw him. 'Little Katie' as he'd always called her, in the soft voice with the flattened vowel sounds. The thoughtful eyes in their smoky sockets that took in everything yet reflected very little, like a black hole of intellect, soaking it all in. And now she found he'd been visiting Mother all this while in the quiet, understated way he'd always had, asking for nothing, seeking no applause, self-deprecating and golden-hearted, just as he'd always been. A great wave of melancholic nostalgia swept over Kate as the train rattled back through the Sussex countryside towards the smoke of home. Francis Pitt, her first true love; what wouldn't she give right now to see him again?

The Barclay-Davenports were on their way out, Rowena dolled up to the nines in aquamarine silk, her hair for once as well coiffed as a princess's, her ears and neck ablaze with the fabled diamonds. Ronnie, beside her, wore a dark dinner-jacket and sported a white carnation; together, as always, they made a striking pair.

'Off to Glyndebourne,' said Ronnie gruffly. 'If only we can beat this blasted traffic.'

'Oh goodness, darling, there you are!' trilled Rowena, giving Kate two smacking kisses on either cheek. 'Funny, I thought you were home already. I swear I heard your doorbell ringing and ringing and I assumed you must be expecting someone.'

Her eyes were sparkling and her face lit up; in party mood she shed at least thirty years. Kate laughed.

'No, I'm only just back. In fact, I've been down that way myself. If I'd known you were coming, I'd have waited and joined you. What are you seeing – Deborah Warner's disputed *Don Giovanni*?'

Rowena nodded and pulled a face.

'Hated it last season,' she confided, 'but this time round they say it's improved. I certainly hope so, darling, but whatever happens we'll have a good time. We always do, don't we, my love?' she said, as Ronnie opened the main front door and ushered her solemnly out into the street. Kate laughed as she stood in the doorway and waved them off.

'I only wish I had your energy,' she said. They were like a couple of bright young things, the Barclay-Ds, brimming over with *joie de vivre* and energy enough to spare for the whole building. She slung her canvas carryall over one shoulder and trudged to the lift, trying, as she always had to these days, to obliterate the memory of Netta's ghastly corpse spreadeagled on the floor in a pool of her own blood. Now who, she wondered, could have been ringing her bell? She still knew practically no one in London and, in any case, casual visitors were not inclined to drop in without first letting her know.

*

Septimus Woolf was patrolling the corridors, walking on silent feet from floor to floor, keeping an eye on things generally as he did at least twice a day, checking that all was in order. As usual, the building was shrouded in silence, with the torpor of decades upon it like a dust sheet. It felt like a genuine step back in time; he could imagine the original Victorians going about their business behind closed doors.

He thought about Amelia, whom he'd always liked, and Heidi and Netta, all slaughtered on the premises. The lift had been cleaned up and the police had done their bit, so that things were back to normal, more or less, and life went on in the usual way. Without any solutions, of course, but that would be expecting a bit too much. How rum it all was, to be sure. He'd thought about it endlessly, as doubtless they all had, but still it made no sense. They were all quite harmless, those three rather pathetic women, so what possibly could have inspired a murderous killer to unleash his venom on them in particular? Septimus could think of at least two more deserving victims, starting with Mrs Adelaide Bloody Potter. Unless that was the point of it, their very ordinariness a salient clue. It was worth considering.

From somewhere downstairs a bell was ringing, and he realised it must be the porter's lodge.

'Just coming,' he called gruffly over the banisters, then walked swiftly down two flights of stairs to see who wanted him now.

The figure in the hall was grey-haired and portly, dressed on this sweltering day in an unseasonably dark suit. As he turned, Septimus saw with a jolt the purple silk stock and plain white neckband, and a thunderbolt of apprehension shot right through him. My God, the Bishop! Now what was going on?

'Your Grace?' For the first time in years, Septimus was severely shaken, and things he preferred to forget came flooding back.

'Septimus, dear boy.' The Bishop was beaming that familiar, absolving smile and holding out both hands in a gesture of forgiveness. 'Come,' he said, once Septimus had bent stiffly and kissed the ring, 'is there somewhere we may go for a proper talk? It's been so long and there's a lot we have to get through.'

There was nowhere else. After a moment's hesitation, acutely aware of his greatly lowered status, Septimus opened the door to the porter's lodge and ushered his eminent guest inside.

Kate couldn't stop thinking about Francis and his touching allegiance to her mother all these years, even though she'd known nothing of his regular visits. She wondered whether Bruno did and thought it unlikely. She couldn't imagine that Lindy wouldn't have used it against her in some way, another demonstration of how the family meant more to her ex-husband than she did herself. Thinking of Francis naturally led to Ramon, and she felt the familiar shiver of fear at the thought that he now knew her whereabouts and might even still be in London, seeking her out. She remembered that ringing doorbell and her blood ran cold.

The third time he hit her was also the last, she had made quite sure of that. It was the day she came home unexpectedly early, with a bit of a migraine, longing only for a quiet lie down in a darkened room, away from those flickering computers. And found him already there, entertaining a 'research assistant', a black girl with stylised dreadlocks, the longest legs imaginable and a supercilious nose.

'Meet Bessie,' he'd said, the whole time grinning, and Bessie had grinned along with him, all the time adjusting her suspender while he was still stuffing his shirt tail back into his pants.

'I'm going to have a lie down,' Kate had said, heading for the bedroom, but the bed wasn't made and some of Bessie's stuff was still in there. And even as she stood there looking, she'd heard this asinine creature laughing and Ramon whispering and telling her to wait. Then he'd followed Kate into the bedroom and given her a shove, and said she was an embarrassment when he was working on a story. And that he and Bessie were going out, most likely to continue their 'conversation' in some downtown bar. And not to wait up since he might not be coming back. All she'd cared about right then was her splitting head and the sharp white lights in her eyes, so she'd fallen supine on the bed and slept for several hours without another thought.

Until, much later, she'd awoken to the sound of his key in the lock and the certain knowledge that something quite dreadful was going to happen. He'd hit her then, slowly, methodically, and using full force, shattering her cheekbone and dislodging two back teeth; then kicked her as she lay on the floor, damaging her spleen and cracking four ribs.

'And that's just for starters,' he'd told her with satisfaction. 'Wait till I've had a shower and some sleep.'

She'd locked herself in the spare room without making a sound, wrapped herself in the duvet and suffered in silence, knowing she ought to be seeking a doctor but that her life was worth nothing if she did. She saw it out. The next day he was off at the crack of dawn to Chicago, and Kate had feverishly packed two cases, all the time nursing her wounded ribs, phoned in an excuse to the paper, and disappeared by cab to a nearby friend, where she'd managed to lie low for a full ten days, undetected, while the superficial damage healed. Until she could face the flight to London. And freedom.

Kate looked into the shop at lunchtime on her way back from the bank, just to say hi to Connie. They stood examining a new consignment of Victorian lustreware wall plaques, snapped up by Connie in a moment of brilliance in a house clearance sale in the Old Kent Road.

'They're absolutely priceless,' said Kate, enchanted.

'Not exactly Amelia's taste, I know,' beamed Connie. 'But I had to have them, don't you think? And I know the tourists will go ape for them.'

'I love these old sampler messages,' said Kate, as she dug through the newspaper-lined box. '*Prepare to meet thy god.* Imagine sitting there stitching that as a demure young maiden; enough to blight your whole life.' The one she particularly liked said *Thou God, see'st me*, on a pearlised cream background with a pink lustre surround, a slightly wonky herald angel suspended sideways overhead with a trumpet.

'I'll take that one, if I may,' she said. 'Just the thing to hang over the loo.'

It reminded her of her childhood and all those ridiculous fears of being watched and the Baby Jesus coming through the wall. She was feeling quite light-headed, and all of a sudden, in a lightning flash, she saw for herself the connection between Bruno and Ramon. Larry the Lamb dressed up as the Big Bad Wolf; that was all it really was once you got it into perspective. She looked at Connie and laughed out loud with the sheer delicious force of such an unlikely revelation.

'What?' said Connie, not understanding, and right at that moment the door clicked open and the chiming bells announced the presence of another. Kate turned, her face still alight with laughter, but the expression froze as she came face to face with her mystery woman, dressed this morning in pure ice-white linen with a black cashmere sweater knotted casually round her neck, picking up the sleek blue-black tones of her hair.

'Hi!' said Madeleine into a silence you could cut with a knife. 'Remember me?'

'That's cute,' she said, when they still didn't speak, looking over Kate's shoulder at the plaque, then taking it casually from her hands for a closer inspection. 'I love all this old Victorian kitsch. I'd ship it back to Canada like a shot if only I thought it would survive the journey.'

Connie, remembering her manners, pulled herself

together and showed her the rest of the collection, taking the heat off Kate for a while, allowing her to gawp without being seen. Her mystery woman, large as life, coming in here just as casual as could be. What could it all mean – surely more than just plain coincidence?

'What kept you?' asked Connie, aware of Kate's rapt fascination. 'You were going to come back to see the Meissen collection upstairs.'

'I'm sorry,' said Madeleine, 'my fault entirely. I had to leave town for a couple of days and it momentarily slipped my mind. What are the odds, do you suppose, on my wangling an invitation up there right now?'

'Not a chance!' said Connie, rather too quickly, and as Madeleine raised one stylised eyebrow, found herself stumbling through the whole traumatic story of Netta's murder while Kate watched unnoticed from the sidelines. Whatever she's pretending to be, she was thinking, she's not what she seems, no way. Netta's murder is not news to her. And furthermore, she knows diddly-squat about European porcelain, I'd bet my life on that.

Madeleine asked routine questions about Netta's death, and Connie answered them by rote, but while the Canadian woman showed the right sort of horrified interest, and although her responses were suitably shocked, to Kate's alert ears they did not sound sincere. Also, nothing further was said about the Meissen, which was odd considering it stood quite a strong chance now of being for sale. Her first impression had been on target; whoever Madeleine might really be, she was faking it.

*

Miles and Eleni were in bed together, thrashing about in the tangled sheets where they'd been for an hour or more, having it off despite the soaring temperature. The sheets were none too clean, he noticed as he came up for air, but Miles was too far gone to care; all he wanted in the world was to thrust deeper and deeper into that luscious, honeyed, all too willing flesh. Eleni's long, perfumed hair was all over the pillow and in his mouth and everywhere else as he pummelled the glorious pneumatic breasts and drove between the elastic thighs like a creature demented. From across the rooftops the sonorous clock of St Mary Abbots chimed seven.

'Jesus!' cried Miles, crashing back to earth. 'It's surely not that time already!' He'd promised Claudia that morning to take her to a Prom; well, he'd blown that now. More lies, more fictitious meetings at Lloyd's or the Hurlingham Club. These days Miles was having difficulty keeping track of what was actually true.

'Relax,' said Eleni, rolling silkily against him. 'We've hardly begun yet, *cheri*.'

'Where's Demeter?' asked Miles suspiciously. The old woman had definitely been there when he'd arrived; it was she who had opened the door and shown him silently into the drawing room, smiling all the time that ingratiating, gold-toothed smile, returning minutes later with a glass of ouzo and a plate of Greek delicacies to keep his strength up during the inevitable wait.

Eleni shrugged. 'Out?' she suggested. 'In the kitchen? Who cares?' and ran long, sinuous fingers expertly over his flagging penis. 'Time to get going again,' she whispered wickedly, and swung herself athletically upwards to straddle him like a dying horse. Oh Lord.

Miles knew there would be all hell to pay when he finally managed to break away and totter back downstairs to the marital home. Claudia was barely speaking to him as it was, what with all the lies and evasions she instinctively knew she was getting, but what was he to do? His financial situation could not be more dire, and the rich little Greek girl's family fortune was his absolutely final chance of digging himself out and eluding ruin. If only he could work out a way to get his hands on it. She was leading him a right merry dance, he could see that now, but even if it did turn out to be a blind alley, there was just no way he was going to quit. Her amazing body, her unquenchable appetites, her raging sexuality had got him like a drug; all he wanted to do these days was fuck her until he drooped. And as far as the little wifey was concerned, lying was in his blood.

The telephone rang in the other room and Demeter came to the closed door and called out something in Greek.

'Later, later,' shouted Eleni languidly. 'Tell him to call again in an hour.'

It had broken the spell. Miles rolled away from her with a heart like lead and groped on the night table for his cigarettes. A quarter to eight; he was definitely in the dog-house. He sat up and lit up and tried to get a grip on his senses before he had to re-enter the real world and face his wife.

'Who was that?' he asked suspiciously, sounding edgier than he intended. Eleni, stretched out beside him like an odalisque, shrugged eloquent shoulders and rolled her eyes.

'Who knows? Some guy. What is it you English say, another poor fish from the sea?'

She lay there quite shamelessly, glorying in her nakedness, and before he knew it, he was stroking her thigh and feeling the heat return between his own legs. He stubbed out the cigarette and leaned towards her, but this time Eleni was calling time. She put up one hand and caressed his sweaty face, then rolled off the bed and on to her feet.

'No more tonight, darling. Time to go home.' She raised both arms above her head and stretched luxuriously, then slipped into her satin robe and left the room.

'Demeter,' he heard her calling, and then, in the distance, the definite sound of someone dialling a number.

He sat on the edge of the bed, cursing as he knotted his tie. For him the evening was already half-shot and all he had left to look forward to was a hangdog return to an accusing wife, and the same raft of worries with which he had started. While for Eleni, ever-youthful, the night was just beginning. Which of her many swains was she favouring with her company tonight? In the distance he could hear the sound of fast chattering, punctuated every now and then by her melodic laugh. To Eleni life was a perpetual game, with not a worry in the world more serious than choosing which particular gown to wear and on which lucky sucker to bestow the honour of picking up the tab. Right on cue, as he was trying to flatten his hair with her silver brushes, she reappeared in the doorway, still swathed in satin.

'Miles, angel,' she said, 'how much money have you on you?' He stared at her uncomprehending but for once she was in a hurry. She indicated his wallet, still lying on the night table, and snapped her fingers impatiently. 'Quick, look. I need to know how much money you've got.'

He opened it obediently and pulled out four twenties and a ten, which Eleni unceremoniously swooped on with delight.

'Okay, Demeter,' she shouted through the open door. 'Run me a bath and order a cab for ten. And tell Ricardo when he next calls that I am dining with the Queen of Greece but will meet him later at his club for a nightcap.' She gurgled with delight as she pulled open the doors to her walk-in wardrobe and started hurling clothes to the floor as she searched for something appropriate to wear. 'Oh, and then you can come and fix my hair.'

She turned an angelic smile on Miles, who she'd momentarily forgotten was still there, and blew him a kiss from her fingertips.

'*Au 'voir*, Miles *cheri*,' she said. 'And please forgive me if I don't see you out.'

'"He's out of my life . . ."' sang Kate as she cleaned the flat, aping Michael Jackson, and then remembered that it was quite a while since she'd last seen her cat. She called him. In the kitchen, in the echoing hallway, out of the open scullery window, all to no avail. She toured the flat, checking all the windows, in case he was in one of his regular snoozing positions on the sill; nothing there, though she noticed in passing that the watcher was back at the window across the way.

She opened a tin of Whiskas and rattled the spoon on his dish, refilled his water bowl, replenished his litter, to make things as normal and as much like home as she could for when he chose to return. She wasn't seriously worried; it was typical cat behaviour and the poor chap was undoubtedly feeling the heat like the rest of them. But, like most males, she was pretty sure he'd come home when he was good and ready.

Right on cue, she heard in the kitchen the familiar thump of something heavy landing, and there was her beloved, rebellious cat, growling fiercely over something he'd brought in, something he was now tugging and dragging across the floor towards her. Kate walked towards him with caution; it was quite large, whatever it was, and she hoped it wasn't another injured bird. It had taken her weeks to get rid of the feathers last time and the splashes of blood down the white kitchen wall remained stubbornly there, despite any amount of vigorous scrubbing.

This, however, looked more like a lump of chicken, or perhaps a pork chop, stolen from somebody's kitchen. Oh dear, not again; could she never stop this pampered animal from thieving? Her neighbours would think she underfed him, would not understand that scavenging was in his blood.

'What's that you've got there?' she asked as she advanced and Horatio, still growling, stood alert over his prey, daring her to come any closer or take it away.

Kate took one disbelieving look then grabbed hold of the doorpost for support. It couldn't be, but it was; with senses reeling and a rapidly rising gorge, she backed into the bathroom and was violently sick. For what her beloved pet was nonchalantly playing with was a severed human hand.

30

The police were there in minutes, along with Digby Fenton and Gregory, whom Kate had called in her initial panic, and the Barclay-Davenports, who, having heard Kate's horrified screams, were in there plying her with medicinal gin. The hand had been neatly severed at the wrist, as if by a sharp surgical instrument, and was in good condition, light-skinned and almost certainly female. It bore no rings or other obvious identifiable characteristics.

'But where on earth did he find it?' asked Digby, studying the cat, who was being consoled with an early, unscheduled bowl of Whiskas. 'Can he get down to the ground from here?'

'I don't think so,' said Kate, still feeling very queasy.

'In any case,' pointed out Gregory, reasonably, 'he could hardly have carried something that size back to the fifth floor in his teeth.'

'So he must have found it somewhere in the building,' mused the detective inspector. 'But none of the bodies is missing a hand, and we are not missing a body.'

'As far as you know.'

All eyes swivelled to Gregory, who was sitting there

quite calmly, giving Kate a bit of a back-rub because she looked all knotted up. He glanced up at them innocently.

'Merely stating the obvious,' he said.

An officer placed the hand carefully in a polythene bag and took it away for lab analysis while the DI stayed on and asked endless questions, many of them re-covering territory they had been over many times. Kate sat slumped on the sofa feeling dreadful, while the rest of them stood protectively around her and Gregory continued to give her gentle massage. They discussed the areas to which the cat had easy access.

'There's always the roof,' said Ronnie. 'I often see him up there when I'm out watering my tomato plants.'

'Which means the whole run of the roof, the other side of the building as well as ours.'

'How does he get there?' asked the DI.

'Out of the window,' said Kate. ' I always leave the one in the kitchen open, and in this hot weather there's none of them closed.' She caught Digby looking. 'Yes, it's okay, don't worry, I've had them all fixed. Right after Heidi's murder I got Banhams in and they put burglar locks on everything. They only open the statutory five inches, wide enough to let in some air and give the cat easy access but too narrow, they assured me, for a human head.'

'So he goes from here along the windowsill and, presumably, up the pediment at the front and on to the roof from there?'

'Or up the fire escape at the rear. He has a number of choices, he's an enterprising fellow.'

'And on this level he can visit how many flats?' The

DI was making a meal of it and his younger subordinate was scribbling away.

'Just my two direct neighbours, Eleni and the
Barclay-Davenports. But he does also often go down
the stairs and in through people's front doors when
they leave them open.'

'But not this time?'

'Not on the return journey, no. He came in the window while I was standing there. He could have come
from almost anywhere, I suppose.'

This wasn't really getting them anywhere but the
policeman persisted.

'And who's downstairs? On the fourth floor, that
would be.'

Everyone looked at each other.

'Heidi. And Netta. Both dead,' said Digby slowly.
'And Mrs Adelaide Potter. Oh, and that little Japanese
man from Toyota who's scarcely ever there.' Deep
silence.

'And me,' said Gregory, reminding them.

The DI studied his sidekick's notes, then wandered
from the room and looked out of all the windows in
turn. At one point, in the office, he turned to Digby
and beckoned him over.

'What goes on over there?' he asked, indicating the
opposite window one floor down where someone was
standing quite motionless, apparently watching.

'Don't know,' said Digby, 'that's the other half of the
building. They have their own lift and are a law unto
themselves.'

'But they could have access over here?'

'Across the roof, yes,' said Digby. 'Though it's not

strictly legal. Because of insurance stipulations,' he explained.

'There's one other thing,' said Kate, starting to feel better. They all turned and looked at her. 'There's a tunnel,' she said, 'from one flat to another. Carrying the electric cables and the water pipes, the porter said. Look, I'll show you.'

She opened the door to her stationery cupboard, pulled aside a pile of cardboard boxes and revealed the hidden thirty-inch door. Everyone crowded round. The DI knelt down and inspected it, opened it to reveal the darkness beyond and beckoned to the minion to hand him his torch.

'A tunnel,' he muttered, stroking his chin. 'Have you any idea where it leads?'

'All round the building, according to the porter. If you were slim enough you could crawl along it and end up in my kitchen. I'll show you the other door. And then, presumably, if you were really ambitious, you could crawl on into Eleni's flat next door. And so on, like in the sewers.' She shuddered. Forget the sewers, all they had was rats. Think of the spiders.

The policeman gave Kate a contemplative look. For an awful moment she feared he was going to ask for a demonstration, but instead he rose to his feet and closed the door.

'And there's a tunnel like this on every floor?' he asked.

'Presumably.'

This time his blistering look was entirely for the minion.

'So why was I not informed of this before?'

The poor young man looked embarrassed and confused as he flicked through the pages of his notebook, fruitlessly searching for something he knew wasn't there.

'You really should have known,' said Kate, in his defence. 'I told the porter weeks ago and he said he already knew. He must have told someone amongst your colleagues. It's an obvious point of entry, surely?'

'Indeed.' The detective inspector looked grim in the extreme as he led the way out of the office into the hall. 'I suggest we adjourn these enquiries now,' he said brusquely. 'There are questions I need to ask back at the station.'

'Is it all right if I keep my cat?' asked Kate politely. 'Or do you need him for fingerprinting down at the Yard?'

'Just fancy,' said Rowena half an hour later, as they sat back in their own comfortable sitting room with Kate, whom they'd kidnapped as they didn't feel she should be on her own, and Gregory, who'd just popped in for a quick one before he went back downstairs, 'we've very possibly a murderer in our midst and we still haven't a clue who it is.'

'I'd put my money on the Ayatollah any day,' said Ronnie darkly, doing the honours with the drinks. 'After all, just look at her. Friends with all the victims, living right smack between two of them and with a wicked, poisonous soul to boot that would probably kill without hesitation. And now we know about the tunnel, we even know how she got in.' The Barclay-Davenports' own access to the fifth-floor tunnel was effectively blocked by a vast Chippendale sideboard in one room and the grand piano in the other. Even after all the years they'd lived in the building, they had never been aware of its existence, which was probably also true of most of the other tenants.

Kate pondered. 'Isn't she more likely the poisoner kind? And would she have the strength to inflict actual physical damage? Amelia was strangled, which must take a fair bit of muscle, while Heidi and Netta were both bludgeoned to death. Not, I would think, the work of a frail old lady, much as I hate to throw doubt on your obvious solution. Though come to think of it,' she added, 'she does always carry a walking stick with a suitably knobby top.'

Rowena laughed. 'Drat, and there was I thinking we had it all sewn up. I'd have really enjoyed watching her taken off in a tumbrel, too. More drinks, darlings? And won't you stay for supper? We've clearly got a bit more brainstorming to do, since that nice policeman doesn't appear to be having much luck.'

Gregory stretched and said he ought to be going, and all Kate wanted, now she was finally relaxing, was her bed, to catch up on some sleep.

'Will you be all right in there on your own?' asked Rowena, walking round to her door with her.

'Never better,' said Kate. 'I'll scream if I need your help.' Then cursed herself for her crassness, though Rowena appeared not to mind.

'Come on down,' said Beatrice on the phone. 'There's someone we want you to meet.'

It was the following evening, at around seven, and

Kate was just putting the computer to bed. 'Right now?'

'Yes, if you're doing nothing. And stay to supper if you've no other plans.'

Kate was pleased. She really enjoyed the company of Beatrice and Lily and loved the calm tranquillity of their elegant apartment. She washed her face and ran a comb through her hair, then examined her full reflection in the mirror to see if she needed to change. Her shirt was cleanish and her jeans were in good order; smart enough for the ladies downstairs, who always dressed down at home. Horatio was sitting on the edge of the bath, nonchalantly washing one paw. Kate wagged a stern finger at him as she left the room.

'Now you stay home tonight, young man. No more gruesome forays, thank you very much.' *Eurghh*, just the memory still made her stomach lurch.

Lily opened the door with a beaming smile and ushered Kate into the living room, where Beatrice was relaxing with a stranger. Not quite a stranger, though, Kate saw as she stood up.

'Hi,' said Beatrice, giving her a kiss. 'Meet Madeleine Kingston, a friend from Ottawa.'

Tonight Madeleine wore sleek leather pants with a silk shirt, and high-heeled cowboy boots with silver inlays. She smiled at Kate and held out her hand. Kate observed that her cherry-red nails matched her lipstick exactly. She was so surprised to see the Canadian, she hardly knew what to say. The fantasy mystery of Madeleine's haunting had become such a joke between her and Connie that it was hard to keep a straight face when confronted with the real person. She could hardly challenge her and demand to know what her business was.

'Yes, I've seen you around,' was all she could come up with.

Madeleine nodded. 'In the antiques shop in Holland Street. I was there in search of some early European porcelain,' she explained. 'Someone in this building – was it Netta Silcock? – apparently had some valuable pieces which Connie Boyle thought might interest me.'

'Yes, she lived upstairs,' said Beatrice. 'Until she was bludgeoned to death in the lift.'

'So what has happened to her flat?' asked Madeleine. 'And all her possessions, are they still there?'

'Sealed up by the police,' said Beatrice, 'while they do further investigations and also find out who's responsible for her estate.'

'So,' said Kate slowly, as light began to dawn, 'Netta's flat is sitting there, exactly as it was, untouched, and no one any longer has access to it except the police?'

'Right.'

'Or someone on the same floor thin enough to squeeze through the tunnel.'

They stared at her.

'What precisely are you getting at?' asked Madeleine, suddenly alert, shedding like a snakeskin the rich Canadian dilettante.

'I'm not quite sure. I just wonder if the coppers are smart enough to have looked in her tunnel. Provided it's not been blocked up.'

'*Cherchez la femme*, you mean?'

'Something like that. Or the body.'

'She's a bright one, that one,' said Madeleine much

later, after Kate had eaten and returned upstairs. 'She might help us solve it yet, if we're lucky. Though I'd still prefer you continued to keep her in the dark. It's fairly vital that she shouldn't know more than she does. Though I strongly suspect she has tumbled to me; there's a certain knowing light in her eye that wasn't there before.'

'Don't worry,' said Beatrice, 'you can count on us. Apart from anything, too much knowledge can be dangerous. There have been enough deaths as it is.'

He was pleased when she gave him the update.

'And she's not scared?'

'Doesn't seem to be. Merely intrigued.'

'Still hanging in there, doing her own thing?'

'So I gathered.'

'And she wasn't alerted, didn't know why you were there?'

'Don't think so.'

'Hmm.' He pondered awhile. 'So you think it's safe to continue as planned?'

'Guess so.'

Again the pause. 'Right, that's settled then. Action stations as before.' And when he smiled, she was surprised how much it improved him.

'You look like a lady who could use a bit of a treat,' said Connie brightly when Kate opened the door. 'Come on, switch off that bloody computer. We're going for a picnic, just the two of us.'

'Where's Gregory?'

'Off on one of his jaunts. Iceland, or somewhere like

that. A thousand sparky words for the *Toronto Star* –
beats working, I suppose.'

It was another glorious, golden evening – would this
summer never end? – and St Mary Abbots' bell-ringers
were just beginning their Thursday night practice.
Connie was holding an efficient-looking thermal bag,
with two promising bottle tops protruding at one end
and who knows what goodies lurking under the lid.
She wore shorts and a cropped T-shirt and high-topped
sneakers and looked utterly delicious and ready for
anything.

'Do I need a sweater?' asked Kate undecidedly.

'In this weather?' shrieked Connie. 'Are you crazy?'

They swung along Holland Street and into the park,
where the whole world seemed to be congregated, yet
with room enough for them all to fit with no noise, no
hassle and none of the near-boiling-point feelings you
might find erupting in Central Park. Groups of black-
clad ladies from the Middle East strolled near the
Round Pond with their children in tow. People of all
ages flew kites and controlled miniature sailboats,
while a legion of rollerbladers strutted their stuff on the
Broad Walk. And people walked their dogs, or sat solitary under trees reading, or stretched out in the fading
sun, or simply walked and looked and enjoyed.

'God, I love this city,' said Connie, echoing Kate's
own thoughts. 'I miss the buzz of New York but this
really is something else.' Even in the middle of a heat-
wave, the grass was that much greener, the air clearer,
the general tone of everything less fraught. Children
played gently close to the cygnets and baby ducklings;
dogs chased sticks right into the water and came out

spattering drops all over but left the livestock alone.
There was a feeling of general *bonhomie* all around,
brought out by the fine weather.

'It can't have changed much since Victorian times,'
said Kate. 'You can just see them, can't you, bowling
their hoops along these paths while Nanny sat fanning
herself on one of those benches and the band played
stirring patriotic marches on the bandstand over there.'

They bypassed the Round Pond and headed towards
the trees, this side of the Italian fountains but far
enough from the skaters and footballers to find a quiet
dell with a couple of handy deckchairs. This was, most
certainly, the life. Connie handed Kate the corkscrew
while she laid out various packages on the grass at
their feet; chicken legs, tomatoes and fresh bread, tiny
Scotch eggs and minuscule pork pies. Enough, Kate
protested, to feed half a regiment. With superior chilled
Australian Chardonnay to wash it down.

Connie kicked off her sneakers and turned elegant,
well-tanned toes to the sun.

'I can't get enough of it,' she said. 'This has to be a
vintage year.'

She was just so happy, Kate laughed to see her pleasure. Life was certainly treating Connie well: the shop
was flourishing, the second cousin appeared in no
hurry to move her on, she was trying out for a part in
the latest Ayckbourn success. Best of all, she had
Gregory, and after almost two months things were as
glowing as ever. A record for Connie. Even Jacintha
appeared to be lying low; neither hide nor hair had
been seen of her in Kensington Court for weeks.

'Quite right too,' sniffed Connie. 'Probably too

embarrassed to show her face, and understandably. What kind of a poor sap runs after a chap as obviously as that? Has she no pride, or what?'

Kate agreed. When Jacintha raised her head again, as she surely must since she'd gone to all the trouble and expense of buying a lease in the building, who else was left for her to hurl her cap at? The suave Digby Fenton, of course, with the elegant wife. Or the little Japanese gentleman who never stopped smiling and nodding, or the handsome Father Salvoni in his well-cut soutane. Or, come to that, even Septimus Woolf. He was certainly a distinguished-looking man, no question of it, cloaked, as he was, in his aura of mystery.

'Which reminds me,' said Kate, 'you'll never guess what I saw today? Our porter deep in conversation with a bishop.'

'You're kidding.'

'Not at all. They didn't see me, but I saw them. Walked behind them, in fact, along Church Row when I was heading to Annie's for a trim and blow dry. As large as life and as intimate as brothers. Strolling together, heads down, towards the church.'

'How do you know he was a bishop?'

'Because of the thing he was wearing, silly. A purple-coloured dickey with his clerical collar. And a bloody great pectoral cross around his neck.'

They ate in silence while they contemplated this marvel. That was the wonderful thing about life, you just never knew.

'He's a decent man, Mr Woolf,' said Connie. 'One of the best, salt of the earth, that kind of thing. Not bad-looking either, in an austere, ascetic sort of way. Brainy as hell, I would think. Not at all the type you'd expect to find being a porter.'

'Exactly what I've always thought,' said Kate. 'What do you imagine his secret is? There has to be one, a man like that.'

'Fallen on hard times,' mused Connie. 'Reformed alcoholic? Bigamist on the run? You never can tell with that sort of bloke. Writer doing research? Train robber? International spy?' Now they came to discuss it, all of these seemed possible. 'Undercover policeman?'

They rocked with laughter like two silly schoolgirls as they ate their chicken legs and drank their wine. Later, however, when Kate was alone it didn't seem quite so absurd.

They dropped their rubbish in a bin, then strolled by the Serpentine as the orange sunlight gave way to a sky of velvety blue shot with crimson streaks. The children had all gone home to bed and even the rollerbladers were thinning out. For once no one was swimming, for the lido was closed and a notice warned you off.

'You couldn't drown in water this shallow,' said Connie.

'Harriet Shelley did,' said Kate.

'Harriet who?'

'Percy Bysshe's first wife, ignoramus,' said Kate, though she could see that her benighted friend was still none the wiser. Ah well. These Americans had a lot to learn about good old British culture but she couldn't be bothered to tease her about it just now; the evening was so peaceful and perfect.

The air was balmy and pleasantly fresh; a light

breeze disturbed the foliage round the water's edge. From Rotten Row came the satisfying thud of two army officers exercising their mounts. A solitary angler still sat motionless, chancing his luck against the hooded grey shadow of a heron, watching unseen from a clump of willows.

'I feel so happy,' said Connie ecstatically, 'that if I died tonight I'd still be satisfied.'

'Don't talk like that,' said Kate, alarmed. There'd been too much dying around her just lately. 'For God's sake, don't tempt providence. You've so much to live for, you're only just beginning. Think of the future, of your career. Of Gregory.'

'That's just it,' said Connie, sobering slightly. 'I'm not really sure if we have a future. But let's not talk about that tonight.'

31

The truth was, Connie was not nearly as happy as she appeared, though she tried to put a good face on things, particularly around Kate, who had always been such a brick. Poor old Kate had taken some pretty nasty knocks just recently and Connie had long had a sneaking suspicion that she was not entirely immune to Gregory's charms herself. True, she tried valiantly to hide her feelings, and friendship could surely not be much more selfless than that, but Connie caught the occasional wistful look and the sudden flush of pleasure when Gregory entered a room or spoke her name. And why not, indeed? Gregory Hansen was about as dishy as a man could be and if she thought she'd made a unique discovery, she was plainly deluding herself. There was Jacintha Hart and the Ali McGraw lookalike for starters, not to mention an endless string of others he must meet and dazzle in the normal course of his life, not just here in London but wherever his travels took him. Added to which, Kate had seen him first, so, theoretically, had a prior claim.

Which made her backing off that much more remarkable. It certainly would not have happened in Connie's New York circles, where the law of the jungle still prevailed and men that eligible were very rare indeed. Connie would have liked to be able to put her arms around her friend and get her to confess the truth. But what good would that do, and besides, it just wasn't on. Kate would simply curl up with embarrassment, the British stiff upper lip and all that, and Connie's generous gesture would be bound to be misinterpreted. All she'd be saying would be: 'Hard luck, sucker. I've got a guy and now you haven't.' Best to keep her mouth shut and leave Kate with her dignity.

Which wasn't it at all, of course. What she really wanted, more than anything, was to discuss her disquieting gut instinct that Gregory was slowly cooling towards her, though how she knew this was hard to say. It was not exactly anything he had done or said; just a vague uneasy feeling that their big romance was going slowly off the boil. They'd been together eleven weeks, and in her first flush of enthusiastic passion, Connie had assumed they'd be living together by now. Why not, indeed? They were both free, straight and over twenty-one. Not to mention great companions and dynamite in bed. What else was there?

One of these days, however dilatory the second cousin might be, Amelia's estate would have to be settled, and when it was, the flat would be put on the market, with all its contents. Much though she'd love to buy it herself, Connie didn't have that sort of money. In any case, that wasn't what she wanted. What she did want was perfectly natural and straightforward, to live with Gregory. To begin with, things had simply raced along and Connie was planning interiors and mooning in jewellers' windows the same as every lovesick maiden since time began. She was thirty-three, with a string of emotional disasters behind her, but her luck must surely change some time, so why shouldn't Gregory Hansen be the one?

After all, he was nine years older, plenty old enough to settle down, and they appeared to have so much going for them – a shared sense of humour, appreciation of the good things in life, a certain element of itchy-footedness, plus a North American heritage in common – that it ought by rights to have been pretty much plain sailing. She was an actress, he a journalist; there was nothing they couldn't do together, nowhere in the world they couldn't go. Connie dreamed of a blissful nomad life with him, at least for the first few years together before the babies started to arrive and they set down permanent roots somewhere.

But lately she had begun to sense that things were not quite as intense as they'd been, that Gregory was somehow pulling back. And that really scared her. These days, whenever she suggested something, he seemed to be busy or have alternative plans, and when she'd offered to join him next time he flew to Toronto, he'd seemed almost alarmed and mumbled some excuse which just didn't make any sense to Connie. It would be fun to go back to the States together, to visit the scenes of his youth along with hers. That was the sort of thing people in love did together; she'd be proud to show him off to her folks so why was it he didn't appear to feel the same?

Just natural caution maybe. She longed to discuss it all with Kate but feared that voicing her doubts might make them real. She tried to convince herself it was all

in her mind, but it wasn't, she knew it, and it was starting to drive her mad. When Jim had gone, the split had
been mutual and no one's feelings were more than
dented. They had simply run out of steam; even the
divorce had been amicable. But this time things were
entirely different. Connie was deeply and passionately
in love; even the thought of ever losing Gregory was
more than she could bear.

He was off on his own on one of his trips right now
and she really couldn't see why he couldn't have taken
her with him. She was earning a nice little income
these days, courtesy of Amelia's shop combined with a
thin flow of acting jobs that kept trickling in, and
would gladly have paid her own way. Iceland at this
time of year should be nice, away from the discomforts
of overheated London, and she wouldn't have cramped
his style on the press trip. In fact, she was sure she'd
have been an asset. She got on well with most people
and liked a good time. But he hadn't suggested it and
she hadn't liked to press, so here they were, parted
again, with Connie's plans no further advanced as the
summer ticked by and the days began to grow shorter.

Take his keys, for instance. All the time they'd been
together, she had been hinting that he ought to give her
a set, but so far nothing had happened. Which was
patently ridiculous since she spent at least three nights
a week in his bed, cooked most of his meals and really
needed easy access in order to keep things running
smoothly. As it was, half her clothes were hanging in
Gregory's closets and some of her kitchen equipment
(well, Amelia's) now resided on his shelves. It was a
cosy way of life and she liked it quite a lot but she

would have been a whole lot happier if they could only share everything on a permanent basis.

So this time, while he was in Reykjavik for five days, Connie was taking things into her own hands. The season was drawing to a close and much of Gregory's flat needed a good sorting and cleaning. She itched to get her hands on his curtains and loose covers so had hijacked Bonita, who cleaned for him occasionally, and borrowed her keys just for a couple of days. Bonita had been doubtful but she knew how close the two of them had become and had not been able to argue with Connie without seeming rude.

'I'll give them back as soon as I'm through,' Connie had promised cheerfully. 'It will be our secret, yours and mine, and think how pleased he'll be when he sees what I've done. Spruced the whole place in his absence, which should also make your job a lot easier, without the residue of years to trip over.'

'Oh dear,' Bonita had confided to Septimus, 'I hope I've not done wrong, letting her have them. He's very much a private person and likes to keep himself to himself. But she was so persuasive, what could I do?'

'Women,' said Septimus, heartily sick of them all. 'They're all much the same. Always meddling and making trouble. Look at Pandora; look at Eve.'

Most of his problems were due to women, and now the Bishop was back on his case, adding to his turmoil by giving him more to think about. Why couldn't they all just leave him alone, secure in the cosy little backwater of his porter's lodge?

Upstairs Eleni was also having a turn-out but hers was

a lot more drastic than what Connie had in mind. There was altogether too much police presence in this building lately; too much coming and going to be healthy. In addition to which, the bills were piling up, and lately there had been a number of unwanted callers who had put her on her guard. Calls from casual suitors or infatuated men were one thing, but when her creditors started to close in, drastic action was called for. Demeter had also alerted her to the presence of a stranger, a tall, rather striking, elegant woman who seemed to be paying a little too much attention to this building and what was going on inside. Eleni had a very sharp eye and recognised trouble at a thousand paces. Immigration or the bailiffs; one thing or the other, she'd stake her life on it.

'Time, Demeter, to be moving on.' They'd had a good run for it, had stayed longer than intended because the flat was comfortable and central and she liked this building and some of its occupants. But even that began to be a liability after a while. Take Miles, for instance. He was behaving lately like a foolish young puppy, throwing discretion to the winds, and sooner or later there was bound to be a showdown, if only with the jealous wife. Eleni had little time for Claudia, who she considered snobbish and aloof, but she didn't much relish the thought of tangling with her, especially as Eleni knew she was in the wrong.

Time to move on. She'd found them another stopgap in Bryanston Square, a spacious first-floor flat with absentee owners and a peppercorn rent (an academic consideration since the Papadopoulos family rarely paid for anything), where they could lie low for a month or so, and mix with a different set until things blew over. Each time she left the building, Eleni took a big bag of clothes and deposited them in lockers at Paddington Station ready for the final flit. No one must know they were about to depart. Bills were unpaid, a quarter's rent owing, and she didn't want to be held responsible for the wear and tear on the flat. Most of all, she was keen not to risk alerting Miles, for then the balloon really would go up and there was no imagining the resulting catastrophe.

The sole person she did trust was Bonita, and to her she donated a great pile of clothes. She liked the pretty little Spanish woman; they were both foreign nationals cheating the Government and therefore sisters under the skin.

'Are you going on a trip, Miss Eleni?' asked Bonita, wide-eyed at her own good fortune. Eleni was considerably taller, but Bonita was a whiz with a needle, and some of these clothes were hardly worn. Pressed and mended, for Eleni was careless with her clothes, she could sell them for a nice little profit in the North End Road or amongst her needy compatriots in Kentish Town.

'For a short while,' conceded the Greek, 'but I'd sooner you didn't breathe a word to anyone. Not even Mr Woolf, if you please.' She made up some story about not wanting a fuss made, but Bonita recognised a moonlight flit when she saw one. Well, good luck to her and that doughty old mother. The old lady worked her fingers to the bone and put up a good show, but she didn't fool Bonita. She'd seen the light of maternal pride in the wise old eyes and respected her for going to such lengths to stay with her child and watch over her. She would miss Eleni – they all would – for she brought a breath of fresh air to the building, but she would respect her confidence and her privacy.

'You're not going away?' asked Rowena, dismayed, coming home with the shopping just as Eleni was leaving with a load. Eleni hesitated. She loved Rowena and hated to lie to her, but what else was she to do? This was the way she had lived since childhood, on her wits and on her back when necessary, surfing across all obstacles, seizing whatever opportunities she could.

'Just a fast trip back to Athens,' she said glibly. 'My aunt is sick. We are needed at home.'

'Is Demeter going too?' Rowena had long been intrigued by this set-up and the odd role the older woman seemed to play.

'Oh yes,' said Eleni carelessly. 'What would she do here on her own?'

'She could have a bit of a rest,' said Rowena firmly. 'Take things easy and put her feet up for a change.'

Eleni smiled her seraphic smile and kissed her neighbour warmly on both cheeks, Greek-style.

'Demeter loves to work,' she said easily. 'She'd be lost without it.'

It felt quite odd to be letting herself into Gregory's flat without him there, even though she was certain he wouldn't really mind. And why, indeed, should he? She was only doing what any woman would, caring for his interests in his absence, preparing to give him a big surprise. All the windows were closed and the flat felt airless, so the first thing she did was throw a few open to get a good draught going. Then she picked up his mail and piled it tidily on his desk, and went around methodically gathering ashtrays and dirty glasses. He ought to get a dishwasher, she'd been nagging him for weeks, but there was detergent under the sink so she soon had them clean and put away.

She took down his laundry bag and put it by the door, ready for the launderette, then gathered all the towels she could find and piled them on top. The kitchen was more or less tidy, she'd given it the once-over last time she was here, and she'd only changed the sheets last week so they could be left for now. The curtains next. If she was going to do it, she might just as well do it properly. She found a set of steps in the kitchen and climbed up and took them all down. Well, why not? She'd lug them all round to the laundry in Holland Street and hope they could get them done before he returned.

It was hard work but she was beginning to enjoy herself. Nothing like a bit of sweated labour to give a girl an appetite, and it helped to fill the aching void caused by Gregory's absence.

You're getting soft, she told herself. No guy's worth this much trouble.

But she knew that wasn't true. It was oddly uplifting to be doing all this for him, and she looked forward to his pleased surprise when he returned and saw what she'd achieved. We ought to get those chairs re-covered, she thought, and smiled as she realised how natural the plural seemed. Eleven weeks together; soon it would be three months and they could have a quarter year's celebration. Perhaps they should have a party, a public

affirmation of their love, just for a few of the neighbours.

Kate, of course, and the Burdetts, and Digby and
Olive Fenton; she checked them off as she worked.
And the darling Barclay-Davenports and those two
ladies in sensible shoes, and the ravishing Greek, provided she could keep her hands off Gregory. What
about Jacintha Hart? Connie pondered as she moved
into the study and balanced herself precariously on
Gregory's desk. She unhooked the grimy net curtains
and found herself outlined against the glass for all the
world to see. Gregory had the identical view from here
that Kate had one floor higher. She caught a glimpse of
someone at the window across the courtyard but when
she found her balance and looked again, the figure had
gone.

Which brought her back to the party list and the
tricky question of Jacintha. On the whole, Connie
thought not – though she definitely had the upper
hand and there was sometimes strength in magnanim
ity. Jacintha was a pathetic creature; look how she'd
crumbled when first confronted with Connie. If she
made an ally of Jacintha, perhaps she'd be less of a
threat. Or else she could invite the husband too; now
that really was worth thinking about.

She rolled the curtains into a ball and tossed them
into the doorway, then scrambled down, careful not to
step on Gregory's papers. She already had at least one
load but now she'd started, she might just as well go
on. She took a closer look at the chairs, which were
covered in an unattractive dark print in russet and
maroon but were still in quite good nick, apart from

the ingrained dirt. A dry-cleaning was really all they needed. Better to hold off buying new things until their future was settled and they could plan together.

'Now, who on earth's that?'

'The American. Kate's friend. The one who runs the antiques shop.'

'What's she doing there?'

'Caretaking, at a guess. With him away.'

'What on earth's she up to?'

'Spring-cleaning from the look of things.'

'At this time of year?'

'Some women are like that. Especially when in love.'

'I wouldn't know.'

The covers came off easily, once she'd worked out that they had zips down the sides, and Connie worked merrily away, cushion by cushion, folding and piling, until she had a whole other load waiting to be lugged round the corner.

'Well, Mr Hansen,' she said cheerfully. 'Don't ever think I don't have your best interests at heart.'

She decided to do the sofa as well – in for a penny, in for a pound – but that she found was a lot more difficult, since she had to wrestle the long cushions from their covers. Somehow she'd never done this before, slut that she was. She only hoped she'd be able to work out later which bit went back where, but it was too late now. She managed eventually, and all that was left was the main cover. She undid the zips and gave a great jerk, pulling it off in one satisfactory sweep, revealing the pathetic iron frame beneath. As she dragged it into a neat rectangle and started to roll it up for carrying, something dropped out of the folds of cotton and on to the floor at her feet.

It was a passport but not a British one. When she saw the Canadian insignia on the front, she assumed it must be Gregory's, but if that was so, what was he travelling on now? She picked it up and flicked through its pages. *Alice Ruth Sorensen*, it said, and the face that looked right back at her from the photograph was Ali McGraw's.

On her second trip to the laundry round the corner, Connie ran into Eleni in the lift. Eleni was wearing a surprising number of clothes for such a hot day and was accompanied, unusually, by her deferential servant, Demeter. Both women laughed when they saw they were equally burdened.

'Off on holiday?' asked Connie breezily, as she stacked her dry-cleaning on the bench and held the door for the others to leave. Eleni's smile was positively dazzling.

'Something like that,' she said, kissing Connie on both cheeks. '*Au 'voir, cherie.* It's been great knowing you. Have a good life.'

There had to be some explanation, but for the life of her, Connie couldn't think what it could be. If Alice Sorensen had left without her passport it was logical to suppose she must still be somewhere in these isles, yet Connie had not seen hide nor hair of her in months, certainly not in the past eleven weeks. And even before that, Jacintha had been much in evidence. If those two temptresses had ever locked horns, Kate would be bound to know and have passed it on. Most odd. She'd thought the passport might be an old one but the expiry date was 1998. She gave up trying to think of an explanation and simply left it on Gregory's desk. None of her business, she told herself sternly, and if she started asking questions he'd think she was jealous.

After she'd lugged everything to the Holland Street laundry, she went into the shop for a few hours' catching-up. Normal trade was slack at this time of year but the casual tourists more than made up for it, and it was worth staying open for the occasional erratic spender. She had hung the Victorian lustreware plaques in an eye-catching position close to the window and had already unloaded two, in addition to the one bagged by Kate. Inspired by what she'd been doing to Gregory's flat, she grabbed her beeswax spray can and a clean yellow duster and set to work, improving the patina of everything around her. What Connie particularly enjoyed about this work was the sheer tactility of it all, the textures and visual delights and aromas. Contact with the actual living past; a joy and a privilege to be handling such fine things.

So much hard graft had quite tired her out, so after a while she thought she'd have a break and settle down to something less exhausting by catching up on the book-keeping. It was after eight and the evening was closing in as she sat comfortably slumped in Amelia's button-backed chair, sandals off, ice-cold can of Budweiser at her elbow, listening to the distant laughter of bright young Kensington things drinking across the road at The Elephant and Castle, gathered out there in the early dusk like starlings nesting, just as they used to do in her distant youth. It was a comforting sound and another reminder of why she loved this city so much, the villagey feeling of the small Kensington back streets as familiar and cheery as the Brooklyn where she'd grown up.

She'd forgotten that she'd left the door unlatched and was surprised to hear the familiar ding-dong of the bell. Now who on earth could that be out there now, long after normal closing time, disturbing her privacy? People could be so thoughtless. She left her sandals where they were, ran fingers through her riotous curls then pushed her way through the bead curtain to confront the intrusive stranger.

'Hi, honey!'

The surprise could not have been greater. A great wave of happiness swept over Connie as she ran into the welcome arms opening to embrace her.

32

Lady Wentworth was appalled. In this morning's mail she had received a curt letter from Miles, telling her she'd sustained an overall loss with Lloyd's of almost a quarter of a million pounds, and requesting a cheque in immediate settlement. She hobbled to the telephone and rang his number but the machine was on; he had obviously already left for work. She didn't know what else to do and her poor old heart started to pound like a hammer. Up till now she had looked upon Miles with benevolent fondness, like a favourite nephew who never failed to delight her with his charm, intelligence and ingenuity. She was less impressed by the chilly wife, but even that was all right. Claudia was simply socially insecure and would, presumably, mellow with time.

Miles had been a comfort and a boon in the past few months and Lady Wentworth had been able to relax in the certain knowledge that her perplexing financial affairs were finally safely in the hands of somebody she could trust. Furthermore, he had always promised that money invested now would grow, and that she might even double it within the space of just a few years. Lady Wentworth was eighty-four. It was reassuring to know she need no longer worry; that Miles's shrewd investments would see her comfortably taken care of for the remainder of her life. So grateful was she, she was even considering altering her will and making Miles and Claudia its principal beneficiaries. She had no children of her own and liked the idea of watching their family grow, once Claudia put aside this foolish notion of a competitive career and settled down, as any good wife should, to giving Miles a proper family life.

And now this. The cold black print on the paper she held in her quivering hand was brutally lucid and brooked no misunderstanding. Lloyd's of London, that hallowed institution, demanded her money. She had only a few days in which to get it together or else goodness knows what the penalty might be. Images of Newgate jail flashed before her mind's terrified eye and she began to whimper helplessly like a puppy, clapping her hands to her ears in anguish and dropping shakily into a chair when her legs gave way. She'd been trying to talk to Miles for weeks now but lately he'd seemed to be strangely abstracted, almost abrupt in the way he'd brushed her aside. She would have talked to Netta, who had been in the same boat, but Netta was dead. The only ally she had left now was Mrs Adelaide Potter, but Lady Wentworth would sooner lie in a pauper's grave than stoop to discussing anything so personal with the widow of a draper. She knew she'd never hear the end of it, and pride meant more than peace of mind, at least in this case.

Slightly rallied by this acerbic thought, she pulled herself together and struggled into the kitchen to make herself a cup of tea. She was overreacting, she was sure she must be, and soon Miles would ring and reassure her and it would all turn out to be a misunderstanding. But even as the kettle boiled and she lifted it with a palsied hand and poured hot water shakily into the silver pot, reality struck and she knew it wasn't so. Lloyd's of London had lasted three centuries and was one of Britain's finest institutions. Her father had been a Name before her and his father before that. When they called in their debts, they had to be paid; that was how the system worked and there were no two ways about it. What chance had a frail old lady against power like that?

When Miles finally realised that Eleni had flown the coop, the cold hand of doom clutched at his heart and he thought for a moment he was finished. He'd finally done it and fluttered too close to the sun, and in his dying fall he knew he was bound to take others with him: Claudia and Caroline and the girls; Lady Wentworth and possibly Chuck Moran. Already the Serious Fraud Office was on to him, the news had filtered through last night, and now it could only be a matter of time. He sat in his Canary Wharf office and looked down for a moment at the river, crawling sluggishly beneath his windows, twenty-seven storeys below. If it weren't for modern architecture and the hermetically sealed windows, he could always take the gentleman's way out . . . but Miles was no gentleman and was not going down without a fight. He stuck his head round Claudia's door, where she was sitting frostily at her desk, dictating letters to her secretary.

'Just popping out for a while, old dear,' he said. It

was quarter to one. 'Could you pick up some supper? Oh, and make sure that all our insurance policies are paid up?' He laughed in response to her frozen expression and blew her a kiss from the door.

'Toodle-oo,' he said as he headed for the lift. She wasn't the easiest creature in the world but he knew he was bound to miss her.

Septimus was sitting quietly in his lodge, minding his own business and trying to come to terms with the latest happenings and the Bishop's bombshell, when he heard a familiar whistling outside and Rhodri O'Connor hove into view, clutching the familiar brown paper bag. Hell and damnation.

'Are you in there, auld sport, and would you be after joining me in a touch of the hair of last night's dog?'

Septimus opened the door. The Irishman stood there, visibly swaying, shirtless beneath his uniform jacket, his underpants pulled up over the top of his trousers, his braces visible above his vest. Lord protect him from the likes of Adelaide Potter.

'You'd better come in,' said Septimus gruffly, and pulled him smartly out of sight of the main hallway.

Rhodri's face was a fiery red and the bottle he so craftily concealed was already half empty. His breath reeked of raw spirit and his voice was slurred. God alone knew how he still hung on to his job; Septimus could only suppose that the residents the other end must be a lot less pernickety.

Settled together in the confines of the small sitting room, Rhodri unlaced his shoes and prepared for a good jaw.

'So they've found another body?' he asked, offering the bottle.

'Part of one.' Septimus shook his head. The Bishop's visit had unsettled him and given him much to ponder on.

'Is that the case? Sure and they're some rum characters around, not only in this half of the building.'

He told Septimus of his own queer couple, stuck up there in a cramped third-floor sublet, scarcely ever coming out, not even for a breather.

'I don't know what they're up to,' he said, 'but it really is most odd.' She always so spectacularly smart, he a real man of mystery in a raincoat and a pulled-down hat. In this sweltering weather, too, when it was almost too hot to breathe.

'Do you suppose they've a chainsaw up there with them?' he asked with a cackle. 'These days you simply never know.'

And he belched companionably and wiped his nose on his sleeve.

Because he was in a hurry, he hadn't time to waste with the car park so risked sticking the Porsche right outside the main front door and prayed to the gods to be spared enough time to grab the essentials and make his dash, without any of those tiresome parking officials intervening. These days they swaggered around like members of Franco's army, looking for all the world as if they were armed. No one was about, however, not even the porter, as he slid through the hall and took the lift to the third floor. He was wary of running into Lady Wentworth, though this was the hour she usually took her nap, or Chuck Moran, who should be safely incarcerated in his office

He really regretted the loss of Eleni but was confident he'd catch up with her somewhere or other when things had cleared and he was good and ready. He and Eleni were birds of a feather; chancers on the great highway of life with more in common than she could possibly be aware. Once he'd fixed this immediate crisis, he'd maybe go in search of her, but in the meantime he hadn't a lot of time to waste. He slipped into the flat, grabbed a suitcase from the top of the wardrobe and started stuffing essentials into it: underwear, shaving kit, a couple of Savile Row suits, plus a thick file he kept in the safe concealed in the cupboard in his dressing room. He checked the time – three-fifteen – then dialled the airline and listened to news of incoming flights: Karachi, Delhi, Sydney, Singapore. In his wallet he had seven hundred pounds in cash, together with assorted credit cards and a couple of passports in different names, so for the time being at least, the world really was his oyster.

He grabbed his Burberry, went back for his Ray-Bans, and was out of there in under twenty minutes. What he'd do about Claudia he'd have to figure out later, once he was safely on a plane and away. At least she had a job and wouldn't starve – unlike Caroline and the children, but he blocked his mind to that. Whether he'd ask her to join him later still remained to be seen; it depended on how she reacted initially and how successful he was in tracking down Eleni. He humped his various pieces of baggage to the lift, went back to lock all the various safety locks and then, on an impulse, posted the keys back through the letterbox. He wouldn't be needing them where he was going, and at least it would serve as a warning to Claudia that he wasn't ever coming back.

The street was virtually deserted as he closed the front door behind him and went to open the car boot. Two short trips and he'd be away; he hoisted his bits and pieces into the boot, threw his raincoat in on top of them, and carefully closed the lid. Then stopped in his tracks, stunned with annoyance, for someone was standing peering into his car, someone in an unseasonable black wool coat and flat, forbidding hat. Mrs Adelaide Potter.

'Going somewhere, young man?' she rapped out authoritatively as she leaned on her umbrella, stern as a sergeant major on parade, foursquare blocking his access to the driver's door. Miles muttered to himself in exasperation, shooting a fast glance at his watch. This sort of interference he could well do without. It was time the irritating old biddy learned to mind her own damned business. If she didn't stop jawing and get out of his way PDQ, he'd risk not getting to the airport on time.

But he managed to hang on to his temper and paste a cheery smile on his face. Always make a good show of it, that was what his expensive education had taught him.

'Just a fast jaunt up to Birmingham,' he said smoothly. 'Back in time for lunch tomorrow, if the traffic's not too dire.' And I can get past you, you interfering old trout.

Mrs Potter was still peering.

'Seems a lot of luggage for an overnight trip,' she said accusingly, just as if she were the beak and he on trial for his life. 'Claudia going with you, then? I don't see her around.'

Shit. 'No, not on this occasion, I'm afraid. Far too much to do in the office and it's strictly a business meeting. Dreadfully dull stuff. Not one of the junkets she really enjoys.'

He smiled winsomely, hoping to get away with it, but Mrs Potter was nobody's fool and never gave credit when it was possible to avoid it.

'Claudia's not been looking at all well lately,' she said through tightened lips. Her hard grey eyes, sharp as the marcasite at her throat, bored into him and recognised his guilt.

'I hope you've not been giving her cause for concern,' she said, shifting her gaze to the briefcase clutched in his hand. 'You and that foreign trollop on the fifth floor.'

Miles was aghast. Was there nothing this nightmarish old harridan didn't know? His hand tightened defensively on the bulging briefcase and he instinctively swung it at her as he advanced towards his car, indicating that she should move sharpish, that she was in his way.

'And another thing.' Mrs Adelaide Potter's voice grew shriller and a rictus of something that might have been amusement distorted the thin face as she stood her ground on monolithic legs and dared him to advance.

'What about Lady Wentworth?' she spat at him. 'You've been leading her a right merry dance. Leaving before you've cleared up your mess, are you? Like you did with Netta Silcock and those other poor fools who trusted you? I wonder how much that wife of yours knows about your carryings-on and what she will say when it all comes out.'

Arms akimbo, she was openly mocking him now, the ghastly semblance of a smile on her witchlike face. Cross me if you dare! was the message she was giving, but Miles had had enough and was not going to let anyone, particularly this old crone, stand in his way.

'Fuck off!' he said succinctly, as he pushed her roughly aside and fumbled with the key to the driver's door. But Mrs Adelaide Potter had not been terrorising her troops all these years for nothing.

'Officer!' she shrieked, regaining her balance and waving her umbrella at a passing squad car. 'Arrest this man. He has just assaulted me. And while you're at it, I'd take a look inside that briefcase he's clutching. Enough evidence there to incriminate him properly, I wouldn't be at all surprised. Hanging's too good for the likes of him.'

The tramp in his rat's nest on the corner watched the scene with his customary basilisk stare. Whatever he was thinking, he wasn't about to divulge it, but for once, there was definite amusement in his eyes.

'I'm sorry,' said Lady Wentworth pitifully, 'I still don't understand what you're trying to tell me.'

After a dreadful day spent cowering on her bed, she was further confused by this sudden eruption of Mrs Adelaide Potter at full throttle, wearing her hat and waving her stick like a wizened Boadiccea on the warpath.

'Well, let me in then and put on the kettle, and I'll tell you all about it.' Whereupon the formidable old woman swept right by her and into the sanctum of Lady Wentworth's front room, shedding the stick on the way as though she had no further use for it. There was a light in Mrs Potter's eye that was not usually there, and for the first time in their acquaintance, she was looking positively elated. Lady Wentworth was quite impressed, and her battered spirits cautiously began to revive. If there was a battle to be fought, she'd certainly be there, if only to defend the honour of her father and his forebears. She'd even go so far as to don her Red Cross uniform if what Mrs Potter was gabbling at her was to be believed. But Miles, poor Miles; in police custody? And could he really be responsible for all these murders, as Mrs Potter was trying to suggest? Surely not. The thought was too painful even to consider. And what about Claudia, had anyone told her?

'All in good time,' snapped Mrs Potter imperiously. 'Just bring the tea, and some of those Fortnum's biscuits, and I'll start at the beginning.'

'It's getting out of hand.'

'I know. But there's not a lot we can do right now.' She'd been on one of her forays to investigate. *The street was blocked with police cars, she reported. All hell had broken out at the other end.*

'What is it about this building? What's going on?'

'Search me. It seemed so dull and respectable.'

'If this is Kensington, you can keep it.'

'Big city life. Guess it's always like this.'

'Well, the sooner we can get out of here, the better.'

'You know something? I'm beginning to think you're right.'

The sergeant entered the room, bearing a tray of good old English tea. She gestured to him dismissively: 'Stick it over there.'

Then, turning on him in sudden fury: 'It's all your fault. If you and the other plods hadn't made such a pig's ear out of this inquiry, we'd both be long gone by now and I, for one, would be up in the Adirondacks, catching up on my skiing.'

The sergeant shrugged expressively. What could he say? He was as weary of the investigation as she was, more so really. And he and his Metropolitan pals were additionally irked by the intrusion on to their patch of this bossy Canadian and the grave-faced suit who was the other half of her team.

The first thing Claudia knew about it was when two gentlemen in discreet dark suits called at the office and requested an interview. The card they sent in turned her pale with apprehension; she curtly dismissed her secretary and went out alone to confront them.

'So where is he now?' she asked much later, as they strolled by the river out of respect for her privacy. She'd known there'd been trouble but this exceeded her wildest fears. Miles in custody, caught in the act of leaving the country? With financial papers that should not have been in his possession at all? It just couldn't be. There was nothing he'd done that she didn't already know about. She was, after all, not only his wife but his personal assistant as well. His business was her business; that was how they worked. How could all this possibly be?

She heard her voice tail off in a pathetic whimper but the officers counselled her calmly not to say a thing she might regret. Her husband was in trouble enough; no need to make it worse than it was already.

'Can I see him? Where is he?'

'He's with the City Police right now. The Serious Fraud Office is waiting to interview him. We'll have to see, it's most irregular.' But she could tell they were softening; in her anxiety, her beauty was quite compelling.

Miles felt a regular fool when the door was unlocked and they came to tell him his wife was waiting outside.

'Do I have to see her?'

'Afraid so, laddie.'

But he hadn't had time yet to perfect his story, and facing Claudia would be far worse than facing anyone, including the beak. He'd let her down and now he knew it. As long as he kept her in the dark and escape was still possible, he'd gone on hoping. He'd been in corners tighter than this in the past and still leapt free. No point in disturbing the little lady if it wasn't absolutely essential, and for Miles Burdett hope had always been an unquenchable wellspring.

'What am I going to say to her?'

'That's up to you. But you've only got fifteen minutes, so better make it quick.'

Claudia looked ice-cool in a natural linen shift, her dark hair glossy and perfectly groomed, looped neatly behind her delicate ears. She wore no make-up. For almost an hour she'd been pacing up and down, but now she was face to face with her recalcitrant husband, she'd suddenly run out of words to say.

Except: 'How could you?'

'I did it for you.' The smile was just as ingenuous, the eyes behind their owlish lenses as schoolboyish and disarming as the day she first met him. He was wearing his second-best suit, and his tie, as usual, flaunted a gravy spot. The officer waiting patiently by the door glanced meaningfully at the big wall clock and Miles remembered he hadn't a lot of leeway; that this could be the last real time they'd have to talk in the foreseeable future.

So he told her everything, at least as much as he dared, and watched her expression turn from blank to disbelieving; saw sheer incredulity enter the magnificent eyes.

'I can't believe what you're telling me,' she said at last.

'It's the truth. Every word. Check it out, if you want confirmation. I don't deserve you and I never did. All I can say by way of mitigation is that I always loved you and was a desperate man.'

Whether she'd be waiting for him when he finally came out again – if he ever did – was doubtful. The way she was looking at him now she'd probably do anything to prevent their paths ever crossing again. And he couldn't, in all honesty, say he blamed her. She was far too good for the likes of him; the lovely Eleni was much more his style.

'Whatever happens, good luck to you,' he said, but

she turned without a further word and indicated that she wished to leave.

Well, I certainly blew that one, thought Miles ruefully as they led him away.

33

It was almost lunchtime and still there was no word from Connie, so Kate unbooted the computer and went to have a look. They'd arranged to meet that morning at the health club but Connie simply hadn't shown. Unusual, but there was bound to be a reason. It was not like her to be unreliable. The heat was finally abating, after all these weeks of stifling humidity, and Kate felt quite cool and jaunty as she stepped into the street and headed up the hill towards Holland Street.

'Hi,' said Madeleine, falling into step beside her. 'Are you, by any chance, going to the shop? Mind if I walk along with you?' To mark the slight cooling of the weather, she was wearing an unstructured pantsuit in a greeny-beigy unpressed linen, and high strappy sandals that had to be uncomfortable but looked terrific.

'That was a terrible thing that happened to you,' ventured Madeleine after a while. 'Your cat bringing in that mummified hand.'

Lord, the way news got around.

Kate stopped dead in her tracks and confronted her elegant companion with suspicion. 'Now how in the world could you possibly know about that?'

'Oh,' said Madeleine, looking suitably vague. 'Wasn't it in the papers?'

No, thought Kate darkly, it most certainly wasn't. There's more to this than meets the eye.

'I thought they'd arrested someone yesterday,' she said. 'There was a rumour they'd caught him red-handed, right outside the building. Or so our resident nosy-parker, Mrs Adelaide Potter, was claiming. I certainly hope it's true. It's been going on for far too long and we're all getting scared to go to bed at night.'

If it was true, they'd presumably be speaking to her soon because of the hand. The less she thought about that, the better, but she would, of course, do anything within her power to help the police tie up this nasty situation.

Madeleine listened impassively, wondering how much she should divulge. But they'd reached the shop already so she put it temporarily on hold.

The sign said *Open* and the bell gave its usual friendly dingdong welcome but today, for once, no Connie came bursting through from the back, rubbing her work-stained hands on her apron, geared to make a killing. In fact, nothing stirred.

'Odd,' said Kate, going through into the inner sanctum to take a closer look while Madeleine stayed outside and pottered about the shop. Connie's desk was littered with papers, and a couple of leather-bound ledgers lay open, with Connie's uncapped pen lying on top. There was an opened can of Budweiser on one side and Connie's familiar thonged sandals lying in odd corners where they'd obviously been casually kicked.

But no Connie. Where on earth could she have gone, without her shoes, leaving the shop door unlocked and the account books open and lying around for the most casual of callers to see? And, Kate now spotted, her house keys on the corner of the desk, along with her cigarettes. Oh my God . . .

She pushed her way back through the bead curtain but Madeleine was there ahead of her. The seventeenth-century carved oak chest that Madeleine had so much admired on an earlier visit was covered now with piles of Victorian plates, recently unpacked from a couple of crates in the corner, and stacked in no apparent order in fairly hefty piles all over the beautiful carving. Not like Connie to be so careless, particularly with a piece that valuable.

'Here,' said Madeleine urgently, staggering across the shop with a pile of the plates. 'Give me a hand with these. Quickly, now.' And she very nearly dropped them in her haste to get the lid cleared.

The mistletoe bough, the mistletoe bough . . . But already they were too late.

So must Lord Lovell's bride have looked when they finally raised the lid on her ingenious hiding-place, decades after the wedding-night frolic which resulted in her mysterious disappearance. Except that Connie was only newly dead, and the look of pure terror on her face would live for ever in the memories of the two stupefied women who found her. She lay in the musty, camphor-scented box as neatly as a sleeping child, flat on her back, her legs folded sideways to accommodate her length. Her skin was waxen, her curls luxuriant and the weals around her throat beginning to fade. Her brilliant, mocking, heavy-lidded, damson-black eyes were staring open and the luscious mouth that smiled so easily was rictured into a silent scream. But the image that would stay with Kate forever, in endless tortured nights of broken sleep, was of her hands. Open, clawlike, on either side of her head, the beautiful, cared-for nails broken and torn, ingrained with splinters and blood.

'My God,' said Kate, in a low, low voice as terrible realisation dawned. 'She was still alive when the lid was shut. She must have been in there all night.'

And then she passed right out, unable to cope any longer.

Strong arms held her as she struggled towards the light, and a soft, calm voice, so familiar and dear, murmured comfortingly in her ear and gave her the courage she so badly needed to bring her back to her senses. Gregory? Thank the Lord for that. She was still lying on the bare wooden boards but someone had thrown a rug over her and placed one of Amelia's tatty cushions under her head. As her brain began to clear and sense returned, she became aware that the shop was now full of police and a blue and white ribbon had been stretched across the street outside, sealing it off to general traffic and passers-by. Two squad cars were parked half on the pavement, and an ominous plain white ambulance reminded her of what had occurred.

'Connie . . .'

'Lie still.' Gregory's voice was calm and steady as he gently pressed her back on to the cushion then moved aside to allow access to an earnest-faced policewoman with a notepad.

'We're going to have to ask you a few questions,' she said. 'Were you alone when you found the body, and when exactly would that have been?'

Madeleine? Kate raised her head again and shuffled into a sitting position. Gregory moved to sit beside her, supporting her shoulders with his arm. There were three uniformed police officers and a couple of plain-clothes men in the shop, besides Gregory and the policewoman. But no sign of Madeleine.

'No, I was with Madeleine.' The woman looked blank. 'Madeleine Kingston, we arrived together. Didn't you see her? Who called you out?'

'A woman dialled 999 and said there'd been an accident. When we arrived there was no one here but you and the body. We couldn't understand what had happened. I'm afraid you're going to have to come down to the station.'

Kate glanced worriedly at Gregory, but he closed his hand over hers and gave it a gentle squeeze.

'Just a formality, I'm sure. I'm here to vouch for you and to tell them about Connie.' Now that she was focusing, she saw that his face was haggard and ashen and began to take in what they both had lost.

'Oh, Gregory.' Tears filled her eyes and she covered them with her hands. 'What a dreadful thing. I can't tell you how sorry I am . . . you were both so happy. How come you're here, anyhow? I thought Connie said you were away.'

'Just passing the end of the road in a taxi on the way in from the airport. I saw the police cars and came to investigate.' He nodded towards the doorway, where his familiar briefcase and laptop were standing. Poor man; just back from the Reykjavik trip to find his future shattered and his life in ruins. It was a wonder he could cope at all.

They'd finished doing their initial investigation and the police officers were beginning to disperse. The policewoman helped Kate to her feet and out towards a waiting squad car. Gregory followed.

'Mind if I come too?' he asked, and the woman mutely agreed. He was, he explained, Kate's closest friend as well as a long-term resident of Kensington Court. And, in a kind of way, next of kin to the deceased. It was the very least that he could do.

'That's it, we have to go in there now. We can't risk wasting another minute.'

'Not so fast. Pity to ruin it now.'

'What the hell are you talking about? There's a human life at stake!' Again that unexpected flash of anger that always caught her off guard. Interesting, this man; in other circumstances . . .

'Wait a little longer. We're very nearly there.'

'Too dangerous. I'm not prepared to take the risk.'

'It will be all right. Let's not ruin it after all these months of planning, just by acting impulsively.'

'But what if . . .'

'It won't. She's far too level-headed, as you well know. She won't let it happen and neither will we.'

'I only hope you're right.'

They let her go after a couple of hours, since there was really nothing she could add to what they had already deduced. She had gone to the shop in search of Connie and found her dead in the heavy oak chest, its lid weighted down with piles of china, put there to prevent her breaking out. It was horrible; whenever Kate reran it in her mind, a feeling of faintness and nausea swept over her. She remembered her mother telling her all those years ago that the single most frightening thing she could imagine would be to be buried alive. That was what had happened to Connie, her dearest friend in the world; the thought of her lying there alone all night, terrified and trying desperately to free herself, was too terrible to contemplate.

'How did it happen?'

'Someone must have overpowered her in the office, semi-strangled her – hence the marks on her throat – and placed her in the box while she was unconscious.' The detective inspector was as appalled as Kate. It was the nastiest murder he had ever encountered. It was hard to believe that anyone that evil could continue to walk the streets.

'And you say there was another person present?' The DI's subordinate was taking copious notes.

'Yes,' said Kate, puzzled. 'Madeleine Kingston. I can't think where she vanished to. She was with me, helping, when we lifted the lid.'

'This woman is known to you?'

'Yes.'

'And where may we contact her?'

Kate shook her head. She just didn't know. Madeleine remained a total enigma who strayed in out of the blue when the mood took her and just as mysteriously vanished again.

'Somewhere in Kensington Court,' she said vaguely. 'But I've no idea which number.' Then, blessedly, inspiration struck just as they must be thinking she was nuts. 'Beatrice Hunt at number twelve,' she said, relieved. 'She'll know.'

But she missed the fleeting glance of comprehension that passed between the two uniformed men.

They were almost through. She didn't want to ask the question but something inside her drove her on. She simply had to know.

'How long would it have taken her to die?'

'Hard to say precisely. Perhaps a couple of hours. Depends really on her level of panic; the calmer you are able to remain, the less oxygen you use up. But from the state of her fingernails . . .'

Kate sobbed, and Gregory gently enfolded her in his arms.

'Try not to think about it,' he said, and she nestled her head against his chest, longing to bring him comfort too. She was being so weedy when he was so strong, yet – for Christ's sake – he had lost his lover. Where did he find the strength to support them both? How could he possibly be so saintly at a time like this?

'Can we go now?' he asked the DI, who nodded.

'For the while at least, sir. The sergeant will drive you both home.' But don't leave town without first notifying us; that part was pure routine and didn't worry Kate. All she wanted was to help find Connie's murderer, and as fast as possible before it could happen again.

'What sort of sicko . . .?' she started to say in the car, but Gregory hushed her.

'Not now, sweetheart,' he said, pressing his lips to her hair. 'We're both too shook up to take it in. I won't tell you to forget but try at least to put it on hold for a while. For me. And also for poor old Con. Thinking about her suffering can't help right now, and we've both got to keep up all our strength for the things we're going to have to face in the next few days.'

The family, the funeral, the endless enquiries starting all over again. What could it be about Kensington Court that made it seem so cursed? Kate turned gratefully into Gregory's waiting arms and tried to lose herself in his reassuring presence.

34

The house was large, though rather on the shabby side, with a pleasant rambling garden with a rusty swing close to the front gate. One of the girls answered her knock and looked faintly stricken when she recognised Claudia. Claudia, conscious of the delicacy of her mission, had deliberately dressed down in a Donna Karan T-shirt and last year's Moschino jeans.

'Is your mother at home?' Emily – or could it be Rebecca? She never could get the hang of which was which – ran anxious fingers through her wayward hair, as thick and springy as her father's, and looked as though she were considering telling a lie.

'Who is it?' called Caroline's voice from somewhere in the garden, and the first Mrs Burdett came strolling round from the back, pushing a laden wheelbarrow, a pair of secateurs stuck into her belt.

'Claudia! How nice!' she said mildly, dropping the handles of the barrow and rubbing one muddy palm down the side of her slacks in order to shake hands. 'Mima, don't forget your piano practice,' she added, and Claudia cursed herself again, thankful at least that she hadn't made the worst possible boob of actually addressing the child by the wrong name.

'What brings you here?' There was nothing hostile or accusatory in the question; just vague interest, as if it were the most natural thing in the world for a high-powered dynamo, who divided her time between fashionable Kensington and even more trendy Canary Wharf, to be meandering through Clapham Old Town on a Thursday afternoon.

'I thought perhaps we should talk. Since we're all now in the same financial boat. Or out of it, rather.'

Claudia suddenly felt awkward and slightly at a loss for words. Her intentions had been quite noble and she had set off after lunch to try and make amends in some way, to forge a bridge where none had existed before between the two sets of survivors of the Burdett case, which looked like heading towards making world headlines before it was through. Now that she was here, though, she felt a bit of a fraud and could suddenly see things clearly from Caroline's standpoint – the brash, smug second wife crassly intruding where she had not been invited and clearly had no right to be. It would not surprise her in the least if Caroline told her brusquely to shove off. Particularly since Caroline was perfectly aware of Claudia's own role in Miles's business affairs. In her eyes, she was doubtless as guilty as him; ignorance, as the law would say, was no defence.

Caroline, however, had no such malice in her soul and simply smiled faintly and pushed the fair hair from her eyes.

'Well,' she said vaguely, dropping the secateurs into the barrow as if in an act of truce. 'You'd better come inside then, hadn't you, and have some tea.'

*

Kate was wandering with Gregory in the park. She still felt too weak and ill even to weep but he'd managed to prise her out at last by saying some fresh air would do her good and she needed to get the roses back into her cheeks.

'You sound just like my father,' she said with a faint smile, and he squeezed her elbow and told her he was here to protect her. They strolled along the Flower Walk like some middle-aged couple and watched the last of the tourists photographing the squirrels and posing in front of the still-shrouded Albert Memorial. Connie always told the Japanese that the squirrels all had rabies and the pigeons were nothing more than flying rats. At the thought of Connie, another spasm of pain shot through her and she had to bite her lips to hold back the tears.

'Cry if you want to,' said Gregory, without even looking. 'Anything that will help ease the pain.'

He was still dry-eyed himself but she saw from his pallor how much he must be suffering inside; she marvelled at the amazing selflessness that could put her feelings first at a time like this. Everyone was being so supportive, and she was beginning to realise – with a certain wonder – how many solid connections she had already made since she first flew into this city as a frightened refugee on the run.

Connie's mother had presented the biggest problem, but Gregory had valiantly dealt with that. She had wanted to come straight over but he'd managed to talk her out of it. She hadn't much money and was certainly in no condition to fly. There couldn't be a funeral until police enquiries were finalised; he had gently persuaded her into waiting until then.

'Poor lady, she was beside herself with grief,' he said. 'But I'm positive I gave her the right advice. There's nothing she can do here just now and it's best if we let her remember Connie as she was.'

Not as they'd last seen her, that was for sure. Kate impulsively halted Gregory in his tracks and stretched up on tiptoes to give him a heartfelt kiss.

Septimus Woolf was sitting in his porter's lodge, jacket off, shoes unlaced, catching up on the racing news in the early edition of the *Standard*. It was mid-afternoon and the building was asleep. After all the comings and goings in the past few days that was more than a relief to him, though there was still quite a lot of muffled banging from the fourth floor where the police were following some lead they had not thought fit to share with him. Which was perfectly all right as far as Septimus was concerned; the less he was told, the harder he would be for the press to grill, and he was getting awfully tired of those disgusting little rodents creeping in on him from all directions, forever looking for yet another angle on what was fast becoming a tired old story. He smiled to himself grimly; if they only knew.

It was one of the reasons he'd tried so hard to discourage Rhodri O'Connor from dropping in quite so frequently for a whisky. He enjoyed the Irishman's company in moderation, but was growing weary of constantly having to bat off his endless questions. He had no idea who had murdered whom in this great old archaic building. And even if he had, he'd no intention of giving it to the other porter to flog for a couple of big ones to the *News of the World*. Septimus had come here, six years ago, in search of shelter and a tranquil life. He was beginning to think he'd made a terrible mistake, but where he moved on to from here, only God could tell. He smiled at the thought, more apposite than he'd intended, and it was then he heard the light, soft foot-fall in the hall and sprang automatically back into porter mode, grabbing his jacket and buttoning it as he leapt for the door.

She stood in the centre of the entrance hall, and the filtered sunshine from the glass fanlight over the door softly illuminated the faded gold of her hair. She'd aged a little and put on weight but he'd have known her anywhere, even with her back to the light She wore a coat too heavy for this weather, and the single suitcase that rested against her feet was old and bulging and held together by a leather strap.

'I'm sorry,' she said, by way of explanation, register-ing his frozen face, 'but someone was just going out and let me in.'

Her legs were heavier and her ankles swollen but the voice was unchanged, low and vibrant, with just that hint of a foreign catch that had always made it so excit-ing. Surely, dear Father, he had died and gone to heaven, and never again would he mock the faith of the Irishman, O'Connor. He stood automatically buttoning his jacket as she remained there in that shaft of light, more blessed to his ageing eyes than the Virgin Mary herself, made flesh. Anna, his Anna . . . but it had to be just another dream.

'Septimus,' she said when he still didn't speak, 'I've

made my decision, after all these years, and left him finally. If you'll still have me.'

Jemima was actually quite good on the piano and, as she listened, an old enthusiasm began to return to Claudia. They sat in what passed for a conservatory, drinking tea, surrounded by muddy boots and rollerblades, piles of old gardening magazines and a ball of green twine, amid the pleasantly pungent warm odour of tomato plants, while the solemn notes of 'Für Elise' wafted through from the drawing room. Caroline had listened, in her detached, slightly fey way, and now there was really not a lot more to say except that, yes, it was tough on them all that Miles had gone under quite so spectacularly. And so soon.

'Not that I didn't see it coming,' said Caroline reflectively.

What? Claudia sipped her tea and wasn't really sure that she'd heard aright. Caroline thought for a while, a soft, sardonic smile refreshing her fading prettiness. She twisted a strand of honey-blonde hair around her soil-stained fingers, then gave a sudden gurgle of delight.

'He never really had any bottom,' she said, looking like the fresh-faced deb she once had been. 'Great for a first husband and procreator of the tribe, I suppose. But absolutely no staying power when it came to the flat.'

Claudia hesitated. She wasn't certain she could trust this woman, but who else was there to unload to?

'So you don't think he could have had anything to do with the murders?'

'Miles? Shouldn't think so, no – not for a moment.

He just hasn't got that sort of bottle.' There was almost a note of wistfulness in her voice.

It was then that Claudia, seeking diversion, joined Mima on the piano stool and revived an old talent. When Emily and Rebecca returned with Angus, their soon-to-be new stepfather, they were amazed to find the house full of light and a veritable festival of old Scott Joplin melodies bouncing forth from the old joanna. Caroline laughed at their expressions, shrugged her shoulders in amused complicity and wandered off in the direction of the kitchen to see what she could rustle up for supper.

They had done almost nothing but it seemed to have been a long, hard day and now Kate was back at Gregory's, slumped exhaustedly upon the sofa while he checked his messages and fixed them both a strong drink. Grief, Kate was discovering, had that effect, a soporific grey blanket that deadened the senses and allowed one to drift in and out of reality, between the recurring bouts of sharp, searing pain. A little like the aftermath of a general anaesthetic, she supposed; if you took things carefully and quietly and didn't allow yourself to think too hard, you could coast along this way quite nicely, probably for as long as it took.

The closest she had ever got to her mother was the night her father died. He slipped away in the early hours of a Whitsun weekend, of an unimportant operation he needn't even have had, when the whole damn country had firmly closed down until after the Bank Holiday. Bruno was off on one of his endless cricket tours and could not be contacted. Kate was there, still living at home, and had experienced her first taste of being truly adult by having to deal with the hospital and the undertaker while her mother wailed and lamented and paced the garden till all hours, unable suddenly to cope. That night, after hours of mindless television, they had taken a dangerous walk up over the cliffs, hanging on to each other's arm for safety as the sharp sea breezes buffeted and tossed them and the plaintive cry of the curlew voiced the desolation they both were feeling but could not express.

The wind had blown away a lot of their despair, and by the time they returned to the safety of the house on the cliffs, Grace's eyes were shining once more and her cheeks were ruddy with cold. They had shared a hot toddy in the kitchen by the stove, then mutely, without even discussing it, Kate had climbed into her mother's bed and they'd spent the night, huddled together like spoons, sustaining each other's awful grief with the physical warmth of their bodies. Natural healing, she supposed, was what it was.

And then, of course, on the following day Francis had arrived unexpectedly, drawn back, by some unacknowledged primitive cognisance which told him he was needed, from the scientific conference in Cologne that Dad had told him was so important. He had taken over in his calm, understated way and Grace had breathed more freely again, knowing she had a man about the place. Kate often wondered how much Bruno had been damaged by missing out on the catharsis of his father's final passing.

Now, in similar circumstances, Gregory and Kate supported each other in their sorrow by huddling together on the sofa with their drinks. An insistent banging was coming from the flat next door and finally raised Kate from her reverie.

'What on earth's going on in there?' she asked. 'Surely that's Netta's flat?'

Gregory nodded wearily, and massaged his temples with his fingers. 'I really don't know,' he said. 'They started while I was off in Iceland and I've not seen anyone yet to ask. I presume they've already settled the estate and some new owner must be moving in. You'd think they'd have some consideration, though, and hold off their refurbishing till a decent hour. If it worries you, I'll ask them to stop. As it is, I can't believe they haven't yet incurred the wrath of the mighty Ayatollah.'

Kate smiled. 'Don't bother. I couldn't sleep, in any case, and I doubt you can hear it from upstairs.'

Gregory's arm encircled her and pulled her firmly against his chest. She didn't resist. An instinctive inherent loyalty to Connie told her that this display of affection wasn't serious, that Gregory was simply leaning on her in his own poignant hour of need. And why should he not? He had been so stalwart and so brave throughout the ghastliness of the past few days; sooner or later it was only natural that he had to deal with his own raw needs and allow his deeper feelings to surface. Kate would be there for him, of that there could be no doubt. Apart from anything else she might feel, this much she owed to Connie.

The truth was that Mrs Adelaide Potter had been much diminished by the series of violent deaths, she had

Carol Smith

shrunk to only a shadow of her usual virulent self. Amelia, then Heidi, then Netta and now Connie. Four solitary women, living on their own, all within the same supposedly safe confines of this legendary, rock-solid building. It was frightening in the extreme but not nearly as scary as the apparent failure of the police to come up with anything tangible whatsoever in the way of evidence or any sort of lead. Digby Fenton, who liaised with them closely, was forced to admit when bearded by Mrs P that they were very little further on than they had been when poor Amelia died. No finger-prints, no *modus operandi*, nothing.

'You mean they are daring to say that that reprobate, Miles Burdett, is not responsible for the murders?'

'That's about it.'

'But I caught him more or less red-handed. Which is more than the rest of your useless bunch could do.'

Digby nodded, conceding her point. 'Nevertheless, he is no longer under suspicion. At least, not for that. The last murder happened while he was in police custody. Thanks, I may say, to your good self.'

'It's just not good enough.'

'Maybe. But at least they admit to being totally baffled.'

Mrs Potter huffed and snarled, then took herself down to the second floor where Lady Wentworth trembled behind her barricaded door, though these days her private demons were far more terrifying than any lurking mass murderer in their midst.

'Let me in!' commanded Mrs Potter sharply, knocking on the sturdy wood with her heavily knobbed stick and brooking no argument from within. Lady Wentworth eventually opened up and Adelaide was shocked to see how dramatically she had aged in the past few days, leaning feebly against the wall with one shaking hand, having difficulty even in wrestling with the door. She followed her through to the small, cramped sitting room which looked as if it needed a good going-over.

'I've discontinued Bonita's services,' explained Lady Wentworth meekly, seeing the direction of her gaze.

'Why, she's not dishonest, is she?' asked Adelaide, brightening. The merest whiff of scandal was sufficient to revitalise Mrs Potter.

'Oh no, of course not, she's a dear, dear girl. I just felt that, well, I don't see as many people as I used to and it's not worth her while just tidying up after me.'

She looked around helplessly at the piles of old newspapers and yesterday's tea tray on a side table, still uncleared. She was shaking so much she had difficulty in standing and Adelaide took her firmly by the arm and propelled her across to her favourite chair.

'There, take a seat. You do look poorly.' There was a gleam of satisfaction in the old harridan's eye as she found herself finally face to face with evidence of the autocratic old lady's vulnerability. She glanced at the sherry decanter – it was just after twelve – but saw, for the first time ever, that it was empty.

'Given up drinking too, have you, while you're at it?' And Mrs Adelaide Potter sat down sharply and forced Lady Wentworth to tell her the truth. Some of it she had already deduced, of course, but the extent of Miles's treachery took even her aback. Though nothing would induce her to reveal it.

'I'm not at all surprised,' was the uncompromising

response once Lady Wentworth had endured the humiliation of baring her soul, and for once Adelaide found herself in the unusually sweet position of being able to lecture her. After all these years, too, and she only a draper's widow.

'To tell the truth, I never did trust that Miles Burdett. Far too cocky by half, with that condescending wife, no better than she should be.' She tightened her thin lips and nodded her head in pronouncement, hands firmly clasped on the top of her sturdy stick.

'So what are you going to do about it?' she said. 'You can probably sue him for everything he's got.'

'Not that I would,' said Lady Wentworth with quiet resignation. 'But I'm afraid there's likely to be nothing left. The newspapers say he's in custody for fraud. I doubt there'll be any compensation where I'm concerned. He apparently owes millions and I am just one victim amongst many.'

'What about Lloyd's?'

'You may well ask. They'll still want their pound of flesh, you can be sure of that.' She was just twenty-one when her father had made her a Name. It was an extra birthday present, more valuable even than the perfectly matched pearls. 'One day,' he'd said, 'you'll realise the true worth.' He had certainly never warned her of anything like this.

Now that it was out in the open, Lady Wentworth was feeling oddly relieved. Sharing a nightmare, she found, did make it easier to face. She had never approved of this aggressive old termagant but she needed company and Adelaide Potter was all that was left.

'Tell you what,' said Adelaide, unexpectedly benevolent, struggling to her feet. 'I'll just pop upstairs and get a bottle of sherry, then we'll see what we can do about sorting out your problems.'

'I thought he might be the one that's been doing the murders,' she admitted later, once they were settled with their drinks and a plate of Rokka biscuits. 'If he's that dishonest, he's no doubt rotten through and through. I'm still not entirely convinced. I've watched his comings and goings, him and that no-good Greek strumpet on the fifth floor. And, come to think of it, I've not seen *her* for a day or two. You don't suppose . . .? I'd better alert the police.'

'Oh, surely not. I can't believe it.' Compared with the bogeyman of the bailiff, what was a rampant killer between friends?

Lady Wentworth still had a soft spot in her heart for her recalcitrant young friend and found it hard to believe him guilty of anything more than simple youthful carelessness. But she could tell from the set of the other woman's jaw that any argument would be in vain, and these days she no longer had the energy to do much beyond staying alive. The way she was feeling now, the end of the line for her was likely to be a debtors' jail.

'Well, you can't be too sure,' said her sour companion. 'And until they catch the real culprit, we'd as well stick together. Two old ladies, alone and defenceless in our own separate flats. Natural targets for a demented killer like that. After all, who else is there left?'

There was, of course, Kate. They had forgotten about her.

*

It was getting late and even the banging had ceased. Raising her head from Gregory's chest, Kate saw that it was almost one.

'I ought to go.' But she wasn't too convinced.

'Stay.' His arms tightened around her and his lips met hers in a kiss that was no longer just that of a neighbourly friend. She felt a powerful desire surge through her, tinged with shame that she could feel this way so soon after Connie's death.

'Connie . . .' she started to say, but he stopped her words with another kiss.

'Connie wouldn't mind,' he said. 'She loved us both. She'd expect this to happen and it's something we both need.'

So soon? But into Kate's head came a clear vision of those bright, mocking eyes and the luscious smiling mouth. Connie Boyle had had a real appetite for life and at all times pushed things to their ultimate edge. Kate could hear her voice urging: 'Go for it, hon,' and knew then and there that the thing she wanted most, a craving that ached right through her, was to lie with Gregory Hansen that night and let him make love to her properly.

35

So here they now stood, Gregory and Kate, after all the tragedies and heartache, the fear and flight and misapprehensions, safe together at last, facing each other by Gregory's rumpled bed next to the wall of books. All of a sudden a crippling shyness overwhelmed Kate and she found she could no longer bear to meet his eyes.

'Come here, you,' said Gregory softly, drawing her into his arms and cradling her head against his chest. 'We've waited so long, let's please not waste any more time.'

She could feel the beat of his heart under the old plaid shirt, steady and reassuring, just like the man himself. Oh, she missed Connie; she guessed she always would. But right at this moment she knew for certain that this was the right thing to be doing, that she and Gregory were destined to be together.

'Happy?' he asked, rumpling her hair, and she looked up at him at last, with eyes that swam with emotion, and silently nodded her head.

He laughed. 'All of a sudden it's Little Miss Shyness, is it?' he said gently. 'What is this? Don't you remember me? Just good old Greg from downstairs, the one who's always been there for you.'

If Kate felt suddenly awkward, she needed to have no fears about him. Gregory knew women and how to make their bodies sing as surely as he knew his own. With sure, practised fingers he removed Kate's clothing, every stitch, and she just stood there like a bashful child and let him.

'You're beautiful, you know that?' he said in admiration, gazing with frank appreciation at her small, perfect breasts and milk-white skin. Kate wished, as usual, that her thighs were just a little thinner but they didn't appear to be putting Gregory off his stroke, quite the reverse. He ripped off his shirt in one fluid movement and lifted her on to the bed. The bed where he'd lain so often with Connie, but she tried not to let that thought intervene. Now he was stepping out of his jeans and she, in turn, could admire his strong, well-muscled thighs and what hung between them, at the moment surprisingly passive. She closed her eyes and allowed him to caress her, with gentle, fluttering kisses all over her thirsting skin until every one of her nerve ends was on fire and she was almost at screaming point, longing for him to carry her to climax.

But it didn't happen. His kisses were deep and filled with a desperate yearning; the fingers stroking her breasts and teasing her nipples danced to a rhythm in tune with her own quickened breathing, yet Gregory's smooth torso remained cool and unexcited while the hand he guided to that place between his legs found he was still not fully erect.

It didn't matter, not to her it didn't. They'd been

through so much together just lately that it was not surprising if he were having a few difficulties now. She ached for him to penetrate her properly and carry her over the edge, but even just lying there, luxuriating in his caresses, was balm to her injured soul and making her heart sing. Gregory, however, she could feel, was growing tense.

'Goddammit,' he muttered with a muffled curse, 'I can't think what the hell can be wrong with me today.'

She kissed him gently and smoothed his brow but he brushed her hand away abruptly, as if she were starting to irritate him. The fingers that caressed her willing clitoris grew rougher and he bit her nipples with an alien fury that excited yet also slightly repelled her. This was no Gregory she'd ever known. She found herself withdrawing slightly, even growing a little afraid.

From somewhere through the wall she was conscious of a muffled knocking, but Gregory seemed oblivious as he held her down and rammed himself against her.

'Gregory, wait — you're hurting me,' but he no longer seemed to hear her as he focused solely on achieving his own pleasure. He ran his fingers over her cheeks, down her neck and lightly round her throat. His blue eyes were filmed with a strange intensity and now he was really beginning to breathe faster, while sweat slicked the pounding body that imprisoned and held her down.

'Gregory, please wait.' Her voice was urgent but Gregory simply laughed, a tight, unpleasant chuckle, and increased the pressure on her constricted windpipe.

'What a pretty, breakable little neck you have, to be sure,' he said in the voice of Red Riding Hood's wolf. 'I could finish you off with just one flick of the fingers, did you know that?'

His eyes now were mocking and his smile quite nasty; for the first time ever she saw ugliness in the handsome face. She was finding it difficult to breathe and thrashed from side to side as he continued to hold her in a vicelike grip.

'Like it rough, do you?' he asked with a sneer, tightening the pressure and ramming himself into her; suddenly, she found, powerfully, frighteningly erect.

She screamed and he hit her, and immediately she froze. This was not the charming neighbour, Connie's lover, she had grown to trust and love. This was some terrifying stranger, and when she dared to look again she saw madness in his eyes.

'I guessed you were kinky for a bit of the rough,' he taunted. 'When you told me about the Latin lover and I recognised the syndrome. Once a victim, always a victim, my dear. What a good thing he got bored with you and left the pickings for me. In any case, I'd been saving you up for last.'

His low-pitched laugh was now quite sinister, and the hands that had caressed now pinched and twisted. Kate was writhing in pain yet unable to scream; Gregory's forearm was still pinned tightly across her throat as he massaged his now flaccid penis back into life in an effort to ravage her again.

'You've probably guessed by now,' he said, stopping for a breather. 'The truth that's been staring you all in the face for so long. What arrogant fools the police are, to be sure, with their bumbling Victorian methods and impotent long-windedness. Talk about taking candy from babies. I had to keep on doing it just to keep them on their toes. I gave them about as much leeway as I could but they never really rose to the challenge.'

He released her throat and ran his fingers through his hair, the normally mild blue eyes now electric with excitement. 'Guy Bartlett was the only one who got even remotely close. Good old Guy, what a great mate he was until he got wind of what I was up to and started breathing down my neck.' He was visibly sweating now, suddenly alarmingly and ecstatically aroused. She watched him with a horrified fascination.

'It was a shame I had to get rid of him – I miss the intellectual challenge – but in the end there was no choice. As it was, I left it as long as I dared. Till he was all but on to me and about to blow the whistle.'

Kate wriggled in aggravated terror, trying in vain to break free. 'You!' she said, in a barely perceptible croak, longing to be able to rub her throat but finding her hands still pinned.

'Me!' he agreed, with a blistering smile. 'First Guy, then Amelia, then Heidi, Netta, Alice and poor Con.'

'But why? Why them? I can't see any sense in it.'

'Does there have to be a reason? Simply because they were there. Got to keep your hand in, you know, for when some really worthwhile prey chances by.'

'But why Connie? She loved you, she really did.'

'I know she did, such a bore. They always get like that after a while, these women. Take them out a couple of times, and before you know it, they're all starry-eyed and thinking of moving in.' The smile was modest and self-deprecating, a glimpse just visible of the man she had thought she knew. 'The trouble with sex, my dear, is that you always have to be on your best behaviour. And that gets tedious after a while, as you'd quickly find out if you weren't such a tedious little prude.'

The slick of sweat had gone from his chest and the fanatical light was fading from his eyes. Now he looked almost back to normal, the kind, adorable, familiar Gregory she had grown to love and rely on these past few months. Reasonable Dr Jekyll reclaimed from dangerous Mr Hyde. Soon, she felt, the frenzy would abate; if she was careful, she could slide from under him, grab her clothes and quietly steal away. She must have made a small, instinctive movement in that direction because suddenly he was on to her again and crushing her down with full force.

'Not so fast, young lady. Where do you think you're going? You surely didn't think I'd be fool enough to let you escape after all I've just told you. Mad I may be, but I'm certainly not daft.'

His laugh was light and amused and the look he gave her full of affection. He bent and softly kissed her on the lips, then slid his fingers back to her throat where they resumed their casual caressing. Amelia, Heidi, Netta, Alice, Connie. And Guy. Whom she'd never met but had heard so much about. In whose flat she lived and in whose bed she slept. Hope died in Kate's anguished mind. If he'd slaughtered Connie, whom he'd once claimed to love, as well as his best mate, Guy, what possible hope had she?

Gregory was enjoying himself. He left her lying

there and paced the room, lighting a cigarette and flicking the match back at Kate, still supine on the bed, too terrified to move or even think any more about making a run for it.

'Apart from Guy, who was my buddy, Alice was the one I regret most. After fifteen years, I'd got used to having her around. And she almost made it, she really did. There's nothing like distance for keeping the flame alight, as you would have known if you hadn't been so stupid and pursued that poor fellow across the Atlantic. But like the others, she went too far in the end so that ultimately I had no choice.'

He was standing at the window now, back towards her, peacefully inhaling smoke, chatting as normally as if they were having tea. Kate moved cautiously, careful to make no sound, and cast her eyes round wildly for some means of escape while he was off his guard. It might be her imagination but it seemed there was movement behind the wall of books.

'As it was, it got pretty nasty, and drastic means were called for in the end.' He almost turned but something in the courtyard distracted him. Of course, the tunnel. How could she have been so dense? That was why Gregory had built his barricade in the first place, to disguise the obvious access to Netta's flat next door which he'd needed to camouflage once he'd realised the police were on to it. Frenziedly, she measured the distance from here to the wall. Even moving like greased lightning, she stood no chance of breaking through all those books without him catching her first and finishing her off. Which, from what he was saying, he wouldn't hesitate to do.

'Disposing of the evidence was the hardest part. It always sounds so simple when you read about it in books, but have you any idea how tough the human body is to dismember? Plus, who would have thought she'd have so much blood in her?' He smiled wolfishly, stubbed out his cigarette and turned his full attention back to Kate.

'Would you like to see how I actually achieved it?' he asked softly, advancing to the bed. He stood over her, smiling gently, holding out one hand to invite her to follow him. And, docile as an automaton, Kate rose obediently, ready to follow him to the next atrocity.

'Wait,' he said, with unfeigned concern. 'You'll catch cold if you don't cover up.' He crossed to the corner of the room where he had tossed her clothes, and solemnly handed her his shirt to cover her nakedness. Then he took her once more by the hand and led her into the kitchen.

She had never really focused on it before, but the kitchen was a model of tidiness, as spartan and pared down as an operating theatre, with gleaming aluminium tops and plain white work surfaces. Gregory crossed to a door right next to the sink and swung it open to reveal a shallow walk-in closet with a gleaming display of chef's equipment slotted inside the door, ranging in size and efficiency from an array of serviceable knives right up to a Chinese cleaver, on which Kate's terrified eyes now fastened. Oh my God . . .

'My *batterie de cuisine*,' explained Gregory proudly. 'I may not be any great shakes at cordon bleu, but I'm a bit of a dab hand when it comes to wielding a weapon. Ask Netta, ridiculous woman. Ask Alice.'

He was still holding fast to Kate's hand but she didn't resist, there was no strength left in her. She watched, mesmerised, as Gregory released her hand and took down the cleaver to display its sharpness on the edge of his thumb.

'See,' he said proudly, showing her the thin line of blood he had drawn, then cast around for something more tangible to work on. He took a wooden spoon from the jar by the stove, placed it carefully on the chopping block, then raised the cleaver and brought it down sharply in a single clean cut, splintering the wood and sending the end flying across the room.

'See,' he beamed. 'How simple it is provided you keep your equipment up to scratch.'

He looked at her quite tenderly, yet with a speculative gleam in his eye. He raked his glance across the shining rows of knives, then drew her closer into a lover's embrace.

'Come here,' he said more softly, 'and let's decide what we are going to do with you.'

Kate thought desperately. She was almost down but not quite out. Screaming would be counterproductive, she was pretty certain of that. Knowing what he'd said about other women, he'd have no tolerance if she made a fuss and would probably simply dispatch her all the faster. In a last desperate bid for survival, she decided to play it his way and nestled closer to his bare chest, choking back a crazed urge to burst into hysterics. Instead, in a curious reflexive action, she licked the drying sweat from his skin and was rewarded with a light kiss on the top of her head as Gregory ran practised fingers along his armoury while he made his choice.

'Which end shall we start at?' he mused, nuzzling her neck and glancing down at her perfect, pink-tinted toes, while Kate swayed dizzily against him, almost too aghast now to stand.

There *was* some activity from behind the wall. Now she could hear it quite distinctly – as could Gregory. Slowly drawing out a deadly carving knife with a narrow sliver of a blade, he released her momentarily as he turned towards the bedroom door. With one great explosion of sound, the whole wall of books erupted slowly inwards like a dynamited building and came crashing to the floor to reveal a black-clad figure in jumpsuit and balaclava. At the same moment, the doorbell started to ring insistently, shaking Kate from her traumatised lethargy.

'Answer that!' rapped out Madeleine at her crispest, pushing back the SAS headgear to reveal ruffled black hair and a chalk-white face with eyes alight with electric excitement. 'And then get the hell out of here!'

Four uniformed policeman, all armed, came crowding into the room, followed by the lugubrious figure of the DI and, inexplicably, Beatrice Hunt. But Kate didn't wait for an explanation. Shaking with terror, on the verge of hysterics, she shot straight past them into the corridor, only to cannon into a silent figure standing motionless in the open doorway of the neighbouring flat. Oh my God!

'Careful now,' he said, as two strong arms prevented her from falling. 'Calm down and come with me. You're quite safe now.' And he led her back into the room where Gregory was now sitting, naked, on the edge of the bed amongst an avalanche of books and surrounded by policemen. A cool Madeleine Kingston, virtually unrecognisable in her serviceable black jump-suit and SAS hood, had got him pinned with the snout of a cold Luger stuck firmly against one kidney. Now she addressed him formally in ringing tones.

'Gregory Shaw Hansen, on behalf of the Royal Canadian Mounted Police,' she pronounced, 'I hereby arrest you for the murder of Alice Ruth Sorensen. With twenty-three other cases to be taken into account.'

'And about time too,' said Francis Pitt, with an arm round Kate, taking off his glasses and polishing the lenses.

Where to begin? They were seated now back upstairs in Kate's apartment and Kate, looking like a child of ten, was dressed demurely in her pale blue terrycloth robe, with her hair all straight and slicked back from the shower, while Beatrice, in Civil Service grey, handed out coffee and generally bossed everyone about. Gregory had been taken away, handcuffed, by the Metropolitan Police. And Madeleine, as the offici-ating officer in charge, had gone along too to make sure the charges stuck and that the RCMP had first crack at the prisoner they had been tracking so assidu-ously for so long. Francis, as an independent party, had been allowed to stay, though Madeleine had cau-tioned him about letting out too much too soon before they were certain where they stood in the light of British law. As if he needed to be told, after all he'd gone through already.

Kate sat there on the corner of the sofa, nursing her coffee mug between numbed fingers and studying with

a kind of awe the face of the wimpish husband she had
so gravely underestimated. Francis Pitt, his skin taut
and pale, fair hair flopping forward in the familiar boy-
hood way, was holding the floor again as he so often
used to, trying to explain what was really pure science,
way above the heads of all his listeners with the possible exception of Beatrice. And where, come to that,
did she fit in? It was all too confusing to grasp in a single take.

'Home Office, dear, Division C2,' said Beatrice, on
cue, with her acute radar. 'And no, to answer your next
question, I didn't move into the building specially, it
was all far more serendipitous than that. Just fancy, all
those dreary years waiting for a career break, then who
should come along and drop right into my lap but one
Gregory Hansen, serial killer *par excellence*, one of the
most wanted criminals in North America. Couldn't
have planned it better if I'd tried.'

Yes, but . . .

'That's about enough for one night,' she continued.
'We have to reconvene in any case in the morning, so I
suggest you all get a bit of sleep now and any further
questions will simply have to wait.'

Bit by bit they sorted it out next day, sitting around in
Beatrice's spacious living room while Lily glided
silently back and forth, keeping them all provided with
cups of strong hot coffee. They'd found Alice
Sorensen's body, or parts of it at least, chopped up and
neatly packaged and stashed away in the section of the
maintenance tunnel that connected Netta's flat to
Gregory's.

'We have your cat to thank for pointing us in that direction,' said the DI. 'In some of the flats these days the tunnel has been completely obscured. It is in Amelia's, though not in Heidi's.'

'Which is how she came to be battered to death in an apparently impenetrable flat?'

'Precisely. Our murderer on that occasion could not have been nearer – just two doors down. We simply didn't figure it out because we didn't then know about the connecting tunnel. Which he is slim and fit enough to crawl along.'

'And the wall of books in Gregory's bedroom . . .' said Kate. The detective nodded.

'Erected in haste to conceal the entry point when he realised it could only be a matter of time before we found it.'

'But Madeleine – where does she fit in?' Today Madeleine was back in obtrusively elegant plain-clothes, a close-fitting two-piece in violet wool that bore the unmistakable stamp of highest French couture. She studied her immaculate crimson nails for a moment, then glanced round the room and flashed a brilliant smile.

'RCMP at your service, chaps. Madeleine of the Mounties, that's me. We'd been after that blighter for years and years, since he started murdering random women in a trail of mayhem that led right across northern Canada. For a year now we've had a bit of a lead but nothing tangible we could make stick. And we didn't want to pick him up for fear of putting the wind up him and forcing him to change identity again. So I came over, as an undercover gal, and we set up our surveillance post in the other wing of Kensington Court, in a flat that just happened to be unoccupied at the time.'

Kate's eyes swivelled to her silent ex-husband, who thus far had contributed not a thing. He sat hunched up at the far end of the sofa, dressed this morning in patched tweed jacket and regulation cords, looking every inch the swottish academic she'd married.

'And Francis? Where on earth does he fit in?' Surely he hadn't really joined the SAS – though right at this moment she was prepared to believe almost anything. Madeleine turned to look at her colleague, who was studying his shoes and forbearing to comment.

'Doctor Pitt was good enough to join us after we first sought his help at Jesus College, when we needed a leading psychopharmacologist to help us look into the mind of the clinically deranged mass murderer. As you will know, his speciality is forensic.' Kate didn't but she let it pass; it was five years now since she'd last been in touch with Francis, and had no way of knowing the details of his research.

All eyes turned to him now and he waved his hands vaguely and just looked uncomfortable. 'Drugs and things,' he muttered incomprehensibly, and was not apparently prepared to expand. Madeleine smiled at him with real fondness.

'It was when he discovered the identity of one potential victim that he was persuaded to step out of his ivory tower and join me in the field.' She nodded at Kate. 'By one of those weird coincidences that happen more often than you might believe, we found you living right above our man – and that, as far as my learned friend here was concerned, was all it took.'

Francis was picking at a cuticle and looking acutely embarrassed. His eyes, when he raised them to Kate's, were bright with emotion behind the thick lenses, and she realised with a jolt of shock that he must, after all, still have feelings for her. After all this time and the way she'd behaved. She was still absorbing this startling discovery as Madeleine continued.

'Over there, in our makeshift listening post, we have all the most advanced equipment modern science can provide. We were the eyes and ears of Interpol, if you like, watching and waiting for Gregory Hansen to make that one fatal mistake.'

'Well,' said the DI, who knew most of this already, 'you certainly took a few catastrophic risks. Four more dead while you had him under surveillance? Even on police averages, that's going it a bit, wouldn't you agree?'

'Five, actually, with Alice Sorensen,' said Madeleine calmly. 'But don't you see, until we found her severed hand, we still hadn't a shred of evidence and nothing we could pin on him that was likely to hold water. Then, with Netta Silcock's place conveniently empty, we were able to take it completely apart and discover some of his gruesome leavings.'

'Stashed in the tunnel in a rather careless fashion,' said the DI. 'By that time he was getting overconfident and really believed he could continue to outwit us. And you know how co-operative he's been all along. Down at the station at the slightest provocation and always highly visible at the scene of each crime in turn.'

'But surely the Mounties always get their man?' interjected Kate, and everybody laughed, breaking the tension.

'Sure we do,' said Madeleine with an easy smile. 'We may take our time, but we get there in the end. Rather faster, if I may say so,' she added pointedly to the DI, 'than some of our British counterparts in this fair city.'

The Englishman was not amused, but Kate hurried on and changed the subject.

'So it was you all along, apparently watching me?'

'Me and the Doc, yes. I kept look-out, he sat further back, out of sight of the window, operating the complex watching and listening contraptions.'

'I'd actually encountered the blighter before,' interjected Francis mildly, by way of explanation. 'Years ago when I was in Canada doing research on the effects of certain drugs on the human brain. They roped me in then and I suppose you might say I've been on the case ever since. Fascinating stuff. Never known a case like it.'

'But if I could see you – and I always could – how come Gregory did not? He was directly opposite and most of the time working at home like me.'

'Elementary,' said Madeleine. 'You could see me because I let you, because it didn't matter. But when Gregory entered his own apartment we got a warning signal from his burglar alarm. When the red light flickered we picked it up and were neatly hidden away by the time he entered any of the rooms we overlooked.'

'Brilliant.'

'Sufficient,' said Madeleine. 'I only wish we'd been able to save the others. Particularly the last one, poor

Connie Boyle, who I must confess I had really got to like.'

Automatic tears filled Kate's eyes but she brushed them away. No time now for sentiment, particularly when she realised how close she had come to death herself. One last thing.

'And Beatrice?'

'Just happenstance, as I've already explained, but I do work, rather conveniently, on international criminal policy, specialising in the extradition of fugitive offenders.' She beamed at Madeleine and Francis. 'So we all worked together as a neat little team and I couldn't be happier that we eventually got a result.'

'Which is why you had me down to meet Madeleine.'

'Yes. Any information she could pick up was potentially useful to the case.'

'So where do we go from here?' asked Kate, and Francis gazed back at her pointedly but offered no comment.

'Where indeed. To court, eventually, once all the legal rigmarole has been dealt with. You'll be our star witness so we'll have to keep an eye on you. Though I doubt you'll be in any further danger now that that animal is finally under lock and key. But we'll almost certainly have to fly you to Canada to give evidence.'

Kate thought fleetingly of Ramon and her narrow escape there; she wouldn't dream of mentioning it, but there were more of them out than in. From this point on she was staying away from dangerous men. She smiled at her husband and saw him visibly thaw. Well,

time enough for making her apologies there once all
this brouhaha was over.

'Well,' said the DI, closing his notebook with a snap,
'I reckon that winds things up for now. We'll be asking
you for a detailed statement, so don't leave town,' he
said to Kate.

Where on earth would I be going, she reflected
silently, when everything I want in the world is in this
room?

36

As an early Christmas present that year, Francis gave Kate an expensive sound system, with a set of speakers for every room.

'Before you think I'm being overly extravagant,' he said, 'don't forget that I hope to be using it too.' And to prove his point, moved his vast collection of mediaeval music up from his Cambridge digs.

'We're going to run out of space at this rate,' said Kate, with a feeling of contented inevitability. 'Maybe we should consider buying the flat next door and knocking a hole through the wall.'

'Why not, indeed?' Francis was in negotiation with Imperial College, less than half a mile away, and might well be spending most of his time in Kensington soon. 'Half this building seems to be on the market, as it is. We may be able to get it at a knockdown price.'

It seemed unbelievable that in only a year, this place had begun to feel so very much like home. They were spending Christmas here together, just the two of them, but motored down to Sussex one Sunday in December to get her mother's blessing and wish her the compliments of the season.

'So you're back together,' said Grace approvingly as

Kate arranged the Christmas roses and Francis poured the sherry. 'And not before time either.' There was little point in producing the carefully thought-over non-committal speech about it being early days and letting things take their course, et cetera; there would be no pulling the wool over her mother's eyes, loony though she may be these days.

'Well, I'm glad,' said Grace, leaning comfortably on Francis's arm as he helped her to her chair. 'There's enough nonsense in life as it is without wasting any more time.'

Bruno arrived unexpectedly as they were waving goodbye, his filthy Land Rover pulling up alongside Francis's vintage Triumph Roadster.

'Good heavens!' he boomed. 'Thought it might be you. Recognised the car.' He was out of his own heap of junk and fussing round theirs, tapping the hubcaps, testing the bumpers, trying a tentative blast on the antique rubber horn, while Francis sat passively behind the steering wheel, thoughtfully watching him but making no pronouncement. He'd known Bruno as long as he'd known Kate and was just too decent ever to take sides.

After an age of inconsequential chat about mileage per gallon and chassis suspension, Bruno finally noticed his sister sitting there and gave her a nod.

'Giving her a lift somewhere?' he asked without much interest.

'Something like that,' agreed Francis benevolently. Bruno's eyes grew beadier.

'Not back together, are you?'

'Something like that.'

'Eurrgh. After the way she treated you? Must be out of your mind. Did I ever tell you she failed her geography O level?'

'I believe it was once mentioned. And I also seem to recall she used to suck her thumb.'

'He can't help being a bit of buffoon,' said Francis sympathetically as they drove away. 'I'm afraid poor Bruno is a bear of little brain. And imagine what life with Lindy must be like.'

Kate beamed and would have thrown her arms around him if it weren't for the traffic. Then she remembered.

'By the way, who was it?' she enquired. 'The beautiful woman on your arm last time they saw you?'

Francis pondered, then broke into a grin.

'Shortly before Christmas last year? One guess.'

'Not Madeleine?'

'The very same. She had just arrived in this country, knew no one, so I took her with me when I went to visit old friends. Lindy was positively spitting with curiosity, so I'm afraid we played it up a little, just for the fun of it.'

For the rest of the journey home Kate purred inside. What a difference a year could make. For the first time in aeons she was actually looking forward to Christmas.

'Come with me,' said Francis mysteriously on Christmas Eve. They'd done the tree, a magnificent seven-footer, covered it with matching ornaments in cream and silver which gave it the look of having been touched by moonlight, wrapped all the presents and tucked them away underneath; even stuffed the turkey and made the cranberry sauce.

'No one actually makes it any more,' said Kate, 'but I want this year to be extra special. And I found the cranberries in Sainsbury's.'

It wasn't quite snowing but the sky looked promising and the temperature outside had sunk to a healthy chill. After supper with Beatrice and Lily they were going to midnight mass, but first, Francis said, there was something he wanted to show her.

'Put on your boots,' he directed, 'and wrap up warm.' Then he took her arm and steered her up Campden Hill, round the corner where the old water tower once stood and into the exclusive square at the top. It was exactly like stepping back into the past and Kate stopped dead in her tracks, spellbound. Not an electric light was burning throughout the whole square but every house was ablaze with candlelight, their curtains pulled back to reveal the glowing interiors.

'Magic!' she breathed. 'How on earth did you know?'

'Lily told me – and there they are now.' He waved. 'I said we'd meet them up here around seven. It's an ancient custom that takes place every year. Pretty impressive, don't you think?'

And indeed it was. By prior arrangement, each householder had lit white candles at the window, in a lessening number the higher the floor. The effect was breathtaking, like the inside of a vast cathedral. It was only surprising there weren't more people out tonight, to share in the enchantment of the moment. Apart from Lily and Beatrice, the only other living creatures in sight were a group of carollers clustered beneath a lamppost, adding the final detail to the Christmas-card feeling of the scene. And right at that very moment, the first few flakes of snow began to fall.

Kate, holding tight to Francis's arm, was ecstatic. 'Thank you,' she whispered against the cloth of his sleeve.

'For what, ninny?'

'For giving me another Christmas to remember.'

Supper was superb and afterwards they played Trivial Pursuit. Normally Kate had no time for organised games but Beatrice and Lily made it so much fun, and they all felt in the mood for a bit of light-hearted entertainment. It had been a fairly horrendous year, all told; each one of them, for their own separate reasons, was heartily glad to be seeing the back of it. At half-past eleven, Francis looked at his watch and they all, by mutual consent, got back into their coats and made tracks round the corner to St Mary Abbots, lit up like Aladdin's cave with its main doors thrown open, welcoming its worshippers to this special midnight service.

Handsome Father Salvoni stood inside the doors, shaking hands and receiving the congregation, with a special welcome for each of his four neighbours.

'It's not usual to see you honouring us,' he twinkled, kissing Kate on either cheek and pumping Francis's hand.

'Well, it's rather a special occasion for us,' said Francis. Tonight they planned to renew their marriage vows, in a private ceremony just between the two of them. 'It's just as well I never got round to divorcing you,' he had said when he asked. 'Sometimes, you see, a bit of dilatoriness doesn't go amiss after all.'

He had bought her an antique eternity ring which he planned to give her last thing, before they went to bed. Francis's love for Kate had never wavered and this time round he was taking every precaution to ensure he never risked losing her again.

Tonight the church was packed and the congregation rose as the choristers came singing up the nave with their swinging censers followed by the priests in their ceremonial robes.

'That's the Bishop of Kensington,' whispered Beatrice. 'The one in the cope with the purple cassock underneath.'

Several of the neighbours were dotted around the church: the Barclay-Davenports singing lustily in the second row; Lady Wentworth leaning on a stick behind them; Olive and Digby Fenton further back, smiling and nodding as they spotted Kate and her party.

'Look!' said Kate suddenly, clutching at Beatrice's sleeve. And there, near the back, was Septimus Woolf with a plump, pretty woman at his side.

'Well,' said Beatrice, after several moments' examination, 'there's a turn-up for the books, if you like. I knew there was some trouble in his past; if only I'd known it was quite so healthy.'

'Trouble?'

'Tell you later.' And with that the whole congregation burst into the first carol.

Septimus had never been so happy as he stood there,

facing his Saviour, with Anna at his side, on the most important night of the year, his faith and the woman he loved both restored to him. It was a little miracle, of a kind he'd thought never to see, and on Boxing Day they had a date with the Bishop to sort out the final details of Septimus's new life. For ecumenical as well as church thinking had eased considerably since that fateful day, eight years ago, when the archdeacon had fallen in love with a married woman and been forced to renounce both his faith and his calling.

'Would you really give it all up for me?' she had said, but there'd been no choice. In Lincoln the church elders had been of one mind: Archdeacon Woolf had sinned in his heart and was therefore no longer worthy to preach the word of the Lord. After a great deal of heart-searching, Anna had returned to her home and family in Baltimore, leaving Septimus a ruined man, standing alone on the edge of the smoking crater that had been his life's work.

'Thank you, Lord,' he said silently, bowing his head. 'You have shown your faith in me; I will not betray it again.' Early in the New Year they would be moving to Cornwall, to a small country parsonage overlooking the sea. It was only a humble living but Anna had a little money and neither of them was in any way worldly. Essentially, it meant they could start a new life together, something he had never dreamed of in those far-off days of the bitter backbiting and corruption of cathedral politics. His new parishioners would be getting a shepherd who had been through the fire and survived, while Kensington Court would once more be lacking a porter.

'Darlings!' said Rowena, linking arms with Francis and Kate, as they strolled back together through lightly falling flakes, their hearts still ringing from the magnificent anthem. 'Join us, please, for a late-night drink. It's Christmas Day already and time to start the celebrations.'

They awoke next morning to the merry peal of bells and small, impatient feet transversing the duvet, reminding them that it was long past breakfast time.

'Merry Christmas, darling,' said Francis.

'Merry Christmas, both of you,' said Kate, handing them each a stocking and then climbing back into bed for the fun bit. Horatio got yeast tablets, a pingpong ball and a new catnip toy, which he straightaway unwrapped and carried away. Francis got socks and other mundane things, but also a small Victorian picture frame, in the shape of two hearts entwined, carrying both their photographs. A bit on the schmaltzy side, maybe, but it truly reflected the way Kate was feeling now.

'Your real present is under the tree,' she said, suddenly shy. Her heart was so full she had nothing more to add. After all she'd been through, she'd emerged more or less unscathed. She would never, ever obliterate the awful happenings of the past few months but Christmas was a time for rejoicing and all her wildest dreams were coming true.

At noon they all had to be down at the Fentons', for their annual drinks party. Last year, Kate remembered, she'd been so lonely; a frightened exile knowing no one and scared of her own shadow. She'd fantasised about invading Kensington Palace and seeking the company of the damaged princess. Twelve months later all that had changed. She walked down the stairs, holding hands with her distinguished husband, to be received with kisses and shouts of welcome into a room full of people who cared for her and felt like family.

Digby welcomed them with a bottle of champagne, but there were all sorts of other drinks, and acres of finger food. Ronnie and Rowena were there already, and Beatrice and Lily followed them through the door. Lady Wentworth was sitting in the corner, rather surprisingly in deep conversation with, of all unlikely people, Mrs Adelaide Potter.

'Don't say a word,' hissed Rowena, naughtily. 'But she's reduced to that since all her friends are dead.'

It was wicked but too close to home to be funny, and threw a momentary pall over all of them.

'Sorry,' said Rowena, rolling her eyes theatrically. 'Me and my big mouth again.'

Things were moving bewildering quickly for Lady Wentworth, who was quite a lot frailer than she liked to project. She already had an appointment to meet with Dr Mary Archer of the Hardship Committee, though what good that could do she was yet to find out, and now Mrs Potter was suggesting they join forces and live together in solidarity against loneliness and old age. Whatever next?

'Two can live as cheaply as one,' said the old harridan briskly, hustling her advantage. But the truth was, she was mortally scared. And too proud to confess it, even to someone more vulnerable.

'To absent friends!' said Digby gravely at a suitable moment, and the whole assembly raised their glasses in silence. To Guy, Amelia, Heidi, Netta, Connie . . . even Alice Sorensen, whom none of them had really known. Also to lovely Eleni, who appeared to have done a disappearing act, and the enigmatic Demeter who was, they now discovered, her mother.

'Well, of course she was, how stupid of me,' said Rowena. 'Such devotion between them, it was staring me in the face. I only wonder why they kept it such a secret.'

'Part of the act,' said Ronnie. 'I hate to shatter illusions, my precious, but Demeter doubled as both madam and maid.'

And to Miles, of course.

'How is the poor boy?' asked Lady Wentworth, but nobody knew. The last they'd heard he was still in police custody, undergoing questioning and awaiting bail, though his chances of getting it seemed slim in the extreme.

The doorbell rang, and to everyone's astonishment, in walked Jacintha, looking slightly sheepish and accompanied by a much older man. Olive welcomed her and introduced them both around – Jacintha and Clifford Hart from number seven. Jacintha had persuaded her stick-in-the-mud husband (here a sideways coquettish glance and girlish simper to show she was only teasing) to spend Christmas in London for a change. After this party they were off to the Dorchester for a long, leisurely lunch without any clearing up.

'Or cooking either,' she said with vehemence. 'That's the worst part, don't you agree?'

She almost hadn't dared show her face here again, but she'd signed the final papers and now there was no going back. Particularly with Miles in his present predicament; now she understood his reasons for so much speed and secrecy. She was still reeling at the news about Gregory, and the shock and disgust had affected her so badly, she'd been forced in the end to confess everything to Clifford. Who had taken it on the chin, in true Brit spirit, and also surprisingly well. He'd always known, of course he had, that he'd never really possessed her heart. This frightful business brought everything out into the open and would get worse, he had no illusions about that. They had already both been interviewed by the police, the Canadians as well as the local chaps, and Jacintha was set, whether she liked it or not, to be subpoenaed to Canada when the trial finally got underway. It promised to be a lengthy, distasteful business and neither was looking forward to it, but he'd stay loyal to the little lady because she'd already been through so much. And there was just a possibility – and he was, in truth, a closet romantic – that some time in the future she might even find it in her heart to love him a little.

And then Claudia walked in and a hush fell over the room. She was on her own but holding her head high, the light of fiery determination in her fine eyes and a slight flush on her sallow cheeks. Olive stepped forward and kissed her, and Digby did the same.

'My dear, some fizz,' he said firmly, handing her a glass, then took her protectively by the elbow and escorted her around amongst his guests, daring any of them to speak out of turn. Miles might have revealed himself to be a bit of a cad but you couldn't help admiring his ingenuity, even if he did get caught, and there was surprising solidarity where his wife was concerned. At least they'd cleared him of the far worse crime, all those horrible murders. It was unanimously felt that Claudia had had a raw deal; no one with any delicacy was anything but sympathetic. But that wasn't going to stop the Ayatollah, even without her cohorts to support her.

'Well, I'm blowed,' said Mrs Adelaide Potter, puffing herself up in indignation like an adder and preparing to give the minx a slice of her tongue on behalf of Lady Wentworth, her new-found ally. 'Brazen hussy, daring to show her face here. Has she no shame?'

But for once no one was listening. Everyone turned their backs on her, and even Lady Wentworth shuffled away. It was Christmas Day and the bells were pealing, time for happy endings and renewed hope for a brighter new year. Everyone grouped instead around Kate and Francis, and Kate turned instinctively towards Claudia as she hovered and drew her warmly into their circle. It had been an eventful year for all of them. She had found a husband but lost a dear friend. There would still be room in her life for another, for she'd learned the value of true friendship and knew that love was not always enough. Kate looked forward, belatedly, to getting to know this cool but interesting young woman who had suffered as much as she had, in her different way, but seemed to be holding her own.

'What's to become of Claudia?' asked Ronnie later, as they all shared the lift back to the fifth floor. 'I was stuck in the corner with the awful Mrs Adelaide P and couldn't catch all that was being said.'

'Don't know,' said Rowena, 'but depending on what the law has to say, I think she'll hang in there and try to make a go of it. At least it's a roof over her head for the present, though from what Beatrice was saying it mightn't be for long. Depends whose name is on the lease, I suppose. And what the verdict is against poor Miles when he finally comes to court.'

It was unbelievable how fast events could tread on each other's heels; already the Gregory bombshell had pushed Miles and his little adventure quite into the shade.

'And tomorrow,' said Kate, 'she told me she's taking her stepdaughters to the ballet. Isn't that great? I hadn't realised they were so close. It's good to know she's still got family around her at a time like this. I know how dismal it can be to be all alone.' And then she had a sudden thought and clapped her hand over her mouth in dismay.

'What?' asked Francis, pulling her close.

'It's only just occurred to me, what with everything that's happened. I wonder what did happen to Ramon? And if he ever really was in London or simply just trying to scare me.'

'Whatever, may it be the last we ever hear of him. Otherwise he'll have me to answer to. As it is, I've lost too many precious years simply by being a fool and not recognising what I'd got.'

Amen to that, thought Kate with her head against his chest. She did love happy endings and wanted everyone to share in her own new-found happiness. If only Connie could be part of it . . . but she'd put off thinking about her until tomorrow.

She stood at the window late on Christmas night, after the turkey had been carved and consumed, the Harrods plum pudding doused in best brandy and set alight. They'd even pulled crackers – just the two of them – before snuggling down on the hearthrug with the cat, to smooch and cuddle and do the things lovers do, with a dish of walnuts, a bottle of Glenmorangie and the video of *An Affair to Remember* that had been one of the presents under the tree.

'You know something,' said Francis pensively, taking off his glasses. 'I do really love you, you little fool. Always did.'

And she knew from the way he kissed her that he was telling the truth.

HIDDEN AGENDA

Carol Smith

Devastated by the shocking news that an old schoolfriend, Suzy Palmer, faces execution in Louisiana for the murder of her children, London rabbi Deborah Hirsch enlists the aid of her former classmates in an attempt to get her off. The Suzy they've known and loved all these years could never hurt a fly; she can't be anything but innocent.

As Death Row draws steadily closer, the friends slowly piece together what has happened. Aided by Miss Holbrook, Suzy's feisty former art teacher, and Markus, a jazz musician who's following the case in New Orleans, they recall their thirty-year friendship – and realise that even more shocking than Suzy's plight is the knowledge that one of their number has betrayed her.

978-0-7515-3635-5

HOME FROM HOME

Carol Smith

Oppressed by the aftermath of September 11th, New York novelist Anna Kovac answers an ad and exchanges her elegant townhouse for a villa in Tuscany. With two friends from England, Genevieve and Candy, she moves there for the summer to finish her book.

Life in their rural paradise is bliss and all three women rapidly adapt to Italian life. Until mysterious things start to happen over which Anna has no control. Her credit card inexplicably exceeds its limit; text vanishes from her computer screen. When her New York architect and friend, Larry, falls from scaffolding to his death, she panics and rushes home, only to find that the locks have been changed and she cannot get into her house. Someone appears to have stolen her identity, emptied her bank account, sold her possessions – even abducted her beloved father.

Who is the stranger whose advertisement she took entirely on trust? The situation takes a darker twist with a second violent death . . .

978-0-7515-3533-4

FAMILY REUNION

Carol Smith

As her eightieth birthday approaches, Odile Annesley, who
has been living alone in France for forty years, contacts her
scattered grandchildren to give them details of her will.
The five granddaughters see it as the perfect opportunity
for a family get-together abroad. Solid Clemency, the
perfect wife and mother; London property dealer,
Madeleine; Paris dress designer, Elodie; academic
Canadian, Isabelle; poor, deprived Cherie, the misfit. And
Harry, the golden boy. Each has grown up in their own
world but, like all families, the shared characteristics are
there. Then the killing starts, the secrets spill and it is clear
that one of them is very different indeed . . .

978-0-7515-3916-5

UNFINISHED BUSINESS

Carol Smith

The brutal murder of golden girl Jinx McLennan, early one Sunday in her exclusive Kensington house, shocks the neighbours and triggers a police inquiry that delves deep into her colourful past. Single, childless, Jinx nevertheless had it all – brains, popularity, her own successful business, plus a wide-ranging network of lovers and friends. Closest of all were her own small design team, the surrogate family who'd been with her from the start: devoted, long-suffering Dottie and her artist husband, Sam; gentle, reliable Ambrose, the team's backbone; Wayne, the zany trainee with the outrageous lifestyle; and Serafina, hot on the fast track, who wanted everything Jinx had, but now. Plus millionaire genius, Damien Rudge, the goose who laid their golden eggs. The trail goes cold until, in a shock revelation, it turns out to be a case of mistaken identity. The wrong person has been murdered. Out there somewhere is still a crazed killer with unfinished business – a killer who will have to kill again.

978-0-7515-3999-8

Other bestselling titles available by mail: